What others are saying about
13 Days: The Pythagoras Conspiracy

This was a very fast-paced book! I couldn't put it down! It is a superb blend of the oil business, current events, and international intrigue. I felt like I was experiencing a front-page news story.

**–Kathy Norderhaug, former
international oil executive**

Starks grabs the reader from page one with this well-researched page-turner.

**–Harry Hunsicker, author of *Still River*
and *Next Time You Die***

Very realistic. Thankfully, most weeks aren't as intense as these are.

–CR, oil company vice president

A great thriller in the tradition of John Grisham and Dick Francis. Full of interesting insights into the energy business, **13 Days** features a tightly woven plot and vivid characters.

**–Mike Barron, retired energy CFO
and senior vice president**

Heart-stopping terror in the oil patch, Starks has crafted a thrilling read.

–Michael Levin, author of forty-five books

For more information, see author's Web site: **lastarksbooks.com**

13 Days

13 Days

The Pythagoras Conspiracy

To: Lynda

Best, L.A. Starks

L.A. Starks

Brown Books Publishing Group

A New Era in Publishing™

13 Days
The Pythagoras Conspiracy

© 2006 L.A. Starks

Manufactured in the United States.

For information, please contact:
Brown Books Publishing Group
16200 North Dallas Parkway, Suite 170
Dallas, Texas 75248
www.brownbooks.com
972-381-0009
A New Era in Publishing™

ISBN1-933285-45-1
LCCN 2006924646
1 2 3 4 5 6 7 8 9 10

This book is dedicated to my family, to the memory of Karen Phillips, and to all who care for New Orleans.

Acknowledgments

A book lives within a community of people who support it. What a wonderful community I have.

Thanks so much to current and past Pentad critique members Helen Holmes, Carol McCoy, Art Bauer, Gary Vineyard, Dr. William Carl, and Janet Carter. Half Price Books of Dallas cheerfully hosted us.

Special thanks to the editors and publishers at Brown Books Publishing Group who believed in and made the book a reality: Milli Brown, Kathryn Grant, Deanne Lachner, Chad Snyder, Margaret Bell, and Lauren Castelli.

The last few miles can be the hardest. This book would not have come to fruition without the expert advice of Michael Levin. Two other key supporters were Bill Rich and Michael Lucker. The encouragement and insight from each came at just the right time.

I also appreciate the efforts on my behalf made by Holly McClure.

Ann Champeau edited early drafts, Chris Roerden later ones, and Christine Fowler completed the line edits with timely grace. Linda Lewis reviewed plot lines while she learned life in Malaysia. Ruth Ratliff advised on dialect details. Suzanne Frank helped widen my scope.

Authors Ben Fountain, Bonnie Ramthun, Rick Riordan, and Zoë Sharp had kind words of encouragement. Thank you.

PJ Nunn and Clara Mizenko provided great expertise with publicity and Web site design, respectively.

I appreciate the many people who provided technical assistance.

Dr. Daniel Horowitz, of the Chemical Safety Board (CSB), provided helpful detail. I refer interested techies to an excellent video Web cast produced by the CSB explaining the BP Texas City Refinery explosion. Both the CSB and BP made fully public the results of their investigations.

Ed Uthman, MD, consulted on forensic pathology and on autopsies; D. P. Lyle, MD, gave advice on oxygen therapy and hydrogen sulfide treatments; Starling Reid, MD, consulted on emphysema.

In addition to their editing, Helen Holmes, Art Bauer, and Gary Vineyard provided expertise drawn from their respective fields of: public relations; piloting and lawyering; and working as a DEA Task Force Sergeant.

Former utilities manager Danne Dannenmaier provided technical assistance as did two engineering consultants who prefer to remain anonymous. Thi Chang offered technical and editorial comments.

I particularly appreciate my fellow energy biz travelers: Mike Barron, Dan Elmer, Larry Gros, Toni Hennike, John Lehman, Kathy Norderhaug, Cynthia Rogan, Bob Stibolt, Julius Zuehlke, and others too many to name.

Special thanks to my friends and family. My parents supported me without waver, and my husband, Joe, offered his usual, always-valuable perspective.

Except for the hurricanes and the risk posed by the concentration of oil refineries on the US Gulf Coast, the events and people described in this book are fictional. I do not purport to represent any actual events. All errors are mine.

Key Characters by First Name

Adric Washington, Centennial refinery crude and catalytic cracking unit supervisor

Alex Stinson, Houston Police Department officer

Armando Garza, Centennial refinery contractor

Bart Colby, TriCoast refinery manager for second TriCoast Houston refinery

Brian Tulley, refinery services vendor

Cari Turner, reporter for the Gulf Coast Herald

Ceil Dayton, Lynn's younger sister

Claude Durand, TriCoast vice president of communications, French native

Cody Laughlin, Centennial United Steelworkers (USW) union representative and refinery operator

Cy Derett, Lynn's boyfriend

Dwayne Thomas, Centennial refinery operations vice president

Dr. Emilio Martinez, Harris County medical examiner

Farrell Isos, Centennial security guard

Gina Vardilla, Investigator, US Chemical Safety and Hazard Investigation Board (CSB)

Henry Vandervoost, TriCoast executive vice president for European refining

Jay Gans, Centennial crude-supply vice president

Jean-Marie Taylor, Centennial environmental and safety vice president, New Orleans native

Jim Cutler, Special Agent, FBI

Kyle Hennigan, Investigator, CSB

LaShawna Merrell, Centennial refinery operator

Lynn Dayton, TriCoast executive vice president of US refining; supervisor of all US TriCoast and Centennial refining employees

Marika and Matt Derett, Cy's children

Mark Shepherd, TriCoast's chief of security

Mike Emerson, TriCoast chief executive officer (CEO), Lynn's boss

Pete Merrell, LaShawna's husband

Preston Li, TriCoast engineering manager

Reese Spencer, Centennial refinery manager, long-time friend of Lynn Dayton

Riley Stevens, Centennial chief financial officer

Robert Guillard, assistant to the technical advisor in the French Ministry of Economy, Finance, and Industry

Sara Levin, TriCoast chief financial officer

Shelby Darling, Centennial administrative assistant

Skyler Knowles, Centennial refinery operator

Tyree Bickham, TriCoast general counsel

Xin Yu, Sansei liaison

Notes for Understanding

Hydrogen sulfide (H_2S) is a colorless, potentially deadly gas routinely produced in oil refineries when sulfur is removed from crude oil, gasoline, jet fuel, diesel, and heating oil. H_2S never leaves the refinery. It is converted to a safer, more useful, solid form—elemental sulfur.

The OSHA safe limit for H_2S is a maximum of 10 parts per million (ppm) over eight hours. Low concentrations of 100–200 ppm irritate the eyes and upper respiratory tract. A half-hour exposure to 500 ppm results in headache, dizziness, staggering, and other symptoms, sometimes followed by bronchitis or pneumonia. Higher concentrations paralyze respiration. Exposure to 800–1000 ppm may be fatal in half an hour. Even higher concentrations can be fatal instantly.

Pythagoras was a Greek mathematician and philosopher who lived from 582-496 BC. He is best known for the Pythagorean Theorem, which states that the sum of the squares of the short sides of a right triangle equals the square of the longest side, the hypotenuse.

Pythagoreans—Pythagoras and his students—discovered the relationship between musical notes could be expressed in numerical ratios of whole numbers. Indeed, Pythagoras and his students believed everything was related to mathematics. They were the first to describe something we now take for granted—the abstraction of numbers. For example, two stones plus two stones equal four stones is abstracted and generalized to 2+2=4. Pythagoreans believed whole numbers and their ratios could account for everything in nature, and that these geometrical relationships were sacred. One Pythagorean belief which resonates today is equality of the sexes.

The group of students that gathered around Pythagoras was similar to a cult in its communal living and its insistence on secrecy. A student named Hippasus challenged Pythagoras by postulating the existence of irrational numbers, such as the square root of two. When, in the eyes of the Pythagoreans he worsened the crime by publicizing the disagreement, he was killed.

Layout of Centennial Refinery Showing Key Locations (Not to Scale)

Houston Ship Channel

Docks and Cranes

Crude Storage Tanks

Utilities Area

Control Center

Catalytic Cracker

Catalytic Pretreater

Atmospheric Distillation

Vacuum Distillation

Gasoline, Jet Fuel, and Diesel Tanks

LPG Spheres

Flares

Farrell Isos' Guard Shack

Refinery Truck Parking

Lab

Centennial Office Building

Front Parking

Security

Fence

La Porte Highway

Simplified Refinery Process Flow Diagram

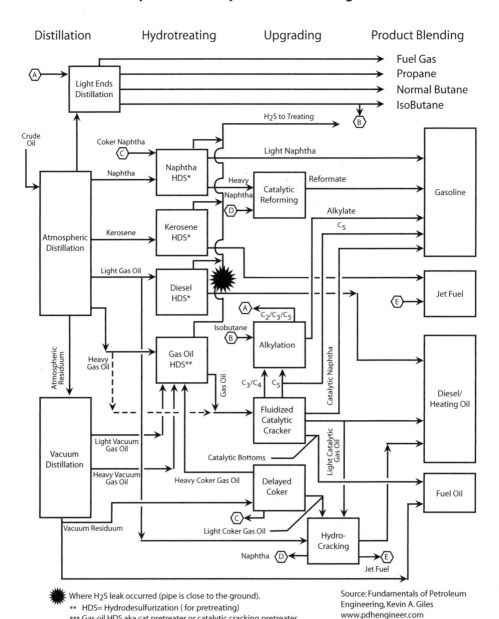

Where H₂S leak occurred (pipe is close to the ground).
** HDS= Hydrodesulfurization (for pretreating)
*** Gas oil HDS aka cat pretreater or catalytic cracking pretreater

Source: Fundamentals of Petroleum
Engineering, Kevin A. Giles
www.pdhengineer.com

1.

Thursday morning, Houston, Texas
Summer

What's wrong with the flare?" Lynn Dayton, executive vice president for TriCoast Energy's US oil refining operations, pointed to one of the giant, sentry-like structures visible through the refinery's conference room window. The yellow flame should have been soaring at least fifteen feet above its 120-foot stack. The three executives meeting with Lynn turned to look a quarter mile away at the feeble smear of orange and smoke.

Lynn's job had traditionally been held by men, a tradition hard to change. Khakis she'd thrown on at four thirty this morning for the flight to Houston hinted at her long runner's legs. "Is a unit down?"

"I'll check." Reese Spencer's short, white hair seemed to bristle to attention. He hurried out of the conference room with his cell phone. She'd hired Reese, ex-navy pilot and long-time friend, to run this refinery she had convinced TriCoast's board to buy just before it hit bankruptcy court. She'd promised the board she would make it profitable by refitting the refinery to produce more gasoline at lower cost.

Four weeks left. A blink of an eye compared to the time required to find the perfect piping changes that would increase efficiency, make the calculations, bid it out, get the welders on site to install it, and restart the unit, hoping the whole time the fix worked and you didn't have a fire on start-up. A nanosecond when it took weeks to find additional crude-oil supply, unload tankers, run the crude, pipeline the resulting gasoline to wholesalers, and get paid. *And you're the only one in this room who cares if you don't meet the deadline because you're the only one who'll be toast.*

This too-small flare meant yet another setback.

A group of the refinery's executives, including the two resentful people in front of her, had also tried to purchase the refinery in a management buyout but hadn't been able to raise the cash.

A frown pulled at Dwayne Thomas's tobacco-stained lips. Lynn glanced at him and the woman sitting next to him, angled back in metal-frame chairs.

She wondered if she could get all four of the VPs to pull together before she and they lost their jobs or worse, were reassigned to suffocate in Special Projects. "We want to answer questions about the merger of Centennial with TriCoast. Where are the others?"

Dwayne hacked a smoker's cough and clamped his ham-sized hands together. "Riley Stevens told me he had a morning meeting."

Riley's probably at a banker's breakfast. If he valued his job he'd be here. Lynn had met the Centennial CFO only twice. But in the last few weeks she had heard rumors about his attitude toward women.

Jean-Marie Taylor, a six-foot-tall woman who was VP in charge of safety and pronounced her name "John-Marie," nudged Dwayne and rolled her eyes. "And Jay's on a golf course somewhere."

They're accounted for so your worry is irrational. Hurricane season was about to start. Luckily, only a few TriCoast employees had been missing after Katrina. But it took weeks to find their bodies.

Dwayne kept staring out the window. Lynn followed the gaze of the operations VP. An easy-to-read beacon of the refinery's health, the flame atop the ten-story, needle-like structure telegraphed in a glance whether operations were normal. The same flame was still too short, too skinny. Dwayne turned. "Lynn, when you combine your existing Ship Channel refinery with ours, how many of us will you fire?"

What will you say this time to reassure him? "We need everyone. Now more than ever." *Except one.*

2

"I don't mean now. I mean . . ."

"Five operators down!" They heard Reese's yell just before the wail of hydrogen sulfide alarms echoed off every tower, exchanger, and furnace.

The three of them jumped up and rushed to the window, as if they could spot the source of the poisonous gas. But they knew hydrogen sulfide had no color.

"Where?" Lynn strained to hear over the high whine of the alarms.

Reese sprinted in from the hallway. "Adric thinks the emission is at a pretreater." *That's why the flame on the flare is so short and skinny.* The control center supervisor, Adric Washington, had likely turned off oil flowing into the pretreater to isolate it. By stopping the oil he was stopping the production of deadly gas.

"How many souls on board?" Reese asked quietly.

Souls on board. What a pilot says when the plane's going down.

"A hundred and twenty of our own. Thirty-five contractors." Dwayne wrapped big hands around the rim of his hard hat. "We gotta go see."

Jean-Marie blocked the exit, hands on hips. "Stay here and don't panic."

"You can't stop us," Reese said.

"Yes, I can." And she could. The safety officer pulled up to her six-foot-plus height. "The operators don't need you big cheese in the way."

After she strode away toward the refinery gate her command kept the room silent and motionless for only a moment.

"Now look at it!" Lynn ground her teeth in frustration as she put her hands on the conference room window and wrenched sideways for the best viewing angle. Pressurized liquid spilled out of a smaller flare and ignited as it hit oxygen and heat. Bright orange fireballs splattered the ground. She felt the glass vibrate against her fingers. *We have to help those who might be hurt!*

"I can't let my men drop like flies!" Dwayne shouted, echoing her thoughts. "I don't need Jean-Marie's permission to go into my own refinery. Reese, you?"

Exclusion happens. Lynn interrupted, "Adric thinks the release is near the catalytic crackers. We'll detour around them. Let's find our folks."

"You're too pricey a chief to take a chance out there," Dwayne said.

"Taking chances 'out there,' as you call it, is one reason I am the chief. We'll go together. Reese has a truck."

She grabbed a hard hat and safety glasses from a peg board in the bright white hallway. She and Dwayne raced outside to an old, red refinery truck with Reese and crammed themselves into it.

The truck rattled as the former navy airman ground gears. A guard waved them past razor wire fence and through the gate separating Centennial's office building from its several acres of giant, spiky refining hardware.

Lynn heard the normal thunder of gas and liquids rushing through masses of pipes all around. Hot, sticky air swept in until they rolled up the truck's open windows.

The processing towers were clumped in one area. Huge vessels two to five stories tall, each with manhole-sized inlets and outlets, were connected by bundles of either battleship gray or shiny insulated pipe. Pipelines of various diameters formed trellises over the roads. A complex network of more piping, heat exchangers, chillers, compressors, and pumps filled between the towers like metallic kudzu.

Everything had a number. Rushing through the C-200 area, they all jumped as a siren blast ricocheted off every exposed metal pipe, drum, and vessel in the refinery.

"Pull over!" Dwayne shouted. "That's the H_2S alarm again. We could be in the middle of another release!"

"We'll be safer at the control center," Reese said. He gunned the engine.

4

Staring over the black asphalt between the silver pipes, Lynn saw five mounds she at first thought were sacks of blue jumpsuits. "No! Stop! Our people are over there!" *Oh Lord, none of them is moving.*

Reese braked so hard his passengers braced themselves against the dashboard. Dwayne reached across Lynn to open the door but Reese yelled, "Don't get out! You need respirators." He gunned the truck again and they screeched up to a bright yellow kiosk.

"Hot zone!" Lynn shouted when they jumped from the truck and grabbed their equipment. Rotten-egg odor filled her nostrils. *It'll be even deadlier when you can't smell it once your nerves are paralyzed.*

"Drive to the control center," Lynn told Reese. "Tell Adric to clear a space near the lockers. We'll drag them in. We can't wait for body boards." She flipped on her oxygen mask which made voice communication no longer possible.

Dwayne put a finger between the mask and Lynn's face to check that her respirator was sealed tightly. She did the same for him. His practiced care with this simple safety gesture touched her.

They ran toward the bodies.

Two limp forms lay motionless next to an orange flag at the huge metal drum known as the catalytic cracking pretreater. Another operator was draped over the big bypass valve wheel. Two more lay twenty feet farther. *Hydrogen sulfide for sure.*

Thousands of butterflies wanted out of her stomach. Lynn told herself to stay calm. *Slow down. Don't screw up. Everyone's depending on you.*

She saw the first person. His shirt was pulled up over his mouth and his eyes were open.

Maybe they're just unconscious. Maybe the concentration's not high enough to kill them. Have to get them out and start CPR. Lynn pointed to a gap in the pipe near the valve and dragged her finger across her throat. *The source.*

Dwayne nodded and pointed toward the bodies farthest from the gap, the ones most likely to survive.

He knelt next to a man, Lynn behind a woman lying face up. They hoisted the operators under their armpits and dragged them toward the control center. Steel reinforcing in the toes of the woman's boots caused her feet to splay out and hit the ground. The boot heels scraped mercilessly on the cement pad and caught in cracks as Lynn dragged her. The woman's hard hat banged into Lynn's chest with each step. She tried to forget that the most she'd lifted in a weight room was forty pounds. She tried not to think the words "dead weight."

Her mask began to slip on her sweaty face. *Surely Dwayne didn't loosen the seal when he checked it.* She smelled sour gas but didn't dare lay the woman down to tighten the seal. If only she could make it to the control center.

She spared Dwayne a glance. Intent on moving another victim, he grunted, his face revealing only the strain.

They were still fifty yards from the cement-block control center when Jean-Marie, Adric, and a man Lynn didn't recognize ran past. Also bulked up with respirators, they were looking for victims, too. Lynn nodded toward the pretreater valve.

The harder she panted, the more the sulfurous smell seeped into her nose. *Twenty yards to go.*

Reese held open the door of the control building that led to the lockers. She looked over her shoulder to make sure Jean-Marie and the others found the remaining operators. *Can't leave anyone behind.*

Lynn pulled the woman in, laid her down on the tiled floor, and cradled her head as it rolled to one side. She ripped off the mask she'd put on only minutes before, pressing her fingers to the woman's smooth, brown throat, then to her wrist. *Where's her pulse? God, help me find it!* The woman's black curls were damp against her head. The smell of hydrogen sulfide steamed from her skin.

"I can't feel anything," Dwayne yelled.

The door opened. Jean-Marie, Adric, and the third man dragged in the other three operators. They looked even worse than the woman Lynn was treating.

"Medics are on the way. They said to focus on the ones we can save." Jean-Marie's words tapered off until they were almost inaudible.

Lynn pumped the woman's chest through her thick blue shirt. Nothing. When she glanced up she saw heads shaking. Lynn kept pushing. "We have to try harder!"

"Christ, none of 'em has a pulse or is breathing," Dwayne said.

"My man's got a heartbeat!" Adric shouted. "Help me!"

Lynn pumped the woman's chest again. She hadn't breathed nor had her heart pumped a beat during the time Lynn had been with her. Probably not for fifteen to twenty minutes before that.

"We have to help the ones we can save," Jean-Marie repeated.

Lynn made the horrible choice she had to make and placed the woman's hands across her chest. Her palms were already cool. She shuddered and moved next to Adric. Her throat burned with the sob she stifled.

Adric's black forehead glistened. He shook the man's thin shoulders. "Are you okay?"

No response.

Lynn tilted the man's head back and lifted his chin to establish an airway while Adric put his ear next to the man's nose and mouth so he could listen and watch his chest.

The door to the adjacent room opened and other operators crowded in. "What's wrong?" "Who's hurt?" Voices rose to shouts.

"Get them out!" Lynn heard panic in Dwayne's yell. The voices stilled and the door closed. The heat from the extra bodies abated.

Pinching the man's nose shut, Adric breathed twice into his mouth.

"Come on buddy, you can do it," Lynn implored.

"Breathe, goddamn you! Breathe!" The big engineer knelt over another body nearby.

Still no response. Adric repositioned the man's head and blew breath into his lungs again.

Lynn heard a gasp. *Thank God.* She clamped an oxygen mask to the man's mouth. The man gasped several times more and coughed. Every person in the room sighed deeply, as if holding extra air for him. Adric leaned against the lockers.

"He's going to make it," Dwayne said.

The applause stopped as soon as it started. *We saved only one, not five.* The muscles in Dwayne's arms convulsed.

Lynn stood up and moved back to the woman she'd brought in. The woman wore no ring because safety rules forbade jewelry. *Wonder if she's married. Has kids.* Sifting out thoughts of her own boyfriend and his children, she clasped the woman's cold hands, then those of each of the three men on the floor nearby. Tears she'd been trying to hold back gathered in her eyes.

"Let's get him next door to the monitor room and wait for the ambulances," Dwayne said. "It's not good for him to see these others."

"But Reese, would you . . .?" Lynn didn't have to complete her question before Reese nodded. He would wait behind with those they hadn't found fast enough.

She and Adric carried the lightly built man into a room lit with dozens of glowing screens. They laid him on a pallet of raincoats.

"Dwayne, have you met this man?" Jean-Marie asked.

"Armando Garza. Contractor, but he used to work here full-time. Knows Centennial as well as any of us."

The now-conscious man stiffened, tried to sit up, and fell back. He clutched the oxygen to his face and took longer, deeper breaths.

"Easy, *cher*," Jean-Marie said.

After a few minutes, two operators boosted Armando up and led him to the eyewash basin.

"Water's the next course," Dwayne murmured to silent nods. They'd all seen mild hydrogen sulfide poisoning before. Usually the victim went to the hospital, rested awhile, then stood up and went back to living. This was much worse.

The bigger operator braced himself and clamped his arms around Armando's chest. The other held the man's head over the basin. They opened jets and water shot into his face. Armando jumped back when the water hit his eyelids, then slumped to allow his face and eyes to be flushed.

Lynn asked Adric what had happened.

"My operators went out about eight thirty to do a pipe inspection. I can't believe it. Not all four . . ." He stopped, choked.

A cramp knifed through Lynn's calves. A cramp as fast as a light switch being flipped. She stretched up and down through her toes to ease the excruciating clutch, a physical betrayal of the emotion she always had to hide.

After a few minutes over the sink, the husky operator tilted the man's head back and the other rinsed his eyes with saline solution. Then they led him to a shower around the corner.

A squinty-eyed man pushed in next to Adric. His mustache almost covering his big teeth, he was the stranger who'd helped Jean-Marie and Adric with the victims. "Like Adric said, the operators had left for rounds. Armando was standing around telling jokes and got a call-out to the cracking unit. When he radioed his crew chief for help, they notified us because we were a half mile closer. Said they thought it was H_2S."

Adric recovered his voice and picked up the story. "After the call, I had my crew turn off flow, then sound the alarms."

"I'm glad you were right on top of the situation," Lynn said.

Turning off the oil had also cut the gas flow to the flare and explained the flare's dimming they'd seen from the conference room, as Lynn had assumed. *This refinery still has its expert operators. But what caused the leak?*

"Armando lucked out today," Dwayne said. "But he's the only one who . . ."

The scream of ambulances drowned out the rest of his words.

2.

Thursday morning, Houston

Reactors: vessels in which raw feeds are transformed into chemically and structurally different products.

Catalytic cracking: key process for converting heavy oils into more valuable gasoline and lighter products. Average reactor temperatures are 900–1000 degrees Fahrenheit.

Six-foot-tall Jean-Marie cracked open the outside door and pushed four medics inside. "The H_2S level is too high for you to be outside without air packs."

The ambulances' sirens were still, but before Jean-Marie slammed the door, sounds of steam hissing through valves and oil roaring through pipes filled the room.

Adric took two of the medics around the corner to the locker room, where the four dead operators were lying. Lynn brought the second team of medics to Armando, who sat with a few other men and women. Still attentive to their jobs, many eyed the computer monitors that showed the vital signs of the massive equipment outside.

Reese directed other anxious operators, who'd taken shelter inside when the hydrogen sulfide alarm sounded, to the break room nearby. He followed them in and closed the door. Lynn had asked him to find out what they'd seen in the minutes before the alarms sounded. She also wanted to give Armando and the medics the space they needed.

Propped in a chair near several glowing screens, Armando rested his feet on a cardboard box. A fresh jumpsuit several sizes too big draped his body. Despite the oxygen, his breathing sounded sloshy. When he tried to stand he fell back into the chair.

Lynn knelt and put a hand on Armando's thin shoulder to keep him seated. "Take it easy. You have plenty of time now."

Adric came in from the locker room. One of the medics asked, "What can you tell me about Mr. Garza's exposure?"

"Normally that stream runs five hundred to a thousand ppm of H_2S," Adric said. "He was exposed for six or seven minutes."

Crushing amyl nitrate capsules, a burly medic held them to Armando's nose and told him to inhale deeply several times. "It'll pull the sulfur out of your body," he explained.

Armando seemed to use all his strength to breathe in. He struggled to hold his breath for several seconds but began coughing. The medic helped him calm his wheezing cough, then finished logging the frail man's stats to the hospital.

Lynn watched Armando with concern. "We need to ask him a few questions while his memory's fresh." She hated saying it.

"We'll keep it easy," Dwayne added, with a pleading note in his voice.

"Only a few." The burly EMT gave them a sharp glance and unfolded a wheeled stretcher.

"Got call out for . . . cat pretreater. Me specifically," Armando rasped. "When I got there . . . saw two men down. LaShawna tried to . . . pull them away." He choked.

Lynn waited until his choking cleared. *You don't want to press him, but you have to size up the situation so no one else gets hurt.* "They fell, too?"

He nodded.

"You smelled hydrogen sulfide?" Dwayne asked, one big hand tapping his own nose.

"Couldn't. But, odd . . . bypass valve in wrong position." He stopped to catch his breath.

"Last question," the big EMT said. He prepared to lift Armando onto the stretcher.

"So all the gas normally flowing through the main line should have been shunted over to a bypass line but wasn't?" Lynn asked.

He nodded. "H$_2$S coming out of pipe opening we're repairing. Held my breath . . . got to valve . . . closed it."

"You saved the rest of us, Armando," she said, talking past the lump in her throat. "Thanks."

Armando's words raced through her mind, and snags started to appear. The open valve? *Probably a maintenance mistake.* High H$_2$S? *It's a high-level stream, especially since the new diesel we're making requires removing most of the sulfur. But why hadn't the H$_2$S alarm—designed for just this occurrence—sounded? And why was the H$_2$S level so extremely high, apparently higher than 1000 ppm, that it was almost immediately fatal?*

"Make way." The EMTs eased the rasping man onto a stretcher and put a respirator mask back on his face.

"You were lucky we found you so fast," Dwayne said.

Where did Dwayne learn his people skills? Enron? "It's amazing he reached the bypass valve at all," Lynn said.

Armando shook his head wearily. "Almost didn't."

Through a window Lynn could see Jean-Marie outside. The tall woman paced from the control center to the drum-like pretreater about 100 yards away and back, taking hydrogen sulfide readings on a monitor clipped to her belt loop. When she opened the door for the stretcher, her mask muffled her words but her gestures were unmistakable. "Get him in the ambulance, get in, and shut your doors. Quick."

After the medics left, Reese came from the break room and stood in front of the open door, listening.

"Damn it, I axed you to keep the door closed."

Jean-Marie spoke in what Lynn recognized as the distinctively nasal, Yat accent. New Orleans natives often sounded as if they'd just shipped out of Brooklyn and were called Yats for their characteristic expression, "Where y'at?" *Wonder if she had family in New Orleans. Are they in Houston with her now?*

Jean-Marie flung herself all the way inside the control room and took off her respirator mask and air pack, again revealing a delicate face that almost took Lynn's focus away from the woman's six-foot stature. Jean-Marie wiped at a sweaty imprint on her forehead from the hard hat cage.

"What's the H$_2$S concentration?" Reese asked her.

"For true, it's off the charts at the gap in the pipe." In Jean-Marie's accent, "for true" came out as "f'true." "About three thousand parts per million. Too high for most high-sulfur crudes. Even fifty feet away readings are a thousand ppm. I can't believe Armando survived."

Shit, the safe limit is only ten parts per million. We're sky high. "What are your directions for everyone here?" Lynn asked.

"The hydrogen sulfide is below the explosive range, but I don't have to tell you it's still a killer." Jean-Marie glanced at the monitor on her belt loop. "No one outside except to change shifts. Respirators and personal monitors for short trips, suits if you're out for long. I'll mark the hot zone. Obviously it's more dangerous to turn off the whole refinery than keep running so I won't order a total shutdown."

Everyone knew that most refinery fires occurred during start-ups. Oxygen could slip into a hydrocarbon line, form a combustible mixture, find a spark, and burn or explode.

"How long until it's safe?" Dwayne asked.

"When the H$_2$S concentration drops below twenty ppm. Depends on the wind and humidity, but probably a few hours. Give it over-night." Jean-Marie shouldered her air pack, donned her mask and hard hat, and ducked through the outer door.

"I'll put the word out," Adric said, moving to the computer. After keying the message into the company-wide e-mail/voice-mail system, he slipped into the break area with Reese and the other workers to give them the news.

For several minutes Lynn had heard no noise from the locker room, where the four operators lay on pallets. Her chest felt hollow.

She and Dwayne joined the second team of medics, and their slow movements told everything. One medic, a woman with well-developed biceps, shook her head. "They were all dead within a few minutes, if not seconds."

"Damn it," Dwayne said.

Shit, you should have been faster.

"The Harris County medical examiner is on his way," Bicep Woman said. "We need his approval to take these bodies to the morgue."

Bodies.

Plastic whispered its awful secret as the medics unfolded black bags that seemed far too big.

3.

Thursday morning, Houston

Pretreater/hydrotreater: large vessel or series of vessels in which hydrogen reacts with sulfur and nitrogen to remove them from crude oil and refining intermediates like gas oil.

The control center's front door creaked open again, and three figures entered quickly, removing their masks. "We all got back to the office at the same time and decided not to wait any longer," Preston Li explained to Lynn. Preston was Lynn's TriCoast trusted engineering manager. A statistical genius, he was the one making the efficiency suggestions Dwayne found so odious. *Mainly because they aren't his.* Preston hunched his shoulders, a posture that Lynn had learned signaled his feeling of urgency.

Lynn heard Jean-Marie outside swearing again. So did chubby Riley Stevens, just arriving, face flushed. He lumbered back to shut the door. The finance veep for Centennial, Riley would be redundant. TriCoast already had a CFO, Sara Levin, and plenty of up-and-comers to take her place when the time came. *And if he's the harasser you've heard described, he's out of here. Fire him. No. "Sever" is the word you're supposed to use.*

Riley pushed out his large stomach, bulldozed the door shut with it, and burped.

"Lovely, Riley. Bacon or sausage?" Jay Gans' aroma of lavender soap offset Riley's belch and Dwayne's tobacco-smoke-saturated clothes. Jay, in charge of oil supply for Centennial, completed the original four-person Centennial management cohort that had run the refinery before TriCoast bought it. They had wanted to buy it, too.

Lynn motioned to Reese and the group of Centennial people to gather in the monitor room. Everyone stood in front of her, crowding around the blinking screens. Tears streaked through dirt on several faces.

"For those of you I haven't met, I'm Lynn Dayton from TriCoast. Four of our operators are dead. They appear to have been killed by a high concentration of hydrogen sulfide. Armando Garza, whom many of you know, is being taken to the hospital. I think, and hope, he'll recover."

As she spoke the men and women shifted on their feet, work boots grinding the cement floor. A falling metal tool clanked a warning. Lynn saw pain and shock on their faces, and a look of the same numbness she herself felt. "My concerns are the families, and you. It would be much more dangerous for us to shut Centennial down and restart it than to keep operating. However, all flow through the affected pretreater and Cat will be rerouted temporarily.

"Don't go outside unless you're using a Scott air-pack and a personal H_2S monitor. Wear a full-body suit if you're going to be out more than five minutes. Adric, Jean-Marie, or Preston will tell you when conditions are safe enough for you to stop wearing the gear. We hope that will be about twenty-four hours, three shifts from now.

"All the families have to be told in person as soon as possible. We'll check our files for their addresses and emergency contact numbers. I need eight volunteers, two each, to leave and meet with the families."

Dozens of hands went up. Adric made selections.

"Riley, Jay—call Armando's relatives and have them meet you at the hospital." Lynn turned back to the group. "If TV, radio, your blogger and IM buddies, or the newspapers contact you, we might not have talked to all the families yet, so have them call Claude Durand in Dallas, TriCoast's public relations VP." She wrote the Dallas number on a white board, and tried to tamp down her dread about the visits. *What can you possibly say? No words will bring back the wives, mothers, husbands, and fathers.*

"What are you going to do about this?" A jumpsuit-clad woman, one of the shift operators, gestured broadly.

Lynn included Dwayne in her glance. "We have plenty of people here and at TriCoast to investigate this accident so we can prevent another like it."

The operators drifted away, faces slack and shoulders dropped. When some of them donned respirators and left the control room for their stations in other parts of the complex, a gust of warm Gulf air tinged with rotten egg odor swept in.

Lynn motioned Preston into Adric's office, closed the door, and told him everything that had happened since she'd first heard the alarms. She was grateful to have him here. Preston was sympathetic, thoughtful, and hyper-competent. Even his cologne—a leathery-smelling one—was easygoing. When she got to the part about the failed resuscitation of all but Armando, he shook his head and closed his eyes.

He agreed to call Claude immediately, repeat the broadcast of safety warnings for the next three shifts, and arrange counseling. "I also want to speak to operators informally, see if they've seen or heard anything unusual," he added. "Oh, and the *Gulf Coast Herald's* already tried to reach us. I'll remind the receptionist to direct calls to Claude."

Now for Mike. Her boss needed a heads-up. Michael Emerson's official title was Chief Executive Officer, TriCoast Corporation, but his self-proclaimed title was "shit-stopper." Or as he put it, "I don't send it down the org chart and I don't send it up to the board."

Using the phone on Adric's desk, she punched the number only a handful of TriCoast executives knew.

"Mike, Lynn. We had an accident at our new refinery. Four operators killed, one injured, and the refinery's in partial shutdown." She turned away from the glass that separated Adric's office from the monitor room. *There's always a lip-reader.*

"How about the families of the victims?" he asked.

She explained the in-person notification process and added, "Reese and I will also meet with them after we've talked to the police and the medical examiner. Claude will prepare a statement."

"Anything the families need, they get. What was the cause? Is it something that'll be trouble at our other refineries, too?"

"It appears to be a straight-up accident, a valve left open that should have been closed," Lynn said. "But I have a bad feeling about it. Even though it seems to be only a maintenance slipup."

"I can't merely trust those 'feelings' of yours, even though they're usually right. Get the cause objectified, quantified, and corrected."

"Absolutely."

Then Mike's tone turned harsher. "Jesus, Lynn, this is the refinery you convinced us to buy for $400 million? The one you bet your career on turning around in a few weeks?"

"Three months since purchase is what we agreed. I still have a month left." *He's memorized that deadline. Anyway, with prices so high and some capacity still lost to hurricanes, your real deadline is ASAP.* A calf muscle cramped and she jumped from the chair to stretch it.

"Do you think your old guy can handle it? Why don't we get Bart over there? And when will you have my Congressional testimony ready?"

Mike had been reluctant to hire Reese from the outside, particularly since the ex-navy man was not acquainted with, as Mike put it, "the TriCoast way." Bart managed TriCoast's other Houston refinery and would run both once they were connected with piping and software. A contract with Pemex, the Mexican national oil company, that could help keep the refineries supplied for years, rode on the outcome. Reese had fifteen months left in his contract to manage Centennial. *If we can fix Centennial.*

"Of course Reese can handle it. You know his record for putting red-ink refineries in the black. You have several weeks before your testimony. Claude can phrase it best, anyway." Claude, a French native, was one of the smoothest public relations VPs she'd ever met.

Pacing, she accidentally kicked a metal trash can and caught it before it tumbled.

"Remember you're on tap for the next board meeting to explain your oil-supply situation. You all set to clarify the contracts with the Russians and the Mexicans? The board won't give you a pass just because you're tall, blonde, and the latest wunderkind."

This time she kicked the trash can on purpose and let it fall. It made a satisfyingly loud ring. "Say what?"

"It means be ready by next Wednesday to explain whatever the hell's going on down there and everywhere else in your refinery system. And that Mr. Sierra Club keeps making eyes at you. Maybe he thinks he's won you over."

"Maybe he likes the way TriCoast's refining division, under my direction, maintained a top efficiency rating despite oil shortages and hurricanes." *And kept your ass out of trouble.*

One more person. Lynn called Angela Harding, a long-time acquaintance who was now chair of the US Chemical Safety and Hazards Investigation Board, or CSB, in Washington. "Bad news, Angela. We had an accident at this Houston refinery we bought called Centennial. Four people killed, one injured."

"I'm very sorry to hear that."

"I don't want to knock heads with you on this; I want your help so we don't have any more deaths or injuries. I assume you'll be sending your investigators. Can you get someone to the Centennial offices here in Houston tomorrow morning at ten?"

"We're always understaffed, but given your circumstances I might be able to free up a few people."

"They'll have our full cooperation."

"Hang on."

Lynn heard conversation on another line. While she waited, she e-mailed the Centennial VPs and Adric, requesting them to prepare for a CSB meeting tomorrow and to bring any evidence or records they considered relevant.

Angela's voice was warm. "Kyle Hennigan and Gina Vardilla can make it. Jeff's based here and Gina's in Houston. I'm afraid they know the way. They've been to Centennial before."

"Only once in the last few months," Lynn said.

"That's not true. We've been out three times in the last six months. I don't have the reasons in front of me, but no one was hurt. I admire the hell out of your safety VP, Jean-Marie Taylor, but it looks like Centennial—now TriCoast—needs to spend more money and time on your safety issues."

Lynn closed her phone and turned to see Preston's curious glance. "Didn't our due diligence only turn up one safety violation here?"

He nodded. "Everything important would be in the public record. I'll check it again, as well as our private files from Centennial."

❖

She looked at the readouts. Red, blue, and green console numbers displayed steady flow from most sections of the refinery. The first catalytic cracker and its pretreater were dark, flatlined. *Like your four people.*

She smelled the cigarettes favored by Centennial's operations VP before she heard him shuffle up from behind.

"What were we doing making that much hydrogen sulfide? If it had exceeded the flammable limit, it would have exploded like a goddamn backdraft."

"Ye-es." She hesitated.

"But what?"

"The refinery shouldn't have even hiccupped. This morning you told us Centennial has been running the same volume and mix of crudes for a week. I don't understand how the H_2S spiked so high."

"Yeah," Dwayne said. "And I sure don't understand why someone opened that bypass valve to the main line, knowing a leak could kill people."

4.

Thursday, late morning, Houston

Residual fuel oil (resid) contains the heaviest parts of the crude that settle at the bottom of the vacuum distillation tower. Coking minimizes resid yield by producing petroleum coke, which looks and is used like coal.

The smells of the morning's strong black coffee and deep-fried doughnuts filled the cement-block control center.

When a county medical examiner and a police officer pushed open the door, other smells drifted in with a humid gust: the heavy, thick oils that would become asphalt and coke, the lighter oils that would be made into gasoline and jet fuel. The familiar odors reassured Lynn.

A faint current of hydrogen sulfide also trailed in, provoking her apprehension. What had caused a hydrogen sulfide leak from one of the deadliest, highest-concentration sources in the refinery, a leak so severe it took the lives of four people? *You'll never fix the place. It'll be so long TriCoast for you. And how will you support Dad or Ceil or yourself then?*

Thick dark hair covered every inch of the medical examiner's exposed skin except for his clean-shaven face. After he finished examining each victim in the locker room—Lynn still couldn't call them "bodies"—he nodded his release to the sunburned police officer. Lynn's sob caught in her throat.

Jay and Riley had gone to the hospital to meet Armando's

relatives, Preston to the glass headquarters building to call Claude. Reese, Dwayne, Jean-Marie, and Adric joined Lynn in waiting for the medical examiner's discussion.

"I think we'll find straightforward H_2S poisoning as the cause of death," Martinez said. "Tell me how the victims' exposure occurred."

"The operators were out for a routine pipe inspection," Adric replied, knotting his mahogany-colored hands together.

"What kind of safety training does Centennial require?" Martinez asked.

Jean-Marie spoke up. "Same as everyone else on the Channel, *cher.* Daily safety meetings. Weekly review of common or new hazards. H_2S accident response training once every three months. But Dwayne, did you change crudes, maybe to West Texas Sour?"

West Texas Sour contained more sulfur than many other crude oils, so when it was refined it produced more deadly hydrogen sulfide. *Even so,* Lynn thought, *none of the gas should have been leaking from the open hole in the pipe. We can't explain that with a variation in crudes. Is Jean-Marie redirecting the inquiry because she made a mistake?*

Adric replied to Jean-Marie's question. "We're running the same mix we have for the last week: 30,000 barrels a day each of Ecuadorian Oriente, Arab Medium, and Kuwaiti Export; 10,000 a day of Qatari Dukhan to top off."

Lynn helped Adric hoist the control center's respirators onto a shelf, their hands aligning them precisely with the edge. Lynn placed the ones she and Dwayne had used with them. All of the respirators would have to be checked to make sure they were still intact, with no rips or leaks, before they could be used again.

"How about the H_2S alarms and analyzers?" Martinez asked. "Are they in good shape? What are their detectable limits?" Lynn was glad for the medical examiner's no-nonsense questions.

"F'true the detectable limit is one part per billion with a response time of ten seconds," Jean-Marie fired back, as if she had answered the question many times before. But the rest of her reply surprised them. "But Adric had to manually sound the H_2S alarm. That shouldn't have happened."

"We should look at the alarm," Lynn said.

"Right now," Martinez agreed.

"Use the self-contained breathing apparatus so we can talk," Jean-Marie said. "In the closet behind you."

"Scuba?" Dwayne snorted. "I don't see any water around here."

"Same idea, lets us breathe and talk, but we'll be in toxic gas instead of water."

"Toxic. My favorite," he mumbled.

A man with a wispy red mustache appeared, seemingly from nowhere. Though he wore a Centennial security guard's uniform he didn't look old enough to buy beer.

"Farrell Isos, with security," the man told Martinez. "I'll come with you to take fingerprints and make sure the police get a copy of the report. It may help the investigation if the fingerprints belong to one of the operators who died."

Farrell's quite security conscious. Good.

"It was an accident," Dwayne protested.

Was it? Who reset the damn bypass valve? Dwayne?

The six put on facepieces like those in the respirators they had just used, then strapped pressurized air cylinders onto their backs. Jean-Marie checked each person's sealing flange to make sure the mask fit tightly and showed them how to use the speaking diaphragm. Recalling how her mask leaked before, Lynn checked it for a tight fit to her face. They walked into the hot, sticky morning and ducked under the tape cordoning off the pretreater.

"Show me where you found the victims," Martinez instructed, his voice ghostly.

Adric pointed. "Armando Garza, the one who survived, was right here on top of the valve wheel. I can't believe he closed it before he passed out."

Nor do I. Did Armando really get a call?

"Two other operators were close to the valve and two were about twenty feet away," Lynn added, remembering the scene.

Farrell put on gloves and carefully lifted the orange tag from the valve.

Lynn bent closer. The scrawl on the tag, instead of describing its required position, showed a series of illegible scratches. *Not good.*

Adric swung around to a gap in the pipe with freshly cut edges. At the gap, the pipe ran parallel to the ground, about seven feet high. Since gaseous hydrogen sulfide is denser than air, the gas had pooled below the pipe and concentrated even more.

Dwayne poked toward the gap with his mechanical pencil.

"Because the bypass valve was out of position, not all the hydrogen sulfide flowed to the bypass line," Jean-Marie said, indicating the gap again. "Some headed down this pipe and out into the air."

The hydrogen sulfide alarm was mounted about six feet west of the pretreater and a foot off the ground. Shifting her air cylinder around, Lynn kneeled and planted her arms on the cement to look more closely at it.

"Get up!" Jean-Marie shouted, the speaking diaphragm magnifying and distorting her voice into a tinny shout. "That's where the concentration is worst."

"I have to see this." Lynn bent her head to examine the underside of the alarm. Nothing wrong, nothing out of place. "You're certain the alarm didn't sound in the control center?"

"No," Adric said. They could hear his heavy breathing. Lynn wondered if she should have allowed him out here after all the exertion he put into resuscitating Armando.

The medical examiner crouched near Lynn and made the same examination she had. "I don't see anything visibly wrong either."

His confirmation disturbed her. "How about you, Farrell? Does Security have a log of anything unusual?"

His red head shook as he finished dusting the bypass valve, PT416. "I had the midnight-to-eight shift. All fine."

Jean-Marie turned to Reese. "If you want to examine the rest of the equipment, wait until tomorrow when H_2S levels aren't so dangerous. You won't have to wear these or worry about running out of air."

"You're a good safety nanny," Dwayne said to her.

"Don't you mean pain in the ass, *cher?*" Without waiting for a reply she stalked back to the control center, her oxygen tank bouncing on her back.

Reese laughed. "Interesting woman."

"She *is* a damn pain in the butt," Dwayne said, watching her go.

"Can't give it up, can you?" Jean-Marie's voice transmission floated back to them.

With Martinez watching them, Lynn wished they'd saved the show for another time. Jean-Marie reminded her of her sister, Ceil. Same gutsiness. Lynn hadn't seen her sister since she left Dallas some months ago.

The heat and hum of computers filled the monitor room, contrasting with the ominous silence of the shut-down catalytic cracking equipment outside.

"We have to get our units to full volume ASAP," Dwayne said. "We're losing money every minute."

She judged the boundary of Dwayne's personal space and planted herself inside it, inches from him. Dwayne stepped back.

"I want this refinery profitable, too. My career depends on it," she said, keeping her voice low and controlled, "but not at the cost of more lives or injuries."

Dwayne's huge hands brushed back a few of his gray hairs. "My wholesalers are begging me to send 'em more gasoline."

"Right now we need to visit some families."

Reese waved them toward the door and the old red truck. This time Lynn slid into the middle and Dwayne took the window seat.

"Reese, take us by the office before we go see the families," Lynn said. "I want to change into a suit."

The drive back to the refinery headquarters was a slower reprise of their early-morning race.

Racks of overhead pipes cast cool shadows. Lynn had the comforting feeling of enclosure from multi-story towers, pipes, compressors, and chillers. She felt the rich heat of black carbon atoms packed together, waiting to be separated, combined, and made more palatable to cars, trucks, jet engines, and industrial generators. Especially cars.

Reese said, "Lynn, I need your direct involvement. The map of what you hired me to do has changed. Help us find out what happened."

For twenty years she'd known and liked Reese, a contemporary of her father, who now ailed with emphysema. When she was a student living with flying cockroaches in a New Orleans shotgun house she'd worked for the ex-navy man at his Mississippi River company to pay her Tulane tuition. Lynn had kept in touch with Reese during her many moves and rapid promotions through TriCoast. Meanwhile, he turned two more refineries profitable. When the board of directors approved her plan to acquire Centennial her first call was to Reese. He agreed to head it up until it could be connected with Bart's refinery a few miles away on the Houston Ship Channel.

Now she felt squeezed in the middle in more ways than one. "I have ten meetings scheduled early next week, including one with the board of directors."

Reese glared at her with narrowed, icy eyes she'd seen only a few times. "Nothing you're doing is more important than the safety of the people here."

She felt her shoulders stiffen. With a motion indicating Dwayne, she said, "He and I just had this discussion, with me sounding like you. But TriCoast has several experts who can help, starting with Preston Li. I'll get other folks lined up."

"I don't think we want anybody else unless they can do heavy lifting." Dwayne banged his fist on the passenger-side window. "Hell, if our own people had been working instead of contractors, this wouldn't have happened."

"You're forgetting who closed that valve." Lynn slid her elbows back against the seat. Both men moved to give her more room.

"Oh hell, Armando used to be one of us, so he's different," Dwayne said.

Reese avoided the lingering hydrogen sulfide gas by driving the long way to the gate, past the blending and packaging warehouse, past the alkylation spires and reformers, near the white, twenty-foot-diameter, bulbous liquefied gas spheres.

"A world traveler like Lynn probably doesn't even have a Texas engineer's license," Dwayne grumbled. "And I don't have time for endless analysis and approval meetings with a bunch of TriCoast suits."

"I don't have time for them either," Lynn shot back. "I've had my professional engineer's license for several years. What about you? Is yours current?"

He blinked. "Of course."

"Dwayne." Lynn spoke slowly so he wouldn't mistake her meaning. "I have a lot on the line here. So do you. We have to play on the same side to figure out what caused this apparent accident. If you're not with me, find another team. Now."

He didn't respond.

"Think it over." She knew he wouldn't change his mind about her or accept the TriCoast acquisition of his refinery during the next few minutes. *He's an important player. But he's gotta get his head in the game.* She heard the routine screech of 200-pound-pressure steam escaping from a valve and longed for the same relief.

"Let me off here," Dwayne said before they reached the security guardhouse. "I need to talk to the crude-storage operators."

She waited until he'd shut—more like slammed—the door. Evidently the need for relief was mutual. "Tell me he's not always so difficult."

"He kept this refinery together when there wasn't any money to do it. It would be one bent, grounded piece of metal if not for him." Reese turned the truck toward Centennial's office building. "Scary stuff is happening in his personal life. His wife has been in and out of the hospital several times with breast cancer."

Lynn felt as if she'd been punched. "I'm sorry to hear that." The ache of losing her mother to bone cancer gripped her chest, and she had to remember to breathe.

Reese knew his way around the neighborhoods where the dead operators had lived. Rain drummed on the Taurus's roof as they drove from Deer Park to Pasadena, suburbs near the refineries with *taquerias* and Señor Cellular stores that some Houston natives would prefer didn't exist. Lynn's fingers strayed to the collar of her silk shirt, a luxury she wouldn't have dared glance at when she was growing up, let alone consider buying.

At the first house, Lynn and Reese saw confused children who'd lost their father. At another, they felt the hysterical anger of a wife who'd lost her soul mate. At the third, they witnessed the numb despair of aged parents bereft of the adult child they'd expected to outlive them—and continue caring for their increasing medical needs. She mourned with them. She thought of her own father and swore to herself that losing her job was not a chance she could take.

Spanish moss drooping from trees formed a dismal arch over the street where until this morning LaShawna Merrell lived. The street looked like the one where Lynn had grown up.

Ragged grass slid over broken curbs.

Her stomach roiled as they parked in front of the small house. Railroad ties framed the lone tree in the yard. Surprisingly rampant bird calls were nearly drowned out by the noise of traffic from nearby LaPorte Freeway.

When she followed Reese up the slanted porch steps to the house, her legs felt heavier than when she'd dragged LaShawna's body to the locker room. Was it only this morning? She stepped around gardening tools and pressed the doorbell. It was answered by a middle-aged African American man wearing a black suit, bleached white shirt, and tie.

"I'm the funeral director for Mrs. Merrell's service." He showed them into the living room, then sat down at a nearby pink vinyl card table and typed on a laptop.

A red-eyed man introduced himself as Pete, LaShawna's husband. "I'd get up to shake your hand but, as you see, I can't." Two children, one a wide-eyed toddler and the other a pigtailed grade-schooler, had wound themselves around his legs. *They're about the same age as Cy's kids.*

"Met you at the company picnic a few weeks ago, Pete," Reese said, reaching around the children to shake the man's hand and give him their business cards.

Pete put the cards aside without looking at them. He continued stroking his toddler's back.

"Maybe the funeral director can take your children to play in another room for a few minutes so we can talk," Lynn suggested, her voice as gentle as she could make it.

As if he'd had to do this before, the man in the bleached white shirt unclamped the children from their father's legs and took them to an adjoining room.

She heard the grade-schooler say, "Here's our book about the astronauts, about Dr. Jemison and Michael Anderson."

Reese and Lynn moved their chairs closer to Pete. "I wanted to tell you how sorry we are about LaShawna," Lynn said. "We tried to revive her."

"Must not have tried hard enough."

Pete's arrow of anger reached its target. Lynn couldn't speak, still feeling the vibrations of the woman's boots scraping across the cement. *If only you'd found her, all of them, sooner.* If only it hadn't happened at all. If only.

"The Hispanic guy lived," Pete said, with as much expression as if he were reciting the alphabet.

"Three other people died, too," Reese said.

Pete leaned down to massage his ankles. When he straightened, his eyes flashed. "You got to find out what happen to LaShawna. She is—was—careful. Sound tense when she call this morning before breakfast."

"What about?" Lynn asked.

"Tol' me she seen some wetback actin' funny. He ran off from the steam shed, she say, when she yell out to ask who he be. Shit, maybe that was Armando."

"Did she know Armando?"

"Worked with him before he got laid off and had to join the contractor."

"Armando seemed as surprised as everyone else," Lynn said. *Shut up about Armando. This man wants to talk about his wife.* "Let me understand. LaShawna went in early this morning?"

He nodded. "Said they was having coker problems—coker fillin' up fast. It's the wetback's fault. Armando killed my wife. I'll find him in the hospital and choke the life outta him!" The arrow of anger had become a spear.

No one else had reported seeing anyone out of the ordinary. Lynn knew about crazy from the time when her mother was dying. For months she was convinced her mother's doctors could have found the stealthy cancer cells earlier.

"It musta been that wetback. She took all the safety training. She didn't make mistakes." He turned aside, choked, tears slipping down his face.

Their school-aged daughter peeked around the corner. She fingered a green plastic butterfly on one of her cornrows. "Daddy, when will Mommy be home?"

"Sweetie, I been telling you, Mommy can't come back this time." He motioned her to him, encircling her in his arms.

"Why, Daddy?"

"God turned her into an angel."

She looked confused, and her voice rose. "He can't do that. I need her now. Can't Mommy make me dinner first? Can't I see her one more time? Please, Daddy?"

"I'm sorry, honey. I'll go see her soon, but she can't talk to us."

5.

Thursday afternoon, Houston

Distillation: heating that separates crude oil into intermediate cuts such as gas, naphtha, gas oil, and resid for further processing.

They ate chopped beef on cheese jalapeño bread and drank iced tea from Styrofoam cups twice as big as any car cup holder was ever designed for. The still-crowded all-you-can-eat diner sported an old gasoline pump and framed pictures of Willie Nelson. Its cement floor was black with oil from every chemical plant and refinery along the Ship Channel.

The television news led with a story about how the stations with the cheapest gasoline had run out, a Centennial customer station among them. *You have plenty to do to help your customers.* Reese shook his head at the story, evidently with the same thought.

Lynn wanted to talk about something besides death, planning funerals, and answering questions from medical examiners. She wanted familiar technical conversation, the kind she'd expected to be having with Reese in his role as refinery manager.

"How's the inside group taking you?" Because no one had been willing to fully finance the offer planned by all four of the original Centennial VPs—Riley, Jay, Jean-Marie, and Dwayne—to buy their own refinery, TriCoast outbid them. Lynn's company had owned Centennial for the last three months.

Reese shifted in his seat. "They're professionals."

"I sense some resentment. Don't you?" *But you can't let the resentment affect you.*

"Same series I've always flown. They test me, but not much. They seem capable." He stared at the company names neatly stenciled high up on a white wall. The diner's paper menu announced free delivery to any nearby plant or refinery.

"Union disputes?" They'd passed the sand-colored brick USW union hall on the drive over.

"The usual. The union complains about outsourced work. But Dwayne, who's far from being a union man, complains about outsourcing too. Dessert?"

"Not today." The only choice was pecan pie. Growing up, Lynn had gathered pecans with her family from a local grove for a half-share. At home, she and her sister cracked the tough shells and picked out the meats until their fingers blistered. Her mother's pecan pies were good, but eating so many left her craving variety—key lime, mince, rhubarb, blueberry.

She had turned off her BlackBerry while visiting the families. When Reese went to the counter to pay, she called Preston. "Set up a press conference. We need to get the word out."

"I'll have Claude Durand arrange one in TriCoast's downtown Houston office in about an hour. He'll know who to invite," Preston said.

Reese returned with a wobbly-fresh piece of pecan pie.

An idea had been flitting around, as wobbly as the pie. Finally she grabbed it. "LaShawna's husband said the coker was filling up too fast." The heaviest part of crude oil was often turned into coke and sold like coal.

He nodded, his mouth full of pie.

"That's a new coker. It should have excess capacity. It shouldn't be filling up."

"Centennial's new coker was a strong point when you convinced your board to buy the refinery." Reese wiped his mouth, touching each corner twice. Then he said, "I've seen more difficulties in the last month. Did you know Centennial shut down twice unexpectedly in the spring?"

He might as well have blasted an air horn in her ear. Refineries typically run full bore in the spring to manufacture peak-season summer gasoline. "Shutdowns in prime time? No. The VPs never mentioned it, and I didn't see it described anywhere."

"None of the numbers we saw suggested Centennial was a hangar queen."

She felt a crackly sensation of sunburn when her forehead wrinkled with a question.

"An airplane that's always in the shop," he explained. "The shutdowns must have happened when you were negotiating with TriCoast's board. No one would have wanted to tell you."

No one ever wants to give you bad news. Still, she felt colder as her lack of trust in the Centennial VPs deepened. "Will we be able to make enough gasoline and jet fuel?" Not wanting to appear tense, she slid back in her seat.

He slapped the table. "Every time I turn around the government hands us a new formula. Soon we'll make three hundred grades of gasoline instead of three and sell it in quarts instead of barrels. And that's on the good days when I have all the crude I need."

It isn't like Reese to make excuses. "Everyone plays by those rules."

He didn't respond so she changed subjects. "We need to swing by TriCoast's headquarters downtown. At my request Preston and Claude set up a press conference. I'll make a statement and take questions. Can you back me up?"

"Only for easy Qs." He grinned.

In the car they closed the blisteringly hot clasps of their seat belts as quickly as possible.

Reese drove her past large gas spheres, foaming sludge ponds, gunmetal-gray warehouses, and loading cranes lining the Houston Ship Channel, where most oil companies have a refinery. Along the highway, large storage tanks serve as billboards for Junior Achievement, the United Way, or plant-safety records. Another reason for the massive tanks' placement was to buffer highway travelers and refiners from one another.

She pulled out her BlackBerry and looked at NYMEX prices for crude oil, gasoline, and heating oil. Margins were moving against her. An e-mail from Josh Rosen told her he'd be gone a few days and gave her the number of the person covering for him. She got through to Daniel right away, something that seldom happened when she called Josh. "Lynn Dayton at TriCoast. Why's the 3-2-1 crack spread so bad?"

She heard a long laugh that subsided into gasps, and finally a rough voice, "What's the punch line?"

"Punch line?" she asked.

Reese looked at her quizzically.

"That's the best joke I've heard all day. Sounds like on-camera directions for a porn shoot." Daniel waited. "That *is* your joke, right?"

Only heard it about five thousand times. She gave a quick laugh but thought how much she already missed Josh, who understood the lingo. *This Daniel dude ought to know, too.* "I wish it were that funny. The crack spread tells me roughly whether the refining margin is up or down." She explained it further, and the rookie trader recovered quickly. He described the Russian pipeline leak that had taken 300,000 barrels a day of crude oil out of the market, increasing the oil price.

When she snapped the phone shut, Reese was shaking his head. "That was helpful."

"A newbie. I hope Josh is back soon." She glanced ahead to the buildings downtown. The afternoon's rain had turned them a shimmering, speckled blue. Although she always felt anxious before an interview, the condolence visits had been far more painful.

❖

Cool-white limestone battled hot-red geometric paintings in the lobby of TriCoast's Houston office. Still wearing the same suit she'd put on to visit the families, Lynn silently read through the official statement and likely Q's and A's Claude had faxed from Dallas.

She heard the introduction. She took a long drink of water and walked into the packed meeting room, stepped onto the raised platform, and began. "About three months ago, TriCoast acquired Centennial Refining here in Houston. Four of our Centennial operators were killed today in an accident that left another worker seriously injured. I want to express to everyone again, as we have to the families of those killed, TriCoast's deepest regrets and my personal sorrow.

"The refinery leaked hydrogen sulfide, apparently caused by a misdirected valve at one of the catalytic cracking pretreaters. Several Centennial employees and I arrived at the site within minutes of the alarms sounding. We pulled all five operators into a nearby control center. Tragically, all but one were already dead.

"Your materials give you the full names and work biographies of each operator. Mr. Garza, the injured maintenance worker, appears to have suffered pulmonary edema and is being watched for bronchitis as a result of his hydrogen sulfide exposure. We ask that you not contact him until he leaves intensive care. Each of you has been given TriCoast's annual report showing the size and extent of our operations."

Time to rock and roll. She pointed to Cari Turner, an aggressive woman from the *Gulf Coast Herald* she'd met a few times on industry panels. *Not that your history matters now.*

"Is this the fault of Centennial's prior management or TriCoast's new management?"

And Cari, have you stopped beating your husband? "We view this as a very tragic accident whose cause needs to be fully investigated and remedied."

"When was TriCoast's last fatality?"

"The last fatal accident at this refinery was three years ago. TriCoast's other operations have not had a fatality for five years."

Lynn recognized a *Wall Street Journal* reporter and nodded at him.

"How much will TriCoast be fined?" His voice boomed in the small room.

So analysts can reduce it to a line item in their models? "We don't see the basis for a fine." She pointed to a Houston station's environmental reporter.

"How could such a leak occur if Centennial is meeting government guidelines for safe operations?"

"We're still investigating how the leak occurred."

The severely dressed *Oil and Gas Journal* editor took her usual approach to detail. "What agencies will be investigating you?"

Lynn thought of the potential list: the Coast Guard, OSHA, the Chemical Safety Board, the state EPA, the Texas Attorney General, the Texas State Police, Region 6 Air Quality, the fire marshal, the local district attorney. *But none will proceed fast enough to keep your people safe today, tomorrow, and the next day.* "We've met with the Harris County Medical Examiner's office and the Houston Police Department. TriCoast will proceed with our own internal investigation, of course. And tomorrow we are meeting with investigators from the US Chemical Safety and Hazard Investigation Board, the primary agency for industrial accident investigation." *Though this doesn't seem to have been an accident.*

"Doesn't this jeopardize TriCoast's $400-million investment in Centennial? And the Mexican supply contract TriCoast so desperately needs? And, since it was your idea, isn't your career also threatened?" The question came from another network affiliate's reporter.

Now we know his opinion. "We have numerous supply sources, including exciting developments from TriCoast's own E&P department. Meanwhile, Centennial's long-term opportunities and profitability remain very attractive to me and the TriCoast executive team. Our board fully supports this acquisition. But today our concerns are for our employees and their safety. That's all we have at this time. Thank you."

She made her way past the forest of boom mikes and out to the street, where Reese had sprinted ahead to the double-parked Taurus. As usual, no one else was on foot in heat-soaked downtown Houston.

"Good job," he said.

"Thanks to Claude's preparation. Let's head back to the refinery." After a half mile, she said, "I don't like what LaShawna told her husband about seeing a stranger."

"Change your mind about involving yourself in the investigation?" Reese stepped on the gas to accelerate through a left turn.

She sighed. "How can I look LaShawna's daughter in the eye if I don't find out how her mother was killed? Yes, I'll be involved, more closely than Dwayne will like."

The buzz-cut ends of Reese's hair seemed to flatten. "Dwayne will adapt."

That night, at the downtown Four Seasons Hotel, Lynn made her list. *This is more than a really bad, and it's bad enough, industrial accident. You and Preston and the TriCoast team checked and rechecked this refinery's stats. You didn't miss anything. So how did that bypass valve get closed?*

As she drifted off to sleep, she remembered a night twenty years ago. *New Orleans must be a place God gave, because God sure tried to take it away.*

On Saturday nights, the line of people waiting to eat at the French Quarter's Gumbo Shop stretched down the alley and out to Saint Peter Street. Favored by Lynn's fellow Tulane engineering and architecture students for its cheap, hearty gumbo and jambalaya, the restaurant's banana tree-shaded patio was full of young people taking a study break.

Lynn counted out money on the checked tablecloth for red beans and rice, the cheapest item on the menu. Enough left for the streetcar back to campus. And just enough time to finish the programming she'd contracted to do for Reese Spencer, to pay for the things her scholarship didn't cover. Like this meal.

When she gave her money to this week's impromptu dinner table treasurer, Lynn's friend said, "You can't go yet! We're off to Napoleon House for Pimm's Cups."

All the excuses—not enough money, having to work, needing a clear head to study in the morning—sounded like weaknesses. "I have a date with a friend."

The casually sloppy boy she'd hoped would notice her finally did. His glance flicked over her slight runner's physique, polyester shirt, and wrong-color jeans. He made a comment to the girl sitting next to him, and they laughed.

The New Orleans native on her right spoke up kindly. "C'mon, Lynn. We know what you'll be doing. Just don't get too far ahead of us in thermo." He led her friends in a chorus of good-byes as she pushed away from the table.

"Next week. Next week, I'll stay longer," she promised. She ran southwest on Bourbon, past the bars and dozens of weird businesses she cherished, until she crossed the neutral zone at Canal—the median that was the ancient French-English dividing line, and now where Bourbon became Carondelet. The streetcar clattered and squealed to a stop. Elbowing through the crowd of disembarking tourists and ready-to-party students, Lynn climbed aboard.

6.

Friday, Houston

She had set this morning's meeting with Reese and Bart at dawn because Bart Colby, the manager of TriCoast's other Houston refinery, was an old-style engineer like Dwayne who started the day early. *He's probably already been to the office*, Lynn thought.

She considered integrating Centennial with TriCoast's other Ship Channel refinery, one that showcased state-of-the-art technology. The biggest issue, of course, was what Preston would call a "human factors analysis." Reese and Bart had met several times and got along. But what about everyone else at the two refineries?

If only you'd been able to sleep through the night. When she opened the door to go to breakfast she spotted the complimentary copy of the *Gulf Coast Herald*. "Former Centennial Refinery Off to a Wobbly Start Under New TriCoast Owners" headlined the business section. The article, by business journalist Cari Turner, featured a file picture of the refinery and a description of its deadly accident. Lynn read the story with growing dismay as she rode the elevator to the hotel café for breakfast.

Turner quoted Cody Laughlin, union steward, and an unnamed inside source. Cody said, "They see a tank fire, and the only thing the big brass at TriCoast worry about is inventory loss. Some operators drink hydrogen sulfide and no one cares."

Cody, you are so wrong. And who's the inside source?

The article went on to suggest TriCoast was struggling to merge

Centennial into its portfolio of other refineries, and that Centennial was plagued by numerous financial and operational difficulties, including environmental concerns. *Damn this elevator! Why won't it move faster?* Turner cited Centennial's use of contract labor and the deep pockets of its new owner represented by "junior vice president Lynn Dayton, who so far has not been effectual in addressing the many difficulties." *Junior vice president? Cari's a hack.* According to the reporter, neither refinery manager Reese Spencer nor Ms. Dayton had been available for further comment after the press conference.

And when did Cari call? Midnight? Ever? And who was the unnamed source?

She ordered toast and coffee and waited for Reese and Bart, hoping to calm down by the time they arrived. She decided against calling Cari immediately, but she pulled her cell phone from her purse and left a message for Claude Durand asking him to call her. A fight in print now wouldn't help the families of LaShawna, Armando, or the other operators. *It sure won't fix Centennial as fast as you need it fixed.*

"That story in the Herald this morning was a nasty surprise. Cari Turner never called me. And who's the inside source?" Lynn talked to Reese while they waited for Bart. "Call a meeting on it this morning, if you would."

Reese's tone was reassuring. "I sure hate to see our name in a bad light."

"I'll talk to Claude Durand, see if he can provide her more accurate background on TriCoast than she seems to have . . ."

"Made up?" Reese said.

When Bart arrived, the three of them talked about the hydrogen sulfide poisoning the previous day, the newspaper article, Bart's advice for more training, and what to expect from the CSB and other regulators.

Before yesterday, Lynn's and Bart's plan had been to combine the two Ship Channel refineries as much as possible—people, piping, contracts, suppliers. Reese was the first to bring up the subject of delay. Tenting his hands, he said, "This combination is close enough that we can count the rivets over at your place. But we'll need to postpone, of course."

"We sure don't want to introduce whatever problems Centennial appears to be having into your refinery," Lynn said.

"How long will your investigation take?" Bart leaned forward in his chair, his head down as he swirled leftover bits of egg and sausage with his fork.

"Fast as possible for the sake of everyone there. We'll do first interviews today, hopefully have answers in a few days," Lynn said.

"Isn't this meeting premature, then? I have too many other things I could be doing." Bart looked straight up at Lynn, a growl in his voice.

She returned Bart's gaze with the firmness of her own. "Our investigation will move quickly. In the meantime, putting together exchange agreements, weight and volume balances, and construction plans will take time. You and Reese can start joint teams on those."

After Bart left, she faced Reese. "We have to work this incident as fast as we can. I'm not sure it's an accident."

"You're not going to give me that old woman's intuition fallback, are you?"

Then she knew how much discussing Centennial's troubles with Bart, both colleague and competitor, had hurt Reese. He had always believed in her abilities and the soundness of her decisions.

"Never thought you to be old-fashioned, Reese. Malcolm Gladwell calls it the power of thinking without thinking."

"Fancy words for snap judgment."

"Believe me on this. Something more than just an accident occurred at Centennial yesterday."

If she was to investigate quickly, that also meant she had only a few days to complete her evaluation of the Centennial executives instead of the several more weeks she had counted on. *You have to find out whom you can trust.*

She had spoken with them a few times before the acquisition. But Tyree Bickham, the company's general counsel, had urged her to limit discussions because of his antitrust concerns. If the acquisition didn't go through, he reasoned, TriCoast and Centennial could be accused of exchanging and using information to gain unfair advantage over their competitors. *But his limits are a damn hindrance to you now.*

"Let's talk more about the folks at Centennial. Tell me what I don't already know about Jay Gans."

What she already knew was that Jay's position in charge of the refinery's biggest cost was crucial. A scratch golfer with sun-darkened skin who always smelled of soap, Jay would remain Centennial's chief of oil supply for now. But Centennial had too few suppliers and too much oil in storage; it was one of the opportunities for savings that had led her to buy the refinery. With TriCoast's wider network of contacts and better negotiating strength, Jay could bring the costs down.

"You remember he's a Texas A&M chemical engineer?" In the Gulf Coast petroleum industry, that made him the equivalent of a well-placed archbishop. "They must really teach 'em to scrub behind the ears. I always wonder what scent he'll come in with next."

Lynn felt her face relax in a smile. "His CV said he'd been buying the refinery's crude about six years. And that golf tan. He must play a course somewhere at least once a week. Either he started out as a par golfer and it helped his supplier relationships . . ."

Reese changed lanes. "Or all the business golf improved his game."

"Hmm. So not much new with him. How about Jean-Marie and Dwayne?"

"Despite their prickliness with one another, they agree on what's necessary to stay in compliance."

"That's one reason this incident, whatever it is, is so surprising." She moved the sun visor out of the way. "Tell me more about Jean-Marie."

Reese explained that she'd married and divorced twice, and now seemed married only to her work of keeping Centennial in compliance with environmental and safety rules. That her immediate New Orleans family was one of the lucky ones living in Algiers who hadn't lost their house to floods. But that her other relatives in St. Bernard Parish had lost everything.

"She's threatened to shut down the refinery if she ever considers it a necessary safety measure. So she's doing her job, even if she is abrasive," he concluded.

Lynn finally remembered why the woman's face was so familiar, and felt even more sorrow about the New Orleans disaster. Her alma mater had sustained millions in damage. It had reopened as quickly as possible, but to do so had slashed curricula and combined colleges. "Jean-Marie was one of the best students ever to go through Tulane's engineering school. I walked by her photograph hundreds of times." In the engineering school's main breezeway, Jean-Marie's had been one of the first women's pictures in a chronological parade of men's photos. Each represented the graduating student who had earned the highest grade point average.

But Jean-Marie was several years older. "I'd have guessed she'd be running a refinery now instead of filling a staff job."

"Maybe there's a personal difficulty."

"Maybe she didn't get the opportunity."

"You going soft on me?" Reese asked. "She should have spoken up about what she wanted to do."

"There's only so much speaking up you can do before you're labeled—I believe your word for it is—abrasive."

"Ease up, Lynn."

"Reese, you understand as well as I do that the starting line isn't in the same place for everyone."

After conferring with Reese and Claude about the *Herald* article, Lynn called a meeting of the Centennial executives late in the morning to discuss it.

She stood front and center. "I'm sure you've heard about or seen the *Herald* article this morning. Claude Durand and I asked Cari Turner to identify her unnamed source, which she won't agree to do, no real surprise. We also sent her a point-by-point rebuttal, which Claude prepared, that highlights our improved financial and operating statistics. Needless to say, I don't want Centennial or TriCoast in a defensive mode with the press."

"I'm preparing a press release, too." Riley patted his large stomach as if to reassure himself it was still there.

"Run it through Claude and have him issue it."

"Why?"

Is he faking or is he really this clueless? "He's the communications VP," Lynn said. "He's the spokesperson for TriCoast and he's the only one authorized to speak to the press."

Riley's face colored slightly. "Bureaucracy."

"Get used to it," Jay said. "What else should we do?"

"Keep your eyes open," Reese said. "Try to find out who the source might have been."

"Cody's quoted saying the same thing he always says," Jay added, "although I wish he hadn't gone to the paper with it. But why would someone else go after us? Maybe it's someone at TriCoast's other refinery, worried about losing his job. Maybe it's you, Lynn, trying to cover up a bad deal."

She stood still, surprised by the attack but determined to stay cool. Conflict, from minor disagreements to sexual harassment to major negotiating roadblocks, came in a daily variety. She'd found she did best by staying as unflappable as possible. "Wrong, Jay. It's in my best interest for Centennial to do well. And you can be sure if I'd been the source, I'd have made myself sound better."

Jean-Marie snorted in appreciation.

Lynn looked slowly around the room. *Let's play this game.* "Who else might have something to gain? Certainly one of our competitors."

The room started to buzz angrily.

"I suggest," she said over the buzz, "that pointing fingers without proof only slows us down."

Riley jumped to his feet. "Lynn, I hear what you say about not pointing fingers, but the fact is we were fine before you, Reese, and the TriCoast bunch showed up."

Dwayne and Jay nodded in agreement.

"Unfortunately not true." She walked over to him but spoke so all could hear. "In fact, as you told me yourself, the setbacks have been occurring piecemeal. The same one or two factors are behind the H_2S leak, the excess sulfur, and the poor margins. When we can bring all the information together and identify those one or two factors, we will solve Centennial's current problems." *Get all that?*

Silence.

"Aside from avoiding a repeat in the press, what else should we consider?" Reese asked.

Jean-Marie spoke up. "I talked to the OSHA rep this morning. She wants updates. F'sure she'll be here to investigate, probably with an initial penalty request of half a million dollars."

"Oh, that helps the bottom line," Riley said.

"Goddamnit, Riley, is that all you ever think about?" Dwayne exploded.

"Someone's got to," he answered, with a sidelong glance at Lynn. Her BlackBerry buzzed and she glanced at the message.

"That's enough, everyone," she said. "Talk to me individually this afternoon if you have more questions. Right now we have visitors, two investigators from the CSB."

L.A. Starks

When Kyle and Gina entered the room it was apparent they were a well-matched pair of opposites for their investigating posts. Shaggy-haired Kyle towered over Dwayne, and even Jean-Marie, at about six-foot-six and 250 pounds. His easy smile belied his physical size. Gina was petite, stunningly dark-haired, with a firm set to her jaw that suggested she was strictly business. Both carried laptops and stacks of well-marked research about Centennial. Lynn was glad the CSB chairman had assigned two no-nonsense types.

Jean-Marie, who knew both Kyle and Gina, introduced them to Lynn, Preston, and Reese. "And you've met Dwayne," she concluded.

Lynn welcomed them. "We have every interest in determining the factors and the root cause of this incident as quickly as possible. We realize your investigation will take some time, and that the full CSB board ultimately has to vote on the root cause.

"We can't wait for the vote. We expect you will immediately share with us anything you find that presents us with any kind of threat or danger. Let me start with a question that arose yesterday when I talked to Angela."

Lynn turned to Jean-Marie. "From our due diligence effort, we understood that there was only one incident in the last six months for which the CSB was called in to investigate. Yesterday, Angela mentioned that CSB investigators have been here three times during the last six months."

Jean-Marie's eyes narrowed, but Kyle spoke first. "It's something you should be happy about; Jean-Marie called me to come out and chat about some accelerated corrosion she thought she and Dwayne were seeing in some of Centennial's pipes and valves. It was strictly preemptive. She was trying to avoid an accident, and I was able to supply industry statistics from our database."

Okay. Good news about the CSB, bad news about the corrosion. "I'm glad you were ahead of the game, Jean-Marie. What did you conclude?"

"That the corrosion is indeed more advanced than it should be.

50

It's localized, and we're watching it. But we haven't uncovered what's causing it yet, *cher*."

Why does "cher" *from her sound like* "baby-doll" *from some of the men you used to work with?* "Tell me about the reported incident in March."

"We had some valves closed on a unit start-up that should have been open," Jean-Marie said. "Overheated liquid filled a splitter and went to the blowdown drum. The drum geysered out and formed a flammable vapor cloud at ground level. Lucky for us, it didn't ignite, but two of our contractors were injured."

"We made recommendations and saw complete compliance from Centennial," Kyle added. "Jean-Marie enhanced manpower on the start-up crews and provided extra training. She and Dwayne reconfigured the unit and tied the drum into the flare system so that any future flammable vapor would be burned off. Centennial also checked to make sure the contractors' trailers and trucks were kept well away from the process areas."

Lynn knew that all their suggestions were lessons learned from an unfortunate BP start-up accident in which nonworking overflow indicators and closed valves allowed a tower of light hydrocarbons—pentanes and hexanes—to overfill. Redirected by valves found closed that should have been open, the light liquid hydrocarbons had been vented to the atmosphere where they'd formed a vapor cloud that rapidly spread. A spark from an idling truck ignited explosions and pressure waves that had killed fifteen and injured one hundred and seventy.

Those killed had been contractors working near the tower in trailers. Unlike control centers, trailers are not designed to withstand the equivalent of a large bomb blast.

Lynn looked around and saw that all in the room remembered the same terrible accident.

Among the many changes since then, Centennial, TriCoast, and other refineries now encouraged their workers to make short trips on foot or by bicycle to lessen the likelihood of an engine spark igniting a vapor cloud as had happened at BP. While the first rule of refining is that oil and gas be contained inside pipes and vessels, and they usually are, the three elements needed for fire and explosion—hydrocarbons, oxygen, and a spark—are always in such close and dangerous proximity in a refinery that containing them can be like riding a rocket.

Ironic that we have to pedal bikes in a place that makes gasoline.

"We need to hear from each of you about what you saw, heard, smelled, or thought—everything leading up to yesterday's accident," Gina said. "You each have different thoughts and impressions, so Kyle and I will talk to you one by one. Lynn, if you'll go with Kyle, and Jean-Marie with me." Dwayne, Reese, and Preston would also be interviewed, and then Kyle and Gina would start the field interviews.

"Dwayne can introduce you to Adric Washington and his crew on shift at the time. You also need to talk to Cody Laughlin, the USW union rep," Lynn said.

"Cody will just say he needs more people," Dwayne said. "Of course, I say the same thing myself all the time, but the CFOs always shoot me down."

Jean-Marie rolled her eyes. "I make sure we get what we need to do our job safely."

Do you? Lynn thought.

"I have to talk to Mike face-to-face, catch up with the other refineries. Then I'll fly back here." Lynn spoke with Reese as they crawled through Houston traffic in the rental Taurus.

"Is one of the TriCoast pilots waiting for you at Hobby?"

She pictured the small plane that had brought her to Houston yesterday at five in the morning and nodded.

Traffic slowed, then stopped, giving her a sense of being trapped. Talking about New Orleans had reminded Lynn that, given Houston's flat, marshy coastal plain, a 15-foot storm surge from the Gulf of

Mexico could strike 50 miles inland. She remembered the 100-mile-long traffic jam between Houston and Dallas in which so many of her TriCoast friends had been caught.

The car's air conditioning faltered. Reese wiped sweat bubbles from his forehead with a white handkerchief. Thick, grainy black smoke rose about two miles ahead.

Lynn's leg cramped suddenly. She flattened her foot to wring out the pain and stared ahead to see the source of the smoke. Hoping it wasn't TriCoast's second Houston refinery, her concerns escalated in a different direction.

The flash of red and blue lights in the side view mirror alerted her moments before three ambulances raced by on the freeway shoulder.

She took a deep breath and strained to locate the source of the fire. "There it is!" Her cramped legs loosened. "Tank fire at Meletio."

Meletio Refining was about four miles from Centennial and a mile from TriCoast's other Houston refinery. The huge orange blaze dwarfed the people and machines visible around it. Black smoke formed an acrid wedge above what she estimated had been a 75,000-barrel storage tank. Her next calculation was so automatic it was involuntary. *More than three and a half million dollars smoked, plus downtime and profit loss.*

Firefighters from the refinery and from the fire departments of Houston and Pasadena were spread cautiously away from the berm surrounding the half-melted tank. Its perfect white cylindrical profile was now black and gray, rolled and melted halfway down into a wavy, worthless heap.

Four ambulances raced out of Meletio's gates, toward Pasadena Memorial Hospital.

"Usually no one's injured in a tank fire," Reese observed in a voice thick with tension. Despite all the oil in storage—essentially tons of the rawest of fuels—nonstop safety training on the Channel meant most fires were contained quickly with few or no injuries.

They stopped and started a few more times until they passed the Meletio Refining Company's entrance and traffic sped up.

She called Adric for news and relayed it to Reese. "Three people killed, ten injured. Pieces of the metal staircase and the measurement platform at the top separated and fell about a hundred feet, turned into shrapnel."

"Terrible!"

Lynn, too, felt her eyes narrow behind her sunglasses as if that would change the news. She forced them open.

Reese exited the freeway and headed toward TriCoast's private airplane hangar. He was silent when they passed swampy water and drove through a chain-link gate to stop at the sheet-metal building that served as the company's hangar.

She reached for her door handle. "Reese, I'm concerned we don't understand what's happening at Centennial. The faulty alarm bothers me. This fire at Meletio bothers me. The Ship Channel has lots of accidents—we're all just sitting on big ol' fuel tanks, but I think something else is up. We need to be careful."

She settled back when the Beechcraft took off for Dallas. TriCoast used this plane and four others like it to fly short hops to Midland, Houston, Lafayette, and Tulsa. Garden spots of the world. *But that's where the oil is. Never Paris, Hawaii, or New Zealand.*

She called Mike to tell him about the day's events.

"Thanks for handling the press conference yesterday. I saw it. You did well. Who's running the investigation?"

"I am." She waited through the CEO's disapproving silence.

"You don't have the time. Get one of the hazards people to head it up."

"Too important."

"Toss it to someone else as soon as you can," he grumbled. "Prep for the board meeting. Check in with your new best friends at Pemex on the supply contract. If you think they don't want to work with a woman, get Bart to take over the negotiations for you."

And then take over your job. "Everything's fine with Pemex. I need to address this situation with Centennial."

"Don't piss around on it too long."

Returning to her primary concern, she sat in the airplane seat, fell back on her years of analytical training, and wrote on a pad of graph paper:

Issues

1) H_2S leak and concentration too high, nonfunctional H_2S sensor
2) Continuing Centennial operating problems—sulfur, making product specs, coker filling up, pipe corrosion
3) Meletio tank fire possibly related

Possible Sources

1) Neglect of safety
2) Deferred maintenance
3) Union prestrike action
4) Deliberate sabotage from known or unknown group

Who/Motivations

1) Riley—job redundancy
2) Jean-Marie—cover up safety mistake
3) Dwayne—resentment, wife's cancer main concern?
4) Cody/Adric/Skyler/union—prestrike action
5) Outsider
   a) Armando/LaShawna mentioned, but attacks specific
   b) grudge
   c) environmental or safety extremist
   d) consultant—Brian Tulley, etc.
   e) unknown third party with inside connection

Lynn stared at the list for a while and shuddered. She would plan her next inquiries while in Dallas tonight and resume them when she returned to Houston tomorrow.

She called her father, then Cy. She could hear Cy's son, little Matt, crooning almost-two-year-old almost-words in the background. "Wuh wuh wuh."

"I'd like to come by, but I have to see Dad."

"Come over after that."

"I'll be there as soon as I can," she said, unsure of whether he wanted her to spend the night.

No one else but the pilot was on the plane. Lynn closed her eyes and replayed the scenes with the families. Two children would never again have their dinners fixed by LaShawna.

7.

Friday evening, Paris
Seven-hour time difference between Paris and US Central Daylight Savings Time

What is wisest? Number.

-**Pythagoras, 582-496 BC**

Robert Guillard?"

"*Oui.*"

"Centennial's down. Part of it." The American's voice honked over the phone.

Robert twisted in his chair to confirm his door was closed. It always was, as in most French offices of any importance. "Then we'll release part of the payment." He would check the Rabbit's version before giving the banks his instructions. He looked at his watch. Still morning in the States. Plenty of time to transfer money. The eurodollar exchange rate made the transaction more affordable than it would have been a few months earlier.

"Four people killed. One injured?" It sounded like a question.

"No additional for casualties," Robert replied in careful English.

"I forgot. Stay in touch, munshur. Uh vwah."

Stupid Americans. Unable to speak French, barely even English, and proud of it. He wondered if the Rabbit would be able to carry out the second plan.

Robert fingered a stack of telephone messages, each beginning with a different country code. His full screen of new *courriel*, e-mail, showed sender servers from five continents. In his work at the French Ministry of Economy, Finance, and Industry, Robert had learned that each nationality, and each ethnicity within each nationality, had at least one useful weakness.

He applied that knowledge to his after-hours work. The Americans he met, like the Rabbit, were easy to understand; they were drawn by the scent of money. The Asians, like Xin Yu, were more interesting. They wanted to exercise power or serve the community good.

But he, Robert, was the person with the broadest vision. And he was the only person in France, or elsewhere, with the will and intelligence to implement his dream of developing energy for worthy emerging countries. Domination of the world's primary energy source carried ultimate responsibility, and ultimate power. He was equipped for both.

If only he could get the stupid Americans to work faster so he could meet Xin's deadline in eleven days. Then Xin would continue to fund him, and he could force the brilliant, beautiful Mademoiselle Dayton to partner with him.

He'd matched Lynn to his plan months ago. Although many people had her level of refining experience, which he needed, few refining executives had as obvious a vulnerability as she had in her idealistic younger sister. He picked up a report from his desk and scanned Lynn's personal data: mother recently lost to cancer, father sick with emphysema, boyfriend a widower with two small children. If his strategy with Ceil didn't work, Lynn had many other useful weaknesses.

He smoothed a wrinkle in his tie.

At the strike of the hour, Robert heard the technical advisor in the French Ministry of Economy, Finance, and Industry close his door and leave.

He knew he could rely on this punctuality. Punctuality so un-French it was treasonous. On the days the advisor was in, no matter which meeting he was obstructing, he extricated himself by seven o'clock, claiming an out-of-office evening appointment. So Robert, assistant to the technical advisor, generally left fifteen minutes later.

The café was a few kilometers away, in the seventh arrondissement. Tonight, no one seemed to be following him. He stopped by a store window and glanced at his reflection and at the ones of those around him.

Robert's frequent girlfriends told him they admired the contrast between his jet-black hair and his Dresden blue eyes. His rare smile was wide, buoyant, practiced. His body was as lean as a coyote's.

As he resumed walking, Robert thought again of Lynn Dayton. The Rabbit had to shut down Centennial Refinery completely. Then he would take care of the others. Fortunately, most were near Centennial. But they had to act quickly. Xin Yu had made it clear that the Asian refining consortium Sansei and its associates would pay only for the next eleven days of capacity removal. Robert needed Sansei's money to carry out his vision of building refineries in certain deserving Third World countries.

He needed Lynn's expertise, too. Robert had scouted for refiners when he attended a New York conference on behalf of the ministry. Lynn Dayton had caught his attention immediately. Fast rising, gracefully athletic, a woman in a sea of men, confident when she spoke. Then he studied the reports and pictures of her, learned her family vulnerabilities. She seemed inordinately proud of her just-announced acquisition of Centennial Refining.

She was probably at Centennial now, wringing her hands over a few bodies, wondering how she would explain the mishap to TriCoast's impatient board of directors.

He wondered if the young woman he expected to arrive in Paris this week would come to the café tonight. Enticing Ceil Dayton into his circle was key to recruiting her more valuable sister. Through his contacts, he had already arranged both an incident to force her out of Gabon and a job with the International Energy Agency as an enticement to bring her here, to him. Unknown to her, he had supplied his friends with her plane fare and exact directions. Graphs of probabilities and standard deviations ran through his mind. In the end, he was fairly certain Ceil would "bite," to use one of the few American expressions he liked.

His small group sat around a table near the fountain, served by their regular waiter.

"*Salut!*" Robert cheered, joining the group.

"*Comment allez-vous?*"

"The usual."

He took his seat and the discussion resumed in the French dialect of food. They had waited for him before ordering and so now they talked about the fricassée of quail, the pink grapefruit with Ceylonese tea sorbet, the leg of lamb with tabouli, and the baked plums with vanilla ice cream.

"Tonight you should have the quail and the plums," their waiter advised. "And the 1986 Guigul Côtes du Rhône."

The fountain splashed behind Robert. He smelled the other plates of the day—seared monkfish, roasting duck, apple-purée tarts. With total concentration, he debated the menu with the others for several minutes.

Robert's position at the ministry gave him the cover and high-level access he required. This group was his policy group, his thinking group. Sansei, the Asian refining consortium, financed his operation. The Rabbit and other assistants carried out his elegant strategy. None knew of his plans for Lynn. All players overlapped only through him. The intersection of his circles produced a set of one.

A fragile May breeze kissed the terrace. The air was clear and clean, the kind that comes from nuclear power, he thought. His thought flashed to a woman he considered as useful and interesting as Lynn, Anne Lauvergeon. There must be a way to fit her, the attractive chief executive of a French nuclear-engineering company, into his plans also.

The men and women of his group bent toward him in postures of complete attention. Their conversation was low and intense.

"The French have been leaders for centuries. Look at our magnificent history, our engineers, our mathematicians, our lovers, and our artists. Our Tour d'Eiffel is but one superb illustration of our mathematical and engineering artistry. It's time we reminded the world."

"Marianne," said one, referring to France's iconic symbol of liberty and reason, the symbol of the French Republic itself.

"Descartes," said another.

Robert noticed a woman pulling up a café chair at the rear of the group to face him. His glance took in her worn blouse and fashionable, though threadbare, skirt.

Was this the woman, Ceil Dayton? She resembled Lynn, but her unwashed hair and skimpy clothes didn't match his expectations. No congruence. Would she default to a banal American smile?

She didn't.

Maybe she was Anglo-Saxon. Or German.

He had to be completely certain this woman was not another of Sansei's operatives, sent to watch him here.

"My friends," Robert said, "we know that all language is a construct. We know that science and scientific language as a subset is even more artificial."

"You are a graduate of X. How can you say that?"

"I did not say pure mathematical language."

"Ah, Robert." One of the men sighed with satisfaction.

The most celebrated university in France, "X" stood for the École Polytechnique. Established by Napoleon near Paris to provide an elite corps of engineers, X accepted only 350 students a year. After earning a high school baccalaureate—no easy feat itself—an aspirant to X prepared two to three years before taking its pure mathematics entrance exam. Its graduates were guaranteed the highest positions in French government, business, and society for the rest of their lives.

"If anyone knows, I do."

Robert waited until a camo-clad gendarme, one who'd shaved his head bald as part of his aggressive armor, walked past. "We understand that capitalists in all countries use this language, this science, to justify control. We must find a way to use their governments—the same tools they use to reinforce their oppression—to benefit people born without the advantages of white race, male gender, or upper class."

Succulent brown rabbit and spicy lamb arrived at the table.

"*Bon appétit!*"

The woman had not ordered. Maybe she couldn't afford to.

Thinking she might be Ceil, Robert invited her to their table and offered shares.

Robert watched her swallow. She savored her food instead of bolting it. He'd made a mistake; she had to be French to appreciate food as she did. Maybe she was from the country.

Finally the woman spoke, in perfect French. "Do you discuss your concerns theoretically night after night or do you have plans?"

Definitely an American, Robert thought. *No patience for abstract thinking.* "We believe the Americans should reduce their petrol use by continuing to experience its true, high price. The OPEC-American coalition should set aside the resulting extra oil and sell it at a discount to worthy underdeveloped countries. Those countries would resell it at market price to finance their own refinery construction."

Heads nodded. They had agreed on this policy statement long ago. Robert would never need to tell the others the truth about Sansei's backing and what was expected in return, or that the policy statement was merely a diversion.

"How could you possibly do that?" she asked.

"Who are you?" he challenged, using an American shortcut he'd learned to like.

Her lips formed a small, luscious curve. "A believer."

❖

The group broke up at nine, even though summer sun still lingered on Paris streets.

Robert strode to the woman in the frayed skirt. "You spoke well. Who are you?"

"Ceil Dayton. You're Robert Guillard, aren't you? Let me be frank. I need money. My dear friends in Gabon said you could arrange a job for me at the IEA. They bought me a plane ticket to Paris and told me how to find you."

At last. He widened his eyes. But he wouldn't tell her he'd been expecting her, or express pleasure that his Gabonese contacts were more effective than the Rabbit, or show his satisfaction that she'd done his bidding. One more test. "I am Robert Guillard. You are from where?"

The woman sighed, as if this were a difficult question. "The States, but as I said, I've just arrived from Gabon. Peace Corps."

He substituted a visage of surprise for the pleasure he felt. "The IEA does pay more than your American Peace Corps. And yes, given your experience as described to me by our mutual friends, and your fluency in French and English, the IEA is interested in speaking with you. Where are you staying?"

"Goutte-d'Or."

"I'll go with you. You should find a better place."

"You mean I should avoid the drug dealers?"

He nodded. For Ceil Dayton and what she meant to his plans, he would make the time for the long underground journey.

They strode through the outside lights of several other cafés and past the classical Dôme des Invalides that housed Napoleon's tomb. She seemed to understand the city, directing him down the stairs at the white-tiled Invalides Métro station.

When the train arrived, he stepped onto it and offered his hand. Ceil grasped it lightly, allowing herself to be pulled in. The train took off, their car now almost empty of passengers but still humid and sweaty.

"What did your friends say?" he asked innocently. He'd made the arrangements weeks before.

"I . . . I had trouble in Gabon. My friends, a couple there, said they had spoken to you about it and that given my background in the industry and my fluency in French, you could have a job waiting. They directed me to you, bought my ticket."

All as he expected. He studied the overhead banner advertising "Learn Wall Street English." *It'll be a short class when all they teach is swear words*, he thought. At Strasbourg St. Denis they changed to Line 4.

"What do you do?"

A typically annoying American question. Never, *who are you? Only, what do you do?*

"I have a position at the Ministry of Economy, Finance, and Industry. I visit New York often." The security precautions had become more arduous, the US bankers more unpleasant since the Iraq invasion, but the ministry required the trips. Late at night, after the drinks and mediocre dinners with his official capital-market hosts, he often spoke with the Rabbit and the others.

After a short ride they reached Barbès Rochechouart. "Here's my stop."

Ceil kicked a crumpled paper on the sidewalk. He hadn't been here in a few years, but the place was still a slum. He thought it close in spirit as well as proximity to the Périphérique. Beyond the Périphérique no one important lived, despite riots from people attempting to protest otherwise. He would persuade her to move to a better location. "What led you to quit the Peace Corps?"

"Paris is the best city in the world," she said.

She was sidestepping his question. He wondered how rough his mercenaries had been and mustered the kindly voice he'd learned from the Americans. "Do you have family here?" he asked, though he already knew her father and sister were far away. He'd settled on the IEA job for Ceil to draw her sister, Lynn, closer.

"No. They're fine without me, though."

Her audacity pleased him. She took foolish chances, like her sister. "Call me tomorrow and I will make final arrangements for your interview." He wrote down his number.

Stopping at the door, she said, "*Au revoir*, Robert. You are very kind to a stranger. I will call."

Robert relished the millions of people Paris drew to its embrace. After leaving Ceil and enduring the long Métro ride back from the 18th arrondissement, he sensed one of those millions following him.

He was not far from the Palais Royal. He turned a corner, stepped into the shadow of a doorway, and watched as a dumpy man came around the building after him. The man's head twitched when he didn't see Robert. He scanned the boulevard for a few seconds, then trotted back around the corner.

Robert waited. When the man didn't reappear, he slipped through the iron gates of the Palais Royal, just as the watchman closed them. He threaded through the barrel-like, striped posts his fellow citizens called "mushrooms." He was home.

The dumpy man's clothing gave him away, Robert thought. A Frenchman would never appear in public looking less than perfect.

❖

Robert's girlfriends had swarmed him ever since his acceptance into X was published in the newspapers. They knew he could go everywhere, especially in the highest circles. And his wife, Thérèse, was as beautiful and intelligent as the icons Heloise or Marianne, Robert thought. A reward he deserved.

He heard his wife's silvery voice. "Robert! I have been waiting here for you." When he entered their bedroom, she let her robe fall open. She drew him to her, slowly removing his clothes, then her robe. Soon she pulled him inside in long, fierce arcs.

8.

Late Friday night, Paris

What is truest? Most men are bad.
                    -Pythagoras, 582-496 BC

After their lovemaking, Thérèse slept.

Robert sat at his restored antique desk. He remembered how relentlessly his parents scolded him. Weak-willed Americans might claim family dysfunction, resulting in the need to display anger on a reality television show or assuage the "hurt" with expensive therapy, but discipline and order were the French norm. Indeed, he considered Americans pathetic for not experiencing such strictness. And the scolding had stopped once he'd brought home top-of-class standings. By that time he'd progressed well beyond his parents' intellectual level; he had discovered the wisdom of Pythagoras.

He reduced the computer's speaker volume so as not to wake his wife, even though his desk was far from their bedroom. She was so beautiful. His prize.

She seemed more tired these last few weeks. He hoped she was pregnant. Fathering a child, particularly a son, would raise his standing at the ministry. He visualized the ideal postpartum gift—an Hermès pink wallet-purse from the flagship store on rue de Fauborg Saint-Honore. Unlike Oprah Winfrey, he could expect a warm welcome.

A story on the screen caught his notice. Pirates had attacked ships again in the Malacca Strait near Singapore. Equipped with assault rifles, cell phones, speedboats, and vessels into which they transferred the diesel fuel they captured, the pirates dispersed it through a black-market network of dealers.

Envious, Robert wondered if Xin Yu from Sansei had sponsored this, too. His deadline pressed on him. Could the Rabbit and his *mercenaires* do everything he asked of them in the next eleven days? Could they lengthen the shutdowns? The longer the refineries were offline, the more Sansei would pay him.

He checked press releases on TriCoast's Web site. News of the "accident" had already been posted. TriCoast executive vice president of refining Lynn Dayton expressed condolences to the families, promising to find and correct the source of the problem.

As long as it leads you to me, he thought. He e-mailed instructions to his bank to pay the Rabbit. Partial payment.

As he clicked further into TriCoast's site, one name caught his attention—Claude Durand, director of public relations for TriCoast. Claude, the second-rater. Robert had bypassed him years before when Claude had failed entrance exams for the École Polytechnique, as most candidates did. So he took refuge in the States, Robert thought, haven for the French incompetent.

He flicked his browser to a twenty-four-hour news show and pulled up the short video of the TriCoast press conference. Lynn Dayton again. She must be taking the lead. His plan was succeeding.

He watched it twice, listened to her voice. No tics, no quavers, not even when asked about the wisdom of TriCoast's multimillion-dollar investment in Centennial.

He'd give her and her board more to think about.

Another headline directed him to a tape showing a burning tank capped by a puff of black smoke. The Houston television reporter noted Meletio Refining had suffered a fire that incinerated 75,000 barrels of diesel.

Mon dieu, was that all the Rabbit had managed? A tank fire? It wouldn't even register for Sansei. The Rabbit was proving even more incapable than he'd anticipated.

He looked at his watch. Evening in Houston. It was the time upon which they'd agreed. He spent a few minutes attaching his SV-100 SafeVoice scrambler to his cell phone and punching in the code, knowing the Rabbit was doing the same. The chips in their scramblers would modify and encode their voices. To anyone trying to eavesdrop, their voices would sound like noise. The next time they talked, they would choose a different code.

"Yes."

Bon, the Rabbit was in the hole.

"All went as planned?" Robert asked, although he knew the answer.

"As I told you earlier, the refinery is crippled, almost useless without one of its cat crackers. So when will you send the money?"

He kept the bite of anger in his voice. "I've sent fifty percent of the contract price."

"Destruction or major damage for full price. That's our deal."

"Deal" seems to be Americans' favorite word, Robert thought. *A nation of card players.* The Rabbit had no recourse but to perform, so Robert ignored the comment.

"What does everyone believe happened?"

"An accident. That's how the new parent company, TriCoast, is investigating it."

"And what is this silliness with Meletio Refinery? I thought you were shutting them down. A tank fire is nothing."

"It was short notice."

Such *plainte*, Robert thought. "We don't get paid for a tank fire."

"But I do have some possible new recruits. Uh vwah."

Robert winced at the mangled French. "Good-bye."

The Rabbit punched a few buttons on a calculator and listened to the sound of the night wind skimming off the Channel. Robert could be a jerk. *Maddeningly indirect, never clear on what he wanted, the man has no idea of the risks I'm taking. Ain't Robert's ass on the line. And he hasn't*

come through with all the money. But when he does, I'm outta here. Blow this clammy town and buy an island.

The investigation was no trouble. Though if Miss Lynn Dayton would slow down, become more cautious, it would help the plans. She wouldn't be hard to scare.

And my plans are to be done and gone before the bitch figures what happened.

Done gone. The Rabbit liked that.

❖

The calls were difficult, Robert thought. He had to put himself in an American frame of mind. He had to bark as they did and "take too many short cuts," another of their phrases. Robert preferred longer discussions. He liked the Asians better; they knew the value of thoroughness.

Although he hadn't wanted to involve another group, his own money wasn't enough. So Robert had persuaded an Asian refiners' consortium, Sansei, to finance his plan of constructing refineries in countries that needed them. In return, they asked him to "improve their competitive advantage by reducing capacity," as they put it.

Their request was simple, but massive: bring down as much American refining not already damaged as possible so Sansei could get a permanent lock on the US market with its own gasoline. Its unoxygenated, noxious, low-octane, high-sulfur gasoline. Robert's Sansei contact, Xin Yu, explained that profits from the sales would finance more scientific education in chemistry, electronics, and physics for the underemployed young people of the region. *Yes, the education that seemed to take place mainly in explosives camps,* he thought.

Robert and Xin had reduced their arrangement to a heavily-encrypted arrangement that exchanged millions of euros for destruction of metric tons of refining equipment. Then Robert started recruiting.

Xin had become impatient. He'd told Robert to demonstrate what he could do. This *petit* result wouldn't convince him.

Through the closed window he heard the fountain splashing outside. It was too dark to see the lime trees and too late in the day for the bocce players with their chrome balls. Yet how wondrous, how appropriate, that his view of the quiet courtyard should mirror that enjoyed by French author Colette. She'd called the Palais Royal "*ma province à Paris.*" Now it was his, too.

Robert returned his attention to the screen. The bank training helped with this part of his after-hours work. He brought up TriCoast's financial filings with the US Securities and Exchange Commission and found the most recent annual report.

He stared at the report's photograph of the blonde-haired woman in black pants and a light blue jacket. Pictured with several men, Lynn appeared so self-contained, confident, *merveilleux*. The men, Robert noticed expertly, all looked as if they wanted to trade their khakis and polo shirts for familiar gray suits.

Lynn had the added weakness of being a woman. It would be simple to persuade her to join his cause after the Rabbit shut down Centennial and several other Houston refineries, including TriCoast's second Houston location. Lynn would lose her job, and there'd be no new job to take its place. The US would be importing Sansei's gasoline and jet fuel to replace hers.

He'd try persuasion with her first.

Robert thought of his evening with Ceil. She was here, the most important evidence that his Gabonese contacts had delivered as promised. She was attractive, had some charm. Perhaps she would offer more than merely a method of recruiting her sister.

He congratulated himself on having already identified prospects for her at the International Energy Agency, near the Seine River and Eiffel Tower. The IEA was accepting applications, and Ceil had just left oil-producing Gabon. His colleagues at the IEA had already accepted his recommendation of Ceil. He was not only a graduate of X and École Nationale d'Administration, or ENA, but had interned with the IEA during his ministry training. Having Ceil in place at the nerve center of worldwide oil information would prove convenient for many projects with Sansei.

As he walked down the hall to join his sleeping wife, he thought about how grateful to him Ceil Dayton would soon be for her new IEA job. And how useful.

9.

Friday night, Dallas

The East Dallas house a few blocks from Lynn's renovated gingerbread was too dark. She'd bought this nearby house for her father. She flipped light switches until she found him in his office near the back patio.

"Yes, I hear you," he rasped as he swiveled around. "I'm fine."

"Let me tell you what happened, why I'm late," she said, speaking quickly so he wouldn't feel he had to talk.

His oxygen tank stood next to his chair. By now she'd become used to the plastic tubes running into his nose. But his shirts had again become too tight across his expanding chest, a sign of how hard his lungs were straining. She'd ask Hermosa to buy him larger, more durable shirts.

Her father had worked on pipelines so he recognized TriCoast's culture. "A bad accident," Lynn summarized, deliberately leaving out descriptions of her visits with the operators' families. "I'm concerned about the refinery recovering. I must have missed something big when we bought it."

His eyes followed her closely.

"What makes . . . ye think that?" Her father retained a few words that reflected his Kentucky upbringing.

She'd have to tell him after all. Lynn sat down near him in a leather wingback. "This afternoon I met with the families of the operators who were killed. That was difficult."

He nodded, and in a motion she almost didn't detect, reached over and dialed up the oxygen flow.

"One man told me his wife saw a stranger near the utilities area. Whoever it was ran off when she asked who was there."

"And?"

"I'm worried about the safety of everyone at Centennial. When I told Emerson I'd direct the investigation myself he wasn't happy, but he agreed. He supported the decision to buy this refinery initially, but not everyone did."

Her father's face furrowed into a questioning look.

"Henry Vandervoost in Rotterdam is the strongest opponent. He says TriCoast already has too many US refineries."

"What now?" He swiveled his chair and his oxygen tube bounced back and forth.

"Vandervoost will make a case for TriCoast to bail out of Centennial. If I don't fix operations, the board will want to sell the refinery. I'll be pushed out the door, too. Dad, I'm sure I'd find another job . . ." She left the rest of her critical worry unspoken. *Dad will always need his expensive full-time care.*

"Then it's . . . best ye run . . . investigation."

"Yes," Lynn said. "What about Ceil? Have you heard from her?"

He nodded, breathing more rapidly. "Tonight."

"She called? How does she like teaching in Gabon?"

"Paris."

"What do you mean? Paris, France? The Peace Corps gives recruits time off in Paris? She's supposed to be in Gabon for another fourteen months, isn't she?"

He nodded again instead of talking, a signal he was tiring. She wished she'd cut short the discussion of the refinery accident. *That's your problem, not his.* Where Ceil was concerned they were both involved. As her father grew weaker, even more of the worry about Ceil shifted to Lynn's shoulders.

"Find, talk to her. She's . . . seriously . . . upset. Asked me . . . to visit."

Lynn thought about the effort it had taken her father to add the word *seriously*. How dangerous it would be to put her father on a plane, given his emphysema. "This is a hard time for you to do that."

He shrugged. "Your mother."

"Don't." Ceil had cared for their mother during her last five weeks alive. Shortly after the funeral, her sister had suddenly joined the Peace Corps and left for equatorial Gabon. "Can't be any worse than Dallas in the summer," she'd announced cryptically. Lynn had assumed it was Ceil's way of handling the crushing grief they all felt.

"Not guilt . . . Ceil . . . crying." He pointed. "You . . . help her . . . you okay?"

"I still miss Mom." She sighed. "So where in Paris is Ceil, and why did she go there?"

"Eighteenth?"

"*Arrondissement* is her word. What else did she say?" She shouldn't hurry him but she was anxious to hear his news about Ceil.

"Met man . . . job at IEA? He also told . . . her . . . call us . . . good man."

"The IEA. That's a great place to work. But she seemed pretty set on finishing her time with the Peace Corps." *First things first.* "Did she give you her telephone number and an address? And what's the name of this man? I want to find out who can yank her all the way to Paris from Africa."

He wrote down the information. The man's name was Robert Guillard.

She studied the name but didn't recognize it. It hurt Lynn to say it, but she had to. "Dad, she won't come back. I'll try to find out what's wrong, but sometimes she doesn't even hear me."

He folded his hands and shook his head, his oxygen tube swinging side to side. "No advice. Ye . . . listen. Find out . . . what bad happened."

Lynn felt worry at her father's uncharacteristic alarm and the stirring of her old fierce love for her sister. Despite their age difference, they'd once been close. But long years away from Dallas on assignments for TriCoast had led to a distance as much emotional as physical. Phone calls and e-mail didn't bridge the divide. *And sometimes her name could be "conceal."*

"I'll do my best. Listen, this Centennial investigation is important and it has to be my main focus. I'll ask Hermosa to stay longer while I'm spending so much time in Houston."

He shook his head.

"Yes, you do need her here more. I'm going to Cy's house, then home. I'll call in a few days." She gave her father a quick kiss and received one in return. The thin plastic tubing under his nose brushed against her cheek, and its warmth stayed with her.

Despite her bone-weariness, she wanted to see Cy. She wanted him to hold her and kiss her, and understand her exhaustion. But she dreaded the burden of the discussion she still owed him. *I don't want to talk about our relationship. Not tonight.*

She drove from her father's to suburban north Dallas at nine at night and knocked quietly at Cy's door. He was kind, his children adorable. But she couldn't risk time away from her job. Growing up, she had experienced the long, dull pain that came from delaying doctors' visits until her parents could negotiate payment. Now her father was the one who needed many doctors' visits, with no one but her to pay for them.

Cy's wife had decorated their seventies ranch house in sturdy beiges inside and out. After her death Cy hadn't changed any of the furnishings, thinking the stability might help his children. *Cy needs stability, too. Not your strong suit.*

It was well after Matt's bedtime and close to Marika's. A garlicky aroma from the pizza she'd brought made her realize it had been hours since her last meal.

"Sorry I'm late. Dad had worrisome news about Ceil." She looked carefully at Cy's eyes, which revealed only the fatigue of a thirty-five-year-old lawyer and single parent. She put aside the pizza box and pulled him close, massaging a knot in his shoulder.

"What did he say?" He touched her on a ticklish spot behind her elbow.

Wonder how he's feeling. "Ceil's left the Peace Corps unexpectedly and is in Paris. Her friends in Gabon knew an official there who said, apparently with some credibility, that he could get her a job with the IEA. But Dad also said she sounded upset. She didn't tell him what prompted her to leave the Peace Corps." She brushed her fingers through his hair. "How are you? How are the kids?"

"I just learned about the longest walk in the world. Matt crossed the driveway with a glass bowl." He kissed her.

She leaned into the kiss for a while. "He made it?" She stepped back to open the pizza box. The smell of garlic assailed her more powerfully.

"Yes, but I almost didn't. If he'd dropped it onto the concrete . . . go ahead and eat." He added wryly, "The kids ate early so I ate with them."

Marika's small, sleepy face appeared in the doorway. "Hi Lynn." She waved nonchalantly and turned to her father. "Can I stay up? It's not a school night."

"You have a softball game tomorrow. I'll tuck you in."

As he settled his daughter into bed Lynn heard Cy murmuring, and Marika's response. "Don't say good night, Daddy. Just kiss me when you leave."

When Cy returned, she said, "I heard Marika. What a sweet thing to say!"

He hugged her. "She is wonderful. As are you. I saw your press conference on the six o'clock news. You looked calm."

She'd eaten one rectangular pizza slice. She put the second aside. "Before that I visited the families of the four operators who were killed. They were all in shock."

"That must have been tough." His gaze followed her. "Sit next to me. Tell me about it."

She sank beside him on the worn leather sofa, wiped her fingers on a napkin.

"I couldn't bring anyone back. One woman . . . I tried to save her . . . we all tried . . . Cy, they were already dead." She felt her tears start again.

He moved closer and held her. "You did your best."

But is "your best" good enough?

Cy turned up the volume on the white plastic baby monitor set on the counter. For a minute they listened to the whistle of Matt's little snores.

"Who's handling the investigation for you?"

"We talked to the CSB today. I'll lead the internal investigation."

He shook his head. "It's too dangerous. You have, what, fifty-five hundred people working for you? Surely one of them could lead the investigation."

"Cy, I'm more worried about the safety of everyone there than anyone else. Something in the whole incident is out of kilter. That open valve was not just a maintenance glitch. I can't identify the specific cause, but I'm certain something's really wrong. Preston's working with me. He's good."

She saw an expectant look in his eyes, key to his real concern. "I owe you more discussion."

Cy crossed his arms.

She said, "Look, I feel as relaxed talking about our relationship as you do watching Matt walk with that glass bowl. If I weren't financially supporting Dad—and Ceil when she asks—this would be easier."

She moved away from him. "I've worked at TriCoast fifteen years. I like what I do. The people there are my colleagues, my friends, my family."

He reached over and took her hands in his. Matt's cry through the monitor startled them.

She stood up. "You need to check on him."

"I wish you wouldn't leave. I'd like to talk more so you understand why I think we have a future together, even how my own plans are changing."

"Not tonight."

He put his arms around her shoulders. "I'm sorry. You had such a bad day. The last thing you need is someone making more demands."

The baby boy cried again. She ducked out of his father's arms, touched her fingers to his, gave him the best smile her exhaustion allowed, then left and quietly closed his front door.

Climbing into her own bed, at long last, Lynn thought about how Ceil seemed to have been one of her responsibilities almost from the time her younger sister was born. She remembered the night nearly thirty years ago when that became apparent.

Her mother's despairing sobs woke her.

The girl eased out of her bed. Toes feeling the planks in the wooden floor beneath the worn carpet, she crept down the hallway to listen. The television news murmured something about gasoline lines, the volume just high enough to cover the sounds of her careful step.

"We can't afford both!"

The girl's mother, a bookkeeper straining to pay for whatever her father's pipeline job didn't, sat at a folding table. Paper—the bills they talked about with such worried faces—fanned out like puzzle pieces.

Her mother's hand propped up her head. Her eight-months pregnant body swelled through the back cross rails of the small chair.

"We'll find a way." Despite the tension the girl heard in her father's voice, the stocky man straddled a second chair, sitting as close to her mother as he could. He put a lined hand on her stomach. Black oil stained his knuckles. His hand moved. Lynn had felt it before herself, that strong kick from the baby.

Her mother shifted in the chair. "We can't pay for both the computer training the Tulsa agency tells me I should have and the deposit the hospital wants for the delivery." Her voice sounded scratchy and tired. "I need both. The doctor said that after all the years since Lynn, it could be a hard delivery. But you should see this program! It's twenty times faster than anything I can do on paper. I can make good money if I learn it."

The girl shifted in the hall, staying out of the light. She thought, *if they can't afford me why are they having another kid?*

Her leg cramped suddenly and she fought the urge to cry out. She pushed down through her toes until the pain released. The leg cramps came on without warning. They only seemed to happen when she was sad or mad.

"Lynn must get her number sense from you." Her father picked a clump of red Oklahoma clay from his coveralls.

"What do we do?"

"We'll figure it out, and Lynn will find her path, too. She's not that many years away from getting a good-paying job. She could always go into the army, like her cousins, or the navy, like my friend Reese Spencer."

Her mother put a hand to her stomach, interlacing it with her husband's. "Now you're sounding too serious. She's just a girl. She needs to have fun."

Lynn slipped back down the hall to bed. She pulled out the flashlight and bounced its light across her new, pebbly-rough basketball.

In Houston, the Rabbit made two phone calls. The first was easy, fun even. The second was brief, to an old contact. "She's back in Dallas. She'll probably run tomorrow morning."

"Yes, the lake path."

"Only enough to warn her, slow her down for a few days. Make it look like an accident," the Rabbit said.

"I always do."

10.

Saturday, noon, Paris

At its deepest level, reality is mathematical in nature;
All brothers of the order should observe strict loyalty and secrecy.
                    -ascribed to Pythagoras, 586-492 BC

Gold and magenta decorated every corner of the restaurant Tout
l'Argent, from brocaded valances topping velvet drapes to the
braided runner on the marble entry table. Crystal stemware
gleamed. Silver settings glittered. As Robert waited for the maître d'
to locate Xin Yu's table, he smelled the flamboyance of garlic and the
delicate odors of salmon, asparagus, apple, and basil curling from the
kitchen. Tout l'Argent required reservations months in advance from
both Parisians and visitors.

Robert was pleased at the slight nod of the maître d' that meant
Xin had obtained a good table. There were too many concerns
connected with this lunch to also have to worry about a status drop in
the eyes of his acquaintances caused by a poorly situated table.

"With Monsieur Yu? He is seated already on the terrace. I will
take you there."

Despite the early hour, the restaurant hummed. High-powered
couples, government officials, and businesspeople leaned together,
quietly conversing. As the maitre d' led the finance ministry official to
his table, Robert greeted colleagues at other tables. Most were classmates from X and ENA, now also ensconced in senior government
and industry positions that required them to lunch at restaurants such
as this.

Xin Yu had secured one of the best tables in the restaurant that a non-regular could obtain. From halfway across the room Robert recognized his familiar spiky gray hair and well-cut suit.

Xin did not stand to greet him. Their conversation opened with lengthy, polite formalities. They discussed the menu, first with one another, then with the waiter.

After a while, Xin changed the subject. "Robert, what is your timing on these, ah, capacity reductions?" He leaned back and lit a long cigarette.

"The first one did not go as we planned," Robert said, willing himself to take a nonchalant tone. He plucked pistachios from the aluminum condiment bowl.

"I am aware of that. What will you do?" Xin asked, leaning forward and flicking ash onto the remaining pistachios.

Robert coughed to cover his shock at Xin's insult. "Our person at Centennial will try again. I expect success next time."

"You recall our arrangement?" Xin frowned.

Robert nodded. They'd encoded and memorized it: twelve million euros for every hundred thousand barrels of US refining capacity shut down for two months, with proportionately more pay for proportionately longer shutdowns. When Robert achieved a US shutdown of thirty percent, Sansei would pay an additional fifty million euros. Sansei would also redirect products to Robert's designated seven countries and oversee construction of a complex, five million metric-ton-a-year refinery in each of those countries.

"After today, ten days remain. Unfortunately, you are far from completing your part of the bargain. My colleagues and I, and therefore you, have little time. And you are not the only operation we finance."

"Ten days is sufficient." Robert pulled his chair forward, and kept his voice pleasant as he shoved the pistachio bowl away.

"We may need to condense it to a week. I'm sure you understand why."

When they first made the plans, Robert and Xin decided to execute this operation quickly given the likelihood of interest from the CIA or other Homeland Security departments. Despite the US government's focus on its War on Terror neither Xin nor Robert wished to underestimate American ability to move quickly if alerted.

"So you and I must perform and vanish," Xin continued. "Sansei's contributions to these countries must appear to be the generosity of Sansei's Asian governments." Xin was motionless except for the noxious words he delivered.

"I and my group must share credit for this generosity," Robert demanded.

"That does not seem possible at this time. The money we pay will allow you to promote yourself later when we have progressed to other matters. At present, Sansei must be in control of all public statements so that only the appropriate information is revealed."

"Monsieur Yu, I must insist. Joint credit is part of our agreement." Robert felt heat burn through his body and concentrate in his face.

"Yes, we will take it under advisement. We will talk to you further."

Robert spoke rapidly, "Monsieur Yu, we are risking much. I will continue with the . . . activities, but I must disagree with you about our ability to publicize."

Xin Yu nodded but did not reply directly. He changed subjects, continuing the conversation in a subdued tone. He said nothing else about Robert's request until they left the restaurant.

"As I said, I will discuss your request further with my colleagues. *Au revoir*, Robert."

"Non, Zachary. Bien, Michelle. Ici, Zachary." The nonstop instructional voices of French parents and nannies filled the Luxembourg Garden. Robert had picked the Garden for the reasons most visitors do: its shady planar trees, its children's puppet shows at the Théâtre des Marionettes, its all-comers chess games among the fragrant orange

trees, and its romantic fountain.

Of course this was business, Robert thought, but she might nonetheless be susceptible to the charms of the garden. It happened frequently with women. He'd telephoned Ceil this morning, before the troubling lunch with Xin, and asked her to meet him here in the afternoon.

An old memory needled through his concentration. If he let it unroll it would be over faster. He gave in and braced himself.

The Saturday ten years ago he'd skipped baccalaureate, or "bac," test preparation to walk the Tuileries, not far from where he was now. His eardrums shrank at the remembered screaming, first from his tutor, who had visited his family's apartment that night. "This test is your future."

Then his father shouted, saying Robert was condemning himself to life as a second-class citizen.

But the worst was his mother. "My son, doomed." She stared at him as tears cut new trails on her face.

Variations of that scene were repeated for years, two people always ready to do their French parental duty, to correct each mistake or infraction or impoliteness, any imagined detour from what was studious, polished, and proper.

He hadn't failed the bac. He'd been one of the top scorers. So his parents, not he, were the idiots.

Robert watched Ceil sitting by the Fountain of the Medicis as he walked toward her. In contrast to the movement around her, she was as still as the statues of the French queens lining the garden, her mien opposite from multitasking French women and men.

"Ceil," he called. She calmly looked at him. No silly American smile this time, either. The afternoon sunlight showed her golden hair and lithe figure to full advantage. But to Robert's practiced eye her dress was skimpy and cheap. Despite its long sleeves, she appeared cool and contained.

He sat next to her and spoke with the openness many women seemed to appreciate.

"You're beautiful. You seem at peace here."

"It's a peaceful place." She stretched her legs and rotated her ankles. Her white sandals were scuffed black.

"Speak to me about who you are, your dreams," he said.

Her mouth turned up in a delicious reprise of her sister's face. "You know them. You've already checked everything possible about me."

His heart bounced. Did she truly suspect he had full profiles on her and her sister? "Did you work for oil companies in Gabon?"

"I taught French and English for the Peace Corps. The government wanted English taught to men employed by English-speaking drillers, so I instructed them, among others."

Two old men got up and shuffled away, yielding their table to another pair of elderly chess players.

"But why leave Gabon?" he asked innocently.

"Now you tell me about yourself," she said.

She kept sidestepping the question. Perhaps she was more sensitive than he had gauged. He was eager to hear more details of the incident in Gabon. He'd been told only that it had happened as he'd directed. Except for her shyness on the subject Ceil was giving him no additional information, no signs. "I graduated from X and ENA."

"Impressive. Very unusual."

So she knew about X and ENA. She must be worldly, for an American. He scanned the nearby crowd and saw nothing out of the ordinary. He knew several of the Sansei operatives and didn't see any among the other park visitors and skaters. "I'm assistant to a technical advisor in the French Ministry of Economy, Finance, and Industry. I started my policy group to develop certain Third World assets the ministry is not yet prepared to fund. I learned immediately that what underdeveloped countries want most, besides money, is diesel and gasoline."

He showed her two lists. He'd selected them this morning as the ideal tests of her abilities and of her usefulness to him.

"Tell me what these are," she said, pointing with an index finger. Her nails, Robert noticed, were cut short and left unpolished. Her voice had lifted a little.

"The one on the left is a list of the countries with the most refining volume, and their capacities. The US leads the list."

"Followed by Russia, Japan, China, and South Korea," she said.

"Correct." He realized his voice had taken on a professorial, no-discussion-permitted edge. He modulated it. "The one on the right lists seven of the dozens of countries with no refineries. Each of these would improve economically by having its own refinery."

"Why not China? Why would anyone build in Honduras, or Ethiopia? Cameroon? Laos? You're kidding!" she exclaimed, lapsing into American slang Robert barely remembered. "They'd be bombed or totally scavenged in no time. These countries need everything, not just refineries." Her cheeks reddened.

Ah. Now she is involved, he thought. "Ceil, I've researched this thoroughly. China is already getting plenty of investment from oil companies. These countries are coastal and stable—as stable as many oil-producing areas—with efficient and increasing fuel use. All they need is assistance."

"I know little about this. You should be talking to my sister."

More American banker slang came to his mind: *reel 'em in.* "Your sister? Who is she? What does she do?" He sat back and dropped his shoulders to subtract from any seeming urgency.

"Lynn Dayton. She's the US refining vice president at TriCoast, a big energy company in the States. She lives in Dallas, at least this week she does." Sarcasm iced her voice.

"Will she be visiting you soon?" He moved closer to her again, but she appeared indifferent to the romance of the garden.

"She's always too busy to take a vacation, so I doubt it."

"You must insist."

She gave him a curious look, and he decided he couldn't push the issue of Lynn further on this visit.

Ceil pointed to the names on the second list. "How does your group get gasoline and diesel to these countries? Your activities sound vague."

It wasn't time yet to tell her about the full scope of his operations. "We talk. We persuade. Once our group is sufficiently large, we will lobby the richer governments worldwide, especially your American government. Are you interested in joining us?"

"I could be."

"We don't pay anyone," he said, lying. "But I spoke to my colleague at the International Energy Agency again. She confirmed an interview for you on Monday. She said they were almost certain to hire you." He gave Ceil the interview time and telephone number of his IEA colleague, Michelle Janeaux. Then he put his arm around her shoulder.

She shrugged his arm off. "Just like that I can work there?

"I trained at the IEA for a few months when I started with the ministry. They appreciate what you learned while living in Gabon about oil production and the government." *And Michelle remembers how well she and I connect, both in the office and out of it*, he thought.

"But what do you get for referring me?" She inched away from him. "I can't give you what you seem to want."

"You could help us," he said. "And as for what I want, you haven't been long in Paris or else you would not take my attentions so seriously. Is something troubling you?"

"No." She stood up and smoothed her dress.

After she left, he considered that there was no time left today for his favorite, god-like sport of free-flying. By the time he donned a wing suit and had the airplane take him up, the breezes would be still. But there would be other opportunities as soon as he met Sansei's demands.

11.

Saturday, Dallas

Catalyst: A substance that starts a chemical reaction but which is not itself chemically changed.

Poison: Anything contained in crude oil which deactivates catalysts and equipment.

Lynn lurched out of bed at dawn and pulled on running clothes. *You think better when you run.*

She sat on the cement front porch, pointed her legs into a wide "V," leaned over, and stretched her arms toward each foot in turn. Boston ivy covered one side of her sixty-year-old house. Two bald cypress trees framed the front door. Curved beds of floppy mondograss yielded to spikier St. Augustine about halfway to the street. The azaleas no longer bloomed, but the hydrangeas Cy had planted still showed pink and blue blossoms.

Emerson wanted all his senior executives to live in gated communities, but the diversity of the Lakewood neighborhood in East Dallas had grabbed her from the first time she'd seen it. The influence of the Belgian, Swiss, and French settlers in the original utopian colony of La Reunion lingered to the southwest in street names such as Swiss, Boll, and Nussbaumer.

After her first half mile of running, blood reconnected with muscle tissue and the kinks in her hamstrings slipped away. Her route along White Rock Lake wound past grand old red oaks, weeping willows, and fluttery mimosas. Huge magnolias swelled with white blossoms.

She settled into a steady pace and thought about Centennial a while. She'd handle everything else today and be in Houston tonight.

And Cy. Pain wrapped in a one-syllable name. They'd met when she was serving food and he was providing legal advice to hurricane evacuees. *Each of us trying to resolve our private grief by helping someone else. His wife dead in a car accident and Mom overtaken by cancer.*

Although Cy quickly became a confidante, Lynn expected his interest to fade as he recovered from the loss of his wife. Instead, he pursued her more seriously.

And the sex! A highly-charged, joyous surprise from the beginning. Awesome.

Steamy vegetation around her conspired to make her remember. Crape myrtles budded, soon to blaze pink. Gnarled live oak branches pointed in a dozen different directions. Red and green caladiums, blooming coreopsis, and lantana were all fed by the rich bottomland around the lake. Everything was hot and green, rushing into summer.

She'd married once, a fun-loving man notably less fun when she stopped seeing him through the bottom of a shot glass. She'd divorced after he chose barstool over bedside during her painful miscarriages.

Lynn ran along the lake path at an eight-minute pace, craving water colder than the public fountains offered. She'd wait until she got home.

You started poor, and you've sweated blood for everything you have. Without your income, there'd be no Hermosa to help take care of Dad, no car, no house overlooking the lake, and no safety net for Ceil. You can't do anything to jeopardize your job.

She doubled back at the boathouse for the return loop. A mile later she saw the cyclist. He wasn't supposed to be on the runners' path. Wraparound sunglasses covered his eyes and he wore a funny, full-head helmet with a chin guard, like a hockey mask.

He bent low to his handlebars and bore down. His posture and dark glasses made eye contact impossible.

What's wrong with him? "You're on the wrong path! Get up on the street!"

The man rode straight toward her, his bike cutting a swath as wide as a small car. She hopped left to get out of his way, but the crazy cyclist turned toward her. *This can't be happening!*

She jumped farther left and thought she was clear.

He stuck his foot out and kicked her hard in the upper thigh, knocking her to the ground. The brutal pain in her quadriceps was immediate.

"Jerk! Stop!" But the man raced away, legs pumping.

She heard shocked voices around her. "He's got no plate!" "Damn bicyclists."

Other cyclists riding at an elevation above her on Lawther Drive gave chase, but the man in the funny helmet outraced them and disappeared up a side street.

An elderly woman with yellow shorts helped Lynn back to her feet. "They shouldn't let bicycles near this path. What the hell do you suppose he was doing? It sure looked like he was aiming for you, honey."

"No joke." *Centennial is in Houston and you're 250 miles away in Dallas, so two days of bad luck are just coincidence. Except that he was aiming for you.* But runners at White Rock Lake had been mugged. A few years ago a woman had been dragged off the path in the middle of the day and beaten nearly to death. She'd been saved by an alert Dallas police officer who saw an abandoned bicycle and trusted his instincts, finding her in the swampy lowlands several dozen yards off the path. *But dozens of people were out today. They all saw him. It wasn't random.* The pain was too much to continue running. She started the long climb back up the hill toward her house, her thigh throbbing each step.

❖

After she showered, Lynn tried to phone Ceil. No answer, even though it was afternoon in Paris. Then she telephoned Claude Durand, massaging her bruised thigh. "Sorry to call you at home. And thanks for your help with the press conference."

His French-accented English was direct. "I saw it on the six o'clock news. It went well."

She wondered if he knew Robert Guillard. *Like France isn't a big country.* She'd ask him this afternoon when she could see, as well as hear, his response. "Can we get together after lunch to discuss any follow-up? And while I'm there, maybe you can point me to some books or tapes for a crash course in French."

He paused, as if offended. "Fast study? You could spend a lifetime learning French. Why?"

"I'm trying to track down my sister in Paris. It may be urgent."

"Then we will start today."

Lynn hadn't checked her home phone messages last night. According to caller ID, all had come in yesterday.

The last two calls were from the same number, a Houston area code, received while she was flying back to Dallas. Scrolling through them again, she recognized the Centennial Refinery exchange. But the number wasn't Reese's.

She pressed buttons to hear the last two calls. The first yielded only a dial tone.

The second was short and vivid. A low, nasty voice growled, "Hey Lynn, bitches who screw around in refineries don't last long. Especially when they trust the wrong people to help them. And they die such interesting deaths. Better find something else to screw before it's too late."

She skidded into an armchair, then replayed the message. *No need to guess that the bicyclist's assault was deliberate.*

A male voice she didn't recognize. Someone who knew she'd been at Centennial yesterday. Someone calling at eight last night. Someone trying to intimidate her. *Who's the wrong person you're trusting? You've seen Reese and Preston in all kinds of crisis situations, so it's not likely them. Dwayne, Jean-Marie, or Jay? It sure ain't Riley—no way do you trust him.*

Her thigh still throbbed from the bicyclist's kick. Two warnings a few hours apart. From what goons?

She dialed the number from caller ID. It rang without stopping or rolling over to voicemail.

She'd talk to TriCoast's head of security. It wasn't the first time she'd been harassed on the job, and she doubted it would be the last. But she'd never before been physically attacked.

❖

A few minutes remained before the TriCoast executive meeting. She'd requested that TriCoast security chief Mark Shepherd meet her at her office.

One wall of her office was lined with basketball goals adjusted to different heights. She took off her heels and the jacket of her suit so it wouldn't get sweaty, and bounced the ball. Mike objected to the noise, although she noticed that he usually took a few shots himself. He liked to shoot from two dozen feet away, and he often missed.

When TriCoast's CEO, fireplug Mike Emerson, asked Lynn if she wanted the job of executive vice president of US refining, he also told her that at thirty-seven, the youngest-ever EVP, she'd have a lot to prove.

Easy right-handed lay-up. Swish. Who wouldn't want the job of running the corporation's US refining operations, billions of dollars of assets in five refineries? Of course, if she goofed there were plenty of other people—*"management depth" we call it*—ready to take over. Most Lynn had trained, and all wanted the job.

A man whose face showed scars from his earlier boxing career strode into her office. Mark's head was shaven smooth, a look both tough and vulnerable, she thought. "First things first, Lynn. There's a tropical storm, Adrian, forming up in the Gulf of Mexico. We don't know which way it's headed yet, but I'm notifying all critical personnel, including your refinery managers. We'll evacuate the offshore platforms in its path once its direction is clearer. Now, what else is happening? You sounded worried."

When she relayed the news of the hydrogen sulfide leak, the assault, and the threatening phone call, his expression became serious. "I don't see how the leak ties directly into what happened to you today, but I'll make a note that they may be connected. Thought about moving into a gated community? We can also put a tap on your phone and give you a bodyguard."

"Caller ID didn't tell me anything. If you can do voice analysis, maybe that would help. A bodyguard, Mark? I can't have somebody trailing me every time I go buy milk. I have very little privacy as it is. What I have left is important to me."

"A hospital room—if that's where you end up—won't be private, either." He grabbed a ball and sunk a shot.

"I'll consider a bodyguard, but I don't want one now."

He turned in the doorway. "Duly noted, Lynn. Call me if anything else occurs to you or you change your mind."

"Thanks, Mark."

Left-handed lay-up. Into the envelope and through the net. At $325 million plus the assumption of another $75 million of Centennial's long-term debt, she considered Centennial a good turnaround possibility available at the right price, particularly when, despite the newly enacted federal refinery construction incentives, not-in-my-backyard (NIMBY) issues made new refineries so expensive. *Rim shot. She makes it. The crowd goes wild.* The company, Lynn had told the board, consisted mainly of an old Houston Ship Channel oil refinery, which TriCoast could combine with another one nearby that it owned. They'd run the two together as one. They could connect the software, pumps, vessels, and pipes to make them even more efficient as they turned the straw of crude oil into the gold of gasoline, jet fuel, diesel, and ethylene.

She bounced the ball away from the desk, credenza, and bookshelf that occupied the side of her office opposite the goals. Glass curtain walls completed the other two sides of the blue-gray aerie forty-five floors up. More pointedly, like all those around it and the hallways connecting them, her office was pocked with invisible political land mines.

When she finally got approval to buy Centennial, she knew that to turn it around in three months—now with less than four weeks left until the deadline—was to gamble fifteen years of work, her new relationship with Cy Derett, and her time left with her father. *Free throw. A miss this time, folks. Your leg. It still hurts.*

She sat and looked over news summaries from Russia, Venezuela, Nigeria, Saudi Arabia, Mexico, and Iraq. All key TriCoast suppliers. *You should have majored in international politics instead of engineering.*

She clicked to Centennial's on-line blueprints. The sulfur-handling equipment appeared adequate for moderate-sulfur crudes. As she had explained to the board when she lobbied to buy Centennial, its refinery configuration was typical, and it worked fine. At least, it had. *But what about those "unplanned shutdowns," a nice euphemism for "crashes"?*

Locating the catalytic cracking pretreater where Thursday's accident occurred, she willed the drawings to tell her what had really happened. No answer. *Was it a deliberate poisoning?*

She stood and picked up the basketball again. *Dirk Nowitzki in the clutch. Get in the paint.* She pivoted, pulled the ball close to her chest, and arched it toward the middle basket. The ball rattled the backboard and bounced off.

Fortunately, Sara Levin, TriCoast's CFO, would be at the meeting today. Lynn could count on Sara to keep the discussions in humorous perspective. *Speaking of.* Sara's solid figure filled the lower half of the 10-foot doorway. A diamond hair clip barely restrained her shoulder-length halo of dark, curly hair.

"Omigod! It *is* Lynn Swoopes. Playing for the TriCoast Oilers in her khaki uniform."

"Sara! Bounce pass!" Lynn gave the ball a low-energy shove in Sara's direction.

Sara pushed the basketball away. "Are you kidding? Never

touched a team sport and proud of it. Come with me. Let's get this sucker over with."

❖

Thick carpeting, padded walls, and cushioned chairs minimized extraneous sound from the five people seated around a half-moon table in the dark video-conference room. Facing oversized screens, they could see Henry Vandervoost in Rotterdam. Her counterpart in charge of international refining, Henry was her constant nemesis. Despite years of hairstyle changes, Vandervoost had elected to keep his Beatle-like, brown bangs.

"Okay, what have we done for the stockholders this month?" Mike Emerson opened the twice-monthly status meeting as he always did.

"I'll start," she said. *They're all waiting to hear from you anyway.*

"Lynn, in your case, it's what you've done to the stockholders," Henry interrupted. The delay in video transmission slowed his expressions.

"Keep your pants on, Henry, and let her talk," Sara said. Her diamond hair pin reflected the little bit of light in the room.

Lynn summarized the events surrounding the hydrogen sulfide leak, concluding, "Reese Spencer and I have spoken with all of the families of those who died." She saw serious faces and fidgeting around the table and on the screen. Each of them, except possibly Sara, had been in her shoes and knew how painful the talks had been.

"What about lawsuits?" asked Tyree Bickham, the company's general counsel. Short and fierce, he'd attended Howard University on a wrestling scholarship. He'd dropped wrestling for Georgetown Law School and a stint on Wall Street before joining TriCoast six years prior.

"I haven't been contacted yet by any lawyers, but I'll send them your way once I am," she said. "I'm running media questions through Claude." She made eye contact with TriCoast's public relations, or PR, vice president. "He's already helped me by preparing the text for Thursday's Houston press conference."

Claude addressed everyone. "If you get questions, please call me before answering them. TriCoast must offer a coordinated response."

"What caused the deaths?" Henry Vandervoost asked. Lynn knew he was headed toward another gibe about her poor decision making compared to his superior judgment. She allowed time for his voice to carry through the room.

"A misdirected valve leaked highly concentrated hydrogen sulfide. How the valve was misdirected and why the H_2S concentration was so high, even for a pretreater, I don't know, since the accident was only two days ago. I'm heading up the investigation myself with Preston Li assisting. I'll bring in others as needed."

"What did I tell you? Centennial is already a bad buy. We should follow ExxonMobil's example and build a refinery with the Saudis in China. I am well suited to add such a growth project to our foreign portfolio," Henry intoned.

"Henry, I like the idea and we'll consider it when your margins are up to plan," Sara replied.

"You Americans don't understand contending with the Green Party," Henry shot back. As he spoke of the environmentalists' political party active in several European countries and Canada, his voice raced ahead of his facial expression again. "Your Sierra Club and so forth doesn't attempt to close your petrol stations every other week as the Greens do here."

"And you Europeans don't understand hurricanes that can shut us down any time from May to December," Mike said. "On top of that we're in the damn begging business, trying to buy crude or sink our own wells. So, yes, we understand your frustration quite well." He turned to Lynn. "How's everything else?"

Whew. He lit into Henry just the way you always want to. It's better when you're not alone. She recapped her hurricane plans for TriCoast's three Gulf Coast refineries, the performance of the remaining refineries, construction of new capacity, progress in negotiations with Pemex and the Russians, and then listened as the other executives described their operations.

"No surprises from anyone then? Sara, you're not going to send me to jail with some undisclosed financial dealing, are you?" Their standing joke.

"You should know, Mike, you signed the papers," she said wickedly.

He closed with the kind of serious news Lynn always dreaded. "We've been approached by a group of Saudi investors about purchasing a chunk of our equity. The talks are very preliminary, at Sara's and my level only. It's not something we're likely to be interested in. Our stock already has plenty of support. So don't worry."

Yeah, right. You'll stop worrying the day Middle Easterners get comfortable employing women side-by-side with men in the same jobs and paying them equitably.

Except for Henry, they adjourned to the fortieth-floor atrium of the Petroleum Club for lunch. The view was good, the chairs comfortable, the soup excellent, and the waiters attentive. But with the news of potential new investors and the deadline at a worsening Centennial, Lynn expected her enjoyment of the Petroleum Club's luxury might be short-lived.

"How much time will your investigation take?" Claude asked Lynn as they entered his office. Dozens of framed pictures of Claude meeting with international dignitaries lined the wall.

"As fast as possible. Quick question. Have you ever heard of a Frenchman named Robert Guillard? Not that France isn't a big country." Behind the cover of the joke, she saw him stiffen.

"He was a contemporary of mine. Americans think the French are arrogant. He truly is. And brilliant. Handsome, with amazing blue eyes. Usually a wealthy, beautiful woman on each arm. Why do you ask?"

"I've read about him somewhere." She worried Claude would pick up on this whitest of lies.

"I haven't seen him for many years." He sat at his glass conference table and gestured to her to join him. He didn't notice her discomfort; he himself seemed in a rush to speak of something besides Guillard. "And now, are you ready for French lessons?"

"*Oui*," she said, feeling a smile touch her face.

"Stop. The French don't smile without a reason. They don't walk down the street smiling. They're not as friendly as Americans. There's not even a word in French that means 'friendly.'"

"They're rude?"

"No. Reserved. Aggressive. Intellectual. To a Frenchman a smile from a woman means one of four things—you're flirting, you're stupid, you're hypocritical, or you're making fun of me. Which interpretation do you want?"

She nodded. "Right."

"Don't be so agreeable. And how is your French? How much do you speak?"

"*Un peu.* My sister is far more fluent. I'm counting on her."

"Don't. Take this. These are books about the sights and customs. This," he said, handing her a box, "is French-language software for your computer. Do you have a microphone?"

"Yes." She stopped herself from nodding.

He got up and walked around her, staring at her. She felt herself straighten.

"You're not a schizophrenic dresser, are you?"

"What do you mean?" Lynn fingered a button on her sleeve. *Probably time to update the St. John's.*

"Well-dressed at the office, a slob otherwise. If the rest of your clothes are like these and your posture is usually so straight, you'll fit in. A slouchy American wearing shorts and a windbreaker is unfortunately a cliché with truth behind it."

"Okay." Lynn mentally divided her wardrobe into acceptably French suits and unacceptably American shorts and jeans.

"Too agreeable again." He punctuated with a flip of his hand.

"Conversations start with complaint and end with analysis. Don't try to compromise or find common ground."

"So what you're saying is forget everything I've learned about being nice."

"No, but the dominant French view is that life is hard, cruel, and ugly." He sat down and leaned back. "Now, on to lunches, which are anything but. Everything closes from twelve-thirty to two-thirty for lunch."

"Not too productive."

"From your American viewpoint, yes. But what could be a better business setting than enjoying fine food and conversation? It is no different than loosening up on a golf course."

Claude glanced at her and continued. "When you meet a French native, you are not talking just about France today but France with the full weight of its history. Suppose you walk along what is now the place de la Concorde. Your French companion will likely remind you that in 1793 it was called the place de la Révolution, that over thirteen hundred people were guillotined there during the Reign of Terror, and that the square so stunk of gore that oxen herds refused to cross. To a French person that is as immediate as today's news. You have never been to France?"

At her negative reply, he shook his head. "You have neglected a most important part of your education."

"Couldn't afford it. Claude, why did you move to the United States?"

"An important story that illustrates French culture, one that involves Robert, in fact. I'll save it for another time. First, you must understand the look."

"What do you mean?"

He gazed at her levelly, then slid his eyes up and down her body. Despite similar experiences, she felt her face heat.

"Claude, that's . . ."

"Harassment?" he said. "Not at all. That's a Frenchman's appreciation for an attractive woman. Here, you try it with me."

Lynn tried to gaze at him as directly as he had stared at her, but dropped her eyes after a few seconds. "I can't."

"Then you're not ready yet."

She could feel herself shrugging and smiling. "I see what you mean. Thanks, Claude."

"No smiling!"

Entrance ramps to Dallas expressways can be so short that merging requires the same acceleration as launching a jet from an aircraft carrier. Lynn tapped the accelerator of her beloved Maserati Coupe GT to enter the expressway. It responded with a satisfying roar.

After exiting at Mockingbird, her cohort of cars puffed west. Home owners of some of the most expensive real estate per square foot in Texas barricade themselves from the relentless Mockingbird traffic with chest-high grass berms, tall nandina, and crape myrtle trees.

The sun had started to fade as her car twisted and turned past the yeasty bread smell of an industrial-sized bakery. Mrs. Baird's Bakery. Now Bimbo. A telling name change, she thought, applying the English connation to the Spanish word. *Just another Dallas mid-life crisis.*

She was taking a Southwest Airlines flight instead of asking the corporate pilots to make a Saturday night run. Summer-sweaty passengers jammed the airplane cabin. From her laptop computer she pulled a database of refineries and compared Centennial's configuration to those of similar refineries, just as she had before she recommended TriCoast buy it. *Nothing, nothing, nothing out of the ordinary.*

When the airplane nosed down for its nighttime landing in Houston, Lynn surveyed the comfortably familiar mercury vapor lights of the furnace stacks and process towers on the Ship Channel, glistening as if to bring order out of darkness.

She knew it was a false impression.

12.

Saturday, Los Angeles

Mist dampened the pavement of the San Bernardino Freeway just west of Monterey Park.

"This is the most dangerous time on the road, when it's just started to rain," Rennie Nichols announced to her three children, all buckled in the back of their brown Omni Horizon. She lifted her left elbow from the driver's armrest to relieve the ache from two hours of rubbing it against the door.

"They're too young to understand," her husband said, turning to look at them. He winked. Their oldest son winked back.

"It's never too early."

"We didn't have to do your brother this favor."

She heard the scratch of irritation in her husband's voice and gripped the steering wheel more tightly.

Ahead, taillights reddened in parallel waves.

"He needs the help. It's just for a little while. I couldn't pass by the station's prices and not think of helping him."

"The owner must be putting himself out of business," her husband said in a calmer tone, the irritation gone.

She agreed. "It's almost half what I've been paying . . ." The blue Ford F-350 ahead of her stopped suddenly. She ground the brake pedal.

Rennie and her husband and her sons never saw the Yukon that skidded into them.

But they felt the collision well inside their flesh, jarring deep into their bones. They screamed. The youngest son's neck snapped backward.

The Yukon hit high above the little Horizon's rear bumper and crunched into the trunk. It kept coming, pushing the little car ahead of it. The Horizon's trunk lid popped, and its back windshield sprayed glass.

They never saw the spark from the SUV's engine ignite the five-gallon tins of gasoline lined up in the trunk, which Rennie had filled in El Monte at such a wonderfully low price.

A wall of flame swept through the car before it exploded.

After the Los Angeles Fire Department removed the five blackened bodies and sped the hysterical, bleeding teen-aged Yukon driver to an emergency room, the firefighters soaked up what was left of the engine oil on the San Bernardino Freeway with clay desiccant.

They also salvaged part of the identification number from the burned chassis. Los Angeles police later determined the loan for the little, brown Omni Horizon had just been paid in full by Mrs. Rennie Nichols, and that half an hour before the collision she had purchased fifty gallons of discount gasoline in El Monte.

13.

Sunday morning, Houston

Hydrocarbon: any of a large variety of molecules containing primarily carbon and hydrogen and ranging from methane, a gas, to asphalt, a solid.

Sour crude: crude oil containing half a percent or more of sulfur by weight. Sweet crude contains less than half a percent of sulfur. Sulfur in sour crude is removed to meet gasoline and diesel specifications. Its removal produces poisonous hydrogen sulfide gas which is converted to sulfuric acid or elemental sulfur and sold to industrial buyers.

Lynn tensed and reviewed notes in her room at the Four Seasons. *Did you make the right decision to buy Centennial? You overlooked something or something is being hidden from you.* Tyree had restricted her interviews of Centennial employees while she negotiated to purchase their company, particularly since the four VPs were making their own buyout offer. *Damn, if you'd ignored Tyree and talked to more people you'd have a better handle on the place now.*

Hydrotreating reactions are carried out at temperatures of 600 to 800 degrees Fahrenheit and pressures up to 1800 pounds per square inch. The process is even more dangerous because it produces hydrogen sulfide. Lynn's experience told her that if the leak was deliberate, it had been instigated by someone who knew the refinery, someone who could find and turn the correct, highly lethal valve, someone who understood the repair work being done at the unit.

That person could be almost anyone at Centennial, but not likely an outsider. The conclusion was no comfort.

Her cell phone rang. "Cy!" Relief surged through her body.

"I knew you'd be awake at this early hour, even on Sunday. I'm sorry about Thursday night," he said. "I added to your burden. I can't imagine trying to rescue a poisoning victim, visiting the hysterical families, and leading a press conference all in one day. Given the danger you'd been in, I just wanted to hold you even more."

"I'm sorry, too. I couldn't forget those families. Their children reminded me of yours. Then, yesterday started with some jerk on a bike knocking me over when I was running and a threatening call from Centennial Refinery's exchange."

"Are you okay? What kind of threat?"

She told him.

"Have you notified the police or company security?"

"Company security. HPD's already involved, and we're working most with the Chemical Safety and Hazard Investigation Board, the CSB. I may have to go to the FBI. I don't like the pattern I'm seeing."

"Good. So you and everyone else at the refinery may be at greater risk than you were before?"

"Yes, I think so. That's why I'm in such a hurry to investigate and why I have to be in Houston so much right now." *I'm glad he's asking these questions.*

"Can you tell me about H_2S again? I can never keep these chemicals straight," Cy said.

"In practical terms, hydrogen sulfide is always dangerous if it's not controlled, like being burned on a hot stove. You don't stop cooking, you just take precautions."

Cy asked if Centennial's oil produced a lot of the dangerous gas, and Lynn explained that its feed was the same as most other refineries its size. "Centennial runs two-thirds sour crude, which produces more H_2S, and one-third sweet crude."

"Sweet'n'sour. That's easy to remember."

"The products we make the most of, gasoline, jet fuel, and diesel, have almost no sulfur. When we take the sulfur out, we make hydrogen sulfide. And I hate to burden you, but I'm also worried about Ceil. I kept calling yesterday. I finally reached her, or she finally picked up. She sounded cautious, said she was feeling better."

Cy's two-year-old, Matt, seized the telephone. "Waga! Buhldee!"

"Sorry," Cy said, apparently regaining the phone. "I thought about Ceil later. She seemed to like the Corps."

"Yes. She's insisting that this IEA job she's interviewing for is better, but we're still surprised by her change in plans. Something happened in Gabon. She wouldn't tell me, just said she had to leave the country. Something is so wrong that she called my father, which is unusual."

"Sounds like someone is looking out for her."

"Yes. She sounded kind of gushy about him. Name's Robert Guillard. Apparently he knew Ceil's friends in Gabon, so he was able to help them help her leave the country. Ceil's awfully pretty, and single, but she's not stupid. Still, this guy's probably on the make. I hope he's not some kind of pimp. I googled the name to see if he was legit. If I found the right man, he graduated from France's top colleges, married, now has a job in the government, and also does some volunteering with a third-world development group. He interned at the IEA, so it makes sense he'd have connections."

"Dad, let's go!"

Lynn heard a loud, little-girl voice, followed by Cy's calmer explanation. "I told Marika we'd get doughnuts this morning. This new information from Ceil is interesting."

"I won't hold you. I should be back in Dallas in a few days. Cy, I miss you." *Does he appreciate how big a chance you're taking by admitting that?*

"I miss you, too. I love you."

Without stopping to consider the consequences of her words she echoed him. "I love you, too."

Tank farms, processing units, and furnace stacks stretch east and west along LaPorte Freeway. The elegant Fred Hartman Bridge spans the east end of the Ship Channel; the upswept Sidney Sherman Bridge, the west end near downtown. The freeway and Lynn's surroundings made her feel as if her rental car were a race car—complete with high-performance gasoline odor—until a passing eighteen-wheeler launched a chunk of gravel that rattled off her windshield.

Alongside the freeway, massive twenty-four-inch gas pipes poke out of the ground, show off their valves, and dive back down. Farther back from the road, light reflects off the shiny insulation that wraps most of the processing equipment.

On the side road leading to Centennial, one company framed its entrance with pink, orange, and yellow zinnias, red and purple amaranths, and evergreen photinia, along with the sign "Safety Counts." Another company portal featured Asian jasmine, tall pampas grass, and fan palms. Lynn made a few turns and arrived at Centennial's three-story main building. She noted its similar horticulture. *Too bad dropping landscaping from the budget won't flip this place into the black.*

Its safety billboard inaccurately announced, "750,000 Work Hours Without Accident."

Every Houston building wallowed in the dank smell of mildew from the city's persistent humidity. Centennial's main office was no exception.

Lynn had asked Preston to meet her at nine o'clock and Dwayne to join them two hours later. "You're gonna make me scratch awake early on a Sunday," Dwayne griped when they set the time.

It was a few minutes before nine. Lynn searched a refinery telephone directory for the number of Friday's caller. It listed the conference room next to Reese's office. *Anyone could have called you from there.*

Preston parked his immaculate, green Camry. "I brought you an umbrella. You're guaranteed to need it sometime in the next few days."

"Thanks. Let's drop it in the office, and I'll pick up some papers."

Sunday morning. Lynn was unprepared for the sight greeting them when they opened the door to their temporary office on the third floor.

"What the . . . ?"

The room looked as if it had been taken over by a pack of monkeys. Every book, every piece of paper, every disk, every pen, even the printer had been dumped onto the floor. Lynn's stomach churned at the sight of dozens of CDs tossed like silvery frisbees into one corner. *All scratched for sure.*

An odor like pool chemicals penetrated her consciousness. Monkeys who'd been swimming. But Centennial's lab no longer stocked chlorine. *And the refinery sure doesn't have a swimming pool.*

Preston picked up an armful of books and crossed the room to shelve them. "Did you bring in a Brahma bull last night, hold your own rodeo?"

Suddenly he dropped the books and covered his mouth. Pulling Lynn with him, he backed out of the office, then shut the door slowly, as if to avoid jarring anything.

"What?" He'd never acted so crazy.

"Don't go . . . think . . . procedure?"

"Procedure? Preston, we're here to work today. I need those papers."

Preston threw himself against the door to keep it closed and turned to face Lynn. "No, no you don't." His face went uncharacteristically blank. "Wish I could remember . . . okay . . . I'm panicking." He took a deep breath. "You didn't see it, did you?"

"I saw a wrecked office."

"No, on the bookshelf. High on the bookshelf. If it spills, we're dead."

"Preston, WHAT?"

"Hydrofluoric acid, I'm almost sure."

Oh God, not HF. Of the hazards Lynn had trained for, hydrofluoric acid was one of the worst. Many refineries used it routinely for alkylation, but only in highly controlled situations. Lynn remembered the safety instructor from years ago. *"You get HF on you, you won't know how bad it is until it's too late. Worse than sulfuric acid. A hydrofluoric acid burn can't be treated by just flushing it with water. Eats through your soft tissues, into the bones. The pain is excruciating. Man splashed it on his leg, hospital amputated the leg, he still died."*

"How can you tell it's HF?"

"The smell. The reflection of the light off the liquid when I turned toward the bookcase. Even though everything is tossed around, the bottle was out of place."

The smell. That was it. Hydrofluoric acid smelled like chlorine, like pool chemicals. But it was unbelievably more corrosive. If they had jostled the bookshelf, it would have fallen on them, splashed them. Even if they'd identified the liquid as hydrofluoric acid, rinsed off, used the antidote, it could have been too late. "What's it stored in?"

"Don't remember."

If it were metal or glass, they didn't have much time. *It'll eat through those. The fumes could kill us, too.* She struggled to think clearly, and pressed a cramp out of her calf muscle. "Preston, here's what we'll do. We'll open the door, take a quick look at the container, then shut the door. I've got my cell phone. We'll get the security guard here."

"Farrell Isos."

"Yeah, him and a few haz-ops people from the other refinery. If it's as bad as you think, we'll make the cleanup fast and quiet. Ready?"

Preston's mouth set in a firm line. "The gas alone can send us to the hospital. I'll count to seven. Lucky seven."

"Right. Here goes. Hold your breath." Lynn pushed open the door, stared in the direction of Preston's pointing finger toward the bookshelf.

"One . . . two." Lynn saw a clear, three-liter plastic bottle with a jagged edge where its top had been cut off to make a larger mouth. Inside the bottle was a glass beaker, its mouth covered with paper. The beaker, in turn, contained large strips of metal, something that once had been a can. Lynn gripped the door frame on the right and Preston held the door on the left. They stepped back from the doorway.

"Three . . . four." *Focus.* The strips of metal sparkled and made a steady rattling sound as they continued to dissolve. Most of the colorless acid had already flooded into the glass beaker. But it, too, was beginning to leak, bubbling through its sides and bottom. *HF etches glass.* Drops of liquid were puddling in the plastic bottle.

"Six . . . seven . . . and close." They exhaled as Preston shut the door.

"Not so hard!"

They waited and listened, but heard nothing. Nothing that could be a falling, splashing bottle of hydrofluoric acid containing a few strips of metal and a dissolving glass beaker.

"What do you think?"

"Not good. Let's hope the outside plastic bottle holds." *And that we didn't breathe too much of the gas when we first walked in.*

"It should. But the beaker is starting to go, too."

Together they took deep breaths.

"How about those calls?" Preston said.

At least it was a Sunday. Farrell closed off the floor. The space-suited haz-mat technicians from TriCoast's other Houston refinery cleared the office, starting with the hydrofluoric acid.

Preston and Lynn watched as the space suits carted away books, papers, the computer, its peripherals. "Hope there's nothing in there we don't have backed up elsewhere."

Luckily, the acid had been confined to the plastic bottle. After today, only their old office would be off-limits rather than the whole floor.

"Who did this?" Preston asked. "And who would be idiotic enough to handle hydrofluoric acid?"

"Someone must have gotten the acid from the alky unit." Centennial had hydrofluoric acid on-site. Stored very carefully, all equipment and procedures adapted for its highly corrosive nature.

"Were they actually looking for something, or was the mess to distract us so the acid could waste us? Could it have been Dwayne?"

Lynn gasped. "Dwayne! We're supposed to meet him. Like now. I'll go downstairs. Find another office close to this one, and start reassembling everything. Dwayne and I will meet you at the crude unit in half an hour."

Fear ricocheted through her mind as Lynn went downstairs. *Could it have been Dwayne who planted the hydrofluoric acid?*

14.

Sunday, late morning, Houston

Alkylation: a process in which longer-chain, higher-octane molecules are made from shorter-chain ones by reacting them with sulfuric or hydrofluoric acid. Equipment nickname is "alky."

Puzzled, Lynn gazed at cars pulling into the parking lot, not really seeing them. A weathered, green Chrysler New Yorker with a Purple Heart license plate pulled near the door. She went outside to meet Dwayne, interrupting his careful draping of the steering wheel with a white towel.

"Normally, I wrap the wheel so I don't burn my hands after it sits in this blasted sun a while." He slipped the towel off and tossed it into the back seat. "But since you're here, let's skip the glass house and take my car directly to the control center. Where's Preston?"

"He's been delayed. He'll meet us at the unit." *After he's finished repairing damage from acid that could have killed us. Quick, another topic.* "How do you like your car?" Lynn climbed into the leather seat. The New Yorker's odometer showed 120,000 miles. The inside smelled like 120,000 smoked cigarettes. Despite the growing heat, she rolled down her window for air.

"Occasional misalignment, but nothing I can't fix. What do you have?"

"Maserati Coupe GT." She looked at Dwayne. *Did he upend your office and leave the vial of hydrofluoric acid?*

"Why are you looking at me like that? It's a normal question."

She wondered how Dwayne would show guilt. Maybe by attempting a conversation like this one.

"Ooo-eee. You got more'n you can say grace over. TriCoast pays well, does it?"

"Worked hard for it." *Probably a hell of a lot harder than you.* Her suspicion of him turned to self-pity as the shock of the morning came back. *No. Don't show your ass.*

Dwayne rattled on. "Now the wife, she wants me to buy a hybrid or even a newer used car, but I won't do it when I can keep fixing this one. It doesn't make sense to drive a new car to work. Besides the heat, acid still blows into the parking lot from the refinery once in a while."

Lynn flinched. "Yeah. Acid." *Acid everywhere this morning.* Seldom had she been so eager to escape the inside of a car. It reminded her of the ones her dad owned. *Damn cigarettes. Damn emphysema.* By comparison, the refinery's hydrocarbons were rose fragrant.

At the cement-block control center Dwayne nodded to Adric Washington and headed for the coffeepot. Lynn decided to postpone another cup, already feeling adrenalized enough to swim the Gulf of Mexico.

Preston arrived and exchanged are-you-okay glances with Lynn. "Hear about the West Coast accident? It shut down San Bernardino Freeway for hours."

"I haven't even seen a paper yet," Dwayne said, yawning. "Tell me how to make another pot of coffee, Adric. I'm about to finish this one all by myself."

Preston spoke rapidly. "They had a trunk load of gasoline in their Omni. Trying to help a family member when they found some cheap. Got rear-ended by an old SUV on the expressway. All five of the family in the Omni died, including three little boys."

"The whole family died?" *Not more death. You need to hear about life. Life.*

"They should have known better than to carry so much gasoline in their trunk," Dwayne said, putting a combination coffee-and-filter bag into the coffeemaker. When he saw their frowns he added quickly, "But it's certainly eyeball waterin'."

"Throughputs are at ninety-six percent, so tight that any refinery outages will drive up gasoline prices further. And we're coming into hurricane season. If people start panic buying, we could see even more of these accidents," Preston said.

"You're right, it is worrisome. In fact, how are we doing right now? What's the H2S concentration, Adric?" Lynn sipped a cup of water.

Adric checked the coffeemaker's progress. "Jean-Marie measured less than 20 parts per million at about 2:00 a.m., so we're back to normal. Makes me tired even thinking about that time of the night."

"What have you heard so far from the operators?"

"They're paying more attention to the daily safety reviews and suggesting more valve locks. Oh, and some of them want to know if TriCoast's EVP of refining is always so, well . . . attractive." Adric nodded toward Lynn. "Only I don't think that was their exact word."

"I'm sure you gave them a good answer," Lynn said as dryly as she could manage. "We need to check the corrosion on the line out of the pretreater, especially at the bypass valve, see if the hydrogen sulfide's been producing sulfuric acid that could have affected the valve's operation."

They walked outside to the huge steel pretreater vessel.

"I'm not sure if Thursday was a one-time deal or if we have a permanently broken rope." Dwayne adjusted his wraparound safety glasses. "Maybe corrosion's been so much faster it made the bypass valve quit on us."

Preston looked at a diagram. "You have three electrical resistance probes mounted in this line. I'll take readings, see if something's changed from ValveTec's last visit. Then I'll attach a data logger to find out how fast the line is corroding." He located the first metal probe and began taking a reading.

Lynn was relieved at Preston's nonchalance after the tumultuous morning, and knew his thoroughness would require time. *So you have another opportunity for a one-on-one interview. Excellent.* "Since we got Preston started, you and I can adjourn for an early lunch," Lynn said to Dwayne. "Barbecue at Pappas?" The Pappas family had developed several successful chains. Their barbecue restaurants were long-time Houston favorites.

"I'm good to go," Dwayne said.

"What can we get you, Preston?"

He looked up, startled from the depths of a calculation. "Barbecue beef sandwich, of course."

"I'll drive," Dwayne offered.

"Why don't you get us to the office and I'll take us on to the restaurant?" *So we're not sitting in Dwayne's smelly ashtray one minute longer than necessary.*

At the office parking lot they found themselves walking behind a man with tousled hair and an ex-athlete's build.

Dwayne spoke in Lynn's direction. "Cody Laughlin, USW union steward."

The man turned around and Dwayne said, "Cody, this is Lynn Dayton, extra-special refining veep for TriCoast, our new owners."

"Too bad I don't get to whistle or tell you you're cute," he said. "You're probably too much of a ball buster for that. And there's those laws."

"I don't curtsy and I'm not allowed to tell you you're a hunk, either," she replied, "but we're going to lunch. Join us?" Cody might have information that would never make it through official channels.

Dwayne rolled his eyes. Cody saw the expression and grinned. "Don't worry, Dwayne. All your management secrets are safe with me. Just remember—don't get into a battle of the minds. You're unarmed."

"How long will it take you to walk to Pappas, Cody?" Dwayne asked. "'Cause that's what you're about to do." But the big engineer relented and as she drove, Lynn asked Cody about himself.

"High school in Oklahoma. Played offensive lineman, long words that mean blocker. Couldn't play college football. I was too small." His muscular upper body suggested he still lifted weights, and the stomach that hung over his jeans betrayed his training table portions.

"After high school I enlisted, saw some action in Gulf One. I'm in the reserves, so I was called up for Iraq. When they finally let me come back I grew my hair out again and came back to work. Got a sweet little boat and a house with five extra relatives still in it."

They turned in at Pappas's sign. Inside, soft, Spanish conversation mixed with country-western music and the steady whir of ceiling fans.

Dwayne chose barbecued chicken with cucumber salad, lima beans, and root beer. Lynn picked a barbecued, chopped-beef poor boy and iced tea, doubling it for Preston's carryout. The former football player rounded off with the combination of barbecued meats, yams, spicy rice, lemonade, and sweet potato pie.

"Eating light?" Dwayne asked him.

"Not if I can help it," the union man said. After they sat down, he sawed into his pork, the first of his barbecued meats, and asked Lynn, "So what's your take on the H_2S leak?"

"I want to find out why it happened ASAP so it doesn't happen again. I don't want anyone else hurt. Cody, Reese and I heard the coker's been giving you fits."

"Shit, yeah," Cody said. "We need another operator just to run it. Drum fills up too fast." The drum in question resembled an upright torpedo on steroids, twenty-five feet in diameter and seventy feet high.

"How long has it been happening?"

"Getting worse the past three months," Dwayne said, cutting his eyes to her.

"Don't you think these frigging problems are a result of using contractors instead of regular union members who know the refinery?" Cody spoke as if he'd been waiting a long time to say it. "Hell, Armando used to be one of my guys."

Dwayne was usually anticontractor, so his answer was surprising. "I think they would have happened no matter who was there."

Wonder why he thinks the leak was inevitable?

On the drive back to the refinery, Cody asked if Lynn had seen Armando.

"Not since the ambulance took him. You?"

"This morning. He looks terrible."

15.

Sunday afternoon, Paris

obert's ice-blue eyes flicked over his reflection in the mirror. He aligned a few stray, black hairs and smoothed a nonexistent wrinkle in his pressed shirt. *Précision.*

The lunch meeting with Xin yesterday had disturbed him. To come this far, risk this much, for no one to comprehend his genius? The fruits of his long years of sacrifice and abuse?

He shunted aside his anger at Xin. His meeting with his policy group colleagues at an outdoor café in the Esplanade de la Défense would start soon. He would continue to control information to them. They had no reason to learn about Sansei's funding or the actions in the States.

At the café, he nodded at Ceil and said, "It is time for us to become more visible. A small gesture, but a worthwhile one. Several of you have already protested here." With a sweep of his hand, he indicated three tall glass towers behind them that housed the national French oil company, Tolf.

"Yes, Robert, and next time you must join us," one said.

"I am more effective where I am, at the treasury," he replied. "And through my position there, I have learned the best avenue for our next action. Tolf will host a shareholder meeting in two days. I purchased shares in our name. I have a short list of demands for you, Guy, and you, Ceil, to put forward at the meeting. You will request Tolf expand its investment in developing countries. I warn you, security officers will likely ask you to leave before you have finished speaking. Are you able to attend the meeting?"

He noted with pleasure that both agreed.

After everyone left, he turned toward the towering, square Grande Arche de la Défense to head home to the Palais Royal apartment. He was startled at seeing a man with a doll-like face watching him from about three meters away. Given how the man stared at Robert's feet, he seemed to be coveting Robert's expensive shoes. Looking down at his feet, Robert noticed a box from an exclusive jewelry store in the passage couvert Galerie Vivienne near his apartment. He picked it up.

"Yours?" Robert gestured.

The man shook his head.

Robert opened the box and gasped. Inside lay a blood-clotted glob of white he recognized as an ear lobe. Attached to it was a gold earring identical to his wife's. *Mon Dieu! What happened to Thérèse? Where is she? Has she been kidnapped? Killed?*

He looked up to see the doll-faced man running. Robert chased him half a kilometer but lost him in the afternoon crowd of families and tourists.

He frantically called his apartment and when there was no answer from Thérèse, he dialed the emergency number for the police. He finished a breathless explanation and ran across the seemingly endless marble of the Esplanade de la Défense to the Métro station nearest the Seine. The two-minute wait for the train stretched interminably.

Fifteen minutes later, he threw open the door to his apartment. Thérèse was there, calm, miraculously unhurt.

"Your ears?" He couldn't control his voice.

"What of them? You needn't shout. I can hear you without difficulty."

"Are you . . . are you missing a gold earring?"

"No. Why?"

He could feel his shoulders slump. The earring in the ear—whose?—had been a threat against Thérèse. But from whom? Only Sansei.

"Robert, the police were here, but they wouldn't tell me why. They left quickly. What is it?"

"I saw something. I worried you'd been attacked. Where were you? I called and there was no answer, yet you were here when the police arrived."

She gestured toward the Cuisinart chopping blade. "It's very loud. Robert, I found fresh shrimp at the market. Indeed, now the shrimp with wine is ready. Let us eat."

He sat down, disoriented with relief. "You're fine? Truly?" he asked.

Thérèse gazed at him wonderingly. "Yes, of course. But you're not, my love. Sit closer to me."

16.

Sunday afternoon, Houston

Catalytic reforming rearranges the molecular structure of C6-C8 hydrocarbons to yield higher-octane, more valuable products.

Dwayne's fingers spasmed as if searching for a cigarette. Next to Dwayne sat Jay Gans, sun lines around his eyes. Jean-Marie's slump concealed her height, and she tapped the table with a pen. Adric crossed his legs.

Riley Stevens, white haired and short, patted a stomach that rounded to the size of a nine-month pregnancy and stared with a gaze that seemed to Lynn to be permanently fixed on her chest.

Reese and Preston completed the group.

They sat in the same conference room as three days before, when the flare first signaled trouble.

"Will you start us off?" Lynn asked Adric.

He uncrossed his legs. "Everyone's still kind of in shock. I sent the maintenance contractors home for a few days. Talked to my crew and the C shift supervisor but no one remembers anything unusual."

"I still say we're luckier than a drunk at Mardi Gras the H$_2$S didn't ignite or flash back. There'd have been even more deaths," Jean-Marie said.

Adric spoke up again. "You have to get those CSB folks out of our way. They're disrupting our operations."

"They're trying to find out what happened, as are we, to prevent a repeat accident," Lynn said.

"The giant, Kyle, says that at least he doesn't have to wear Level D gear. That got my crew all worried. Turns out Level D gear is pretty much what we always wear—hard hats, safety shoes, safety glasses, but also Nomex suits. So the crew starts thinking if something else happens, we need more Nomex suits.

Jean-Marie broke in. "We have enough, but they're all the same size. We ought to buy more different sizes of them."

That's easy. Lynn said, "Well then, buy them. It's in your budget."

"I keep forgetting that TriCoast is ten times richer than Centennial ever was. With Centennial, we'd have to do a requisition for a box of screen wipes, then wait two weeks while Riley here approved it and complained about not having much cash." Jean-Marie elbowed Riley.

Riley patted his stomach, unperturbed. "We were in a cash conservation mode then. That's why we're still alive and kicking today. So complain all you want."

Adric drew a circle in the air with a finger. "But see if you can get this Mutt and Jeff, I mean Gina and Kyle, out of our hair quickly, won't you?"

You're hearing him, but maybe he's not hearing you. "They're good investigators and I want you to give them your full cooperation. The more you tell them, the more they can help us."

Dwayne clapped his large hands together. "I'll remind you again that we have to meet our gasoline and jet contracts. We're already pushing throughput as hard as we can."

Do you need to buy hearing aids for everyone here? "And I'll remind you again that the safety of the people here is paramount. We can't meet the contracts if we can't make the fuel because we're shut down again." She took a long sip of coffee.

But Dwayne had a point. Most crude oil refineries had been running at ninety-five to ninety-eight percent of capacity, and even that hadn't been enough when hurricanes, or just preparation for hurricanes, shut some of them down between May and December. It was unlike earlier, leaner years when utilization rates were in the eighty percent range. Ninety-five to ninety-eight percent meant less time for turnarounds. The pressure was on constantly to manufacture as much gasoline, jet fuel, and diesel as humanly possible, while meeting the ever-changing specs.

With all the NIMBY issues, building a new refinery in the US was nearly impossible, despite Saudi offers of financing to do so. Thus, existing refineries had to be expanded, and imports from abroad of gasoline, jet, and diesel increased. The difficulty was that the rest of the world's gasoline and diesel often didn't meet US specs, particularly for oxygenated gasoline and the new ultra-low sulfur diesel.

Indeed, all of Lynn's refineries had jumped the hurdle of making ultra-low sulfur diesel, 15 ppm sulfur instead of 500 ppm, because she'd made sure they'd built the multi-million dollar equipment to do so during the past several years.

Centennial had managed it, too. Somehow, Dwayne had found a way in his meager budget to install the deep hydrotreating needed to almost eliminate all sulfur. Lynn was impressed the operating chief had found a way to squeeze out the money.

"Armando is recovering at Pasadena Memorial," Reese said. "His visiting hours are restricted, but he'd appreciate seeing you. Also, Lynn is leading the investigation. Having someone at her level indicates how seriously TriCoast takes it."

Adric shook his head. "More time wasted."

"Adric, you know that's normal protocol," Lynn said.

He was unhappy that she was running a parallel investigation for TriCoast instead of relying on the CSB's inquiry. The CSB might furnish informal results to her quickly, but their formal recommendations sometimes took months. *Your crisis is now, today.*

Lynn looked around the room, holding the eyes of each person in turn. "I have five other refineries, so I'm relying on your expertise and the advice of my engineering manager, Preston Li, whom you've already met. I'll say it again. Safety of the people here is paramount."

Okay, truth or dare. Lynn and Preston had concluded news of the hydrofluoric acid incident would quickly be public, so she wanted to be the one to break it. "You'll notice he and I have moved to another office. This morning we found a container of hydrofluoric acid in our original office."

"No way!" Adric stared at her.

"Stuff will kill you!" Jay exclaimed.

Reese and Jean-Marie looked similarly shocked.

"Someone just wanted to give you a see-through blouse," Riley said.

What a jerk. "I'll give you see-through, Riley, and you won't like where. Get a grip on your zipper," Lynn said.

He glanced around for support. No one returned his glance.

They were all looking at her. "If you hear anything about how the hydrofluoric acid got there or who put it there, tell me, Preston, or Farrell." She sighed. "Now let's talk about Thursday's H$_2$S leak."

"What about Cody?" Jay asked. "Where was he when all that happened?"

"Mr. Football's a troublemaker!" Riley exclaimed, jiggling in his chair.

"Oh, he was here and there, talking to people like he always does. Nothing strange about that," Dwayne said. After Dwayne's and Cody's lunchtime sparring, Lynn was relieved to hear Dwayne defending the union man. *Their squabbling must have been more put-on than real.*

"Why do you think Cody's a troublemaker?" Preston asked Riley.

The CFO wouldn't look at Preston, addressing Dwayne instead. "All Cody ever wants is more money and more job security for the union. He doesn't realize we can't spare either one."

"Riley, I'm over here," Preston said.

Riley leaned back in his chair but didn't respond.

Lynn looked at Riley. "Everyone in this room is on the team. I'm going to assume we're all comfortable with that."

Heads nodded. Finally Riley looked down and said, "Sure."

"Well, Cody and the union are probably clear," Reese said, breaking the silence.

"I'm still really worried about that cat pretreater. We just finished repairing hurricane damage a few months ago," Dwayne said, his voice deepening. "It's not stabilized yet. We lose it again, we can't make enough gasoline, jet fuel, anything. Just as bad, it's sucking up more hydrogen than usual. I'm not sure the reformers can keep pace."

"Time-out," Riley said. "Is there any connection between the pretreater using more hydrogen and what happened Thursday? And what do you mean 'reformers keeping pace'? Why is that important?"

Sensible questions from Riley. At last.

"If we've got a stream with a concentration of H_2S so high it kills people almost instantly," Dwayne said, "then we have a bunch more sulfur somewhere in the system I didn't know we had. The pretreater would be going nuts to pull all that sulfur. It uses hydrogen to react out sulfur and other poisons."

As operations expert, Dwayne was warming to his subject. "Otherwise all our products would be so off-spec they'd be worthless. The reformers supply hydrogen to the pretreater, and if the reformers can't supply enough hydrogen, we buy it from the outside. But it's damned expensive to do it that way." Smoker's breath bracketed his explanation.

He didn't answer one of Riley's questions. "So is the pretreater using more hydrogen a result of the accident?" Lynn asked.

"No. We've been using excess hydrogen for the past few months. We're not running well, but the accident hasn't changed anything."

"What do you mean?" *An operations chief never admits his refinery isn't running well.*

Jean-Marie sighed. "We're not making good gasoline and diesel. We're constantly rerunning what should be finished gasoline and diesel to meet spec."

"Reprocessing is an expense our competitors don't have," Lynn said. "Which specs are you missing?"

"Too much sulfur," Jean-Marie said. "We can't seem to clear it out of the system."

"Okay, okay. These ladies think they know everything, don't they, Dwayne?" Riley chirped.

"The scary thing is, we do." Jean-Marie guffawed.

"I give up. I'm being double teamed," Dwayne whined, looking from Lynn to Jean-Marie. Despite his complaint, his eyes crinkled as if he and Jean-Marie were old hands at this verbal jousting.

"Jean-Marie, your accent is familiar. You must have grown up in New Orleans," Lynn said.

"Born and raised there," Adric complained, "and never lets us forget how much she misses it. Especially now." Although his head was down as he tapped notes into a laptop, Lynn heard the amusement in his voice.

"Oh Lord. Don't go there. I still got relatives I'm trying to help. So I hope you're planning to keep me now that you've bought the refinery," Jean-Marie said.

"Jeez, yes." *Yeah, legally, Tyree wouldn't want you to make promises, but you need everyone here except maybe Zipperman.* "Top of your class at Tulane School of Engineering."

Jean-Marie's nose reddened, as if she was about to cry. "Hurricane gutted the city, then Tulane gutted engineering." After Hurricane Katrina the university had substantially reduced its engineering courses and degrees to pay for repairs and still keep its doors open.

Dwayne started to hum the tune of "Do You Know What It Means, to Miss New Orleans?"

Lynn felt a wave of sorrow at all that had happened to her favorite city. *Gotta move forward.* "So, Dwayne, what else?"

"More downtime in the last month or two than we'd like, or expect."

"Why?" she asked, recalling Reese's surprising news two days ago about excess downtime—downtime that had occurred during negotiations and about which she had heard nothing. *Downtime that threatens your chance to make Centennial profitable in a few short weeks.*

"No single reason. Various equipment failures," he said.

Not a good answer. Is Dwayne really the expert he's supposed to be?

Jean-Marie's phone rang. She listened, said "Yes," and hung up. Then she interrupted in a harsh voice. "You may have all day to shoot the shit, but Channel Industry Mutual Aid just called. Some joker screwed with the main power and the backup cogen at Meletio. First result—cooling water to the front end of Meletio's refinery was cut. They lost the bigger of their two distillation columns. Half burned. They'll be offline for months! They asked me to help." She pulled up to her full six-foot-something, shoved her hair back from her face, and departed, clanging her metal chair against the table.

Dwayne and Reese looked ready to jump up and follow.

More bad news at Meletio. Damned suspicious. "Hard as it is, let's wait and find out what she tells us. We have our own difficulties here," Lynn said.

"What else will you be analyzing?" Jay asked.

"Well, for example, what catalyst Centennial used in the pretreaters and when did you change it last?"

Dwayne tore his eyes away from the door through which Jean-Marie had just exited. "In the guard reactor we're using a silica-alumina base with a little cobalt and molybdenum. The other reactors use the same base but more co-moly. We changed our catalyst last year."

"Oh, Christ!" Riley said. "I hate this mumbo-jumbo."

Dwayne shot back, "Wouldn't hurt you to know it, Spreadsheet Man. Throw out a few words like co-moly and you'd have scared the bankers into giving us lower rates when we needed them."

"You did throw out words like co-moly and the bankers ran

shrieking in the other direction," Riley yelled.

"Let's fly in formation," Reese said, his eyes steely.

"Can we get Catanalyst here?" Preston asked, naming a local catalyst consulting company.

Good ol' Preston. He can always calm an argument. Glad he's on this project.

"They came out two months ago," Dwayne said. "They can tell you about the fresh catalyst but not about what's in there now because I'm not shutting down the unit for them to take a look-see."

"I'll call them and set up a meeting for ten," Adric said, tapping the reminder into his Palm.

"Preston will join us." Lynn caught his nod of assent.

"We're done," Lynn said. "Thanks for your time, folks."

Chairs scratched on the carpet.

She'd gone over what she needed now. Other questions came to mind, but they were best kept silent until she learned more.

"Show us the tape, Farrell." Reese and Lynn had remained in the conference room after the emergency executive meeting. They'd requested a viewing when they learned that one of the young security officer's videotapes might show what had happened at the leaking pipe.

"Ms. Dayton, we haven't been able to afford an upgrade to a digital video recording system for security surveillance. Maybe now with your TriCoast backing we can," Farrell said. He adjusted the settings and fast-forwarded to the time of the accident. "I was telling Mr. Spencer here that the security video screens weren't manned. I was checking the IDs of a couple of contractors at the time. We're lucky this one was in the right area."

As if in a home movie, the four operators—alive then, she thought with a pang—came on screen. They were talking, looking at checklists, and unsheathing measuring tools. Suddenly their faces froze. One ran to the valve a few feet away and the others began to back out of camera range. One man tripped and fell. LaShawna ran toward him, and she fell.

Armando Garza moved into view.

The next few frames were quick.

Lynn could see Armando look at the people on the ground and throw up his arms, then punch his radio buttons. His mouth formed the words "Help! H_2S leak!"

He retched. His safety glasses fell off and his notebook computer slipped from his hands, crashing into the gravel by the asphalt walkway. He stumbled to the bypass valve and twisted it.

Within moments Armando passed out and fell across the valve wheel, left arm crumpling beneath him. She could hardly make herself continue to watch. Deadly minutes accumulated. Finally the screen filled with movement as the respirator-protected figures of Dwayne and herself, then Jean-Marie, Adric, and the man named Skyler appeared.

Farrell turned off the tape.

17.

Sunday afternoon, Houston

After the tape ended, Shelby Darling, executive assistant to Reese and the vice presidents, entered the conference room. Lynn had reluctantly asked Shelby to give up a few hours of her weekend, too, because of their emergency meeting. Gesturing to the blank screen Shelby reported, "The nurse at Pasadena Memorial says Armando isn't doing well."

Lynn turned away from the screen, still considering the video. "We need to talk to him."

Shelby had anticipated her. "He can see people other than his family only fifteen minutes every two hours. His next visiting period is in forty-five minutes."

"Reese, let's go see him. Farrell, I'm glad you found the tape. Tyree, our general counsel, needs to view it."

"Security procedure is I make you any copies you need, Ms. Dayton."

"How long will that take? I'll be seeing Tyree soon."

"Copying will only take a few days," Farrell said.

"Will you also make a copy for the CSB and TriCoast corporate security chief Mark Shepherd? And call me as soon as they're ready?"

"Yes, of course. Three copies, and a fourth backup copy for me." Farrell put the videotape in his briefcase.

Reese and Lynn jogged down three flights of stairs to the front door. The intense heat outside seemed to liquefy the asphalt of the parking lot. Barehanded, they opened the dark, stinging-hot doors of her rental Taurus as quickly as possible.

Since LaPorte Freeway had been designed for large trucks, it ran straight and was easy to navigate. Railroad tracks paralleled its south side and tank farms lined the north. Farther north, hugging the Ship Channel, process towers for several other plants and refineries presented themselves.

Pasadena Memorial spread its parking lots over several acres, surrounded by a dozen fast-food outlets.

The sun continued to bake as Reese and Lynn walked through an entry framed by cedars. Inside, the brown-tiled hall was mercifully cool.

When they entered Armando's room, they were met by the hard squint of a boy Lynn guessed to be about nine. His hands cupped over Armando's right arm. Stretched under a crisp sheet and wearing a cotton gown, Armando looked even frailer than the slight figure with chiseled features who'd coughed himself back to life two days earlier. His face was lined, as if its moisture had been sucked away.

The boy was talking to Armando, who stared back at him intently. Even through his oxygen mask they could hear his struggle to inhale short, shallow breaths.

Lynn recalled all of her father's hospital rooms. She turned her head, hoping no one would see her rub her eyes.

"You must be Armando's son," Reese said quietly.

The boy pulled himself up a little straighter. "Yes, I'm Jesús." His voice was high as he pronounced Hay-soos. "Who are you?"

"Reese Spencer. I run the refinery where your dad had his accident. I'm sorry it happened."

"Was it your fault?" Anger seemed to spend the little energy the boy had left. He started to cry.

Armando touched his arm. "No."

"Jesus, I'm Lynn Dayton. I work with your dad. I'm here to see how he's doing."

"You big guns here . . . to say . . . you're sorry?" Armando asked Reese. His voice came in gasps. That was familiar to Lynn, too.

"Yes. We are very sorry." Lynn answered for both of them. "Armando, you weren't in any condition for introductions when I saw you at the control center two days ago. I'm TriCoast's vice president of US refining." Keeping her voice gentle, she asked, "Can you answer a few questions?"

Armando nodded.

A pastel-smocked nurse in athletic shoes interrupted and addressed Reese in an officious tone. "We can allow Mr. Garza only two visitors at a time. One of you will have to leave," she said, turning to look at Lynn.

Lynn waited quietly, trying to cool the steam she felt sure was escaping from her head. This, too, was like her father's hospitalizations.

Armando nodded to his son.

The boy blinked away tears again and his shoulders sagged. "I'll be back in five minutes, Dad."

Lynn watched Armando's son leave and slowed her pace further. "You saved a lot of other people. Thank you again."

He shook his head. "Not the four."

"You did your best." When Armando didn't answer, she continued. "To make this easy for you, I'll ask yes and no questions. You can nod or shake your head."

Lynn settled until her shoulders rested against the back of the vinyl visitor's chair. "Did you get a call-out on valve PT416 between seven forty-five and eight o'clock Thursday morning?"

He nodded. "Call for me . . . by name . . . to check pretreater."

"Did you know four operators were already there?"

He nodded. "Only a few . . . minutes."

"So you saw them down, knew something was wrong."

He nodded.

"Why didn't you . . ." She stopped and rephrased so he wouldn't feel defensive. "Were respirators available in the control center?"

"Couldn't . . . smell anything."

If Armando had lost his sense of smell after encountering the hydrogen sulfide, that meant its concentration had been so high it immediately paralyzed his olfactory nerves.

"Do you remember if the pipe was marked with an orange flag?" Reese asked.

Another nod.

The flag had shown up on the videotape, although not its color. Because an orange flag meant "to be repaired," no one would be surprised to see the line open. Armando would have assumed, as they all would, that the gas normally flowing through that valve had been shunted over to the bypass line.

"You saw that the bypass valve wasn't completely closed to the main line," she said. "You closed it, switched the flow all the way over to the bypass line."

He shrugged. "Gonna tell me I . . . took too long?"

"Not at all," Lynn said, softening her voice even more.

"I'm still amazed you did that," Reese said.

Armando coughed.

Lynn looked down at her list of questions and tried to summarize so that Jesus could return quickly to his dad. "Did you have any kind of handheld H_2S detector with you?"

Another no.

"You were near the valve about a minute before you passed out." She remembered the scene on the videotape.

He shrugged his uncertainty.

It hadn't been long. Yet they'd found the concentration higher than what she expected even from a high H_2S stream. Several more minutes had passed before everyone was found, so the exposure of Armando, of all five, continued after they passed out.

"You didn't smell H_2S?"

Another no. With the on-site hydrogen sulfide alarm not working and no handheld detector, he'd had no warning. But there were other factors that could have dampened his sense of smell.

"Did you have a cold?"

He nodded.

"Do you smoke?"

Another yes.

Reese interrupted. "You work a potential hydrogen sulfide area when you've got a cold?"

Armando's face pinched together, and he coughed. "Telling me it's my fault? . . . I'm contract. Don't work, don't . . . get paid. Family has to . . . eat. Wasn't supposed to be H_2S." He eased himself against the pillow and turned away, struggling for breath as she heard her father do so often.

Reese is pushing too hard, damn it.

"No," Reese said. "I don't think it's your fault at all. You were heroic."

She watched him walk into the hall, his face torn in grim lines. She waited for Armando to stop coughing and wished they were finished so he could rest. "You worked for Centennial full-time a long time. How many years?"

He held up all fingers of both hands.

"Had you worked on that pretreater before?"

"At least once . . . a month," he croaked.

"Do you recall how many times you've had H_2S exposure sufficient to give you medical symptoms?"

Five fingers.

"Any time before as bad as this?"

He shook his head.

A nurse came in and frowned when she saw Lynn. "You're still here, honey? You need to let him rest."

"Almost done," Lynn said, focusing on unclenching her hands.

"Two minutes." The nurse's shoes squeaked as she left.

"You've had all the required H_2S safety training at Centennial?" Lynn asked gently.

He nodded.

"Mr. Garza, you have been kind with your time. One last question. Did you see anyone else in the cat cracking or distillation areas anytime Thursday? Anyone not on your contract work crew or from Centennial—someone out of place or that you didn't recognize?"

Armando paused for a long time.

"The day before . . . someone in . . . utilities area."

"Who was it?"

"Couldn't see . . . yellow . . . hard hat."

"Thank you for your patience," she said, again making her voice as gentle as she could. She reached out and touched his hand.

Reese returned from the hall. "Armando, I'm sorry about this accident and sorry to have upset you just now. Naturally all your medical expenses are covered. Call us or have your family call us if there is anything we can do. Everyone is pulling for you. We hope you can go home soon."

His son and the nurse returned at the same time. Each displayed a protective mien.

"You need rest, Mr. Garza." The nurse gave Lynn and Reese sharp glances. Lynn was both relieved and sad to leave.

On the drive back to the refinery, Reese said, "This shouldn't have happened. Especially not to someone with Armando's experience."

"Did you hear what he said at the end when I asked about anything unusual?"

"No."

"He saw a person with a yellow hard hat in the utilities area. Why is that unusual?"

Reese whistled.

"What?"

"Refinery protocol is that executives and visitors wear yellow. Everyone else wears a green or blue hat. Administrators, secretaries, and security officers wear white."

"Which executives have yellow hats?"

"I do. So do Jean-Marie, Dwayne, Jay, and Riley. But it could have been a visitor, too."

"Could someone have . . ."

". . . borrowed one? Easily."

18.

Late Sunday night, Paris

Pythagoras believed that each number had its own personality—masculine or feminine, perfect or incomplete, beautiful or ugly.
                    -School of Mathematics and Statistics,
                    University of St. Andrews, Scotland

Thérèse had fallen asleep an hour before, unusual for her. The swiftness of their lovemaking had pleased him, and her too, it seemed.

Two thoughts embroidered the edge of his memory. The ear, like an old-time pirate's. A ghastly, severed ear, delivered unmistakably to him.

And the lunch yesterday with Xin Yu. Xin had mentioned "financing other operations." Did Sansei direct the pirate attacks in the news? What could that mean for him? Perhaps Sansei, like any business, sponsored competition among its suppliers—in this case, its suppliers of sabotage.

He scrolled through news stories on his computer and saw Meletio Refining in Houston had finally been brought down. But he still lagged the schedule he had guaranteed Xin. *Mercenaires* were hard to control, unpredictable. Robert's anger at the Rabbit's incompetence returned. A few words seemed insufficient. He apparently needed to give the Rabbit more complete guidelines.

He e-mailed a message to the Rabbit to prepare for a call and attached his voice scrambler to his cell phone.

"*Bonjour,*" Robert said when the Rabbit answered his telephone. He deliberately kept the bite of anger in his voice.

The Rabbit hesitated. "Uh, is everything okay?"

"Our colleagues are impatient. You finally damaged Meletio. You must now proceed with the third refinery."

"That's quick. I need more time to plan. Hey, I sound like you."

We have no time, imbécile, Robert thought. "*Non.* Tomorrow. You have someone in place?"

"Yes, but the middle of the day? That's hard as hell." Robert heard the Rabbit's teeth clack with caution.

"You are capable. And Centennial?"

"You mean my refinery? Now it's TriCoast."

"TriCoast has another refinery in Houston. If I call it Centennial, you will comprehend best what I mean."

"I hear ya. For a Paris boy you've done your homework."

Robert felt his jaw grinding at the Rabbit's insolence. "And you haven't."

"I'll finish the job. So when's the rest of my money showing up? That would speed up the work." The American's voice screeched.

Robert tugged at his earlobes until he realized what he was doing. "I will advance you fifty thousand."

"Dollars, not euros. No funny euros showing up in my Houston account."

Robert glanced at his computer to remind himself of the exchange rate. Euros were up Friday against the dollar, making his transactions with the Americans less expensive. He relaxed and said, "No euros. A fourth of the total for Centennial. The rest will come when I receive it myself, which won't occur until you shut down Xavier and Centennial."

"People are buzzing about the investigation here."

Robert heard concern in the American's voice. He sat up. "Does anyone realize your involvement?"

"The survivor might." Now the Rabbit's voice rattled with anxiety. Robert held the telephone handset away from his ear for a few seconds in distaste.

"And why are you concerned about him? Apply a Pythagoras project," Robert suggested, layering satin into his tone.

"No, not yet."

"Your concern is what?"

"I don't like the body count going up. Four stiffs at Centennial. Now five more dead and fourteen injured at Meletio. You're there safe in Paris."

"The faster you move, the faster we finish. Not stopping, are you?"

"No." The Rabbit paused, seeming to visit the possibilities.

The answer was clear, but the Rabbit hadn't made the logical deduction. "Zero is not an ugly number. Take the survivor out of the picture."

19.

Late Sunday afternoon and Sunday night, Houston

Heat exchanger: equipment in which a hot liquid or gas gives up heat to a cooler stream. The hot stream is cooled; the cool stream is warmed.

Looking west from LaPorte Freeway, downtown Houston glittered, a mutant, giant offspring of industry and verdancy. Smog settled in for the day. Buildings poked out of the dust like jewels left in the sand.

When Lynn arrived at her hotel room she dropped her briefcase and laptop on the bed. *Probably time to make amends for hours of sitting and pounds of chopped-beef poor boys.*

With a temperature of ninety degrees and a heat index over one hundred, running outdoors, even briefly, in downtown Houston would be an unhappy experience. She pondered what to do next, and recalled she needed to talk individually to Jean-Marie. *Maybe it won't take long. And she probably has an inside view of what happened at Meletio today.*

"Lynn, *cher.* After busting my butt at Meletio, I sure didn't make any plans for tonight. But I could loosen up with some racquetball. You're at the Four Seasons? There's a health club with courts across the street. I'll meet you there."

Lynn vowed to herself to make the game quick so that they could talk over the investigation. *Maybe she'll see a similarity between the damage at Meletio and Centennial.*

Lynn returned e-mails and voice messages from her five

refinery managers. *Good.* Nothing else sounded as urgent as her current investigation. Then she snapped on the heart monitor the company doctor had been reminding her to wear, changed into running clothes, found the air-conditioned skyway, and padded to the club.

"You're at the Four Seasons? We'll charge it back to your room." A trim gatekeeper handed Lynn a locker key, a warm towel, and a rental racquet. Music pounded through the floor. The customary smell of ball rubber reassured her for some reason. Lynn found Jean-Marie already swinging a racquet on the court she'd reserved.

"Lynn, whereyat? You'd think sweating at the refinery would be enough for us, wouldn't you?" The tall woman wiped her face with the sleeve of her T-shirt. After a few quick stretches, instead of volleying, she announced, "I'll serve."

Jean-Marie walked a few steps to the back of the court. The ball exploded off the front wall.

Lynn missed it. She missed the next one when it smashed off the right side wall.

"Two serving zero." With incisive aim Jean-Marie lofted the ball so that it barely grazed the front wall of the court. Lynn raced to it but swung high. The ball bounced a few inches off the floor, almost dead, well under her reach.

You can't find your game. How could all this stuff at Centennial be happening on Jean-Marie's watch as safety VP? How do you get her to be frank?

Jean-Marie seemed to notice Lynn's distraction. "You awrite?"

"I'm always slow to warm up."

"What does your heart rate monitor say?"

No hiding it now.

"One fifty-five? *Cher!* Sit down. You're in too good a shape for that to be normal."

"I'm just dehydrated. That's all." Lynn took a long drink of water to prove her point.

When they resumed hitting, only squeaking shoes breached the sweaty silence.

"Thirteen serving sixteen . . . fourteen serving sixteen." Lynn strained so hard on her returns, she didn't notice how often her body slammed into the side walls. The last few points took several minutes while they traded serves. Finally, Jean-Marie delivered a shot that skimmed the wall. Lynn pivoted to reach it, but let it pass. "Enough for me."

"Sure you don't want to play another game? Show me how good you are?"

"I'm beat," Lynn said as convincingly as possible. *You don't have time to run a marathon in exchange for what may be very little information.*

"Your focus seems a little off." Jean-Marie said.

Lynn couldn't decide if her tone implied sympathy or suspicion so she said, "Drinks?"

"Unanimous."

They toweled off and found the bar.

"You have Dixie?" Jean-Marie asked, and in her question Lynn heard a boatload of longing for all New Orleans had ever been.

The server shook her head. "Still trying to get some. We have a fine absinthe, though."

"I'll take whatever's on tap."

Lynn ordered scotch and soda.

"It's entertaining to see what someone with an undergraduate drinking degree from New Orleans orders," Jean-Marie said.

Lynn laughed. "It's also entertaining to see how much she drinks. So, tell me what you saw at Meletio Refining this afternoon."

Jean-Marie's look sobered. "When I went over there a few hours ago it was a mess. No one knows why they lost power, but the consequences were devastating. Without cooling water everything superheated, went way above the normal temperature range. Lots of melted, warped exchangers, lots of product dumped to the flares."

"It'll take weeks to return to normal."

Jean-Marie sat back, crossed her long legs. "Everybody's in shock, too. With these two accidents, five people have been killed and fourteen injured."

She's counting casualties just like you are. "The folks at Meletio have their hands full. The timing, so soon after their tank fire . . ."

"is awful." Jean-Marie completed.

"Do you see any similarities to our incident?"

"No, but we sure have issues, too. Like I said at today's meeting, *cher*, we're producing more sulfur from the treating plants than usual. Out of our atmospheric resid, we're making well over 300 tons a day of sulfur. We should be making only about two hundred and fifty."

She folded her paper cocktail napkin into tiny squares and tore them off one at a time. "Also, our operators wouldn't have died and Armando wouldn't have passed out so fast except that the H_2S concentration from the pretreater was sky high. Overall, we're circulating more H_2S and sulfur than we should."

Lynn hid her concern so Jean-Marie wouldn't get defensive. "Are units being pushed too hard? Maybe the catalysts are fouling too quickly."

"No. We don't take chances like that."

"Then either a higher-sulfur crude is running or the hydrotreating catalyst is unusually active and more H_2S is being produced." Lynn sat back and wove her fingers together. "Let's think about the second possibility.

"The refinery takes sulfur out at several places in the refining process. So if the hydrotreating catalyst were unusually active, we'd see more H_2S from the cat cracker pretreater but less elsewhere."

Jean-Marie shook her head. "F'sure that's not happening because the gasoline and diesel hydrotreater units are fine. So it must be the crude."

The waitress came back with a second round. Lynn gave her a gratefully received tip.

"Here's another factor that makes me think it's the crude," Jean-

Marie continued. "The operators under Adric have logged the sour crude distillation tower running rough. They're making beaucoup temperature and pressure adjustments every single shift when they shouldn't have to."

Lynn lowered her pitch so her tone wouldn't sound accusatory. "I remember that from our notes. How do we test the crude?"

Jean-Marie explained that Jay sent samples to O'Roark, a Pasadena company who verified crude quality, and that Jay had asked them to do a full round of tests on each of the crudes Centennial had in storage.

"What's he heard?"

"Nothing yet. O'Roark is slow, sometimes two or three weeks, Jay says."

Lynn was appalled. "That's unbelievably slow. We need answers now. Yesterday."

"This isn't anywhere close to your job description, but have you and Preston thought about firing up beakers yourselves?"

"I hadn't narrowed the concern to the quality of crude oil until now. But we can't wait two or three weeks for O'Roark."

Jean-Marie's been forthcoming. Here's the test, though. Lynn took two swallows of scotch and soda. She spoke slowly, so as not to appear anxious. "I want a fellow Tulane engineer's view of the situation at Centennial."

Jean-Marie looked at her with an ice-sharp gaze. "Tulane was years ago. A lot has happened since then, and not just hurricanes. Though Katrina sure as hell turned my family's life upside down, *cher.* Had a houseful for three months. Some of the family returned to Louisiana, some settled here. Shit, they lost everything. In fact, next time you want to schedule some little chat," she looked sourly at Lynn, "we'll try my second cousin's bar, NOLA in Exile."

"I'm in charge of this investigation, which means I have to search every dusty corner that hasn't seen light in years. As a safety executive, what do you really think about what's been happening, Jean-

Marie? At Centennial? At Meletio? Don't you think it's suspicious? Three accidents so close together like that?"

The tall woman didn't answer immediately. She drank the rest of her beer. "You know what it's like to be a woman in this industry. My head is still scarred from all the times I've butted it into a brick wall. When I started at Centennial, managers slipped pictures of women in bathing suits into every slide presentation. Operators asked my bra size. Would I get a boob job? Did I want a date? Of course anybody new gets hazed, but it was mean. I gritted my teeth during the day. Then I went home and cried every night. I thought I was going crazy."

"Those attitudes haven't gone away," Lynn said, sympathetically.

Jean-Marie's voice hardened. "I learned to use my height. Just leaning into people stopped some of the comments. But I also proved myself. People understand me, even my impatience."

Her face relaxed. For Jean-Marie, that was equivalent to a grin. "And the men I started with married, so they quit axing for dates. Big relief."

You've been "axed" on some dates, too.

Jean-Marie dragged an index finger through the water ring on her cardboard coaster. "My point of that pity party is that I have a lot invested in Centennial, *cher*. Glad you're here, glad TriCoast bought the place, but we've been pushing crude for years, and pretty damn successfully. Then you show up, we got an accident, CSB's all hostile. So, yeah, I'm suspicious. But I'm suspicious of you, Preston, Reese, and the whole TriCoast bunch."

Lynn looked at her firmly. "We both have a lot of experience. And mine tells me that the open valve, the H_2S poisoning, and those deaths were not accidental. Either help me prove it or stay out of my way."

To her surprise, Jean-Marie didn't get angry. "I'm not imagining it. You *are* edgy."

You usually don't get your life threatened or your office booby-trapped. But the jerk caller said trusting the wrong person would get you killed. You've probably already told Jean-Marie too much. "We bought this place and I thought I understood what it needed. Help me here. Have you heard or seen anything unusual? Maybe something from the operators or the younger engineers?"

Jean-Marie looked sideways at Lynn, swirled her empty bottle, and placed it on the table.

"One thing." Jean-Marie uncrossed her legs and wiped sweat from her calves. "One of Adric's men said that when the call came in just before the accident about the valve on the pretreater, the caller asked specifically for Armando Garza. And he remembered the call came from an unidentified number instead of Dwayne's office, the way it usually does."

"Did he remember the number?"

"No. Strange things happen. I have to leave. *Bon chans.*" Jean-Marie pulled back from the table and stood. Her claim was true. At full height Jean-Marie could be quite persuasive. Even threatening.

"We can't screw up again," the Rabbit whispered to the Assistant in the Pasadena hospital elevator. "This time we'll make sure."

The Assistant's fingers raked across his forehead to brush away sweat. "You're sure he has an oxygen tank? Why isn't he hooked into the ICU's room oxygen system?"

"I asked when I visited. The nurse said since he smoked and had been exposed to hydrogen sulfide, he was on one hundred percent FiO2 therapy, which they could only deliver with a rebreather mask and an oxygen tank."

"FiO2?"

"Fraction of air breathed in that's oxygen. Where's the substitute tank?"

"It's stored down the hall from his room." The Assistant slipped an operating-room mask over the bottom half of his face.

The elevator lurched to a stop on the third floor. Dim lights shone around them as they exited. Both wore blue surgeon's scrubs and recently printed hospital ID badges. Although the Rabbit was prepared to offer an explanation, they saw no one at the nurses' horseshoe. They swung open the door to the private room. Armando was asleep.

"Here we are, waking you up to give you a sleeping pill," the Assistant joked in a deepened voice. He shook Armando awake and gave him a Xanax tablet and a small cup of water.

"Damn hospital . . . never sleep . . . who?" Armando rasped. He swallowed the pill, then turned over and slept again.

The Rabbit remained with Armando while the Assistant walked to the hospital supply room, loaded a tank scratched with a nearly-invisible check onto a handcart, and wheeled it back into the room. Only they knew it held nitrogen instead of oxygen.

"What if he wakes up and takes the mask off?"

"He won't. The rebreather mask fits more tightly to his head than an ordinary oxygen mask. And the Xanax ensures he won't even wake up." The Assistant grunted, moving the new tank into place.

The Rabbit pulled out a pair of surgical gloves that matched the Assistant's.

Within a minute, they switched the tanks. Within two minutes, the Assistant wheeled the used oxygen tank back to the hospital supply room. Within three minutes, they were in the parking lot.

Ten minutes later, Armando Garza would never have to worry about having his sleep disturbed again.

The room was still dim as they left. So when the Assistant put the surgical gloves back in his pocket, he wasn't aware of the scrap of paper that stuck to them, then fell to the floor.

Lynn didn't need to see the clock to decide it was too early for the hotel's wake-up call.

"Yes?" She heard herself groan. Only 5:00 a.m.

"Lynn, it's Reese. Armando's dead."

Her eyes flew open when she heard his message. She struggled to gear up her brain. "Dead? In the hospital where they were keeping him alive? We just saw him!"

"Someone substituted nitrogen for his oxygen. He was never even able to call a nurse. I've already met the police at his hospital room. They showed me a scrap of paper they found on the floor. It said 'Armando Garza. Room 315. Pythagoras Project.'"

"Oh God. Armando's family. What the hell does Pythagoras Project mean?" Her thoughts broke in a dozen directions. She reined them back.

"I'll be there."

20.

Monday morning, Houston

Assay: a table of data for a specific crude oil that shows raw yields of gasoline, jet fuel, and diesel; density and flowrate; and the weight percent of the oil that is nitrogen, metals, total sulfur, and hydrogen sulfide.

The only comfort offered to Lynn at 6:00 a.m. by unshaven medical examiner Emilio Martinez was that Armando died quickly. Armando's lungs, already severely damaged from years of smoking, had almost shut down after the hydrogen sulfide exposure. "What's unclear is how someone was able to substitute nitrogen for his oxygen."

Reese and Lynn looked at one another, remembering their visit with LaShawna's family. Finally Reese said, "The husband of one of the other operators who died threatened to kill Armando. But it sounded like an idle threat, made when he was upset."

"You know," said the sunburned HPD officer, "I'm seeing you so much you can just ask for Alex Stinson by name every time you call 911. Meanwhile, we'll check out this husband." He took information from Reese on how to reach Pete Merrell.

"This label says oxygen!" Preston leaned over to point to the canister in the roped-off area that had been Armando's bedside.

"We've already tested the contents. Pure nitrogen," Martinez said. "Mr. Garza was likely sufficiently sedated that he was unable to recognize his shortness of breath. His ability to react was reduced so much he couldn't take off his mask."

"Who could have done this?" Preston groaned.

At the remark, Officer Stinson turned on Reese, Preston, and Lynn. "The refinery's one thing, but you're bringing your shit in here, too, causing god-awful troubles for this hospital. Pythagoras Project my ass! You and your Centennial people start giving me more cooperation, and you find out who's behind this before I shut you down."

The news of Armando's compromised lungs made Lynn yearn to go directly to her father's house in Dallas. A telephone call was her only choice. He sounded the same as last time, and asked if she had talked to Ceil.

"I've talked to her once, Dad. She's interviewing today for a job at the IEA. They're interested in her because of her fluency in French and English and her experience in Gabon."

"Ye keep calling . . . please."

But the next time she called the number her father had given her, there was no answer. Lynn tried the IEA. The receptionist informed her that since Ceil had just been approved as a new hire, a listing of her extension was unavailable.

She called TriCoast's Dallas head of security, Mark Shepherd, and updated him on the hydrofluoric acid in her office and the news of Armando's death. He told her that voice analysis of the threatening call she'd received hadn't matched anyone in his databases. He promised to alert TriCoast and Centennial security and ask their help in determining how the acid had gotten into her office. "Someone has you in his or her sights. You ought to think about dropping the investigation, or at least excusing yourself from it."

"I can't do that. More people could be hurt."

"You're not a one-woman show. By the way, did you tell me Farrell has a security videotape he's copying for me?"

"I did. I'll ask him again about it."

She hung up, and wondered if he had been the right person

to notify, particularly given that news of the threats would now be broadcast to the entire security group. *But that's B-school Management 101. Hire the best people and trust them to do their jobs.*

When she called Farrell about the videotape of the H₂S leak, his response was contrite. "Ms. Dayton, I'm so sorry. I understand you and the CSB and Mark are counting on viewing it again, but I must have misplaced it."

Jeez, that's suspicious. "Do you have a backup? Did you get a chance to make copies?"

"Unfortunately, no to both. I'll locate it soon."

❖

Four hours later, Lynn stood in front of the small group of Centennial executives. *The person who killed Armando, maybe the same one who is threatening you, is probably in this refinery. Maybe this room?*

She would make the announcement she, Preston, and Reese had agreed upon, then watch each person and see if one or more of them would correct her about the time of death or the nature of the "complication."

"I have bad news. Armando didn't make it. His system was irreversibly damaged by the exposure to hydrogen sulfide. He developed an acute complication and died at nine-twenty this morning."

"Oh, no!" Dwayne and Riley gasped. Jay dropped his hands in mid-gesture and slumped back in his chair.

"Goddamnit!" Jean-Marie cried. "Damn it, we tried." She covered her face with her hands and rubbed her forehead.

The lines in Reese's and Preston's faces revealed despair. The three of them had talked about nothing except Armando's death since Reese's early-morning call.

"Is his family provided for?" Jay asked.

Riley answered. "Workers' comp and his contractor's insurance . . ."

"Has HPD been notified?" Riley asked.

"Yes, Centennial security officer Farrell Isos is coordinating an outside investigation with Alex Stinson at HPD and Mark Shepherd, TriCoast's security chief," Lynn said.

"We need action now," Dwayne interrupted. "Yesterday a fifth of the operators didn't show up for work. Some of the contractors are keeping their people off-site. The ones here can't handle the extra workload."

"I agree," Lynn said. "But first Reese will call Armando's family. Shelby will give you the details on his funeral once we have them." She motioned to Preston and Dwayne, and they left the room with her.

"Let's review a few numbers in your office, Dwayne," Lynn suggested.

Their shoes squeaked on the rubber-treaded stairs.

"After all my years here, this is suddenly turning into a snakebit refinery," Dwayne said.

Damn right.

The bookshelves, conference table, chairs, and desk of his office were carefully comfortable. Only the old metal filing cabinet defied safe, ergonomic design.

"I have a question about the last several refinery weight balances. There are more pounds of product coming out than feed going in," Preston said after they sat down.

Dwayne seemed to have anticipated his concern. His too-close breath smelled of smoke and coffee. "Think we've violated the laws of physics? Nah. We need to fix our tank calibrations, and we probably overestimated our fuel use. What I do find interesting is that you two are dusting off lab beakers to run a boiling point test this afternoon. Lynn, don't you have a meeting to attend somewhere?"

"Who needs e-mail or cell phones when the grapevine is so efficient?" Lynn said.

"Speaking of grapevine, I hear you played racquetball with Jean-Marie," Dwayne said.

Good Lord. No privacy. The caller said you would be killed because you trusted the wrong people, so you were right not to tell her about the threats you've received. Did you still tell her too much?

Preston tapped his pencil. "Let's talk through the crude supply situation. Centennial has hydrotreating of 80,000 barrels a day and a sulfur plant rated at 350 tons per day. By design, the refinery has excess hydrogen production, although you've mentioned your higher-than-expected hydrogen consumption."

Dwayne's demeanor warmed. "So you know what you're talking about." Apparently he expected less technical expertise from TriCoast's engineering manager.

"What's this bullshit? I think 'pain' rhymes with 'Dwayne' for a reason," Preston shot back.

"I've heard that before." He laughed. "Where were we? Our sulfur cleanup is good. We can take out moderate amounts of all the usual poisons: nitrogen, salts, sulfur, metals."

"So you run the lighter Texas and Louisiana grades all the time and shoot for a low-priced mix of medium and light sour crudes," Preston said.

"Damn straight. We run 50,000 barrels a day of sweet. You're right—mostly from Texas and Louisiana," Dwayne said. "The rest of our crude is sour: 70,000 barrels a day of Middle East crudes. Over the last several years we've increased our purchases of Latin American crudes. Jay just made another good deal on Ecuadorian Oriente, so we've been running it at 30,000 barrels a day."

"You've talked about rough operations," Preston said.

"Seemed to start around the time you all bought this place and Reese got here," Dwayne answered, running his hand through his hair, "not that I think the two are related."

Right. "Which units aren't up to par?" Lynn asked.

"Which one is?" Dwayne sighed. "Let's start with the sulfur plant."

Lynn stood and walked to stretch her legs. Dwayne watched her warily, as if afraid she might move a paper clip out of position.

"Fills up too quickly. It must be overloaded," Preston said. Dwayne stared at him, again appearing surprised he knew this. "A few chats with the operators," Preston explained.

"What else?" Lynn asked.

"Same with the coker," Dwayne said. "It's filling up too quickly also. We're dumping resid into six-oil." The resid would normally be turned into gasoline or diesel instead of high-sulfur, No. 6 fuel oil, which was worth only three-fourths as much. Jean-Marie and LaShawna, according to her husband, had remarked on these issues, too.

"Don't forget the cat cracker." Preston bounced a pen on Dwayne's desk.

Dwayne looked ready to take the pen away. "Yup. I hope it doesn't keel over. And we're losing catalyst activity too quickly."

"You've thought of too much sulfur in the system?" Lynn asked.

That was obvious—the hydrogen sulfide poisoning of the five operators at the catalytic pretreater, the overloaded sulfur plant, the cat operating problems.

"Yes. We're waiting on assays."

Just as Jean-Marie told you last night. Suppliers were supposed to guarantee crude quality. The assays would confirm the composition of the crudes Centennial was running, including sulfur content. Lynn looked out the window at the refinery's tall flares. All normal. "I have an unrelated question. Was there another meeting here Friday night after I left?"

"We had our weekly operations review. Broke out some beer. We talked more about the accident, of course. Then a few of us went to see Armando."

Beer. Not TriCoast standard operating procedure but it should be. "Who was in the visiting party?"

"A big group. The nurse let us all in because we agreed to stay for only a few minutes. Me, Jay, Riley, Reese, Jean-Marie, and Adric."

So they all knew how to get to Armando's room. "What time was the operations review?" Lynn asked.

"Why do you ask?" Dwayne cocked his head.

"I got a bizarre call from the Centennial offices about nine o'clock that night."

Preston whirled away from the computer to stare at her.

"From here?" Dwayne's surprised expression mirrored Preston's. "We were finished long before nine. Our meeting only lasted until seven thirty. We were out of the hospital by eight thirty."

"Who was at the meeting?"

He scratched his chin. "The usual. Myself, Jean-Marie, Jay, half a dozen unit-operating supervisors from the day shift. Reese didn't attend, but he stopped by for a few minutes at the end."

"What about Riley?"

"No, no reason for him to attend an operations meeting, though it would do him some good," Dwayne snorted. "He usually slips off to chow at those bankers' receptions. He did meet us at the hospital to see Armando."

"He could have returned here later," Preston said.

"You don't strike me as the nervous type, Lynn. 'Course you know what they say: 'Just because you're paranoid doesn't mean they aren't out to get you,'" Dwayne offered brightly.

"Oh, thank you." Lynn didn't bother to hide her sarcasm.

"So your bizarre call came after last week's operations review," he mused, unwilling to drop the subject. "Jeez, seems like we're diggin' up more snakes than we can kill."

Preston bounced a pencil off its eraser and checked his watch. "Don't forget we have the ten-fifteen meeting with Brian Tulley from Catanalyst in half an hour."

21.

Monday, Houston

Reflux: a recycle subprocess of a main process such as distillation. Reflux increases yields of desired products.

Gina Vardilla had asked to meet with Lynn before she and Kyle presented their early observations to the rest of the Centennial refinery executives. Lynn had agreed, and requested that Preston Li, her engineering manager, attend also. The four sat in the new office Lynn and Preston were using while at Centennial. Their old one was still off-limits due to the hydrofluoric acid contamination.

Lynn described the circumstances of Armando's death to the two investigators. Both looked concerned.

"Lynn, that could take our recommendations in a different direction, so keep us informed about the progress of the investigation into Mr. Garza's death. Let us tell you what we have so far." Gina adjusted her glasses, and Lynn noticed with amusement that both men gave Gina their full attention. Gina said, "We've only been here a few days so our findings are preliminary. We still have a considerable amount of evidence, computer readouts, modeling, and documentation to examine. That will require a few months."

She told them the good news first. Unlike some other situations the CSB had examined, Kyle and Gina did not see pervasive safety mismanagement at the Centennial refinery. Jean-Marie, in particular, but Dwayne and Adric also, had reacted well in time of crisis. It was clear they were prepared. "In fact, Lynn, I might suggest that you were the renegade, walking into that H_2S cloud without determining whether or not it was in the explosive range."

"I was worried about our people. And we did save one. For a while." She tried not to let her voice rise. *Gina's just doing her job.*

"Yes, but at great risk to yourself and Dwayne."

Kyle interrupted. "I'm sure TriCoast doesn't want to lose one of its most valuable executives."

Lynn shook her head. "Kyle, that's kind of you, but I don't rate a man's life by the numbers on his pay stub."

"Of course. But many lawyers with whom we work do." Kyle wasn't smiling any longer.

Gina went on. "Here's what we know so far from interviews and an examination of the scene. I'll mention three pieces of evidence. Then we have some preliminary recommendations to help prevent another accident."

You don't think it was an accident. But listen to what they say.

"We looked at the bypass valve position, the maintenance tag, the H_2S alarm, and the actions taken by those at the scene. The valve did not have a lock, the maintenance tag was illegible and not logged into any automated system, though Dwayne says he has one, and the H_2S alarm was nonfunctional."

The news that the tag wasn't entered into Centennial's maintenance system unsettled Lynn. She said, "And what about the excessively high H_2S levels Jean-Marie reported? That's a high-sulfur gas, but in her words the H_2S was off the charts."

"We've seen these very high H_2S levels at many refineries producing the new ultra-low sulfur diesel. When you're leaving in only three percent of the sulfur that you used to, that means a lot more H_2S is being made, and much more sulfur disposal is required."

Reasonable, but something still doesn't feel right.

Gina pushed her black hair away from her eyes and continued. "So here's what we suggest for the interim. First, you need redundant H_2S alarms on that pretreater, probably two more than what you have now. Next, you need a more automated maintenance-log system, with some way of verifying that all maintenance requests are included. An illegible tag on a valve doesn't cut it. Third, you need valve locks everywhere, so that the valves can't accidentally be moved out of position. Finally, we still see a lack of compliance here with our urgent warnings to all refineries about the placement of contractor trailers. Lynn and Preston, I count five of them much too close to the units right now."

"That all sounds reasonable. We're happy to comply and appreciate your working fast. Please keep us informed of any other concerns that arise as you examine the evidence. I've arranged for you to brief the Centennial execs in an hour—that'll be Reese, Dwayne, Jean-Marie, Riley, and Jay. I've also asked Adric and Rodney to sit in on that meeting. I'll talk to Jean-Marie about getting the trailers moved ASAP."

After they left, Preston said, "Gina and Kyle were helpful."

"Only somewhat. They're frank about not looking at all the evidence yet. I have a feeling that they'll turn up something else. At any rate, the board wants us to complete our own internal investigation. So you and I have more to do."

Two operators pedaled bikes along the refinery's main asphalt road as Dwayne drove Preston and Lynn from the glass office building to the control center. Other than the bicyclists Lynn saw no one. *Why should that worry you?* Centennial was as fully automated as possible, so it would be unusual to see people outside.

It was another humid day. Even the sun sweated. Ninety-five degrees, ninety-five percent humidity. Zager and Evans lyrics came to mind. "In the year 9595/I'm kinda wondering/If man is gonna be alive."

The air conditioner of the refinery truck Dwayne drove wasn't cooling, no surprise. Lynn had driven many like it—rusting finish, nonfunctional air conditioning, suspension long gone. There would be large sums in Centennial's budget for new trucks. *Which you will be approving only if you still have your job.*

Dwayne rolled down the window for a breeze. They passed a clutch of trailers, temporary outbuildings to house contractors whatever length of time they would be here. A speed bump jolted the truck, and they were at the control center. The noises were the same as always—steam hissing from leaks, furnaces roaring, liquid and gas rushing through pipes. Lynn found their sounds more reassuring than usual.

As Preston led them in, they heard the end of a story.

"Anyway, he chased that little ol' gal all the way to Port Arthur," a man with a stubbly face was saying. Only with his rounded pronunciation, it sounded like "Pote Awfa."

The men-only crowd stopped laughing when they saw Lynn.

She waved the speaker on. "Turns out not only was she married, but she was his foreman on the next construction job there. But don't let me interrupt."

The group laughed. "Gotta do better than that, Brian," said one. "I thought you high-priced Catanalyst guys had the newest jokes," added another.

Lynn walked back to the Port Arthur jokester. "Brian Tulley from Catanalyst?"

"Ooh, baby! She got your number now," said another operator, winking at Lynn.

"Christ, man," Dwayne said, "have you forgotten who you're teasing? She's the big boss."

"And you're Skyler Knowles, aren't you?" she asked the winker.

His mustache drooped over big teeth. He winced and nodded.

"And you helped save Armando Garza by dragging him and the others in here," Lynn said.

"But I saw a plant notice this morning that Armando died of pneumonia, so I didn't do much good, did I?" Skyler looked down.

"The last time I saw him, he was talking to his son. I think you did a lot of good," Lynn said. Her heart sank despite her words. *Why was Armando murdered?*

She turned to Brian and Dwayne. "Let's go to the pretreater, see if we can nail that sucker's problem." Preston stayed behind to ask the operators more follow-up questions.

"Has Centennial been sending you random samples of the pretreater catalyst for testing?" Lynn asked the Catanalyst engineer as they walked underneath the shade of the piping. She felt her face relax for the first time in days as she concentrated on a technical issue instead of emotional ones.

"Yes. No notation of anything unusual in the last three years," Brian said. "And the spent catalyst tested fine a few months ago."

"You think we'd lasso the wrong steer? We don't let our catalyst degrade." Dwayne sounded disgusted.

She ducked under a low pipe. "What's the catalyst deactivation time?"

Brian and Dwayne followed her.

"About a year," Brian said.

"We put the catalyst in during turnaround, so it's been there about six months." Dwayne's face reddened.

"Have you optimized your catalyst?" Lynn adjusted her sunglasses. She was surprised by Dwayne's anger over simple, factual questions. *The catalyst is one key to our investigation. If it's degrading too fast, we can lock in on the crude oil supply or the pretreater operations. Dwayne should know that, but maybe you need to remind him.*

"Goddamn, yes, of course. We ran all the tests about eight months ago. Adric and I worked on it."

"Hang on, Dwayne. We're just going through checklists. If the pretreater catalyst is less active, that explains why we're picking up excess sulfur downstream. If it's overactive, that explains why the hydrogen sulfide was so concentrated that it killed four of our people almost immediately. Now tell me about the catalyst."

"Alumina with an open pore structure and plenty of matrix activity." In a move that seemed affectionately proprietary, Dwayne nudged closer to the big metal cylinders of the pretreaters and patted the shiny insulation.

After asking about crude feed, Brian pulled out a handheld computer and typed in a few numbers. "The probability of catalyst degradation this early is about five percent. Shouldn't happen."

"But operations have been bumping so much it's like wasps in an outhouse. We'll pull a sample and send it to you," Dwayne said.

"It's hard to retrieve catalyst from a working reactor. Are you planning an emergency shutdown?" Brian lifted his eyebrows, showed some teeth.

"Smart-ass vendor," Dwayne said. "No. We'll cut our crude throughput and switch over to pretreater CCPT 402. It has additional capacity. We have to do so anyway in case that tropical storm, Adrian, crosses Florida and makes its way across the Gulf."

Good, the word's gotten out about preparations. "It's not certain where Adrian will hit, but as you might imagine, Brian, we've started our hurricane-watch protocol at our three Gulf Coast refineries," Lynn said. Though it was too early for a category four or five hurricane, the frequency of all tropical storms and hurricanes had increased. Hurricanes Katrina and Rita together had been a one-two punch, from which the industry recovered slowly. Gasoline prices, already stretched to the limit, had bounced up for weeks afterward. Tropical storms and hurricanes presented difficulties offshore, too. Oil platforms broke loose, underwater mudslides ripped up Gulf of Mexico pipelines. Onshore, refineries were shut down or damaged as were the pipelines carrying gasoline to customers throughout the country. *Every point in the system from wells to gasoline tanks can be damaged.*

After Brian left, Dwayne put his big hands up in front of his chest as if to push her away. "I don't care who you are. I don't like having my operation questioned, especially in front of outsiders like Brian."

"I wasn't trying to embarrass you. We're investigating. You've done the same catalyst testing anyone would." Lynn held his gaze until he looked away.

"You mean like a big-shot TriCoast refinery."

So that's what he's worried about. "Sure, like TriCoast. You're TriCoast now, remember?"

They strode next to the pipelines toward the one-story control building. Massive exchangers lined the walkway. Two furnaces stood in the middle of the concrete pad like sentinels.

Preston joined them and the three clambered back into the red refinery truck whose loss of air conditioning was about to be matched with the loss of a muffler.

A security guard stopped their truck at the refinery gate. Lynn recognized Farrell Isos, the short, red-haired guard.

"What's doin', Farrell?" Dwayne shouted over the engine's roar.

"Hello Ms. Dayton, Preston, Dwayne," Farrell shouted back. "Got to check your vehicle. Tools have disappeared, and with Armando's death we can't be too careful. We're inspecting everything."

Sweat dripped from Lynn's forehead while Farrell took his time climbing throughout the truck bed and opening the glove compartment. Finally he said, "Don't see anything. Sorry for the delay."

Lynn unlocked Centennial's laboratory and paced as she talked to Adric on a cell phone.

"My guys pulled the samples you requested and put them next to the door. Do you see them? Sure you want to do this yourself?"

"Yes. Thanks, Adric." She knew his reluctance came from union concerns. But Lynn planned to run the tests herself to get the results she needed quickly and confidentially. She downloaded procedure ASTM D-2892 for crude oil distillation. Essentially a standardized chemistry experiment to boil oil into more identifiable fractions, the procedure would give her answers about the quality of the crude oil Centennial was purchasing—issues that Lynn had raised with Jean-Marie after their racquetball game. This experiment could pinpoint the source of Centennial's operating problems.

A racing form fell from his pocket when Preston came in.

When he picked it up, Lynn noticed one page highlighted. *Surely he's not spending too much time at the track. Even if he is, it's not interfering with his work, so it's none of your damn business.* "I have two samples to run. Can you help me?"

"Sure. I could stand doing something safe and routine for a change," Preston said. "What have I signed up for?"

Lynn said, "You remember D-2892? We're mimicking crude tower C-201."

At Centennial, the hoods were large, dining-table-sized work areas set halfway into the wall. The portion that stuck out was topped from the wall above to shoulder height with a large, sloping chrome cover, shaped like a mansard roof. Fans vented the worktable under the "roof," pulling vapor out of the room to be treated at the sulfur recovery plant. She found two pairs of safety goggles in the open shelves next to the hood and handed one to Preston.

Another man's voice sounded. "Since moneybags TriCoast has bought this refinery, how about reopening the lab and hiring back my people full-time?" Lynn turned to see USW union rep Cody Laughlin lounging near the door. Jay and Jean-Marie accompanied him and relaxed into similar cat-like postures.

"Probably won't happen, Cody, much as we'd both like it to," Lynn said.

"Speaking of research, did your crude assays come back, Jay?" Jean-Marie asked. "Lynn and Preston could skip this test if O'Roark sent you their results."

After Jay shook his head, Lynn suggested, "Make yourselves useful. Wash some glassware for us."

"I just remembered a meeting," Cody said. The three turned and walked away.

"Didn't want them looking over your shoulder?" Preston said when they were out of earshot. "I've never seen a faster allergic reaction to dish soap."

Lynn winked at him as she turned on the vent in the first hood and reviewed the procedure. "Speaking of dishes, we need three-liter distillation flasks with side arms, condenser columns, gas collectors, reflux dividers, a heating mantle . . . the list is on my computer screen."

Preston pulled out one of the gray metal drawers. "Here we go."

Lynn opened a glass-fronted cabinet and was relieved to find the rest of what they needed. She labeled and weighed two distillation flasks and twenty of the dry collection beakers, calling out the weights to him. They smeared fittings with silicone grease and assembled glassware in the first hood.

He repeated the setup with the second set of glassware in a nearby hood and started a new file on Lynn's computer to record their notes.

Lynn opened the first canister. No water had mixed in with the oils. That meant little or no water had invaded the refinery's tankage and lines, so the crude dehydrator was operating efficiently. *Good.* But the sample flowed out more slowly than she expected. "Let's check the viscosity of the crude mix Centennial is running. This pours slower than molasses."

After weighing the flask, she dropped in a magnetic stirring bar and positioned it inside a heating mantle that fit around the flask like a baseball glove. The stirring bar began rotating when she turned on the heat.

Lynn again found herself enjoying the return to a technical pursuit, one that didn't require evaluating political moves or making decisions about people.

The sample temperature rose. Vapor surged steadily up through the distillation column and reliquified in the condensing column. Then the droplets split between the collection beaker and the reflux cylinder.

Lynn looked at her watch. Early evening in Paris. "I'm ducking out for a few minutes to call my sister." She stepped into the hallway, retrieved her cell phone, and tapped in the long series of numbers to reach Ceil.

"*Bonjour?*" came a musical greeting. Just the sound of Ceil's voice brought with it dozens of memories.

"Ceil, it's Lynn."

"Oh my. I was not expecting you to call," Ceil said, her voice flatter.

That's odd. Ceil must know you've been trying to call her. "How are you?"

"Mmm, fine."

So fine she suddenly leaves her teaching post in Gabon and goes to Paris. "Dad continues to be concerned about your sudden change in plans."

"And you thought it was arbitrary, irrational, but so like Ceil?"

"Actually, it seems unlike you. You were the one with the guts to stay with Mom her last five weeks."

"Didn't help."

Lynn could hear the bitterness in those two words. She could almost see Ceil's shoulders shrug. "It was the best anyone could have done." She felt a catch in her throat and talked past it. "Ceil, I'm worried about you. What's wrong? Why did you leave Gabon?"

Ceil paused. "I can't tell you that."

"Was your whole group evacuated?"

"No. No one was evacuated. I just left. Actually, I would like to talk to you about it, but not over the phone. Anyway, maybe I'll be able to stop thinking about it so much soon. Between starting a job at the IEA and volunteering with a development group, I won't have much time to think."

"So they hired you today? That's great!"

"Statistics. Robert Guillard, the head of the development group, got me the job. He said they'd be interested in my Gabonese experience, and they are. But he must have really pulled strings." She sounded pleased.

"That's a fast transition from the Peace Corps. I'd like to come visit. There's one roadblock. This new refinery we bought is giving us fits. We had a leak four days ago that killed four people and put another in the hospital. The man in the hospital seemed to be getting better, but then he died too. Speaking of things I can't talk about on the phone, the investigation is taking a lot of time. Though, since I'm talking to you—you know the West African situation and you're doing stats—do you see numbers about South American crude export sales?"

"Lynn, I'm just starting! I can't call you or e-mail that information to you."

"I don't want to sound dramatic, but it could save some lives. And besides, I do want to see you." Lynn put as much warmth in her voice as she could. "I could be there in a day or two."

"It would mean a lot to me to see you," Ceil affirmed, with what sounded like hope.

Lynn was replaying the conversation in her mind when Preston came out of the lab.

"Have I got something for you! Remember that note in Armando's hospital room? Pythagoras? Did you ever study Greek history or the history of mathematics?"

Lynn shook her head. "I remember the Pythagorean Theorem and that the Babylonians may have developed the same theorem fifteen hundred years earlier. I hope you're not going to tell me about triangles."

"Here's what's interesting," Preston said quickly. "In Pythagoras's time, to be one of his students meant belonging to a secret brotherhood with Pythagoras as the leader. When his student Hippasus came up with the idea of irrational numbers, like the square root of two, it didn't fit Pythagoras's view of the world."

Pricks of sadness from her conversation with Ceil made Lynn impatient. "Why does that matter?"

"Pythagoras believed numbers had an innate harmony that dictated the movements of the very universe. But to achieve harmony, the most complicated number he thought could exist was a fraction, like two-thirds. When Hippasus suggested his own strange new numbers, Pythagoras couldn't accept his error but he couldn't logically refute Hippasus."

"So?"

Preston pulled her back inside the lab and directed her toward a computer. "I'll print it out for you. When his views weren't accepted, Hippasus went public, something Pythagoras and his disciples saw as a complete betrayal."

"I'm sorry, I just had a worrisome conversation with my sister, Ceil. Cut to the chase for me."

"Hippasus drowned at sea. There were lots of rumors, some that vengeful gods struck his ship, but others that he'd been pushed overboard by someone working for Pythagoras and his secret brotherhood."

Lynn felt more butterflies trying to escape her stomach. "Oh no. You're saying Armando must have revealed or been about to reveal a secret someone didn't want known."

22.

Monday afternoon, Houston

Naphtha: The major raw component of gasoline and the crude oil cut closest in boiling range to gasoline.

A secret so important he was killed?" Lynn said. She wondered what else the lost security videotape showed.

They looked at the data for the first distillation cut and noted with surprise that about twenty percent less volume in the light-gasoline cut than expected had distilled.

"Maybe we lost light ends when the sample was taken. Let's see what the next cuts look like." Preston's eyes squinted.

The door to the lab creaked open and Reese walked in with Riley Stevens. "I want to see this in person," Riley said.

"Since you're here, we could use the backup. Want to weigh some beakers?" Lynn asked.

"Okay, I've seen enough." Reese smiled and pretended to leave.

"I hear a tropical storm is forming and may hit Houston in a few days," Riley said. "Why don't we all have a preseason hurricane party at my place, like Jean-Marie's always talking about? Invite Lynn here and some other party gals. Who knows what'll happen when the electricity goes off?"

What a goddamn jerk. "You'll have to take me off your invitation list," Lynn said. "Have I mentioned my ex-husband used to be sumo wrestler Killer-San?"

"Can't blame a guy for trying," Riley said.

"C'mon Riley," Lynn said. "You're being a pain in the butt and you know it. TriCoast's drill on unwanted comments, et cetera, is lay off or be laid off."

"I like the et cetera."

Lynn's reply was interrupted when a sudden loud boom was answered almost immediately by the sound of several smaller explosions.

"Too far away to be us, but someone on the Channel just landed way too hard." Reese straightened, as if ready to report for duty.

Preston opened a door of the windowless lab. "Black smoke about a mile away. That's Polyolefin Chemicals or Xavier Refining."

After a few minutes, Reese's cell phone rang. As he listened, Lynn saw the lines around his eyes set into a mask. "Adric said his operators got calls from friends at Xavier Refining saying it was a boiler explosion at their place. Sounds like there are injuries."

"Injuries? That's awful!" Preston's voice was sharp with disbelief.

Lynn felt dismay at the thought of four Ship Channel accidents—with casualties—in four days. *Too many, too frequent, even for the Channel. Union interference? Not their tactics. Environmental extremists? Unlikely they'd get access. Sabotage looks more and more likely. But by whom, and why?*

"Oooeee! What's going on?" Riley asked. "Now if I were Dwayne, I'd say it's contract labor. No matter what, that's where Dwayne always points."

Reese clasped his hands behind his back, as if at parade rest. "Adric said Xavier is shutting down everything that isn't already knocked out."

The events of the last few days crowded her mind—hydrofluoric acid in her office eating away its containers, the attack during her run, and the phone call: *Bitches who screw around in refineries don't last long. Especially when they trust the wrong people to help them. And they die such interesting deaths.*

"Lynn, you're frowning at something that's invisible to the rest of us. Are you okay?" Reese asked.

Who is it you aren't supposed to trust? Lynn willed her focus to clear. "I'll call the refinery manager at Xavier later and see if he can use Jean-Marie's help."

"What are you finding in your distillation?" Reese asked.

"Too early to tell," Lynn said, giving Preston a silencing look. Riley had whirled around, appearing to listen intently.

After Reese and the sexist CFO left, Lynn said, "We have the light naphtha cut."

Lynn looked over Preston's shoulder at the glowing screen showing the light naphtha calculations. Again less than expected. *Not good.*

Preston shrugged. "These are small volumes. Any error shows up as a big percentage. Let's see what we get next."

But the next cut was no different. In the first three, they had distilled twenty percent less than predicted. That meant the remaining, higher-boiling fractions were larger than they should be. And that meant Centennial's crude was heavier and of poorer quality than it should be.

But was the glitch with all of Centennial's crudes or only one? Since the sample was a mix, she couldn't tell. Lynn stretched out a cramp pulling on the arch of her foot.

The door banged open as Dwayne barged in.

"We're charging admission," Lynn told him.

Dwayne pulled out a five-dollar bill and waved it at them. "Hear that boiler explosion? They made the same mistake we did. They let too many of their good, experienced operators go and brought in a bunch of contractors so dumb they spit upwind."

Preston raised his eyebrows. Lynn suppressed a smile.

"Are you getting the results you expected?" Dwayne asked.

Preston shook his head. "It's still too early to tell, but not exactly what we expected."

Dwayne grimaced. "You must have made a mistake. Do you really remember how to do this procedure?"

"You should try this. When was the last time you did?" Lynn asked. *If Dwayne treats you this irritably, how does he treat his employees? He's probably running off his best people.*

The next three cuts, for heavy naphtha, light kerosene, and heavy kerosene, were closer: ninety to ninety-five percent of predicted. But the continued difference troubled her.

A fog appeared in the flask.

"Sample's cracking," Lynn said. "Let's switch to vacuum pressure to get the last few fractions separated."

Preston connected the vacuum pumping and control system and turned it on. Lynn dropped the pressure and resumed the heat. After reflux stabilized, they watched and measured again. When the temperature rose to six hundred and fifty, they weighed the collection beaker, the distillation flask, and the condensing column.

"Over half the sample is left, when we should have less than half. The heavy atmospheric resid is fifteen percent larger than it should be. Let's take a break and think about this before we do the second sample."

"I want something to drink. You're taking your laptop?" Preston said. It was complaint more than question.

"I've never lost it," Lynn said, "and I don't want this to be the first time. Let's take yours, too."

When the Assistant saw the samples being collected, he notified the Rabbit. The Rabbit then heard about Lynn's big experiment and arranged to monitor it. It was useful to work as a team.

Lynn had a team, too: that mixed-blood, know-it-all Preston Li, probably some scholarship Bellaire-Boulevard success story. But the Rabbit and the Assistant had discovered that Preston couldn't resist a bet.

"They're leaving. Headed for the vending room," the Assistant said into a phone. "The bitch took the laptops."

Bad break, but no time to think about that.

The Rabbit hastened down the rubber-treaded stairs to the empty lab. The Rabbit knew where everything was, having reviewed the layout a few hours earlier in a brief rehearsal. Lynn wasn't the only one with a key to the place.

Using a cloth, the Rabbit pulled open the drawers and found the knife, the big wax block, and the ruler. After heating the knife, the Rabbit measured and cut two smaller squares of wax from the big block, then shoved each wax block into a fan intake in the hood.

"Is Lynn still in here, do you think?"

Shocked to hear another voice so nearby, the Rabbit dropped the knife by the sink and scrambled out the back door of the lab that led directly into the parking lot. The Rabbit jogged to the wooden loading dock and vaulted up onto it to hide.

After coffee, Preston and Lynn walked back the way they'd come across the smoking-hot parking lot.

"I thought you'd never finish talking team bets," Lynn said.

"Some people drink beer. I drink statistics."

"Let's start the second sample." Lynn rebooted the laptops.

"Come on," Preston said. "What are your odds on the Cowboys? Or would you rather talk about the Rangers?"

Lynn was about to answer when she caught a whiff of something familiar. Something dangerously familiar. *Think, don't panic!* First, verify. "Do you smell something?"

"Someone must have left eggs in the refrigerator a few months ago." He coughed and his voice rose. "H_2S!"

"Hold your breath!" Lynn found two air packs and tossed one to Preston. The small respirators had a safe limit of only five minutes.

Step two, protect yourself and others. Locate the source if possible.

"Turn up the fan on this hood." Lynn banged the switch to turn on the fan in the second hood and flipped off the heating mantle.

Step three. Get the hell away. "Let's go!"

She grabbed their laptops and they raced out the door into the heat, rubbing their eyes. The asphalt pavement shimmered and wobbled, a mirage of instability.

She looked at her computer, uncomprehending, as if it might hold the answer. Instead, the cursor on the screen blinked stupidly, as unreal as what had just happened.

"Rotten eggs again." Preston's laugh held the slightest of quavers.

"The samples were exactly the same. In fact, they were the same sample, divided in thirds. The second one shouldn't have been producing more hydrogen sulfide." Lynn spoke deliberately and slowly to fight off a new wash of fear.

"Should I sound the H_2S alarm?"

"No. No point in disrupting everybody, though it would be interesting if this alarm didn't work either. The H_2S came from the sample so there isn't much. We can go in with these air packs. I saw a portable monitor next to the door."

They reentered the lab. Preston grabbed the monitor and activated it. "H_2S yellow. Less than 20 parts per million. Our survival odds without the air packs are good."

"Only good? Tell me they're perfect!"

"As close to perfect as they'll be for the next few hours," Preston said, and they shed the packs.

When Lynn sniffed, she could still detect the strong residue. "Let's take the glassware apart to check for a leak."

But nothing was chipped or broken. "This didn't happen the first time, before we left for a break. Let's look at the vents." She found a flashlight in one of the drawers.

They turned off the fan and Preston shone the flashlight up into the vent of the first chrome-covered hood. She saw nothing unusual.

"We'd better take this vent fan apart to compare it with the one in the second hood." Lynn unscrewed the nuts for the wings that kept liquid from dropping back into the work surface of the hood. The locking clips unsnapped easily. The vent had two motorized fans. Each of its two air intakes measured 4 square inches. Although the fan blades were black from years of greasy hydrocarbons, they rotated easily. "No one has cleaned these."

"Do you clean them in your kitchen?" Preston asked.

"No, I only microwave or eat out."

"So when you host a dinner you check the caterer's calendar first?"

Lynn felt a smile crease her face. Preston's teasing was a relief. "Absolutely." As she expected, the air intakes were clear.

Preston disassembled the second hood vent.

When Lynn gazed up into the intake mouths she saw nothing out of the ordinary. Then she shone the flashlight. *Damn.* She couldn't see past the intakes. Both were plugged. She poked at one with a pen point, and the pen stuck. When she pulled hard to free it, a few white flakes drifted down.

"If that's not dandruff we're in more trouble than I thought." The leathery smell of his cologne came from behind Lynn's shoulder.

"Do you see anything sharp enough to dig it out?" Lynn tilted her head to get a better view of the intakes.

After a minute, Preston said, "Well, not only did I find something sharp, but it's been recently used. A knife is over by the sink."

White wax smeared the blade of a small knife. A large block of wax missing two four-inch-square chunks sat in the open drawer. As Lynn looked closely at the work surface of the second hood, she saw two piles of freshly carved shavings directly beneath the intakes.

Her stomach knotted. "Let's see if we can find gloves and another knife. Also paper bags to store the knife you found, the big block of wax, and what we're digging out of the intakes. Maybe someone left fingerprints."

Preston dropped the smeared knife into one paper bag and the sample block with the missing squares into another.

Touching their surfaces as little as possible, Lynn worked the wax plugs out of the fan intakes. Both fit the cut edges of the large sample block like puzzle pieces. Lynn dropped them into bags also.

"I doubt there are fingerprints," Preston said.

"Maybe whoever did this didn't have time to use gloves." Lynn turned to Preston and looked at him closely. "Why don't you take a break and I'll start the second distillation again?"

"I'm worried about you here alone."

"You're sweet, but whoever plugged the vent already can tell we're still around. I think we were just being warned."

"Just? Just almost knocked out, I should remind you," Preston said, brown eyes sparkling in an undefined emotion between amusement and outrage. "I'll stay here."

"I'm glad you're staying." Lynn patted his arm, restraining herself from giving him a full-body hug of relief. She turned away, and began opening cabinets and drawers to find clean glassware for a third test.

"So who's on your short list of people who want to poison us?"

"I don't know enough of the employees to eliminate people or suspect just one or two. If you ignore for a minute what just happened . . ."

"Ignore! Are you a robot?" Preston said. This time his anger was unmistakable. He accidentally knocked an empty beaker to the floor. It rolled but didn't break.

"Slow down. Who has a reason?" Lynn asked, glad to run through her reasoning and her list with Preston.

"People are upset Centennial is contracting out so much maintenance work. It could be a union disruption—that's happened in other refineries."

"Sabotage occurs during a strike, not an ordinary workday. I've never known the union to hide its concerns. Cody's the rep. He would have spoken up." Lynn greased a new collection flask.

"There's also a possibility of a third-party extremist, or maybe another layoff casualty. Someone with a grudge." Preston typed data into Lynn's computer.

"We can't rule it out, but I don't see much to support it." Then Lynn remembered her conversation with Reese in the diner with the pecan pie and pictures of Willie Nelson. "What about the buyout group—the four VPs?"

Preston's forehead wrinkled. "Come to think of it, I've heard all four—Jay, Riley, Dwayne, and Jean-Marie—say they wish they'd gotten financing."

"Did any of them seem especially upset or angry?"

"No."

"I'm worried about the safety of everyone here. If we don't find some answers in a few days and the refinery crashes, it could kill more people." She suppressed a sigh. "So do this calculation. Compare a mix of four crudes to our results. Make the theoretical mix thirty percent each Arab Medium, Oriente, Kuwaiti Export, and ten percent Qatari Dukhan. My guess is that they don't match what we're supposed to have. Even though they don't blend linearly, the results will be telling."

Preston typed in the formulas and had the results almost instantly. "You're right, they don't match. What we have is heavier. Maybe our proportions are wrong."

"These four crudes are all similar. Even if we drop all of the Dukhan, the lightest, the density doesn't change much."

"Are you saying that we don't even know what crude oils this refinery is running? That Centennial could have anything out there?" With each question Preston's voice rose.

Preston is right. We aren't even sure of the most basic data. We can't panic. "There's probably only one off-spec crude. And out of all the possibilities, we can rule out the crudes that aren't shipped to Houston."

But she understood what Preston left unspoken. The number of permutations was huge. While many crude oil combinations could be ruled out, hundreds couldn't be. They needed to run the same time-consuming procedure on the crude in each of TriCoast's four sour-crude storage tanks.

"Why don't we call Jay?" Preston asked as they washed glassware.

"Not yet. What if he's the one trying to warn us?"

"Poison us. Kill us. Isn't that what you should say? It could have been anybody. The whole refinery knows we're here. We had so many visitors you'd think we announced we were giving away your Maserati."

"Look around. Maybe we'll see someone who's surprised we aren't strapped into an ambulance." Lynn forced herself to chuckle and picked up the paper bags. As they walked out of the lab, she said, "I'll meet you at that office we're using in half an hour."

Can you talk to him? Will he help you, or are you screwing up by trusting him? She climbed the rubber-treaded stairs. In answer to her unasked question, Shelby nodded and Lynn went into his office.

"Let's talk." She took the chair across from Reese.

23.

Monday night, Paris

The restaurant was empty. It would fill later. Robert caressed his book while he waited for Ceil. He opened it and read Simon Singh's passage again: *"It is suspected that irrational numbers were originally discovered by the Pythagorean Brotherhood centuries earlier, but the concept was so abhorrent to Pythagoras that he denied their existence. . . . [Pythagoras's student], Hippasus, was idly toying with the number the square root of two, attempting to find the equivalent fraction. Eventually he came to realize that no such fraction existed."*

He shifted in his chair. Where was Ceil?

He picked up the menu. Hearing a familiar voice, he turned to see two of his classmates from École Polytechnique. He nodded at them and found his place again in the book.

Because Pythagoras had been unable to either accept or logically refute this departure from mathematical harmony, *"To his eternal shame he sentenced Hippasus to death by drowning."*

But Robert considered that removing dissent was to Pythagoras's eternal credit. The world needed to learn the wonders of geometry before being distracted by the esoterica of irrationals. He thought that the master mathematician had simply delayed discovery of irrationals. That discovery came soon enough, a hundred and seventy years later in 330 BC.

The story told Robert that doubters and those of lesser intellect had to be sacrificed for the greater good, foot soldiers in a war. Like those in the States the last few days, and hundreds—only hundreds, not thousands—would be in the next nine days, as the Rabbit and his recruits carried out Robert's plan. And those killed would be mostly foolish, uneducated American proletarian workers, probably none of whom had a college degree, let alone the intellectual armaments of a graduate of École Polytechnique. Not much of a loss.

Ceil sat down before he noticed her. How could he have missed her lithe form, barely sheathed in an electric-blue dress? Perhaps because she blended so well with the Parisians around them.

"Bonjour, Ceil. *"* He rose from his chair to kiss the pale cheek she offered. He congratulated himself on this choice of venue, Royaume. It was near the large chestnut trees off the Champs-Elysee. Plush decor—a gilded ceiling, mahogany-paneled walls, and luminously white linens—complemented two-star food. "I'll order for you."

She started to protest, then pursed her lips. *"Bien sûr. "*

To the waiter he said, "We'll have the smoked mussels, the chicken St. Jacques with beer sauce, the bitter salad, and a bottle of '95 Mâcon Cuvée Levroutée from Jean Thevenet's vineyards. You still have a few bottles?"

"Oui, monsieur. "

At the end of the meal, when their salads arrived, Robert advised, "Take a sip of the wine before each bite of salad." He followed his own advice and was pleased that, as always, the dulcet harmony of the wine with its overtones of honey and lemon soothed the compound bitterness of the arugula and brussels sprouts. Ceil responded with pleasant surprise at the taste combination.

When they finished, she asked, "Robert, what is your purpose?"

"With what?"

"All this. Your group."

"Simple. The world's resources should be divided equitably among all populations. In particular, your American countrymen should use oil less and tax it more, as we Europeans do. Higher taxes would reduce petrol use and clean the air, which even you Americans worry about."

"The States aren't Europe," she said, sitting back in her chair. But she didn't dispute the first part of his premise.

"Remember our discussion in the Luxembourg Gardens," he said. "The tax revenues should be sent to countries like Honduras, Cambodia, Ethiopia, and a few others to build refineries."

"Why not send them aid directly? Or buy oil in their names and ship it to them?"

"Oil by itself is nothing to them. They need to put people to work refining it."

"You sound like my sister. OPEC will object."

He contained a twitch at the reference to Lynn, his true object. "No. Ultimately, OPEC is neutral. It still sells oil. The payers have different names."

"There's so much corruption. The money would be siphoned off. You don't convince me." Her quiet voice contradicted her words.

"Not these countries. I know the officials," he insisted.

"But how can you accomplish anything like this?"

"I have additional means."

"You said 'I' not 'we.' Does that mean the rest of the group isn't aware of all you're doing? What else are you doing?"

"Unlike you Americans, we French don't tell everyone everything. They'll learn, and you'll learn, when the time is appropriate. And now, you must tell me your secrets."

"Unlike you, I have none," she said. But to Robert, her flat tone signaled otherwise. She placed her salad fork by the side of her plate and wiped her mouth, staring out across the restaurant. "This is a lovely place."

"Surely your family is worried," he said, hoping this would lead her to talk about Lynn.

"Yes. My sister called me this afternoon. It's possible she may visit me. But she sounded very distracted."

"What could be more important than visiting you?"

"Some refinery she bought. Five people have died, including last night in the hospital one that seemed to be recovering."

"What happened to him in the hospital? What do you mean?" Robert asked, leaning forward to catch her answer.

"She said the man was on oxygen, and someone substituted nitrogen."

So, Robert thought, *the Rabbit proceeded with a Pythagoras project as I suggested. Competence, for once.* "Is she your only sibling? Are your parents alive?"

"There's only her. Well, my father is alive, barely. Emphysema. My mother died when her bone cancer metastasized to her liver. That was several months ago." Ceil looked away. "I took care of her during her last five weeks. She was in such pain. I was so helpless to relieve her."

Robert reached over and touched her chilly hand, exploring it with his fingers. "I am truly sorry. Let us talk of other things."

She allowed her hand to remain under his, but didn't return his clasp. "Robert, this work. Why so roundabout? Why not use your influence at the Ministry of Finance?"

"The French government cannot force the US Congress to do anything."

"So tell me about the Tolf protest to which I agreed. What is supposed to happen? Why is your group involved?"

"The meeting will generate good media coverage and keeps our views on third world development public. Truly, it is as a game. When the Tolf executives tire of your challenges, they will enforce their time limit on questions. If you choose to keep talking, three or four large men will escort you and Guy from the microphone and out of the meeting hall. Nothing more."

"How does the media exposure help you?"

"Recruiting and funding. We always see an increase after these actions."

Ceil drained her third glass of Cuvée Levroutée. She was drinking less delicately than when they'd started dinner, Robert noted. He signaled for the dinner check and signed it.

When he offered to see her to her apartment she didn't refuse. He tucked his book inside his jacket. On the métro ride to the Goutte d'Or—still that awful place, he thought—she allowed him to drape his arm over her shoulder. He couldn't read her expression, except to see that it had eased.

Without saying a word he started to follow her into her apartment building. She turned, shook her head, and backed away as fearfully as if he were a monster. "*Non*, Robert. I can't. Not now. Not after what happened in Gabon."

He shrugged and said casually, "Another time, then."

But he felt the clenched heat of his angry, rejected body radiate through the darkness like an explosion.

24.

Monday evening, Houston

Lynn had known Reese for almost two decades. Once a navy pilot, his insistence on high standards for jet-fuel performance had segued effectively into an oil refining career. After he'd cleaned up the third refinery, the Venezuelans came courting and made a buyout offer too sweet to refuse, then put their own management in place. Reese's subsequent retirement was in name only; Lynn could tell he itched to resume work. Naturally, he was the one she called to take Centennial once she bought it.

But do you really know him? Has something changed?

He was still in his office, reviewing financial spreadsheets. She related the afternoon in the lab, both the unexpected results and the hydrogen sulfide emergency, putting the two paper bags on his desk and telling him what they held. "Do you have a contact in the Houston Police Department? Besides our friend Officer Stinson?"

His eyes narrowed and his short hair seemed to bristle more than usual. "Lynn, you're scaring someone so they busted your airspace. You're too senior to take these chances. Back off and let the rest of the team handle it."

"I'm too senior not to pursue this. Reese, TriCoast bought this refinery at my recommendation. I can't back off now. In fact, I won't put someone else into a dangerous situation."

"It's just hardware. You're taking this too personally." A tic jumped inside his jaw.

Lynn felt the beginning twinge of a leg cramp. She got up and paced to Reese's window, with its vista of the whole refinery. She took time to scour the plant, left to right, examining each road, tower, and pipe rack. *Why can't you believe him? Reese is the same person he's always been. That jerk in the phone call, telling you trusting the wrong people would get you killed. It almost happened with the hydrofluoric acid, and just now in the lab.*

"Reese, you and I know it's anything but hardware. It's those five people who've died. 'Flown west,' is what you'd say. It's everyone's safety. I need to speed up, not back off, because whoever is doing this is in a hurry. Everyone here is in danger."

Reese sighed. "To answer your initial question, as it happens, I have a friend at HPD I used to see all the time when I played the Sharpstown golf course."

"Can he run prints on this knife and these chunks of wax?"

He smiled. "*She's* a par golfer. But we need to go through Alex Stinson since he's assigned to us. I'll make sure he gets these."

"At the hospital I got the sense Alex didn't want to hear from us again."

"We have to use the system."

"What we have to do is find out who just blew a bunch of H_2S at Preston and me."

"Fair enough. I'll see if she can release the information on prints to us and to Alex at the same time."

"Good. Now, is there anyone in the group here who wanted to buy the refinery and is still angry?"

"They're grumpy sometimes, but no. Do you really suspect them? Lynn, they fly this plane. They wouldn't prang it."

Sometimes Reese's pilot jargon is indecipherable. "Prang?"

"Damage."

"Not unless there's something we don't know about them. Or one of them."

"I don't like creating dissension in our management group."

"But we need to consider the possibility they're involved."

"I can't see any basis for that." He crossed his arms.

Do you need a two-by-four? Usually he gets this stuff right away. Or is he involved with them? "Preston's and my H$_2$S exposure in the lab today was no accident, nor was the hydrofluoric acid that appeared in our office over the weekend. The deaths of five people, one of them in a hospital, for God's sake, are not accidents."

"Do you think this is related to TriCoast's purchase of the refinery?" Reese tightened his lips into a thin line.

"The operating glitches predate our purchase. They started showing up several months previous. No amount of due diligence can uncover what someone takes pains to hide."

"Are the shipping logs online?" Lynn tilted the back of her chair in the new Centennial office until it was against the wall.

"Almost everything is. Let's see what they say." Preston clicked the computer mouse a few times. "Here's what's arrived in the past six months. Nothing unusually heavy, sour, or difficult to process."

"Who enters the shipping data?"

"Shelby. Surely you don't suspect her. Every spare minute she has, she's coaching one of her kids' sports teams."

She wouldn't be the first to conduct criminal activity on company time. Saddened by the thought, Lynn asked, "Does she handle the whole transaction?"

"Shelby is under everybody's direction. She works for Reese, and all four VPs—Dwayne, Jay, Riley, and Jean-Marie. Helps them all with scheduling, word processing, and data entry."

"Who are the suppliers?"

"I don't know, but Jay would. Let's see if he's in."

Lynn tapped the button that turned on the speakerphone.

"Jay? It's Lynn and Preston."

"What can I do for you?" Jay's voice was warm and reassuring.

"We're looking at the online supply logs and wondered who Centennial's suppliers are," Preston said.

"Arab Medium and Kuwaiti Export from Middle East Brokerage. We started an exchange agreement ten months ago with you, with TriCoast. We give Bart the West Texas Intermediate we don't run ourselves, and he gives me Dukhan plus a markup. We started running the Oriente about six months ago. That comes from Latin American Crude Traders. What have I forgotten?"

"Louisiana Light Sweet," Lynn prompted.

"We buy it from various producers at market price."

"How often does Centennial receive shipments?"

"Louisiana Sweet and West Texas Intermediate are piped in continuously. Arab Medium and Kuwaiti Export arrive at the deep-water terminals in shipments of 400,000 to 500,000 barrels and are delivered to us 150,000 to 250,000 barrels at a time. Dukhan comes in 150,000-barrel chunks every so often. We get Oriente whenever I make a deal for it. The most recent was for 400,000 barrels, and 150,000 barrels of it are due on our dock this week."

All the statistics Jay cited squared with the shipping logs on the screen in front of them.

"Thanks, Jay. We'll let you get back to your evening," Lynn said.

"Hey, hold on. Riley just walked in and he wants a word. I'll put him on the speaker."

"Lynn, for a new boss-woman you're working awfully hard. Can we take you out, get a drink?" Riley offered. "We'll even take you to a nice place instead of a Westheimer men's club."

"Riley, men's clubs are my favorite places to negotiate. I do better deals when the people with me are watching the dancers. But I appreciate the consideration."

Preston moved away from the speakerphone to cover his snorts of laughter, and they exchanged silent good-bye waves.

This would be a perfect opportunity to talk to Jay and Riley, see if you can ferret out what they know, discover for sure if you can trust them. Maybe if it's in Jay's venue, he'll be more open. "After I check in with my office, I thought I'd head to Southwyck Golf Course to practice putting and driving for half an hour or so. Do you want to meet there?"

Riley's voice echoed through the speaker. "Did you bring clubs and cleats with you from Dallas, Lynn?"

"I've got cleats. I'll rent clubs."

Jay's golfing prowess was no accident. Most considered it a job requirement. Lynn's handicap was decent, but she needed practice for her time on the courses with some of TriCoast's oil suppliers. Maybe if they shared a round with her at Pinehurst, she'd reasoned, they would be sure to cut TriCoast the same deals they cut her competitors. *But let's hope this doesn't take too much time, and that your anxiety isn't reflected in your swing.*

"If you have distance on your drive, you aim for the houses at the end of the range. Yes, we'll meet you there," Jay said. "Lynn's all set. My clubs are in the trunk. How about you, Riley?"

"I can find a three-wood somewhere in my car."

"Good. We'll meet you at the driving range, then," Jay decided. "After that, we can get a drink. You're staying at the Four Seasons, aren't you, Lynn?"

"Yes." Everyone at Centennial seemed able to identify her whereabouts at all times. *Did someone sew GPS trackers into your bras?*

"We can have a drink there afterwards," Jay said.

"There's a jazz bar Jean-Marie's been after me to try, NOLA in Exile," Lynn said. "Jean-Marie said one of her second cousins opened it when they evacuated from Louisiana. They're trying to raise money to reopen their main place in New Orleans."

"Sure. Hell, I had half a dozen people staying with me until a few months ago. They lost everything," Riley said. "So where's this course?"

Jay answered, "South on Highway 288 until it turns into the Nolan Ryan Expressway. Farm-to-Market Road 518 east to the sign for the Silverlake housing development. Signs direct you to the course."

"As long as I live in Texas I will never get used to six-lane highways being called farm-to-market roads." Riley said.

This investigation is your top priority, but you can't neglect the other billion-dollar part of your business or you'll be pulled from it for sure. Lynn left a message for Mike Emerson, promising him an update when she returned to Dallas. She set a time to meet with Claude, telling him she'd be flying to Paris in the next few days. Then she scheduled teleconferences with her other refinery managers.

"Awrite, there you are!" Jean-Marie greeted Lynn boisterously as she came through the door, ducking her head from habit. "I thought I'd find you in the office. Hell of a situation at Meletio and Xavier. I found out the emergency shutdowns wrecked their cat crackers as well as their main distillation units. A month's downtime."

Then her voice dropped several decibels. "And at Xavier two people killed, five more badly burned."

"Oh no!"

"It hurts them, us, everybody. Plus, no one has any spare capacity. If gasoline prices rise again Congress will be up our ass in a big way."

Lynn didn't want to visualize Jean-Marie's comment too closely. "What else did you find out?"

"Someone sabotaged the electrical system at both places. That's what gave them fits. Their cooling-water pumps couldn't run, and they didn't have enough electrical backup to keep their computer and control systems going."

"Who'd do that?"

"No idea. I've put in some long nights so I'm headed home to sleep," Jean-Marie said. "Just stopped by to see if you'd talked to Armando's crew chief."

"Did you?"

"Yeah. Funny about the call Armando said he got. The chief said he didn't call Armando, that he wouldn't have called him out early morning like that."

"So who called him?"

"Good question, *cher.*"

❖

Lynn decided to take a more rural route than the one Jay described to Riley. She exited at Cullen and glided south past all the flat, familiar scrub until Cullen turned into Old Chocolate Bayou Road.

This time of the year, cars never really cooled. By summer everyone in Houston suddenly remembered favorite relatives living in Maine, Michigan, or Montana.

When she arrived at Southwyck, with its rounded bunkers and stands of pampas grass, she greeted Riley, who was already hoisting his clubs out of the trunk of his car, a black Mercedes.

On the putting green she stretched with the putter behind her back, teed up a ball, squared her stance, and tried to remember everything from the last lesson. She hit the ball fifteen times, but it dropped into the cup only twice. Her drives were no more successful; 125 yards and not one straight. *Jeez, you're off. Those shanks will give you away.* She could see Riley's lumpy back. Judging by the direction of his drives, he'd warmed up far more easily.

She heard a rustle behind her. "It's hard to both concentrate and relax, isn't it?" Jay appeared at the edge of the green.

She hadn't seen him arrive, despite having what she thought was a full view of the parking lot. "Yes, it is." Lynn hoped he wasn't one of those golfers who felt compelled to advise other players.

"I heard you had a ten handicap. Must be harder on an unfamiliar course," he said, genially. "And no, I don't like to get advice either."

Her stomach jumped. *Jeez, he's a mind reader. And your bad drives are betraying your nerves.*

"Have you ever had the yips?" he asked. "Trouble sinking easy putts?"

She nodded. "Feels like it today, for sure."

"Mayo Clinic had a study on that. Maybe you could ask to be in the follow-up." Jay drove the ball beautifully and precisely. His form and follow-through were perfect. The ball flew 200 yards in a straight arc. Riley drove with more power but less direction—about 225 yards with a hook.

Lynn resumed putting practice on another cup, her forehead dripping sweat from the afternoon heat and humidity, Houston's own special double whammy. After she tried all the putting practice cups with little improvement, she moved to the driving range again and teed up next to Riley.

She could feel him watching her. With her driver, this time she hit a dozen straight and short, each about 130 yards.

"Why don't you . . . ?" he started.

"Why don't you and I hit a few more drives? Then we can go." She shot him a keep-away look and resumed hitting, this time with a five-iron. After a while the thwacking resumed at his tee.

"Ready to give up on the toe balls and rainmakers, Lynn? Ready to go, Riley?" Jay asked.

Riley said, "I just need to catch up with all that practice you get during—what is it you call them—'marketing conferences'?"

"You could find the time, too, if you wanted." Despite his heat-absorbing black hair, Jay appeared comfortable in the afternoon heat. His shirt showed only a few dark patches of sweat. By contrast, Lynn had soaked her shirt. *So much for giving an impression of composure.*

"I'll clean up and meet you at the bar," she said.

She drove out behind Jay. His car was a polished, navy BMW in the large seven hundred series.

The refining business doesn't make people rich. How can Jay Gans and Riley Stevens afford their expensive new cars? Even more, how could they afford to park them at Centennial where, as Dwayne pointed out, they risked finish-destroying acid and ash boilovers? *Maybe they'll reveal something at the bar.*

The drive north on the Nolan Ryan Expressway passed hurricane evacuation route reminders. She wondered if, the next time they were used, the evacuation traffic jams would be the fifteen- and twenty-hour nightmares Houston natives had experienced before.

❖

The NOLA-in-Exile bar bumped with the steady rhythms of Preservation Hall and Tipitina's jazz band recordings. A plasma screen television perched silently. Low ceilings reinforced cool relief from the outdoor heat and omnipresent street construction. They found three club chairs and ordered beer and sandwiches. The music switched from the Neville Brothers to the Dixie Chicks in that peculiar gumbo-chili, New Orleans-Texas subculture that had developed in Houston.

You can't stay long. But you have to be here long enough that they relax and talk.

"Lynn, here's a joke you'll like." Riley bounced cheerfully in his chair. "You know why they call them operators, don't you? Because operators know how to turn knobs and open valves."

It was an old barb, dating from the earliest, most sexist times women had begun working in refineries. "That joke's past its sell-by, but I think I can dredge up the response: 'And you know why they call us engineers, don't you? Because we know how to handle operators.'"

"She's got you." Jay laughed.

Then Lynn said, "Riley, have you ever thought about your intent being misinterpreted?"

"Always. Keep hoping I'll get lucky." Riley grinned.

Jesus Christ, how fast can you get this man out of Centennial? He's a lawsuit waiting to happen. "So, how do you like being a part of TriCoast?" she asked them, swallowing beer so cold it barely had a taste.

"I'm still getting used to Reese's pilot talk, and his hours. Sometimes he's out of the office by four thirty in the afternoon to see his grandkids," Riley said.

She nodded. It was the Reese she always pictured.

Riley said, "Reese keeps talking about cutting nickels and dimes. Hell, he wants me to know Jay's job—what crude he's buying, which ones are the best to buy at any given time. And he wants me to know Dwayne's job—how the cat cracker operates. I'm neither a trader nor an engineer. For all I know he wants me to try smoking like Dwayne, too."

Jay nodded, then stared at the bar television as if willing it to turn on by itself. As if he and Riley had already had this discussion many times.

Riley continued. "Dwayne thinks money works like a valve—turn it on and it pours. Until TriCoast came along, I'd been telling our story to a bunch of bankers who couldn't care less. Excuse me." Riley heaved himself up and trotted to the men's room.

"While we're on the subject, what kinds of crude oil are you buying these days, Jay?"

He tugged at his chin. "I just made another deal on 400,000 barrels of Oriente at a dollar a barrel under the market rate. I've been able to do five or six deals like that in the last six months."

"Oriente is great crude. Congratulations!"

His face creased in a smile that lingered. "I learned a few tricks from my dad. Surely you know him from TriCoast, Lynn. Bobby Gans?"

"Bobby Gans, the convenience store CEO?" She should have connected son to father earlier. "I met him once." Bobby Gans had been on TriCoast's board of directors. After TriCoast opened its own convenience stores, the company wanted Bobby's expertise at selling beer and chips for hefty markups. Lynn chauffeured Bobby and wife number three to catch his private plane after a board meeting. "How's Bobby doing?"

"He's dead."

"I'm sorry," Lynn said, shocked. "What happened?"

"Old age. He declined and never improved."

"All that money Bobby had, why are you still working, Gans?" Riley piped in as he rejoined them.

Jay's reply was equally jovial. "I like the business. You'd miss me too much if I didn't show up. Besides, we can't all cash out on our reputation like you did." The two men shared a laugh and high-fived one another.

"What do you mean?" Lynn asked.

"Ask me no questions and I'll tell you no lies," Riley said, and changed the subject.

After Lynn finished her second round, Jay got up, a signal for all. "See you in the morning."

Lynn walked the few steamy blocks to her room, the conversation still bothering her. *What was Riley's secret source of wealth? How did Jay snag so much Oriente?*

"You know you should not drink and think," she muttered to herself. *An old Arnold movie.*

She sat at the computer desk. Even two bottles of beer were too much. *Not like all the practice you got drinking before your ex was an ex.*

She punched the first speed-dial number on her cell phone. "Dad, how are you feeling?" Lynn could hear the ricochet of cicadas. So he was probably outside on the porch with the portable phone.

"Doctor told me . . . lung reduction . . . surgery." He sounded cheerful.

"So you're going online to find out more?"

"Don't finish my . . . sentences."

"I feel I'm helping you if I do. Anyway, you quit smoking a few years ago. That was the biggest step."

"Most difficult . . . still dream . . . about smoking." He wheezed.

She sighed. "Change of subject. Remember when you worked on that sulfuric acid pipeline? What was wrong with it?"

"Ye answer."

"It was wrongly designed for the sulfuric acid concentration it carried."

"Reason?"

"The obvious answer would be corrosion. Since you were an

inspector, you'd say the pipe wall measured too thin, too close to failure."

"But not . . . that."

"No. It wasn't." She suddenly remembered. "You found the source before the pipeline leaked or failed. The operations were so sensitive the excess sulfur disrupted them months before corrosion showed in the pipe wall."

"Why ask?"

"I have a similar problem at this new refinery." Lynn described what she'd learned since they last talked. "Several facts puzzle me. The bypass valve was slightly open to the main line when it should have been closed. The H_2S alarm didn't trigger. The tag on the bypass valve that should have described its position was illegible. The H_2S concentration was higher than it should have been."

"Random?"

No. Not with Armando killed. Murdered. No need to upset him with that.

"Different . . . how is . . . Ceil?"

"I called her but she didn't say much, though she did ask me to come see her. She may have some information useful for my investigation, which I didn't expect. I hope to fly over and back."

"Good . . . important." He was gasping harder.

You shouldn't keep him talking. "Tell me what you learn about this lung reduction surgery. Take care, Dad."

"Ye too . . . I . . . love ye." He took a few short, rapid breaths.

"I love you, too, Dad." She hung up, wishing in vain he was younger and healthier. She called Cy at his office. When he didn't pick up, she left a message. "It's Lynn. I'll be back in Dallas tomorrow, but then I need to see Ceil. She has information for my investigation, and she still sounds upset, asked me to visit. I miss you."

You do miss him. Talking to Cy is calming, even though he's too serious right now. She missed his insight. His touch.

Rubbing her eyes, she brought up e-mail on her laptop. After half an hour, she'd sorted and replied to all of it.

She looked at her root-cause list again. The days since she'd first written it seemed like years. *And you're adding more than you're subtracting.*

Issues

1) H_2S leak and concentration too high, nonfunctional H_2S sensor

2) Threats against me—attack by bicyclist and death threat telephone call

3) Threat against me—Hydrofluoric acid in my office

4) Armando's oxygen switched to nitrogen; Armando, the only leak survivor now dead; "Pythagoras Project"

5) Threat against me and Preston—blocked vents exposing us to hydrogen sulfide

6) Continuing Centennial operating problems—sulfur, making product specs, coker filling up, pipe corrosion

7) How accidents/sabotage at other refineries connected?

Sources

Are not:

1) Neglect of safety

2) Deferred maintenance

3) Dehydrator inefficiency

Could be:

1) Electricity supply—cogenerator synchronization

2) Crude supply

3) Union deliberate action—but what reason? Cody not talking.

4) Other deliberate cause

L.A. Starks

Who/Motivations

1) Riley—job redundancy, lifestyle need
2) Jay—money and lifestyle need
3) Jean-Marie—cover-up of safety mistake
4) Dwayne—resentment, but wife's cancer main concern
5) Cody/Adric/Skyler/union—prestrike action but not typical union pattern
6) Outsider
   a) Armando/LaShawna mentioned, but attacks specific
   b) grudge
   c) environmental or safety extremist
   d) consultant—Brian Tulley, etc.
   e) other
7) Reliant/Centennial/other refiners—careless operations

25.

Tuesday, Rotterdam and Paris

Thyme still perfumed Robert's shoulders. Ceil's rejection last night fueled his passion, and his wife accommodated him. Deliciously. Aboard the train for the four-hour ride to Rotterdam he shivered in remembrance.

Ceil must be brought into line again. It would be different from Gabon. More mathematical.

Robert, along with the technical advisor to the French Ministry of Economy, Finance, and Industry and several of the advisor's other minions—Robert's colleagues—were taking the Thalys train to a conference on hedging the euro's fluctuation in long-term energy contracts.

The advisor himself slept, with the paper containing his speech folded in his hands. Although his large, bald head lolled to one side, his clothes remained sharply creased. Robert contrasted the advisor's clean appearance, even when asleep, with the Americans and their "business casual" clothing. He could always spot Americans by their shambling walk and ill-fitting clothes. Just more evidence of their sloppiness, as if he didn't already have plenty in his dealings with the Rabbit and the others.

He tapped into his e-mail and saw Sansei had deposited more funding into his account. *Bien.* Xin Yu must already know about the Meletio and Xavier refinery shutdowns. It wasn't all they owed him, but it would pay those who needed paying.

Robert replied to his bank officer, specifying another partial distribution of funds, including a dollar-denominated wire transfer into the Rabbit's account.

The land outside his window was flat and abundantly forested. Lace curtains and window boxes thick with flowers frosted every window. The Netherlands was one of the most densely populated countries in the world, and Rotterdam topped it with over four thousand people per square kilometer.

He'd visited the city before. He remembered most the new, glass-walled buildings; new in European parlance, meaning built in the last sixty years. During World War II, the Germans had firebombed Rotterdam repeatedly. Anything not burned down was so ferociously damaged it had to be torn down. Ossip Zadkine's giant statue, *Destroyed City*, memorialized Rotterdam's complete destruction; the anguished metal reach of a powerful man whose loins had been torn open.

Robert allowed the advisor time after he awoke before pressing his argument. "Advisor, may I direct your attention to the topic we discussed last week?"

"I don't recall the topic," the advisor said, fingering his collar stays.

"I believe our government should lead the funding of oil-refining facilities in stable, less-developed countries."

"Which ones?"

Robert showed him the same list he'd shown Ceil a few days before. "Honduras, Ethiopia, Vietnam, Cameroon, Laos, Cambodia, and Guinea-Bissau."

The advisor glanced at the list. "That role is for the United Nations, not for us. God knows what homicidal regimes we'd be supporting. Besides, if they can afford it, diesel and gasoline can be shipped in from somewhere that already has refineries. Surely there are some that are underutilized."

"No, refineries are at maximum utilization, which is why prices are so high. And it's been proven these countries will do better if they own the refining assets themselves."

"I like your idealism, Robert, but this is too complicated. I don't want to be in the construction business in some country I know nothing about."

"It would be simple to learn."

The advisor shook his head and ran his hand over his scalp as if smoothing hair no one else could see.

"Then let us talk again later," Robert said.

"That is enough. We have more important concerns."

Robert gave no indication of his disappointment. With the advisor, no subject was ever completely closed.

From Rotterdam's Centraal Station, they strode to the conference site. The complicated, narrow streets followed the vagaries of the canals. At each intersection the French visitors navigated lights for pedestrians, cars, bicyclists, and streetcars.

Robert walked on the far right, placing the street on one side and the good ear of the technical advisor on the other. He began to tell the advisor about Ceil Dayton—starting with her legs—when he heard a loud Dutch bark a few feet behind him.

"*Rechts!*"

Robert didn't understand that the bicyclist behind him was warning of an approach on the right. As he turned to look, a wide, unyielding metal handlebar poked him in the back and pushed him into a stumble. The bicyclist sped on without stopping.

"*Idiot!*" Robert cursed as he regained his balance and brushed at his clothes and hair. He felt his group's stares and his own never-ending hatred of Lance Armstrong for stealing the Tour de France from French bicyclists.

"Robert, you forget. We are in Holland. Cyclists rule." The advisor smirked.

Eventually they reached the Coolsingel, the city's main boulevard and the location of their conference host, TriCoast Energy's European headquarters. The sleek, linear building blared recent profitability,

Robert thought. Inlaid into the lobby's marble floor was a circular mosaic, about four meters in diameter. Robert admired its highlights of lapis lazuli and peridot.

In the conference room, the small group settled into plush chairs to hear the director of Rotterdam's port authority. Robert found the director's slides more absorbing than he'd expected.

"About fifty years ago a group of ports and industrial areas was created between Rotterdam and the entry to the North Sea. With dikes, dams, and sand deposits, the coastline was changed to add many square kilometers of newly created land, where the petroleum harbors, container terminals, ore terminals, and the Maasvlakte power plant you see are located. Three hundred million metric tons of goods pass through this port every year."

As the director spoke, Robert thought, involuntarily, delicately, but with a surge of interest, of a range of possible accidents. He could convince Sansei to fund another project after the success he would show them in the next seven days. Surely they wanted to sell their gasoline and diesel to Europe as well. He could expand his third world refinery construction list. He would give Lynn more to do. They would travel together.

The director explained that one of the port's features was a "disaster area," a training complex where fire brigades trained for large-scale industrial accidents. The complex included a grounded tanker that was frequently set on fire.

They couldn't train for everything, Robert considered.

"The largest port," the director said, "is the Eighth Petrol Harbor, just outside the Dutch coastline, where Persian Gulf supertankers unload. Nearby crude oil storage capacity is several million gallons."

Robert rubbed his hands, but quickly segued into clapping for the end of the director's introduction and the beginning of the advisor's speech.

When they left the conference for the dinner hosted by TriCoast's executive vice president of international refining, Henry Vandervoost,

Robert again admired the large, ornate lobby mosaic.

"Cosmati design," Vandervoost said, noticing Robert's interest. "The Cosmati were twelfth- and thirteenth-century Italian craftsmen who designed and installed flooring for cathedrals. This is a rare and beautiful design. It's made to look very old, but we installed it when we recently constructed the building."

Vandervoost ushered the group into a waiting line of Mercedes sedans, which sped to Restaurant Parkheuvel. The restaurant, set near the Maas River, boasted furnishings to match its food—creamy, heavy, and ornate.

They lingered over several courses, buoyed with wines.

"Did you hear?" the advisor asked Robert.

"About what?"

"The protest at Tolf. It's been all over the media this afternoon. I was called by the minister."

Robert feigned lack of interest, despite the fact that he'd directed these two particular protestors, Guy and Ceil. "No. What happened?"

"Two people at Tolf's annual meeting said they represented a third world development group. They asked Tolf and all large oil producers to direct ten percent of their production to less-developed countries."

The discussion quickly spread, with the whole group listening and contributing.

"Are they imbeciles?"

"The Saudis, Russians, Venezuelans? No one will even consider it."

"Who would pay?"

"They say the Americans will," the advisor reported. "The protesters, a man and a woman, said Americans should tax their gasoline at the same high rate as Europeans and use the revenue to subsidize purchases of oil by less-developed countries."

"Now that's a good idea. The Americans are wasteful. They think everything is free, especially petrol."

"Not something to which Americans would agree."

"It could be promoted as a conservation measure."

Vandervoost was quick to disapprove, Robert saw. "These protesters. They are everywhere trying to shut down those of us who actually make the gasoline. Who are these people?"

"Are you acquainted with them, Robert?" another of the advisor's minions asked, with what Robert thought might be sly knowledge.

"No," Robert replied, after a moment, "although I think they have interesting ideas." He doubted the others would pick up his hesitation in answering. *So, the Tolf protest went as planned*, he thought. If it seemed that a thousand voices were raising the issue—as had happened in the *Banlieu* Riots—action would become inevitable.

But he had another concern. Robert waited until Vandervoost drank enough to be free with his opinions. "Herr Vandervoost, are you acquainted with a Lynn Dayton who works for your company?"

Vandervoost's face reddened. "This lady Dayton. She thinks only of profits. She speaks always about it. But she just stupidly bought another American refinery, in Houston even, which immediately had a serious accident. I have here far better investment alternatives."

It was gratifying to have his Centennial handiwork discussed. "Does she visit you?"

"No, and I hope she never does."

"What is her background?"

"An engineer, which is good. A business degree, which is bad. She thinks she can simplify everything to a few numbers. Pah!"

"Maybe she has children and will soon quit and leave you alone." This led in the direction Robert hoped.

"She's not married. Only a sister and a dying father."

"These women, they are difficult?"

"Yes, they're too much trouble in a business like ours," Vandervoost concluded and turned to his other dinner partners.

Most of his group, including the advisor, expected to stay on in

Rotterdam, but after only two hours of eating and drinking Robert decided to return to Paris.

"Can't stay away from your wife, Robert?"

"No. And I don't want to," he said, pleased at the cover the innuendo provided him.

Arriving at the Paris station well past midnight, Robert made one stop before returning to his apartment at the Palais Royal.

"*Bonsoir, Monsieur Guillard.*" The guard at 9 rue de la Fédération gave him a quick nod of recognition.

Though few celebrities of his stature, dual graduates of École Polytechnique and École National d'Administration, came by, Robert had spoken with this same guard at these same IEA offices several times before. The guard wouldn't question the hour of Robert's visit. "*Bonsoir.* Do you know where the new American woman, Ceil Dayton, works?"

The guard waved him through and provided her office location.

It was elegant, really. He guessed correctly that the new user ID and password, which were always the same, would still be in effect for Ceil. He clicked into the relevant reports. Only a few numbers were important. Gasoline stocks in the US and a few other countries suddenly became half a million barrels a day higher. He shifted the predicted oil demand a few hundred thousand barrels a day lower. And oil production from OPEC and Russia—well, there were the official numbers and the real numbers. He bumped up OPEC supply by half a million barrels a day, and Russian supply by a hundred thousand barrels.

The reports would feed the IEA Web site, there to be relied upon by OPEC members and international oil companies to plan their production. The approach wasn't as clean and exact as the mathematician in him preferred, nor did it precisely fit his arrangement with Sansei, though he could probably persuade them to include it.

The changes in the reports would make oil refiners, especially those in the US, pause. They made it appear that excess crude, gasoline, and diesel were sloshing around in tankers worldwide. Refiners would then make less gasoline and diesel. It would be some time before the real numbers were discovered. By then, the shortages would escalate further, leaving room, particularly in the US, for Sansei's inferior imports.

The simple beauty was how the falsified changes would be traced to Ceil's computer.

Robert was almost to his apartment at the Palais Royal before he saw the woman. He hoped it was Ceil, but even at a distance he could tell this woman was shorter. She seemed to be hurrying to meet him.

As he started to ask her name, she lifted a long stick. *A bat?* he thought, confused. She slammed it into his shoulder.

He crumpled.

Straightening, he tried to grab the bat, or her. She threw it aside, and it hit the ground with a rolling clatter.

When Robert saw the knife she brandished, he turned and ran. Her hissing command resonated in the heavy night air.

"*Bête.* Shut up you people. No television. No Internet. Next time, I kill your wife."

26.

Tuesday, Houston

Hubbert's Peak: M. King Hubbert was a Shell Oil geologist who, in 1956, accurately forecast the 1970s peak in US oil production. His methodology predicts a similar peak in world oil production in the next few years.

The telephone rang. Lynn swam up from sleep. "Hello?"

No response. Then the voice again. "Sell Centennial and go back to Dallas, bitch, or you and your father are dead."

"Who is this?" She choked on sleepy anger. The line clicked. The digital bedside clock blinked 3:18 a.m.

Although she was still angry, and more afraid than she cared to consider, she wouldn't phone anyone. Still, she wished she could fall back to sleep with Cy's warm, familiar body wrapped around her.

She felt gray dread fill the room. *Who's at the other end of the line? Why are you and Dad being threatened?*

The wake-up call came at six.

This has to stop. After last night's drinking, mild as it had been, Lynn's mouth tasted as if she had eaten a tennis shoe. The call less than three hours ago hadn't helped.

Who the hell called?

All right. You're prepared for smoker's breath this time, Lynn thought as she entered Dwayne's office an hour later.

"Here are the simulation runs," Dwayne said as she settled into her office chair. Judging by the smell of his clothes, he'd had four or five cigarettes already.

She pulled out a tube of mints and offered him one.

"Nah, no thanks. They give me indigestion."

"Smoking doesn't?"

"Nope. Makes me real regular, as a matter of fact."

"Enough."

He smiled at her. "Heard you had golf and drinks last night with Riley and Jay."

"It's too bad this refinery's hardware doesn't work as efficiently as its grapevine."

"No kidding." His tone softened. "And I suppose last night Riley complained about how no one understands him, and how he really ought to be in New York eatin' on the high side of the hog. Sometimes he forgets his shit stinks the same as everyone else's."

"You've heard Riley talk before. And there was this 'Ask me no questions, I'll tell you no lies.' What's that?" She stood and stretched her legs.

"Riley was awarded a huge sum from a lawsuit. His former employer, the bank, charged him with sexual harassment. He turned around and countersued for slander, mental distress, court costs, the works. Faced with that, the bank decided it didn't have enough evidence from the three women who complained. So now he's here, gracing our fair company."

"Wonderful." *More bad news. But it fits Riley's behavior. So Riley's not only redundant, he's a liability risk. What else besides itchy skin does Dwayne have in that head of his?* "How well did you know Armando Garza when he worked here?"

"Well. One of the times when he was having trouble raising money, Riley somehow convinced us to lay off the pipe fitters and machinists and contract out their jobs." Dwayne stood to leave. "I told him we'd be paying twice the old hourly rate for the same work.

Now it's hard to get full-time people. Stupid bankers. We should have kept our men."

"And women. Dwayne, you're so retro. Any bad feelings from the layoffs?"

"Always. But everyone's been through at least two or three."

"What about people outside the refinery? Can they get in here easily?" Lynn asked.

"Possible but complicated. Somebody outside would have to game the system or someone in it."

Post Oak is a shopping mecca on the tony west side of downtown Houston for those who've already pounded out fortunes on the gritty east side. Double silvery arches canopy Post Oak Boulevard for several blocks, emphasizing its high-rent status. Massive silver tiaras crown several intersections. Retail chains fight for location.

Brian had questioned her wish to meet at his Catanalyst office instead of Centennial's, and Lynn had explained she could concentrate better with the fewer interruptions his office would offer. She also wanted to size him up. She and Preston had decided to evaluate anyone with regular access to Centennial's refinery.

Catanalyst's Post Oak offices were housed in a midrise, black glass shell. A moat of green grass, a fountain, and a busy duck pond advertised the company's environmental friendliness. To combat Houston heat, the developer had installed shades on all of the windows, which mechanically rose and fell at programmed times of the morning and evening.

Brian met her in the fourteenth floor lobby. "What's new," he asked when she exited the elevator, "besides what I saw in the paper last week? I noticed you were unavailable for comment."

"I must have missed Cari Turner's midnight call," Lynn said sarcastically. "I'm not surprised at Cody's quote, but I wish I knew the identity of Cari's unnamed source. Did she call you?"

"Yes. I told her we don't discuss clients." He slid a card and opened the glass lobby doors onto an endless array of semi-walled cubicles. Voices competed gently; "*Hola?*" and "How ya doin'?"

"Let's head to my office. I have your results there." His office lay past the outer orbit of cubicles. The same furniture filled it, but it upgraded to full walls, a door that closed, and a picture window with a view of the changing fountain.

She heard the ping of a mail-cart robot as it trundled around, sniffing its chemical path embedded in the carpet while Brian poured coffee for her. "I compared Preston's probe data with our readings eight months ago."

"So you did some research since our last meeting in the refinery and the 'Pote Awfa' joke," she said. She smiled to take the edge off her words.

"You know how it is with the union operators—get along to go along. You had a quick response."

Yeah, I'm a damn comic.

He pulled a graph from a folder on his desk. "Anyhow, the corrosion rate has accelerated. Several factors can cause that. Besides a higher–than–expected level of H_2S, TriCoast's dehydrators may not be doing a complete job."

"That's not what I saw in my initial samples, Brian. They contained very little water. Other possibilities are higher temperatures or a volumetric increase—more sulfuric acid coming from an unexpected source. Now, besides catalyst work, you still do hydrocarbon analysis, correct?"

"What do you need?"

"Pretreater catalyst. Crude oil samples. Pretreater feed and product. If you get them this afternoon, how soon can you give me results?"

"Our normal time is a week, but I can high-pri them. Day and a half."

❖

Dwayne clumped into Lynn's office at Centennial. His red face told her he was rushing. "We switched the flow to pretreater CCPT-402 last night, so we're taking catalyst samples from 401."

"Dwayne, you read my mind. I just met with Brian Tulley at Catanalyst. I told him we wanted to send him some catalyst samples."

Dwayne completed her thought. "So we can find out what's really happenin' inside the pretreater."

"What tests do you want Brian to run?"

He told her and she wrote them down. It was a standard list, including pore volume, nitrogen, microactivity level, and several others. She added a couple of tests that would point to unusual metal poisons such as nickel and vanadium. She didn't expect to find either substance, but if they were present she'd have an important clue to Centennial's troubles.

"I also want him to do some oil analysis for us," she said.

Dwayne seemed not to hear her, so she added, "I need to sample crude from C-201."

"Brian Tulley's getting some business from us," Dwayne said. "Maybe he'll drop the Port Arthur jokes."

"He already has. I need pretreater feed and product samples. I'll wait on those until pretreater 401 is back online and stabilized."

"Easy as catchin' fish with dynamite. If you insist on doing this again yourself, Adric will show you the sampling points." Dwayne turned to go.

"I'll get a truck and meet you at the pretreaters."

"Truck 139 is the only one left," Shelby said when Lynn stopped by to get keys. "It's temperamental."

Truck 139 started easily, although its air conditioning blew only hot, moist air. But when the engine died a half block from the guardhouse, Lynn couldn't restart it. *Of course, since you're in a hurry.* She locked the truck and jogged up to the metal guardhouse building, hard hat in hand, to give Farrell Isos the keys and ask him to call a mechanic.

"Any luck finding the security tape?" She wanted Farrell to understand she hadn't forgotten.

He shook his head.

She ran past the white-hot furnaces, the tall, gaunt propane-propylene splitters and the huge, squat vacuum distillation towers. Her target, pretreater 401, featured a several-story-tall guard reactor vessel followed by two similar-sized hydrotreating reactors. All looked like cylindrical capsules of Brobdingnagian proportion made to stand upright. Dwayne and Skyler Knowles, an operator from Adric's crew she recognized as having attempted to rescue one of the hydrogen sulfide victims, climbed winding stairs to a manhole halfway up the guard reactor. Skyler wore an air pack; Dwayne held an extra one.

She jogged up the toothy metal stairs, planting steel-toed safety shoes firmly on each step. "Good to see you again, Skyler." Lynn wiped the sweat from her hand on the leg of her jeans before offering it to him.

"Two supervisors and one worker." Skyler's thick mustache framed the top half of his grin. "Now that's a good ratio."

"Someone has to pull you out if you fall," Dwayne replied. "Have you checked the inside temperature?"

"About a hundred degrees."

"As cool as it'll get. Sample from four different places on the bed."

The inside of the thick-walled guard reactor was dark, except for the exploratory poke of Skyler's flashlight. Despite his nonchalance, Lynn was well aware that going into the pretreaters carried risks. "Manholes" were barely that because they were so small. The dark, tight quarters brought out claustrophobia many never knew they had. And insufficient oxygen inside the reactors felled many people. Hence the buddy system.

Holding four small plastic canisters, Skyler disappeared through the manhole. Dwayne could barely follow his progress with a second flashlight because the inside of the reactor was pitch-black, the beam of the flashlight sucked away by the darkness. They heard Skyler's measured steps down the rungs of the inside ladder to the catalyst bed, cursing as he missed a rung, then scraping and shuffling for several minutes. When he reappeared at the manhole, each canister was filled with gray catalyst powder.

"Only two more reactors in the train," he said.

While Dwayne prepared the plastic canisters for shipment to Catanalyst, Skyler repeated his sampling at the other two reactors. Then he and Lynn walked to the one-story, cement-block control center.

"Adric, we need to sample the crude oil and the pretreater feed and product. When's a good time?" she asked.

"Now's fine. Skyler knows the sample points." Adric glanced at the glowing unit readouts on the monitors. He turned and looked at the wrench in her hand, then to her. "What are you doing with a pipe-fitter's tool? You're not union." His smile didn't hide his seriousness.

"It's a souvenir. I think of it as a lucky charm."

"Must be a hell of a charm bracelet you have."

She hitched a ride to the office, checked out a new truck from Shelby, and gathered buckets, packing, and sample collection flasks from the lab. The air conditioning in truck 97 didn't work either, and rubber gasketing drooped from the driver's side door. But at least it didn't stall. After she picked up Skyler at the control center, they sampled crude oil at C-201, the sour crude distillation tower. Then he showed her the sample points for the pretreater feed and liquid product.

He adjusted sunglasses underneath his safety glasses and said, "We don't have one of our more experienced operators on this shift, so take the samples yourself when you're ready. The union doesn't need to know. Hey, maybe we could offer you a job. Want to be an operator?"

"Some days I do," she said, honestly, as she wrote the courier slips that would direct the samples to Catanalyst's office.

Leaving Skyler at the control center, Lynn drove truck 97 past the

219

coker, the utilities sheds, the water-treating area, and back toward the office building.

Beneath a humid, sunless sky she saw Jean-Marie and one of her trainee engineers standing on top of cooling tower CT-1 in wading boots and raincoats. Periodically, they stooped and put what Lynn guessed to be temperature probes into the shallow pool of water on top of the tower.

Lynn stopped the truck, yanked open its cranky door, and jumped out, glad for a diversion. "Hey, Jean-Marie," she shouted. "What are you doing? Is that cooling tower giving you fits?"

Jean-Marie looked down from the top of the tower, about thirty feet above Lynn. "Performance check. I keep wondering whether this old tower does its job, so we're comparing the flow and temperature distributions with the manufacturer's guarantee. They gave us better than spec. *Lagniappe.*"

Yat translation. Lagniappe, *"a little extra." Good news, then.* Lynn craned her neck. "Splashing around up there on a steamy day like today shouldn't even be called work."

Jean-Marie brightened. "I like it up here more than inside the tower. Now that's a hothouse."

"Well, I'm glad to see that you're working on operational efficiency."

"You're in, *cher.*" Jean-Marie laughed out loud.

"What do you mean?"

"You used one of the three magic engineering passwords."

"Which are?"

"Consistent, feasible, or efficient. We know you're a real engineer and not just a management goof if you drop one of those words into your conversation every so often."

Lynn laughed but shook her head. "I don't have to prove anything to you."

Jean-Marie's smile broadened, but took on an unfriendly cast. "Oh yes, you do. Now we're sure you get the code."

❖

CEO Mike Emerson had promised her that the trip would be brief, and that it was diplomatically important.

"Of course a trip with Pemex officials to their offshore platforms is important. We'll be buying hundreds of millions of dollars of oil from them. But it's hard to squeeze into my schedule while I'm in the middle of a critical investigation. We can't even think about running their oil until I get Centennial working right."

However, since she was already in Houston, Mike arranged a corporate jet to take her across the Gulf of Mexico to and from the Pemex heliport on the southern Mexican coast during the afternoon, returning her farther north to Dallas in the evening. Lynn asked to see two of the platforms from which ten percent of the oil for Bart's Houston refinery would be produced.

When she emerged from the TriCoast jet into the hot, dry Mexican sun, heavily armed guards walked her across the steaming tarmac to a fortified building. She was pleased to find Bart Colby and Mike already there. They'd also brought Susan Larsen, TriCoast's offshore production safety manager, to evaluate the operations. Three distinguished–looking Pemex officials and a translator greeted her, handed her cards, and smiled as they introduced themselves. She also greeted Mark Shepherd, TriCoast's chief of security, who introduced her to another TriCoast security officer. Mark touched her on the arm and nodded toward the Pemex officials walking beside men with weighty athletic bags.

Yokay. Everybody's walking heavy.

Mark smiled. "This way, please."

Their exit through another stout door took her past water and fuel tanks she estimated to be ten thousand barrels. Each tank, as well as the on-site electrical generating plant, had its own pair of guards, armed with machine guns.

"Job security, Mark," she said.

"Not as expensive as you think down here and it sends a message to the *banditos*, who understand perfectly. But I must say, these birds remind me too much of the medivac choppers in Vietnam. Just stay with me and do what I do." He nodded to someone.

A security man who could have played Pancho Villa made the wagon train "circle up" sign over his head and everyone followed him. When they were close, he smiled and pointed at an idling helicopter that looked like an angry yellow insect. "Your ride."

The other security men motioned them toward a large Sikorsky UH-60. Mark described it as the civilian transport derivative of the military's Black Hawk.

They all ducked under the spinning blades and climbed up into seats in the monstrous helicopter. Security personnel assisted with boarding and buckling, then briefed Lynn and the others about headsets and emergency procedures.

The slow whoop of the rotors increased to a formidable roar until the door slid shut. *Very nice. Plenty of insulation.* The helicopter lifted, tilting forward for a moment, and then the tail swung all the way around. *Like riding inside a bumblebee,* Lynn thought, marveling as always how close everything appeared. She looked out at the blue water foaming onto a white beach. *You can count the waves in the Bay of Campeche.*

While they flew, the trio of courtly Pemex officials talked about existing and future Pemex production, noting that current oil sales to its US customers of about two million barrels a day were expected to be quite stable for the next two years, but then increase.

Susan, the production safety manager, wasted no time, peppering the translator with questions about safety records, hurricane procedures, blowout preventers, and crew schedules. Lynn also appreciated her questions about reliability—"*Si,* very reliable"—and overall platform downtime.

She referred to crude specs and assays. The two platforms they would visit were in the Cantarell complex, the world's second largest oil field behind Ghawar in Saudi Arabia. Cantarell produced heavy sour, or especially dense high-sulfur oil, that was difficult and expensive to refine. Its marketing and pricing designation was "Maya." Part of TriCoast's purchase negotiation with Pemex had been to also secure some of its lighter, sweeter Olmeca crude. *Truly the deal-sweetener.*

Racing low and level, they saw the first massive platform. From a distance, it looked like a champion Lego construction supported by giant cylindrical caisson legs. Its four levels of heavy-duty scaffolding contained cranes, tanks, crew living quarters, and a control room. The platform was topped by a ten-story flare. The pilot in command maneuvered the helicopter downwind, then eased it forward onto the pad at the end of the platform.

As they climbed out, Lynn took in the variety of smells, oil, of course, more sulfurous than usual, but also salt spray, and even tortillas. The sulfur reminded her both of the Centennial leak and the difficulty she and Bart would face turning this very heavy crude into feather-light gasoline and ultralow-sulfur diesel. *Jeez, we'll have to crack so much hydrogen into it, it'll be like trying to beat egg whites into a hunk of sirloin.*

But she knew they would and could do just that. *We need this oil.*

27.

Wednesday, all day, Dallas

"How are your lessons?"

Lynn groaned. "I'm leaving tonight and I haven't had much time. I'm barely sure of which city I'm waking up in, and I don't know what I don't know about French."

"Simple solution," Claude Durand said. His fingers moved quickly over his keyboard. He was faster than anyone she'd seen, except maybe when Preston pulled up his racing statistics.

"Here's the test. I'll come back in five minutes."

"You're testing me?"

"No, you're testing yourself."

She stared blankly at a multiple-choice French language test. *Stop thinking about hydrogen sulfide and hydrogen fluroide.* A few words came back. She scrolled down the screen at an excruciatingly slow pace. *You don't need this.*

Claude returned, instantly it seemed.

"Let's see how you did. According to this, ah, . . ."

"What?"

"Your sister who is fluent in French, is she meeting you at the airport?"

"You mean I shouldn't navigate Paris myself?"

He stared at the screen and back to her, his eyes twinkling. "You might not like where you'd end up, or with whom. Now. Next test."

"I don't know if I'm up to another one."

"Show me the look."

"The look? Oh."

"Yes, the one that says you're a woman, I'm a man, and you find the difference attractive."

She closed her eyes and cleared her mind of all but one thought. Then she opened them and gazed at Claude with an intensity she hadn't allowed herself since she was ten.

He smoothed his shirt almost unconsciously and patted his hair. She thought she saw red along his cheekbones that hadn't been there before.

"Bien. Excellente."

She shook her head, readjusted her gaze, and made it a point to shrug. "So why use the look?"

"It can catch a person off guard. And you need to understand its effect on you."

"My turn for questions. Why all the mystery about schools, Claude? What's so special about, what is it, X and ENA? I don't understand."

"I'm here because of X and ENA." He twisted open a paper clip. "I wasn't admitted to either one."

"So? Lots of students here aren't accepted to Harvard or Yale. They recover, go on to become billionaires."

"You don't understand, do you? In France, your school determines your life—how much admiration you'll receive, with whom you'll associate, whether or not you'll eat in fine restaurants, whom you'll marry, and whether or not your own children will go to good schools."

"Where you go to college dictates the rest of your life?"

He nodded.

"Many people would say the same about the States."

"Non. It is less rigid. Consider politicians or CEOs. Take Mike Emerson's background."

"He had five brothers, his father was a refinery operator in Beaumont, and his mother was a schoolteacher." Lynn sat back in her chair and laced her fingers together. "He started out in geology at Texas A&M and moved all over the country every eighteen months as he was promoted through TriCoast. He and his first wife are divorced and he's remarried."

"A man like that would never become the managing director of Tolf."

"Tolf, France's largest oil company. What sort of person would?"

"A man. I see your eyebrows rising—yes, a man—who'd graduated in mathematics from MIT and acquired a degree from Harvard's Kennedy School of Government."

"Limits the talent pool."

"But for the graduates of X and ENA, the doors are wide open. So every French schoolchild endures what an American would consider torture to earn a position at one of those two schools."

"Speaking of torture, I'm due at the board meeting to explain Centennial."

But first she had another call to make. Increasingly, she felt torn in four directions, not just two. For many years, her career success seemed to satisfy her family, but now both her father and Ceil needed more of her time. Work hadn't become any less demanding. *And then there's Cy. You aren't the first to want to clone yourself.* Lynn returned to her forty-fifth-floor office, stared out one of her big windows into an even bigger blue sky, and dialed.

Hermosa answered the question before she asked. "Your father isn't well. I'll put him on, but just for a few minutes." Lynn heard the rustle when Hermosa placed the phone in her dad's hands.

"Dad, it's Lynn. I'm in town. I'll come see you as soon as I can. Emerson's asked me to a board meeting first, though. How are you feeling?"

"Tired . . . Ceil?" asked the most familiar, loving voice in the world. He sounded weaker and more breathless.

"I'm leaving tonight for Paris," she said, mirroring his abbreviated conversation.

"Post me," he said.

"Cy . . ." she started to say.

" . . . love him?" he asked.

"Yes, but marriage is too big a commitment."

"Cy's . . . different."

An e-mail alerted her to more news in Houston—a fire at the Tier I blending terminal. She called Reese, and he filled in the details. If the board didn't ask about it, she'd be sure to tell them.

While Lynn waited outside the boardroom, she recalled what she knew about the TriCoast board members. Tyree Bickham, TriCoast's general counsel, would attend. There were the inside directors—her boss Mike Emerson and CFO Sara Levin. She'd already reviewed with each of them what she would say, and they were generally in agreement. They described what they'd heard from each board member. But that still left the surprise questions.

The outside directors numbered seven: an oil-pump company CEO, a consumer goods CEO, a former cabinet secretary, a university president, the head of a moderately left environmental group, an international banker, and the CEO of a company that made distribution software.

"Lynn, come in," Sara said as Mike opened the door. "We've all eaten lunch so we promise not to chew you up much." Cast against taller-is-management type, Mike and Sara looked up at Lynn when they ushered her into the room.

She moved around the table, shaking hands, and avoiding the two worn spots in the beige carpet that she knew from prior, embarrassing experience would snag the higher-than-sensible heels of the shoes she wore with her pantsuit.

Taking her seat, she caught Mike's eye and said, "First, we are lining up additional oil supply and, in fact, we saw a couple of the offshore Pemex production platforms in the Bay of Campeche yesterday. Second, you recall our plan and you have our numbers on integrating the Centennial refinery with TriCoast's existing Ship Channel refinery to operate them as one. The piping and data connections are complicated. However, some of them are already in place and we don't anticipate many problems. With them." Lynn paused deliberately, knowing that follow-up reporting on the decision to buy Centennial wasn't why she'd been invited to this meeting.

Integrating the two refineries is a great plan. But to buy Centennial, you spent more than four hundred million dollars of shareholder money and ate the political capital you've grown for years. "I'm here to summarize what I know so far about the incident six days ago, last Thursday morning. You've already been briefed on it. Five people were killed. Reese Spencer and I met with each of the families."

"Any lawsuits yet?" asked the oil-pump CEO, no stranger to lawsuits.

"I'll answer that," growled Tyree Bickham genially. His heavy, gold Howard University ring flashed as he sorted through papers. "We've heard from two plaintiffs' attorneys. One purports to represent four of the operators who died. Another one, just an ol' ambulance chaser we cross horns with all the time, is threatening a class-action lawsuit on behalf of the surviving USW union employees."

"What are our damages other than potential employee lawsuits? Have you calculated those yet?" asked one of the outside directors, a former White House cabinet secretary, leaning back in her chair.

"As with any accident of this kind, the direct costs are less than the indirect costs," Lynn said, consulting numbers she and Preston had projected last night. "Preston Li, our engineering manager, and I prepared an estimate. Labor and materials for repairs, energy costs, chemicals and catalyst recovery, and inventory loss to the flares total about $10 million. But lost margin, contaminated and subgraded product, and demurrage are another $20 million. In terms of lost margin on gasoline, the accidents couldn't have come at a worse time, frankly."

"What you mean by demurrage?" the former cabinet secretary continued.

"Vessels at our dock were required to wait several hours over contract to finish loading and unloading," Lynn said.

"Do you think Reese Spencer is up to running this refinery? I know he's a friend of yours, but at his age, can he handle the media and the quick decisions? TriCoast has plenty of management depth."

Lynn knew this question, from the consumer goods CEO, was prompted by his friend Riley Stevens. Now that TriCoast owned Centennial, Riley's position was redundant and he was angling for a new one. She'd witnessed his lack of management skills and his liability-risk harassment. *This maneuver is another brick in his wall o' severance.*

"Until now, our refineries have been run so well that we've never needed to improve large-scale operations quickly. Reese has more experience with time-sensitive turnarounds of Centennial's size than any of our internal candidates. Our contract with him is for fifteen months. After that I'll move our best candidates into the top jobs at Centennial, people I think can work with Bart Colby, the RM for our existing Ship Channel refinery."

"How does this accident change the economics of the acquisition?" This came from the university president, a man who hated risk in any form and had been the only "no" vote on buying Centennial. "A third of this country's refining is already foreign or committed to Latin American national oil companies, so maybe Venezuela or Mexico is a ready market for Centennial if we need to dump it."

Lynn felt her hands tighten. *You wimp, give me a chance.* "The leak was unexpected. Let us find the cause and fix it before we talk exit strategies."

"What do the CSB, OSHA, and the EPA have to say?"

She expected this question from the sunburned director who headed the environmental group. She counted on him, in fact, to ask it. *Mike's right, his expression when he looks at you is friendly.*

"Appreciative" would be Claude's word. She felt her cheeks warm and hoped the dim light hid them. "CSB has given us some preliminary recommendations, which we've implemented. OSHA has unofficially suggested its fine will be half a million dollars."

"You included this in your damage cost estimates?"

Lynn nodded. Jean-Marie Taylor had seen to that.

"The government's making money in Houston this month," the oil-pump CEO said, clearing his throat.

"I'm glad you mentioned that. Let me fill you in on what's happened down the Channel from us, even though it's not TriCoast business," Lynn said. "Meletio and Xavier have had serious electrical accidents, knocking them off-line and reducing their production. Tier I just had a big fire, reported a few minutes ago. It appears they'll lose 2 million barrels of gasoline inventory.

"My concern is that some kind of concerted action is occurring."

She glanced at Tyree, who was shaking his head. *You have to get the idea out there!* She forged ahead. "If it were union pre-strike sabotage, we'd have already heard from Cody Laughlin, the USW union rep at Centennial. This—I hesitate to use the word—sabotage may even be tied into the Centennial incident."

"Do you really think it could be sabotage? Not just your woman's intuition?" the oil-pump CEO asked. A few other men laughed.

The ex-cabinet secretary looked at Lynn with interest.

Speak up, I can't hear supportive thoughts. "That's why my investigation, and that done by the CSB, is so important. We need to get to the root cause, prevent another occurrence at Centennial, and keep our people safe." She fixed the oil-pump CEO with a hard stare and continued. "I don't think we should overlook any possibility. At the local level, Farrell Isos is assisting with the investigation. TriCoast security chief, Mark Shepherd, is aware of my concerns. He just informed me that he's arranged for me to meet one of his FBI colleagues."

Tyree added, "Lynn talked about security. Let me give you additional background. The Houston Ship Channel has so many refineries and chemical plants that we're constantly under watch. After 9/11 everyone stepped up security. The Coast Guard's made the whole Houston Ship Channel off-limits to small boats. In fact, we're certain the FBI is keeping an eye on things 'cause our own security guys keep tripping over 'em."

Mike stared at his watch. His signal.

"I think that wraps it up," she said.

"If you have any more questions, send them through me or Tyree. We'll get you an answer," Mike concluded. Lynn knew he was freeing her to work, but she didn't want him in her territory.

"Don't let this distract you from the rest of your business." The ex-cabinet secretary's voice was sharp as she dug her elbows into her chair arms to move herself forward.

"It won't," Lynn said, with more confidence than she felt.

The sunburned environmental director gave her an extra-wide smile, one it felt good to receive.

Lynn told her Paris travel plans only to her secretary and to Mike Emerson.

"Tell me again why you're going and when you'll be back? Sure you're not interviewing for a job at Tolf, that Parisian oil company?" Mike had asked, massaging his knuckles.

"My sister has moved from Gabon to a statistics job at the IEA. She has critical information about crude loadings that will help me with the investigation, but I can't get her to talk about it over the phone, e-mail, or IM. If I sit face-to-face with her, she'll tell me. I'll fly over tonight and back tomorrow night, try to stay on this time zone." *Another visit to the realm of exhaustion.*

She expected to meet in an interior conference room, but instead everyone gathered in her office with its floor to ceiling windows. There was so much light it seemed that anything dark or suspicious should shrivel under its heat and illumination.

She sat at her table with Tyree Bickham, TriCoast's chief legal counsel, and TriCoast security chief Mark Shepherd.

A receptionist announced, "There's a Special Agent James Cutler from the FBI here to see you." She ushered him in and shut the door.

When he introduced himself as Jim, she saw that he was her height, but twice as heavy; the pounds that hadn't gone into his trapezius, deltoid, and bicep muscles seemed to have shaped his very square, massive jaw.

Maybe you should rethink the bodyguard offer. This guy could wrestle a bull and walk away with the horns.

Mark and Jim were acquainted, so Tyree and Lynn stood and shook Jim's hand. His glance was three seconds longer than the perfunctory business introductions with which she was familiar. In that time she felt as if he'd brain-tapped every fantasy she'd had about torturing sexist Riley Stevens. Even Tyree and Mark sat up straighter than the alert-but-at-ease posture they used with the TriCoast execs.

Jim smiled at Mark and Tyree. "You guys have something for me?"

Their eyes went to Lynn.

"That would be me," Lynn said.

"Oh. Sorry," he said as Lynn slid him a chair. He sat and took out a notepad while she continued to stand. She began recounting the suspicious leak that killed four operators. She described the threatening calls, the bicyclist's assault, the hydrofluoric acid in her office, and the hydrogen sulfide gassing. She moved on to her concerns about the pattern of "accidents" at other Ship Channel refineries. By the time she finished, she could tell he didn't like looking up at her.

"And she still refuses a bodyguard," Mark said.

"Then I'm glad you're still alive to tell us about it. First off, sounds like you and the Chemical Board have the Centennial accident investigation under control." He emphasized the last two words. "CSB people know what they're doing. I'm sure they'll be thorough."

"But . . ."

He put up a hand. "Except for your claim of this, uh, conspiracy, the thing sounds like it might be personal. Is there anyone who has a grudge against you?"

"Not that kind of grudge," Lynn said.

He thought for a moment. "Who's got your case with the Houston PD?"

"Alex Stinson, a detective who seems pretty antagonistic and uninterested, frankly."

"Well, Houston PD has a lot on its plate right now, especially with all those New Orleans evacuees. Out of one hundred and fifty thousand new people, it only takes a few gangbangers to scare the hell out of the whole city."

He stood up, rubbed his neck, and walked to the window.

"And for that matter, Lynn, our resources are tied up, too." He tapped the glass with a knuckle. "The war on terrorism is occurring on dozens of fronts."

"Look, Jim, I assure you, this isn't about me. We're talking about the five hundred plus folks at Centennial and another two thousand down the road at our other Houston refinery. I'm certain it isn't a personal grudge . . . or even limited to TriCoast."

"That's a pretty bold claim. What sort of security do you have at TriCoast?"

"Basically the same as the other refineries," Mark said. As security chief, he'd answered the question many times. "Background checks, photo ID badges, retina scanners, off-limits areas, razor-wire fence. In terms of software, numerous firewall and antivirus programs, and conversation and e-mail monitoring, if needed."

Lynn knew the list, too. She'd either experienced or been briefed by Mark on all of it.

"Excellent," Jim said. "And the Coast Guard patrols the Houston Ship Channel. As I'm sure you know, the Coast Guard is not exactly shabby. You saw them in action after the hurricanes."

His gaze went out the window and up. "We have airspace covered. We've got TSA now. And don't forget, we're stopping anybody at the border who doesn't look like a roofer or a housekeeper." He smiled at his own humor. "Though that might be something to look into further."

"You think I'm crying wolf," Lynn said.

"Look. Homeland Security receives hundreds of citizen calls and government warnings every day and we check them out. Mark and I go back a long way, so he has a lot of credibility with us. If he calls, I come over. But so far you've given us nothing that smells like intentional sabotage or terrorism."

Lynn wondered if the glow on her face was noticeable. "Have you heard any of that famous phone chatter around here?" she asked.

He shook his head. "We can't just climb up a cell tower and start listening to phone calls between every refinery on the Ship Channel. Or even monitor gossip about your cousin Debbie's two-day marriage like people think we can. In other words, Lynn, I can't connect anything you've given me to the Taliban, Al-Qaeda, a drug cartel, or the hundreds of other usual suspects."

Lynn shook her head. "I see, Jim, but I think the evidence is there, and it needs to be pieced together." *His need for bloody fingerprints and a smoking gun sounds like every fact-obsessed engineer you've met. Not that you aren't one, too.*

Jim glanced at his watch, making it clear he was anxious to leave. "Have you passed all of this evidence on to the other companies?

She looked at Tyree. "For obvious antitrust reasons we can't call them and ask if their security is up to snuff, can we?"

"Definitely not," Tyree said.

"How about this, Ms. Dayton? I'll open a file, and you keep Mark and me posted."

Lynn was silent, waiting to see his direction.

Jim folded his notepad and put it away. "Oh, and you might rethink that bodyguard thing, too. We've got some ladies in better shape and tougher than most men. Hard to believe, I'm sure, but some of them are ex-Quantico instructors."

And have to ask every time I need to go to the ladies' room? "No, but thank you."

"Call me when you change your mind."

After the bull-wrestling agent left, Mark and Tyree were still looking at her.

She sighed. "And why am I having so much trouble with Houston PD? Every time I call Detective Stinson, it's like I've pissed him off. Could you talk to him?

Mark said, "Will do, Lynn, but I think Jim probably has it right. Houston's been experiencing a big crime spike. Stinson and his crew are probably stretched pretty thin right now."

❖

When Lynn arrived at her father's house, he was sitting in a chair on the porch near the door. The late afternoon shadows spared him the more intense heat of the sun. Fat, orange citronella candles, their fragrance deflecting mosquitoes, burned on the stairs to the porch.

Lynn waved as she approached, but he didn't wave back. She strode up the walk, unable to avoid crunching a two-inch cockroach that scuttled underfoot. Her father remained motionless, head down, in his metal porch chair. His oxygen tank was nearby. For a moment she hesitated, but then saw the uneven rise and fall of his chest and heard the whir of the oxygen tank.

Hermosa appeared at the front door and motioned her inside. "He was excited by your call, started walking around. After that he had a long spell of breathing trouble."

"What did you do?"

"Finally he sat down. We talked. He said he wasn't sleeping well, worried about your sister. Then he fell asleep."

"Should we let him sleep there?"

"Yes. He is very tired." Hermosa looked out at him. "Cy's children are cute. He came by earlier, before you called." The older woman's voice held a teasing note.

Lynn turned away to align a crocheted arm cover on a chair. "Why?"

"Wanted to see if he could do anything or if I needed a break." The smile Hermosa gave her suggested she saw herself taking care of Cy's children, as well as Lynn's dad. *She's jumping the gun. Wish everyone would stop pushing.* Despite her irritation at Hermosa's assumptions, Lynn felt warmth spreading through her chest and arms. She was used to discussing Dad's care with Hermosa but not with Cy. *He didn't have to do that. He knew you were worried.* The warmth reached her eyes and they stung.

"You have my cell number if you need me when I'm in Paris. I'll be back almost immediately. You're right, let's let him sleep now."

Before she left, she lifted the plastic tubing out of the way and kissed her father's papery cheek. He didn't wake.

❖

When no one answered Cy's door, Lynn picked her way across the stepping-stones in his side yard through a red, white, and green blaze of giant caladium leaves. She heard Matt's shouts and Marika's splashing before she turned the corner of the house to the pool. A heavy wooden fence walled in Cy's backyard, and another black-mesh safety fence surrounded the pool itself. She could smell the dry, high antiseptic of chlorine. *This time it's really chlorine.*

Marika's coloration mimicked Cy's, while Matt's brown hair and dark eyes seemed closer to those in his mother's pictures. The skin of all three glistened from the water. Lynn couldn't restrain a gasp when she saw Cy's perfect profile on the diving board. *Awesome butt, awesome everything. It's been way too long.*

Marika was the first to see her. "It's bursting with heat today, isn't it, Lynn?" she said. Neon oranges, greens, pinks, and blues striped her bathing suit. "Do you like my new one-piece?"

Definitely a rhetorical question. "It's great!"

"The only place I've seen colors that bright is on poisonous frogs. Are you a poison frog?" Cy grinned at his daughter.

"Daddy! No! Hey Lynn! Guess what! I'm going to a sleepover tonight!"

She exchanged glances with Cy. When he nodded, she asked, "With whom?"

"A girl from her class, Sandra Brock."

"I just hope they don't have corn on the cob. See, Lynn?" Marika proudly curled back her lips to show a wide gap where she'd lost a top front tooth. "And see, I've got another loose one!" Concern suddenly creased Marika's wide-open face. She stood on the steps at the shallow section of the pool, ignoring her brother's splashing.

"Dad, if I lose this other tooth at Sandy's house, will the tooth fairy come there? Will she know where to find me? Will she know how much I'm supposed to get?"

Cy winked at his daughter. "If you lose a tooth and the tooth fairy shows up here by accident, we'll tell her where you are." Behind the wink, Lynn knew Cy was reminding himself to tell Sandy's parents about the loose tooth. Panic about the parental concerns she would take on if she married Cy braided Lynn's thoughts. *But your life will be over while you're worrying about responsibility. When the most irresponsible thing of all is to deny love.*

"Daddy?"

"What, Matt?"

"No tiger in deep end."

"I'm glad you're watching out for them," Cy said seriously. Then he explained to Lynn, "We went to the zoo this morning, and he saw the Siberians splashing in their pool."

"Come 'wimming," Matt invited her.

"I didn't bring my swimsuit. But I'll change into shorts and put my legs in the water."

When she'd done so she marveled at how the cool water siphoned away the stress of summer heat.

"How's the Centennial investigation?" Cy asked, holding Matt at the side of the pool.

"This seems to sound crazy to everyone I tell, but I think something deliberate is up that involves more than Centennial. I met again with our security chief, and he brought in an FBI agent. They think I need to be careful—they want me to get a bodyguard—but they don't see anything bigger than that. I'm fairly sure Ceil has some important data that will help that otherwise won't be public for another few weeks. She won't tell me over the phone, so I have to go see her. Over and back as fast as I can."

Cy nodded.

Marika jumped off the diving board repeatedly. Matt leapt from the side of the pool into Cy's arms, Cy returned him to the side, and Matt jumped again, over and over.

It had been weeks since she'd seen such pure joy. She drank it in.

After Marika left with her friend's family, Cy wiggled Matt into dry clothes next to the pool. In the perverse logic she now recognized as a two-year-old's, Matt proudly thrust out his stomach to show how tall he'd grown.

"Sure you don't want to change out here too?" she teased Cy. "No one but your two-year-old son and I can see you."

"No free peeps."

"No fee peep," Matt solemnly repeated.

Inside the house, Cy offered linguine with pesto. "Just made it. I used the first basil of the summer." He waved toward a patch of leggy plants near the backyard fence. "Plus pine nuts, olive oil, parmesan cheese, and garlic."

She closed her eyes and gave in to tasting the gritty texture of the basil and nuts, the heat of the garlic, and the slipperiness of the linguine.

"I didn't realize how hungry I was. Thanks. And thanks for visiting my dad, too."

"I know you're worried about him."

They played blocks with Matt. Then the toddler arrayed an attack force of small, plastic backhoes and bulldozers and pushed them toward the block buildings, laughing when the buildings tumbled.

As if on cue, Cy rose and called the Brocks to discuss tooth fairy logistics. After he hung up, it was baby Matt's turn. "Time for bed, buddy."

"No!"

"Yes."

"Do you want me to wait here while you put him to bed?" she asked. "I want to."

"Of course." He returned in a few minutes and sat next to her on the sofa. "Swimming made Matt sleepy. He conked out fast. Are you set for Paris?"

"Completely. My suitcase is right there."

"I'm amazed you can pack everything in one bag. The kids and I could never manage that." He sighed. Though his son was asleep and his daughter was gone neither child seemed far from his mind at the moment.

But then he took her hands in his, kissed them, and gazed at her. "I missed you."

"I definitely missed you." She felt a wash of sadness and looked away, unable to keep from voicing an earlier thought. "How do you track it all? I'd forgotten about the tooth fairy. I still don't . . ."

He covered her lips with his, kissed her several times on the mouth, then on the neck. He murmured, "I'm selfish. I want you for me. Whenever you can be here. We'll handle whatever happens." He traced a hand along her back.

Don't stop. "You're changing the subject."

"Yes. I want to change the subject," he said, moving close and enfolding her.

She began unbuttoning his shirt. "There are more interesting things we could be doing." His chest muffled her words.

240

So they did them. For a long time.

When she finally got up, she washed her face and brushed her teeth. A few hours remained before her red-eye flight would depart from Dallas and land in Paris the next morning. "You didn't say anything about my new clothes," she said, smiling.

He mumbled sleepily, "Remind me to look when you put them back on."

28.

Thursday morning, Paris

Then on my lips, where a flame flutters,
a flash of love purified by God himself,
place a kiss, and be transformed from angel into woman . . .
All at once my soul will awaken.

–Victor Hugo

What do you wish, love, quoting me Hugo?" Thérèse whispered.

"You. You again." Robert slid the chemise from her shoulders. He lost himself in a rhapsody of pleasure.

When they lay back exhausted, Robert admired his wife's delicate form. Her flawless white back was turned to him, and he cupped a hand around her hipbone. When she didn't respond, he sank back into the cotton sheets. They were new, striped green and white, with an appropriately high thread count. Thérèse had purchased well. He could feel it in the cool, soft density of the fabric under his legs.

She got up, dressed again, and circled to his side of the bed. Then she gasped. "Robert, what happened to your shoulder? Will you be at ease when I am gone? Perhaps I should not leave you to be with my family."

For many wondrous minutes he'd forgotten that his wife was vacationing for a week with her family, as well as forgetting the deep ache in his back and shoulder. His wife's absence was part of his plan, so he had to reassure her. And the woman with the bat had broken nothing. The angry purple bruise above his shoulder blade showed where she'd struck him.

"An accident. It is much better than it appears. But I have another request, once you return." Robert pushed the pain aside, brushing his fingertips along the back of his wife's arm.

"A dinner party? For the advisor?"

"Yes. In three or four weeks?" He should have time to prepare; he and the Rabbit would be finished in less than a week. They must, to receive full payment from Sansei. A dinner party for the advisor would give him another opportunity to advocate funding refineries in developing countries.

"Robert, those are difficult. It is easy to fail. He and his wife are so demanding," Thérèse sighed. "I will consider it."

If he kept nudging her, and reassuring her, she'd agree. And once she agreed, he was confident he and Thérèse would excel at the tense ritual of hosting a French dinner party, where any mistake was discussed for weeks afterward by those who attended.

The technical advisor had just left Robert's office for another meeting when the telephone buzzed—the first time she'd called him at the ministry, although he'd encouraged her to do so. He heard concern in her cool tones. He shifted back in his chair, closed a file on his computer.

"Something happened, Robert. The numbers on our Web site don't match my entries. When I reviewed my log-ons, I found one timed late Tuesday night when I wasn't here. But everyone suspects me because I'm new, and American."

He could hear her pause to puff on a cigarette.

"What will you do?" he asked.

"We'll issue an online and a written correction. I'll call our major clients. It's a tremendous amount of unexpected work. And my sister's arriving today. I've already told her I can't meet her at Charles de Gaulle, that we'll have to meet later in the day."

Robert straightened his back, forgetting his injury until it lashed his shoulder. He gingerly pulled forward to his desk. "Your sister will be in Paris?"

"She said she's worried about me. I think she also wants me to return to Dallas to take care of our father."

The opportunity had come sooner than he planned. "Shall I meet her at the airport for you?"

"That's a long way for you to go. She's already told me she only wants to catch up on work until I can see her. It's a short visit. I'm not even sure she's staying over."

To implement his plan, he couldn't make Ceil suspicious. "Friday lunch then, if she stays. Musée d'Orsay. The café on the roof."

"*Oui.* And Robert, since I spoke at the Tolf meeting, I've been followed."

"By whom?"

"Three different men. One who watched me for only a day was a Tolf security officer, the one who forced me to leave the annual meeting. But the other two have continued and seem to take turns."

"What do they look like?"

As she spoke, Robert recognized the descriptions of two of the men who'd followed him, one, the dumpy man he'd managed to elude near his apartment, and the other, the doll-faced man who'd left the box containing an earring and a severed ear lobe at his feet.

"They may also work for Tolf," Robert said, not knowing whether or not he was lying. "They should lose interest soon."

"I hope so."

❖

It was too risky to call the Rabbit from the ministry so Robert gave the Rabbit the numeric code for this SafeVoice conversation and returned to the Palais Royal.

He attached his voice scrambler to his cell phone and punched in the code.

"Robbie, good to hear ya. It's been a while. I got the money. How about Xavier and Tier I, eh?"

"How did they proceed?" Robert ignored the Rabbit's familiarity.

"Easy. Easy as pie. Just like Meletio Refining. I've got some contractors up my sleeve—they can get in anywhere. Just say the word."

"The longer these locations are off-line the more we are paid. We have only five days left to complete our assignments."

"No problemo." The Rabbit was surprisingly upbeat. Giggling, even. "Meletio will be shut down two months at least. You'd think a hurricane had hit it straight on."

Robert suddenly wanted to finish the conversation. The clear sky outside his apartment reminded him of his long-anticipated appointment with Lynn.

"How about Centennial? When will you shut it down?"

"That's harder, since I'm right here."

"What about Lynn Dayton and her investigation?" Perhaps Robert could determine if the Rabbit's information matched Ceil's.

"She's running a few tests. Thought I'd see her today in Houston after the Dallas board meeting, but I don't."

And I won't tell you she's headed here, Robert thought, as he disconnected the voice scrambler from his cell phone. He best executed his plans by limiting what he shared. As always, the set of information he provided others would be as close as possible to the null set, the emptiest of sets.

29.

Wednesday night-Thursday afternoon, Dallas and Paris

In the jetway between the terminal and the airplane, the smell of burnt rubber and the evaporative wince of kerosene-based jet fuel reassured Lynn. From the terminal window, she watched the foreshortened shadows that precede the touchdowns of the planes themselves. Their tires smacked the runways and kicked up violent white puffs of rubber smoke, swallowing their shadows.

You need to get back to the Centennial investigation ASAP. Ceil should have useful information for it. And she's hurt in some way she won't discuss on the phone.

During the ten-hour flight, she didn't sleep well, not even during the five hours the plane flew east through the dark. Then it was morning again, and night had been so short.

Despite Claude's warnings about the inadequacy of her French, Lynn planned to find her hotel alone. Because of a sudden work deadline Ceil faced, the sisters would meet in the afternoon.

After navigating customs at the beautiful, confusing Charles de Gaulle airport, Lynn boarded the RER/TGV train for Gare du Nord. From the station it was a taxi ride to the professionally luxurious Hôtel le Bristol. Settled in her room, she made the call she had delayed until being assured of a landline.

Henry Vandervoost picked up himself, a good sign, and greeted her cheerfully. "You're in Paris? Surely you will come on to Rotterdam to see all of my good ideas in person."

"I wish I could. I'm calling because, unfortunately, I'm short East

Coast gasoline. Can we do a time trade—you deliver unleaded 87 now to New York Harbor, I'll reciprocate in two months to Rotterdam?"

"No. My ships are taken."

Of course Henry couldn't help. He never has in the past. But this time his reason was new.

"You know of Sansei, the Asian refining consortium?"

"I've met some of their executives." They'd showed up at refining conferences, formally dressed, taking notes but saying nothing, unwilling to participate as speakers or even in roundtable discussions.

"They've tied up the options on extra shipping capacity for the next six months. I barely have cargo space for my own contracts. My shipping broker said Sansei is also moving large volumes of gasoline to California."

"Did your broker say who Sansei's customers were? Their gasoline doesn't pass US specs."

"He didn't." She almost missed his next words. "Coincidence, actually, that you should call. Someone asked about you a few days ago."

She tried to think of the acquaintances she had in common with Henry Vandervoost. None, except for a few other TriCoast executives. "Who?"

"Robert Guillard."

She swallowed her surprise before responding. *The man who drew Ceil to Paris with a job when she needed to leave Africa, who was mutually acquainted with her friends in Gabon.* "Where did you meet him? How does he know me?"

"TriCoast hosted a dinner here in Rotterdam. Robert attended. He asked about you."

"And you told him what?"

"Only the truth, as always."

She doubted Henry Vandervoost's honesty had been flattering.

"I didn't talk to him long. He didn't drink much of the excellent wines I chose. Anxious to see his wife he said. He left early to return to Paris. But he seemed agitated, as if he had something else on his mind. Maybe someone else."

❖

The hot sun focused laser-like through a gap in the drapes. Two showers and forty-five minutes later, she met her sister at the place Ceil had chosen, a busy outdoor café three blocks from the hotel.

No matter what the distance, time, words, or difficulty since their last meeting, Ceil's warm smile always enveloped Lynn as completely as her embrace.

"Oh, it's so good to see you!" Lynn stepped back and let the impression of her sister's face soak in like a balm, this sister who'd known her through so many salty tears, startled laughs, and pain that Lynn hid from everyone else. "Well, uh, *bonjour*."

"That's a start." Ceil grinned. "But since it's almost evening, how about *bonsoir*?"

"Yes, *bonsoir*. What are you up to? How have you been?" Lynn suppressed dismay as Ceil lit a cigarette. *If she could just see Dad's oxygen tank.* Ceil pushed blond hair out of her face repeatedly, a new habit. Only someone who knew her well would notice the slight tremble in her hand.

"Just working. Let's sit."

"Great!" Lynn forced enthusiasm to cover her surprise at Ceil's sandals. Dirt and scuffs marked them nearly black. In a white slit skirt and a pink broadcloth blouse with three-quarter-length sleeves she otherwise looked the part of a Parisian woman. "Do you like working at the IEA?"

"Yes. This is only my third day there. I cleared up a spreadsheet today." Ceil described how the numbers in her reports were changed without her knowledge.

"A virus?"

"I must have mistyped something."

Now, let's hope she can be as candid as you've expected. "Speaking of the IEA, we talked about what you might have seen concerning South American crude oil exports?"

Ceil crossed her legs. "All the pieces are out in the public domain, so the TriCoast economist may already have reached the same conclusion. We make a few adjustments and have algorithms we apply. As of today, we see heavier six-month-average density of the crude oil landing on the Gulf Coast than in the last half of last year. I understand that usually means more Mexican Mayan or heavy Venezuelan crude."

Hmm. The Pemex officials said that their production levels, most of which are Mayan, were stable, not increasing.

"What about Ecuadorian Oriente?"

"I don't have final numbers yet from their government."

Change of subject. Take it slow. "Ceil, tell me about your last few weeks."

Ceil didn't answer at first, her glance darting to a place on the street behind Lynn's chair, then back to Lynn. "I came to Paris because my friends told me that this man, Robert Guillard, had a job for me, and because, well, I needed to leave Gabon. I was right to trust them, and him."

Robert Guillard again. So far he seems legit, but why the interest in Ceil, and you? "How did you meet him?"

Ceil dipped a spoon into her carrot stew before answering. "I first heard about him from other PCVs—Peace Corps volunteers—and my friends, some French expats in Gabon. They told me he'd discovered a post for me here and exactly how to find him. Not a hard sell; I've always liked visiting Paris, and living here isn't much different. I was a little suspicious because the offer was so out of the blue, but I wasn't in shape to ask questions. My friends even paid for my ticket."

What does she mean she wasn't in shape to ask questions? And is Robert the same man you profiled on the Internet? "What has he told you about himself?"

"He works for the government. He also leads a group that

advocates building oil refineries in third world countries to help them become self-sufficient in energy."

Relying on her sister's experience, Lynn had ordered the same carrot stew. Its salt and onions pinched her mouth. Lynn felt another meaning behind Ceil's words. "Like a technical Peace Corps?"

Ceil nodded.

"So Robert is probably as interested in your Gabonese experience for his group as the IEA is. You were in-country." Lynn leaned over to touch Ceil's arm, unable to believe they were finally together. "It's good to see you," she said again. "It feels like it's been five years."

Ceil put aside her spoon and covered Lynn's hand with her own. "I wish you could have gone with me. If only to help me get groceries!" She laughed. "Each day I had to spend a couple of hours going to market. No leftovers because no refrigerators. I really missed milk, ice. I got so tired of eating manioc paste and boa."

"Boa? As in snake?"

"Absolutely." Ceil's eyes twinkled at Lynn's dismay. "Now. You asked about Robert. He's visionary. And he seems to have money to carry through his plans. He's not just talking about a few English classes here and there."

Ceil's cynicism is new, too. Lynn forced herself to notice something different and felt the hot sun on her legs. Its source was light shafting through the spaces between buildings. Despite the density of the nearby stone structures, none was taller than five stories. *Humane. Human-scale. You didn't fly this far to see Ceil so you could gape at buildings.* "Tell me more about Robert."

"He's a graduate of École Polytechnique and École Nationale d'Administration. That's significant. His day job is assistant to a technical advisor at the Ministry of Economy, Finance, and Industry. The development group he does after-hours."

Check. "A subversive banker?"

Ceil laughed suddenly, drawing stares from sober passers-by. "Yes, I suppose so. You'll meet him tomorrow. His request."

"Ceil, I came to see you. I can't stay through tomorrow. I have to get back to this investigation." Lynn paused. She watched Ceil eat. *How long has it been since we've eaten together? What's happened in the meantime?* Lynn settled herself and voiced the second of the two questions she'd traveled five thousand miles to get answered. "Why did you leave Gabon, and the Peace Corps?"

Ceil pushed hair away from her face again and said, "It was time to move on."

The diffident note in her voice was so unfamiliar that Lynn didn't trust herself to reply. Instead she took several spoonfuls of stew, which she no longer tasted.

Ceil's glance flicked again to a spot behind Lynn's chair. A shadow passed across her face. Lynn started to turn, but Ceil said, "Don't. I see two men I recognize. Let's go to my apartment for tea."

❖

"Who were the men?" Lynn asked when they exited the Métro.

"Don't worry about it," Ceil said hurriedly.

"Did they follow us here?"

"Not tonight, but they have before." She walked quickly and Lynn jogged to keep up.

"Who are they?"

"I don't know." Ceil brushed blond strands out of her face.

Lynn groaned and stepped around two men asleep on the sidewalk. "I came through Gare du Nord this morning. I didn't realize you lived so close to it." *Nor that Ceil lived in such a rough neighborhood.*

Her sister's apartment building presented a flat, unadorned front to the narrow street. From the building next door, Lynn heard the squeals of children. Air brakes screamed and train horns blasted intermittently.

"The fanfares keep me company." Ceil turned the key in a door halfway down the open-air hallway. She started the water for tea and left the window open to the courtyard so they could hear the whistle when the water boiled. "Let's sit in the courtyard while we wait."

Lynn followed her outside through an ancient wooden door. One-room apartments enclosed a brick patio shaded by apple and pear trees. "What do you do with Robert's group?"

"Protests at Tolf, for example."

"Doesn't that conflict with the IEA?"

Ceil's welcome, melodic laugh resonated. "Unlike the States, in France working for the International Energy Agency and protesting an oil company aren't contradictory."

They settled into a couple of plastic chairs on the edge of the sandstone-paved courtyard.

Ceil lit another cigarette. Lynn started to move away from the smoke but restrained herself, though not before her sister noticed. "You've been taking care of Dad."

"I wish you'd stop smoking."

"It's an escape. So was the Corps. I can't sit around and watch Dad die, too." She crossed her legs.

Lynn leaned forward, her own legs heat-sticky on the cheap plastic of the chair. "You did everything you could for Mom."

"It wasn't enough. Dad misses her so much. Don't you see? He won't last a year."

"He's talking about some surgery that might help." Lynn heard her own voice rising.

"You face every reality but this one. I can tell how sick he is just by talking to him. Move on with your life. Get married." She brushed hair out of her eyes.

"Like you?"

"I'm doing something I believe in."

"So am I."

The teapot screeched and Lynn followed Ceil inside. Her small, plain flat contained a bed, a few dishes, and little else. Ceil found and filled two modest china cups, neither of which had a handle.

They walked back outside to the courtyard. As if reading Lynn's thoughts, she said, "The cup won't burn your hand. And it's decaf."

Like she always makes. Lynn felt a storm of fatigue wash down to her bones. *No whining.*

"Boyfriends? Lovers?" Ceil persisted. "The 'lost time' with your ex, as you called it, did you in?"

"You're one to talk. Or is Robert even more special than he seems?"

Ceil shook her head. But her expression eased.

"I've been going out with a widower, Cy Derett. He has two kids."

"Do you love him?"

"Yes, but . . ."

"But what?"

"He doesn't understand what my job requires. I'll probably be transferred out of town in a year or two. And I'd want to go. Two kids, Ceil! I don't have a clue, except to worry I don't have enough patience."

"I don't believe that. You were pregnant once, ready to have kids."

"Stop. I don't want to relive it." But the memory was unavoidable—excruciating pain, blood-soaked sheets, a months-long depression afterwards.

They sat for a while. Lynn remembered the bicycle trips they'd taken in the summer before she started high school. As the older, more responsible sister, she had watched for cars and stopped at all the stop signs. When she gave the "all clear," Ceil would zoom past with her hands off the handlebars and her feet off the pedals. "Do you remember our bike trips?" She wove her fingers together.

Ceil smiled and kicked off her scuffed sandals. "For ice cream. I'd ride as fast as I could and you'd watch traffic for me. It was wonderful! I love riding fast."

You have to try again. "Can you tell me what happened in Gabon? You were so anxious to go there."

Ceil sighed and moved her chair back. She glanced around the courtyard as if to be certain her sister was the only one listening, and lowered her voice. "Like I said, I'd had enough when Mom died. You lost yourself even more than usual in your work. The Peace Corps offered me change. I needed it."

Lynn sat back to give Ceil the physical space she seemed to want.

"In Gabon, I was assigned to teach French and English in Makokou, an inland city where a quarter of the men and half the women are illiterate in any language. Makokou was hit hard during the most recent Ebola outbreak, and the Corps had just started sending people back.

"At first, everything was fine. My teaching went well since I'm fluent in French, Gabon's official language. I was learning Fang, the main native language."

"Was it dangerous?"

"From a health standpoint, yes. Cholera, malaria, yellow fever, river blindness, sleeping sickness, and three forms of hepatitis. But I was vaccinated against all that." Ceil crossed her arms as if to hug herself, then uncrossed them and rubbed a finger along the side of the chair.

"What did you do?"

"I taught children during the day, men and women at night. Men would come to the classes, then go to the bigger cities of Port-Gentil or Libreville and work for two or three months. They'd return to Mankokou and drink palm wine for a few weeks."

Shadows began to fall on the sandstone of the patio, turning it dark brown. Lynn made an effort to match her voice's softness to Ceil's. "Were you there alone?"

"No, like I said, two other people were nearby—a husband and wife team—and as I said, I lived with a host family. The husband and wife were setting up a vaccination campaign. I kept in touch with other volunteers in the region. And the country has a large French expat community, several thousand.

"People seemed happy I was there. I felt good about preparing them for jobs that would pay better. But then." Ceil stopped. She closed her eyes and swallowed a few times. When she opened her eyes, she said, "Then one night, my host family and the two other volunteers left for a remote village to administer vaccinations."

Lynn felt a stir of anxiety.

Ceil frowned. "With the dirt roads and nonstop rain in the rainy season, traveling a hundred miles takes several days. That's if your bush driver doesn't detour too often for a drink." She stopped talking.

Lynn waited. Finally she said, as gently as she could, "Is there more to the story?"

"I . . . I'm not certain I can tell you. I keep trying to decide what my mistake was." Her hand twitched through her hair again.

"You seem as if you've been hurt. Ceil, I really care about you." *God, please let her tell you.*

Ceil's finger rubbed faster on her chair. "That night. The rainy season was almost over, but it was raining that night. One of the girls I taught came to where I was staying. Said she and her friends had a puzzle for me and would I come to her house to answer it. When I stepped outside, she disappeared. Men I didn't recognize surrounded me. One covered my mouth, two held pieces of sharpened bamboo to my throat, and the other two grabbed my arms."

"Oh no. No!" Lynn sat forward, one foot grinding hard into the ground as if she could stop whatever had happened next.

Ceil continued, her head down. "The men forced me into a taxi and drove me what seemed to be a long way from Mankokou. Each time I tried to escape, they caught me and sliced my arm with the bamboo. See?" Ceil rolled up the right sleeve of her pink blouse and thrust out her arm.

Despite the growing darkness in the courtyard, Lynn counted six scabbed-over slashes on Ceil's right forearm. Her stomach began a long, cold slide.

Ceil dropped her head to her knees and retched.

Lynn jumped up and wrapped both arms around her and hugged her, with the dull comprehension that nothing could erase Ceil's experience. Her arms vibrated as Ceil heaved.

"Oh, Ceil! How awful! Oh God. I'm so sorry." Lynn felt tears in her eyes. She went inside Ceil's apartment, filled a glass with water and brought it to her sister. Ceil rinsed her mouth and spit onto the sandstone patio. Ceil, who never spit anything anywhere.

"Finally they stopped the truck. I knew where we were."

"Was anyone nearby?" *Stop. Don't even suggest she could have prevented it.*

Ceil shivered again. "We'd passed a Baka Pygmy camp I'd been shown when I first arrived. But I couldn't get away. I couldn't even scream."

Lynn hugged her tightly, then stroked her arm.

"They pulled me out of the truck. There was nowhere to go. Lynn, I tried. Then they took turns."

Lynn hugged her more tightly.

"They . . . raped . . . me. It must have been only half an hour." Ceil's voice shivered with sobs. "It seemed much longer."

Lynn drew her fingertips along Ceil's cheekbones to wipe away the wetness.

"They left me tied up with palm fronds. Loose enough that I freed myself a few minutes after they left. They left water, but I didn't drink it. I washed myself as best I could, which wasn't very well."

"How did you get back?"

Ceil looked at Lynn with glazed eyes. "I must have walked. I don't even remember. Somehow I found my way back to Mankokou."

"Was there a doctor?" Another cold thought let loose.

"My host family and the other American couple came back the next day. They had medical training, did what they could." She plucked at her hair. "I trusted that girl. I trusted all of them. I heard later her family needed money. She was paid to get me outside."

"How horrible!"

"I couldn't go back to teaching. I wasn't even strong enough to find out who the men were. I should have been."

Lynn shook her head fast. "No! Don't think that."

Ceil sobbed, then caught her breath. "In the first days afterward, it took all my concentration not to stay curled up in bed. So when my hosts suggested I leave Mankokou for Paris to take this IEA job Robert could arrange for me, it was a godsend."

"Have you been tested for . . . ?" She felt a foot cramp start, stood, and flexed her toes until it stopped.

Ceil watched her. "AIDS? Not yet. It's too soon for the test to show results."

"Can you press charges?"

Ceil uncrossed her legs and stretched them out in front of her. "No names. No witnesses. Rape is common. I truly had a native learning experience," she said, laughing without mirth. "No, the Gabonese government doesn't prosecute rape."

Lynn moved closer to her and hugged her again. "What do you want me to do?"

"Don't tell Dad. Don't ask me what I could have done differently. Believe me, I've thought about that every waking minute since it happened."

❖

Lynn waited a few hours until Ceil announced herself tired and allowed Lynn to put her to bed.

Then she made the long trek back across a forlorn Paris by foot, métro, and taxi to the Charles de Gaulle airport. After checking in, she called Mike.

"I was right. My sister needed to see me, so I'm glad I could hear her story. She's . . . had a hard time." Lynn also summarized her sister's information on South American tanker loadings. "It doesn't square with what I've heard from Centennial. I'll get the facts parsed out."

30.

Friday, Paris

In the stillness of the Palais Royal apartment, Robert stroked the feathery pile of gray velvet draperies that shielded his computer screen from the sun's glare.

He and the Rabbit had agreed to limit *courriel*, e-mail, and encrypt it using the BLUE program. So this new one was short:

1) Who's next?

2) Inquiries at Centennial. Action?

Robert consulted his notes on refinery sizes and his online satellite photos of the Houston Ship Channel. Then he thought about the second question. He kept his encrypted response as brief as the Rabbit's original inquiry:

1) Peltzman Energy and Petrochemical. Stanover Refining. Capital Refining. Exeter at Deer Park. Henderson Energy. Strachan Energy, both refineries. TriCoast's second Houston refinery.

2) Stop inquiries with Pythagoras projects if necessary.

Minutes later, Robert was pacing under the large clock on the top floor of the Musée d'Orsay, waiting for Ceil and, finally, Lynn Dayton. The glass roof vaults displayed to great advantage the nearby artwork, the glory of France, something of which Americans always needed reminding. The soft light, particles and rays that were themselves infinitely fortunate to fall where they did, provided the right understatement for the honeyed Monets, Pissaros, Cézannes, and Van Goghs.

Ceil hurried toward him. She was late. She was, he also saw with great irritation, alone.

"My sister had to leave."

"You mean she didn't come to Paris," he snapped, in spite of himself. He hated slippage in his timetable for involving Lynn.

Ceil regarded him coolly. "No. She was here last night but she left."

Robert's hand jerked involuntarily. "What happened?"

"She had to return to her investigation."

Frustration jolted Robert. With great, invisible effort he quelled it. "I'm sorry to miss her. Did she say anything about returning?"

She shook her head as they walked outside to the terrace.

He decided not to let his disappointment about missing Lynn this time interfere with enjoying Ceil's company. They'd have a simple lunch on the terrace and take pleasure from its wide-angled view of the Seine.

Something about Ceil has changed, he thought, as they talked and ate. She seemed annoyingly calmer.

31.
Friday, Chicago

On the south side of Chicago, in the Ready-for-U Mart on 63rd Street, Keisha Jackson shouted at the assistant store manager.

"What do you mean, you got no size two diapers? You're the third store I been to and no one's got nothing. What am I supposed to do, clean up my baby's shit when it falls on the floor?"

"I'm sorry," the assistant manager said, as if he'd been saying this all day, as he had. "We'd sell you some if we could get them. No deliveries because our supplier can't run his trucks. I'll give you a package of size fours if you want those."

"Better than nothing." She shifted her baby around to her hip and pulled out her money while the manager walked back to retrieve the bigger-sized diapers. Keisha gazed into her three-month-old son's brown eyes, smiled, and said, "Think you can stop pooping for a day or so?"

The State of Illinois took matters into its own hands Wednesday. After truck diesel prices doubled because of Houston's refinery accidents, legislators passed a bill declaring an immediate six-month tax holiday of a dime a gallon to cut costs for the state's heavy industry. The governor announced his state's intention to monitor prices to ensure that the rapacious oil companies did not take the tax discount for themselves.

Within hours after the legislation's passage, truckers' onboard software all over the country directed them through Illinois for refueling. When consuming a gallon of diesel every five miles, or thirty billion gallons a year, dollars saved add up fast. Truckers descended in eighteen-wheeled droves, clogging truck stops throughout the state. Drivers used up precious hours of their required daily ten-hour rest periods waiting for turns to refuel.

After a few more hours, the terminals and truck stops began posting notices about empty storage tanks.

By Friday, there was no diesel in Illinois. Not at any price. Not on Interstate 290, the tollways, or even on the linebacker routes of I-55, I-80, I-90, and I-94 that knitted the northern, western, and southwestern suburbs to Chicago's core and to steel country in northwestern Indiana.

The small, gasoline-fueled trucks continued delivering, but their drivers were strained to their limits operating around the clock. They stormed the dark recesses of lower Wacker Drive with their bread, fish, books, and software. But the long hauls, especially the reefers, or refrigerated trucks, stayed away. No grapefruit or lettuce from the Rio Grande Valley arrived at Dominick's grocery warehouses. No automobile parts came into the South Shore plant. No one unloaded regular-guy beer from Wisconsin at the Near North bars. No toys, soaps, boilers, pharmaceuticals, surgical instruments, clocks, clothing, edible vegetables, or thousands of other items moved into or out of the great city, its suburbs, or the rest of the state.

32.

Friday, Dallas and Houston

Lynn raced through the hospital's wide hallway. She'd gotten word on the flight back that her father had suffered congestive heart failure. *Thank God you gave Hermosa written authority for emergency treatment.*

Fatigue cut and sanded the backs of her eyes. She leaned over her father's resting form. She felt Cy's warm hands on her shoulders. "The emergency room doctor told me he'll be treated and rest here for a week, then they want him home with limited activity for another ten days."

"Glad you . . . came, Lynn."

The sound of her father's hoarse voice surprised them.

"I . . . can talk. See Ceil?" Her father raised the back of his hospital bed and leaned forward a few inches.

"Yes," she said, touching his arm with her fingertips, cautiously searching for unpunctured squares of skin.

"How is . . . she?"

"She had a bad accident in Gabon," Lynn said, looking into his eyes. "She's all right now."

"What kind of accident?" Cy murmured.

"A run-in with the locals she didn't expect." Ceil hadn't wanted her sister to give their father details. "What can I get you?"

"You . . . got what I . . . needed . . . Ceil." He leaned back. "I'll call . . . when I get . . . out."

"Rest a while. I'll tell her how you're doing. I'll try to persuade her to return. Dad, I have to go on to Houston."

She put her face next to his. Cy's daughter's words from a week ago were the best she could do. "Don't say good-bye. Just kiss me."

Moving his oxygen tube to one side, he did.

❖

"Hello! It's good to see you guys!" Lynn said, hugging the children with relief outside her father's hospital room. She gave Cy a hard embrace. "Thanks for coming to see him."

"Hermosa called me and told me," Marika said. "I gave Dad the message. Hospitals are important."

Lynn winced at how much the six-year-old already knew about hospitals.

"Daddy buy candy," Matt informed her seriously, looking through the gift shop window.

"For you?" she asked in make-believe surprise. He smiled, sporting a chocolate grin.

"Do you think your dad will get better?" Marika asked.

Her directness made Lynn's eyes prick with needles of tears, and she didn't want to burden Marika. "I hope so. He's been sick a while. Why don't I walk you to your car?" Lynn anticipated the difficulty Cy would have maneuvering his children, especially Matt, through the crowded hospital lot.

"We've had a few more scares recently," she told Cy. She told him about the hood vents blocked with wax, and the dissolving canisters of hydrofluoric acid.

"Who do you think did it?" Sun reflected from Cy's glasses in a dizzying pattern.

You're so tired you could lie down on this cement and fall asleep. "Someone who wants us to stop asking questions."

"With warnings like that, I want you to stop asking questions too."

"Comes with the job."

"You're exhausted. This isn't a good time to talk. But it never is." He sounded remote and measured. After the children got into his

Volvo, Cy buckled up a still-wiggly Matt and checked his daughter's seat belt.

"What's wrong?"

He paused. "We can't go on like this."

An alarm jangled in her head through her bone-numbing fatigue. "Well, I have to return to Houston and finish this investigation. It'll be a few more days."

Cy closed Matt's door harder than necessary. "It's always just a few days, according to you. If you don't want to get married, I need to move on."

She held her breath for a few seconds before speaking. "Marriage is a huge, risky bet. It means compromises. What if we get it wrong? I sure did last time."

Cy got into his car, turned on the ignition, rolled down the windows, punched up the air conditioning, and stayed planted in the driver's seat. "I'm sorry, but the kids need more air. They'll just have to hear us talk. Do you want to sit next to me on the passenger side?"

She leaned against the car in the next parking spot so she could see his face. "No, I'm fine. Perfect example right now. You need to focus on your kids. I worry I won't have time for Dad. It's just me and Hermosa to take care of him. And what if I have to move for work cross-country or out of the country? I already have several times. You wouldn't leave your partnership. I've seen you put in those seventy-hour weeks at the office." She heard the snappishness in her voice and didn't care.

"As a matter of fact, scaling back my hours would be good for me and especially the kids."

"You haven't talked about reducing your time before." She shaded her eyes with one hand.

"Marika and Matt mean a great deal to me. I'd like to spend more time with them."

"Daddy, your kids are hot! Let's go!" Marika shouted.

"We're almost done," Cy said to Marika.

Done now or done forever? "You do have the sweetest kids. But," she whispered, so Marika wouldn't hear, "kids—any kids—are more than a full-time job. I'm not Becky, and I can't be as responsible for them as she was. Dad's care, worrying about Ceil, and especially investigating at Centennial to keep my people safe are all I can handle right now."

"Together we'd have more time for your father than you do alone." He looked up at her. "Who was here in his hospital room when you arrived?"

"You. Believe me, I appreciate it." She stopped leaning and stood up. "But I'm running a set of six refineries with, as you've pointed out to me, fifty-five hundred people reporting to me. I can't sit at home and push buttons and make it happen." Lynn felt cool air coming from the open windows of the car.

He sighed. "I hate having this conversation in the parking lot with your dad lying up there in that room. I love you. I don't want to lose you. But it isn't fair to either of us if we don't talk about going forward."

She started to speak but he held up a hand.

"Don't give me an answer now. We'll talk when you come back to Dallas." He buckled his seat belt.

"We'll talk then," was all she could say before Cy rolled up the car windows. She saw Marika's and Matt's quiet, upturned faces in the back seat.

You're only going a few hundred miles south, but it might as well be ten thousand. Lynn climbed into her Maserati and wiped her eyes.

She awoke to the copilot of the corporate plane shaking her shoulder in Houston at two o'clock. For a few long seconds, she couldn't orient herself to her location or time zone. *Jeez, you need more sleep.*

At Centennial she and Preston reviewed the last few days' events. Jean-Marie appeared, her head grazing the top of their office's doorframe. "I came by because of something odd, *cher*. We send our used catalyst to Texas Cementing Industries."

Preston nodded. "They mix it into their cement brick."

"Their customers have been complaining recently about the brick, that it's weak and it cracks easily. So they called us, axed us to take off the gris-gris."

With Jean-Marie's pronunciation, it sounded like "gree-gree." Lynn hadn't heard the word in years. "The what?"

"Voodoo. But the explanation is easier than some spell. The cracking probably means excess metals, maybe vanadium, in the spent catalyst we sell them. Here's the real gris-gris; none of the crudes we're running has high vanadium."

Preston said, "Maybe we're not running the crude-oil mix we think we are."

Jean-Marie folded her body into a chair and sat, waiting for his explanation.

"The crude mix is worse than it ought to be," Preston said.

Lynn shook her head at Preston. Jean-Marie saw it. "You don't want to talk about this? Why not? We sure as hell don't need more secretiveness."

"We have only one opportunity to get the answer right," Lynn said.

"Try again?" Jean-Marie still sounded angry but she was backing down.

You have to trust her. Lynn took a deep breath. "This conversation doesn't leave this room."

"I'll be the judge of that." Jean-Marie's eyes hardened.

"If you start talking, something else dangerous could happen."

"Are you threatening me?" Jean-Marie demanded.

"No. If I were threatening you, you'd know it." Lynn mustered a quiet tone. *Is she the one you're not supposed to trust? If so, you're about to blow it.* "Last week, Preston and I had a replay of what happened to Armando Garza. Except we were working with a small sample of oil. There was a smaller concentration with a lot less H₂S than the pretreater outlet. So we didn't end up dead or in the hospital."

"Preston, I knew your lab technique needed work."

Preston didn't smile in response.

Lynn described the wax plugs in the vent pipes. The color drained from Jean-Marie's face and neck. "*Mais jamais.* I can't believe it. Who'd do that?"

"Likely the same person who left hydrofluoric acid in our office. Whoever is worried about what we're discovering. Namely, that we're not running the crude oils we think we are."

Jean-Marie turned to Preston. "Have you gone over the shipping logs with Jay?"

"Yes. No discrepancies."

"Why hasn't Dwayne figured this out already?" Then Jean-Marie answered her own question. "He's been distracted, worried about his wife. She's pretty sweet, ya know."

Jean-Marie and Dwayne work together even better than you realize. Good news for a change.

"We've identified symptoms, but not the illness until now," Preston said. "Trouble meeting specs? Adric complaining because his unit's bouncing all over the place?"

"So you think this mystery crude is the answer." Jean-Marie shook her head. "There must be another logical explanation. Maybe you got bad readings."

"I don't think so. What we need to do is run individual distillations on each of the sour crudes," Lynn said. "Maybe shipments got mixed up."

"Maybe Jay is being misled about what he's receiving," Jean-Marie mused. "We're not the only ones having trouble. Peltzman Energy and now Stanover Refining are down for a month. Nine more people killed, fifteen more injured. Electrical outages again."

No way! You weren't gone that long.

"Is Reliant the problem?" Preston asked, naming the electricity supplier to all the Ship Channel refineries and plants.

"They claim not to be."

"Now I'm positive. This pattern of accidents is too frequent, even for the Ship Channel. We don't need anything else to worry about, but it looks like sabotage," Lynn said. *Time to call the ever-helpful Jim Cutler again?*

"No, it's just sloppy operations," Jean-Marie objected. "Everyone here has security. Badges, ID systems, retinal verification, to say nothing of guards, razor wire fences, antivirus programs, and cybersecurity."

"But Lynn's right. This cluster is statistically abnormal. Even chaos has roots in order and definition." Preston wrote out a nonlinear equation in neatly blocked letters.

"Yeah, I studied Lorenz attractors. But the butterfly effect is bullshit," Jean-Marie said.

"You're wrong," Preston said. "Sensitive dependence on initial conditions? It probably explains your behavior. You've always been crazy and you just get crazier." Preston was lashing out as Lynn rarely saw him do.

Jean-Marie didn't escalate the battle. "We must all be hungry. Low blood sugar."

He didn't answer, instead instructing his computer to graph the equation. Long, lazy loops and swirls began to appear on the screen, gradually taking twin elliptical shapes joined at the bottom that resembled a butterfly's wings.

Jean-Marie nodded at the screen. "It's beautiful but I can't fill my stomach on eye candy. How about muffalettas?" She picked up the telephone handset. "Red beans and rice, too?"

"I've been awake with only a nap or two since midnight Houston time," Lynn said. "I have to sleep."

"I'm leaving too," Preston seconded.

"Must be a good race starting up somewhere," Jean-Marie said.

She just can't resist. It's amazing the operators haven't broken her nose a few times.

"You need a life," Preston snapped.

Jean-Marie sighed. "I do. I'd leave with you but I have e-mail and stuff to answer."

Lynn said, "I'll come by tomorrow. We can talk then about what to do with the news from Texas Cementing."

Your day has gone on much too long. The slow drive west on LaPorte Freeway and the steep climb over the Ship Channel at I-610 narcotized her and she struggled to stay awake. Even the Port of Houston Authority sported only gray—gray warehouses and gray loading terminals. To fight her tiredness, she turned the air conditioning to its coldest setting and cracked the windows so the freeway sounds would keep her awake.

Once in her room, she shed briefcase, laptop, and cell phone, turning the television to the Weather Channel.

". . . Adrian now moving north at around thirty miles an hour. Internal winds of one hundred miles an hour make it a category two storm. The weather service predicts landfall on the Texas or Louisiana coast in about forty-eight hours, with the highest risk for Texans in the coastal zone between Port Lavaca and the Houston-Galveston area."

Bart and Reese will likely have to shut down TriCoast's Ship Channel refineries. And if they and others here are off-line, even for a day, you'll have even less gasoline at a time when Gulf Coast refineries are supposed to be at full throttle, making up for the ones that suffered accidents.

Centennial wasn't running at a hundred percent yet. Meletio, Xavier, Tier I Blending, Peltzman Energy, and Stanover Refining were also partially or completely shut down.

Lynn sat up suddenly. She opened her laptop and brought up the US refinery system maintenance database. Within minutes she had the answer. Her suspicion, growing in the last week, was justified; there had never, in any year, been such a large group of refineries out of operation in the late spring. *The nature gods are already harsh taskmasters. Exactly who's trumping them, and why?*

"Stay tuned for more on the approaching storm," the television weatherman said brightly.

33.

Friday night-Saturday morning, Houston

nterfering bitch. Always putting herself where she didn't belong, in the middle of business. Didn't look like she was going to give up easily, either.

The Rabbit called the Assistant. "Pythagoras Project. We don't have much time."

❖

Lynn awoke at 4 a.m., turning from one side of the hotel bed to the other, unable to find a comfortable place.

She kept replaying the conversation with Cy, hoping it would end differently. By 4:30, sleep was a lost cause; despite her best efforts, she'd slipped into Parisian time. She changed into running clothes. At the front desk, the night clerk drowsed.

Lynn ran the few blocks to LaBranch and circled downtown, tacking back and forth as she came to dead-end streets or those crossing under the elevated loop formed by highways I-10, I-45, and US 59. The dense air stuck to her skin. It hadn't cooled much during the night. Fortunately the mosquitoes were still asleep.

Gradual, partial refinery shutdowns for tropical storm Adrian might be a good thing if someone's otherwise trying to sabotage them. Less oil means less fire and explosion risk. Maybe my call to Mark and Jim should wait until after we know Adrian's course.

A faster pace felt natural. The knots fell away, first from her calves, then from her quadriceps and hamstrings, and finally from her gluteals. An occasional truck rocketed through the one-way streets of downtown Houston. She loved the business of making gasoline, but cars were the machined enemies of runners. Either they were driven too fast or, worse, too slowly. The slowest cars usually contained a half-dozen kids with bright ideas about what to say to a woman running alone.

She raced past several more street signs: Brazos, Bagby, Milam, and Prairie. Soon her head cleared and she'd covered the five miles she intended to.

When she returned to her room at 6:00 a.m., her telephone's message light was blinking. Too early for the wake-up call. She hoped Cy's voice would greet her. *Maybe he's reconsidered.*

The recorded mailbox voice informed her the message had been left ten minutes ago. What came next was brief and chilling. "Lynn, it's Reese. Call my cell phone. Jean-Marie Taylor's been shot. She's dead."

Lynn crumpled to the floor, pulled by a force stronger than gravity. *Impossible. You heard him wrong.*

But when she listened to the message again, it hadn't changed. Numb, she punched Reese's cell phone number. "I saw Jean-Marie last night right before I left. What happened?" Her voice broke.

When he answered, he sounded as if he had aged fifteen years. "Last we knew, she went into the refinery about 8:00 p.m. One of the operators on the night shift found her inside the cooling tower. I got the call at home half an hour ago. HPD is here now. So's the medical examiner."

"I'm on my way."

At the razor-wire entrance to the refining compound, two of the regular security officers staffed the guardhouse. The one directing operations from a walkie-talkie scrutinized her. He sipped coffee from a Styrofoam cup.

"I'm Lynn Dayton. Is there another entrance for the main refinery besides this one?"

"A contractor gate about a mile away, but it's locked after four in the afternoon. Not many people try to climb the fence, but someone could have."

"Jean-Marie came through around eight. Anyone else in or out then?"

"The shift changes at ten. That's several dozen people. But no one at eight. When I took over at eleven thirty, I looked at the sign-in sheet and asked about her."

"Did you tell anyone else?"

"Yes," the security officer looked pointedly at her. "I put out a general alert. Everyone here on the night shift knew Jean-Marie was missing."

"And no one saw her once she went inside the gate?"

"Not that I've heard. One strange thing, though. Both doors to the cooling tower were locked on the outside when the operator found her."

Lynn drove slowly to the old redwood, three-cell cooling tower, the same one where she'd kidded with Jean-Marie a few days before. A white HPD cruiser was pulled up nearby. The hot, rich asphalt smell was usually comforting. Today it made her sick.

She stepped up onto the railed platform of the tower and looked past yellow tape through a propped-open door. The inside smelled like moist algae and felt like a cramped attic. Water dripped all around. She balanced on the narrow catwalk. *Hello claustrophobia, my old friend.*

The door at the opposite end of the tower was also propped open and taped off. Light from the two open doors illuminated the wooden catwalk. The cooled-water basin lapped underneath it, large fans roared above. Water dripped relentlessly.

A man crouched close to a form, searching it with a flashlight. While he searched, he talked into a recorder shielded from the water with a plastic case.

She introduced herself to Dr. Martinez.

"I remember you. Sorry and surprised to be here again. I've gotten a lot of Ship Channel call outs the past few days."

With a shock Lynn realized he was searching Jean-Marie. *Not Jean-Marie. Her body.* She no longer wore last night's blue linen skirt and jacket. Instead, jeans and a white sports shirt now bound her, bound her much too tightly because her bloated body had absorbed so much water. A blindfold was knotted at the back of her head. A gag pulled back the corners of her mouth. Her wrists were tied behind her back with a small black cord.

A dark stain spread across her chest. Blood had dripped down her side and into the basin of water below.

Whoever shot her wanted her to suffer. Both doors to the tower had been locked from the outside, the guard said. The water inside roared, so no one could have heard a shot or a scream, even if she had gotten the gag off.

Goddamn. Goddamn it all.

Lynn walked around to the west side of the cooling tower where several men congregated near the platform. Nauseated, she barely recognized Reese and Dwayne, neither of whom looked any better than she felt. One of Dwayne's large hands clamped onto his cigarette as if it were a tube of oxygen.

Reese's nose was red and his eyes bloodshot. "Lynn, I asked Officer Alex Stinson to come back. He has a few other people with him from the Homicide Division. Alex, this is my boss, Lynn Dayton."

"I told you I didn't want to be out here again." The sunburned Houston police officer coughed.

Ignoring his comment, Lynn asked, "Who found Jean-Marie?"

"One of the water-treatment operators on the night shift," Reese said, standing rigidly. "He was making early-morning rounds in the utilities area. As I told Officer Stinson, there's no reason to suspect him."

Dwayne added, "He noticed the east and west doors to the cooling tower had their wooden cross-pieces down and latched. Both doors barred on the outside—that's not standard procedure. The operator opened one of the doors and found her."

"I asked Riley to arrange meetings for each shift. The first one is later this morning," Reese said.

"Dwayne, you were saying no one saw her or anything unusual last night?" Stinson asked.

"No, I said I don't know. Someone could have."

"Are all of the evening shift workers gone?" Stinson asked.

Dwayne nodded, exhaled smoky breath, staring up at the platform seven feet off the ground.

"We can't wake them up," Lynn said. "They need sleep to stay sharp."

"I have to talk to them," Stinson insisted.

"No, it's not safe," she said.

"What's safe about that woman in there?"

"I agree, but I'm not going to risk my other folks, too, by waking them up. Let's see what we can find out today at the meetings."

"Since you won't let me call them, let me ask you. When did you last see Jean-Marie?"

"Preston Li and I talked to her in my office last night. About seven thirty. She said she was staying late to catch up on her mail. She was wearing a blue linen suit and heels, not the clothes she's in now. Is. Was." Lynn closed her eyes for a moment to gather self-control.

"Then you left? Can anyone verify your whereabouts?" Stinson asked suspiciously.

"I went to the hotel and went to bed. Maybe someone there saw me."

"That's not much. We may need to question you further."

"What do you make of this?" Reese asked the officer.

Stinson explained that the gravel didn't hold physical evidence well and complained again, "This woman won't let me call potential witnesses."

Reese blinked. "Officer Stinson, you know how it is on the Channel with shift work and sleep deprivation."

The medical examiner emerged from the inside of the cooling

tower, ducking his head to avoid the low doorframe. His black hair, mustache, and skin dripped, as if from a rainstorm. He walked down the several steps from the platform to the gravel and stood in front of them. "It appears Ms. Taylor died from gunshot wounds to the chest. The bullet cavitations indicate two or three high-velocity bullets. May have been contact wounds. Any soot would be washed away, but she has burns at the bullet entry sites."

"Jean-Marieeee!" Dwayne keened. Lynn remembered how relentlessly Dwayne and Jean-Marie joked with one another and realized how much he would miss her, too. *Goddamn. We'll all miss her.*

Martinez went on. "The untreated wounds to the lungs and the aortic arch alone were enough to kill her. There's no foam around her mouth, so we can rule out the last few hours; this happened earlier. But because the water temperature is so warm, Ms. Taylor's body temperature doesn't indicate anything about her time of death. Once her body is moved out of the tower, rigor mortis and livor mortis may tell me more. The level of water in her body suggests she was inside here not long before she died. She has self-defense wounds—skin under her fingernails and scratches on her arms."

"What kind of fucking asshole would do that to her?" Dwayne exploded. He threw his cigarette to the ground and he crushed it as if he were stomping the body of Jean-Marie's killer.

Reese shook his head, anguish pinching his face.

Lynn rocked on her feet to ease the cramps shooting up her legs. In the middle of the group of stunned, frightened men, she juggled her feelings of anger and shock with the need to reassure them and appear in control.

Her other feeling—so deep it had no end—surprised her.

She was lonely.

34.
Saturday, Houston

Heavy crude: crude oil that is denser, with longer and more complex carbon-hydrogen molecular chains than light crude. Heavy crude costs more than light crude to process into valuable refining products such as gasoline, jet fuel, heating oil, and diesel.

When Lynn reached Mike at home, he wasted no words. "Glad you're back in the country. Stop screwing with Centennial. You and I have a week before we testify on the proposed loosening of the gasoline regs and I haven't heard anything from you about them. Your refinery managers are calling me with their crap because they can't find you."

"Mike, I was only gone one day. I came back ASAP for the investigation, which turned out to be a good thing because my father had congestive heart failure. On top of that, as I told you, my sister passed along some useful, very new data about tanker loadings."

"Sorry." His tone relented. "The jet lag must be killing you. You were hardly there."

"I've felt better." *Like after the last time I slept more than four hours.* "But I called for another reason." Lynn told him about Jean-Marie's shooting and how she'd been found. "Because the air and water are so warm, the medical examiner can't fix a time of death, but he thinks it occurred just after Preston and I saw her."

"You two were the last to see her alive."

"We're the ones who admit it. Mike, she was shot. She didn't just slip and drown. And both doors on the tower were bolted from the outside. There's no way she could have done that, and no way she could have escaped."

"Jesus Christ! Who'd think of such a thing? What's the reaction?"

At least with Mike you can be honest. About some things. "We'll have meetings, talk to everyone, try to calm them . . ."

"But they're scared shitless," he said.

"Wouldn't you be?"

"Yeah, of course. Okay, I'll run interference for you for another few days. But don't forget my testimony."

"And don't forget Claude can help you." *C'mon, Mike!*

"Lynn, like I told you, you have other people working for you who can handle this."

"I need to be on the front line."

"No, you don't." His voice was ferocious. "I don't want to lose you like Jean-Marie."

She hadn't expected this sentiment from a man whose mantra was that anyone could be replaced.

By midmorning, the news spread. Employees, even those not on Saturday shifts, collected throughout Centennial's offices in knots of three and four. Cody, Reese, and Lynn announced a noon gathering at the auditorium, and met a packed house of at least two hundred people. All seats were taken with several employees standing at the back, as well as HPD officer Alex Stinson.

"I'm Lynn Dayton, TriCoast's executive VP of US refining. Ladies and gentlemen, I have a tragic announcement. Jean-Marie Taylor, the vice president of safety and environmental issues for this refinery, was found dead this morning."

Buzzing filled the auditorium. She waited for silence.

"She was discovered locked inside cooling tower CT-1. She was shot. We urge anyone who saw anything unusual last night, or in the last few days, to speak with me, Cody Laughlin . . ." she gestured to the men behind her, "or Reese Spencer."

Cody stepped to the microphone.

His Oklahoma accent rebounded sorrowfully throughout the room. It was strained, not playful as it had been during the lunch she and Dwayne had shared with him, a lunch that seemed years ago. "I want to emphasize what Ms. Dayton has said. If you think of anything, anything . . ." His voice choked off. Reese gently took his arm.

"Please join me in expressing sympathy to Jean-Marie's family and friends," Reese concluded. "We'll take your questions."

Adric Washington stood. Tight curls hugged his head, and his mahogany face glistened under the lights. "I think I'm speaking for several of us here when I ask what's being done for our safety. We've lost six people. My friends at plants around here have told me about several accidents in the past week. And not just injuries. Deaths."

"We're investigating as quickly and thoroughly as possible," Lynn said. "Here's where I most need your help. I repeat, if any of you have seen anything unusual or different, out of the routine, in the last few days, especially last night, let us know.

"The second thing you can do is, as always, watch out for one another. The buddy system is the cornerstone of our safety rules, and it still applies. In particular, if you're here after the end of your shift, be sure two or three people know where you are and what you're doing. We don't know if the person who did this was someone inside or outside the refinery," Lynn said. She tried to force back a cold thought. *The killer could be looking at you right now.*

"Will we get extra security?" a Hispanic woman asked.

"Our security officers will be happy to provide any of you an escort anytime you need it." She looked over at the four of them, including Farrell, and they nodded. "If we decide the situation merits temporary additional security, we'll hire."

A short, dark-haired man at the front, one of the junior design engineers, raised his hand. "I have to ask an obvious question. Is cooling tower CT-1 still operating?"

Lynn grimaced as she realized a question behind his question. *Is some of Jean-Marie's blood circulating through the refinery in the cooling water system? Only parts per billion, but yes.*

"No, CT-1 isn't operating. We shut it down, isolated it, and put the load on the other four cooling towers."

"Are the police going to be in our business, checking on the expired license of Chuck here, or seeing if our cars have been inspected?" With an obvious look at Stinson's uniform, the crew-cut man who asked the question took a punch in the arm from his friend, but sounded doubtful he himself would pass a law officer's close scrutiny.

"Of course I encourage you to follow all laws and regulations, but the police are confining their investigation to the homicide. Requests for interviews will come through Reese or me, so no, you won't be randomly stopped. However, if you're interviewed I expect you to cooperate and answer any questions you're asked."

"Was Jean-Marie really shot or did she just hit her head, get knocked out, and drown? That's almost happened to me, you know."

"I wish I could tell you otherwise, but she died from two to three gunshot wounds to the chest. If you and others have a safety issue with climbing around the inside of the cooling towers, let's address it through the safety committee." She felt a dull pang. *Which Jean-Marie is no longer around to lead.* "Remember what I said about working in pairs."

"This place is getting scary. Since TriCoast owns us now can you transfer us to one of your other refineries?"

"As soon as possible we'll get Centennial's human resources department integrated with TriCoast's and you'll be notified of openings elsewhere. But your strongest qualification for those jobs will be getting this refinery on an even keel, and I ask your help in doing that."

After a few more questions, mostly about funeral plans for Jean-Marie, Lynn closed the meeting and the voices in the auditorium escalated, everyone talking at once. As she stepped down from the stage to the floor, she heard the icy voice of the stranger who had twice threatened her by telephone, " . . . without interference from any damn safety nannies."

He's here! Who is it?

It was Dwayne's phrase but she wasn't sure it was his voice. Lynn spun around, staring through the crowded auditorium and listening, unable to find the person to whom the voice belonged. She edged over to where she'd heard it, but was slowed by several people greeting her. *You can't talk now.* But she did. While offering reassurances and hugs, she listened for the voice but didn't hear it again.

"What's wrong?" Cody asked.

"I heard something unusual, but it's gone." Lynn turned and searched his face. "How are you holding up?"

"Are we going to do more of these meetings?" he asked, flapping his shirt to dry his armpits. "I'll feel better if we don't."

"Almost everyone on all the shifts was here. We'll send a plant-wide e-mail for those who missed it."

She stopped Farrell on her way out of the auditorium. In answer to her questions, he told her that the cooling tower wasn't under security surveillance, and he still hadn't found the leak videotape.

She closed the door to her Centennial office.

Ceil picked up on the first ring. "*Bonjour?*"

"I wanted to tell you about Dad. It's taken so long because last night one of the women I work with was killed, a woman named Jean-Marie Taylor. It's shaken us all up."

"It sounds as if you would be safer here than there," Ceil said.

"Whatever." Lynn strained to keep tiredness and resentment out of her voice. "I saw Dad yesterday as soon as I got in. He's at Presbyterian Hospital with congestive heart failure. He'll be home in ten days or so." Lynn paused. "He'll get through this, but it can't help when he's already weak."

"And you want me in Dallas to take care of him."

"Hermosa and I take care of him. Come back for your own sake. He asked about you. I didn't tell him what happened in Gabon. He should hear that from you, anyway."

"Lynn, I need to be here."

Damn it Ceil, I can't do it all. "So it's my turn to say your work is more important than your family."

"Don't be bitter. You should know the feeling well." Ceil hung up.

She sounds as angry as you feel. Maybe it's part of recovery.

"Brian, it's Lynn Dayton at TriCoast. You're doing some overtime, too. What have you found?"

Brian Tulley at Catanalyst sounded surprised to hear from her, as well he might on a Saturday afternoon. "The latest report was just handed to me half an hour ago. Shall I e-mail or fax it to you?"

"No, tell me what it says and courier it to me at the Four Seasons."

"You sound paranoid."

"Jean-Marie Taylor was killed last night. She was shot."

"Good God! I talked to her yesterday."

"It appears to be somebody who has access to the refinery."

"You don't suspect me, do you?"

"No," Lynn said. *Won't tell him you do.* "I called to ask about your results."

"We tested the catalyst. I talked to Dwayne and Jean-Marie—I can't believe we talked less than twenty-four hours ago. I sent the report to Dwayne. Jean-Marie—Jean-Marie!—suggested we test the sour water for iron. I did and the iron levels are high. That's consistent with accelerated corrosion."

"Consistent with corrosion somewhere, not necessarily the pretreater outlet."

"You got it. Next we found the pretreater samples couldn't come from the crude mix Centennial is running. The samples show more bottoms, with more metals and sulfur. Your electrical resistance probes suggest the corrosion rate in the pretreater gas line is higher than it's ever been in the ten years Catanalyst has been testing for Centennial."

"So we can't be running Dukhan, Kuwaiti, Saudi Medium, and Oriente on the sour side of the refinery," she said.

"Right," Brian said. "Something is making the mix worse. Heavier, with more sulfur and metals. You should find out what you have in those tanks."

❖

The weather remained oppressively overcast. In the last few hours there'd been no further indication of whether the tropical storm would bypass Houston, sideswipe it with plenty of rain, or hit it straight on. If the storm strengthened, the mayor would have to decide soon whether or not to order an evacuation.

Not another evacuation, Lynn thought. She tucked her jeans into her boots and rolled up the sleeves of her white cotton shirt, wishing she could wear shorts. But that didn't fit the safety code. *As Jean-Marie would have been the first to tell you. So let's get a move on. "Awrite, let's check the roux!" is what she'd say. Should go much faster this time.*

After locating four sampling flasks, Lynn signed out truck keys from the security officer who took this task over from Shelby on the weekends. When she arrived at the cement-block control center, she motioned Adric into his office and shut the door. "Thanks for speaking up at the meeting this morning. You're still on shift?"

"I have a lot of scared people here. Or not here. Since some still aren't showing up, I'm pulling extra duty."

Is Adric's sense of responsibility the real reason he's working overtime? Or is he involved with the funky crude? Or even Jean-Marie's murder? I hate suspecting so many people. "I need to investigate further. Can you help me?"

He nodded, flexing his large brown hands.

"I'd like to take samples from each of the four sour crude storage tanks. Can I borrow someone on your crew?"

"Skyler Knowles is on duty today."

"Can Skyler keep a secret? Given what happened to Jean-Marie, this needs to be between you, me, and him."

"Sure." He looked out the window between his office and the monitor room, caught Skyler's eye, and motioned him inside. After Adric explained, Skyler confirmed he would go with Lynn and take samples from sour-crude tanks S1 through S4.

"That's it," she said, "only the sour-crude tanks, not the sweet ones. *A small test for Skyler.* "What's in each?"

"Arab Medium in S1, Dukhan in S2, Kuwaiti export blend in S3, and Oriente in S4."

That's what you thought, too.

The tanks were nearby. S1 was the largest at two hundred and fifty thousand barrels. The rest held one hundred and fifty thousand barrels each. S2 and S4 could be heated so that very heavy crudes could be stored in them without solidifying. Rotors at the bottom kept hot spots from bubbling up by evening the temperature distribution. The sample from S4, Lynn noticed, took a long time to collect. *Maybe a clogged line. But likely that's our culprit. Verify and identify.*

From the tanks, Skyler drove her back across the asphalt roads of the refinery complex to the lab, near the offices. She again prepared to do the experimental crude distillation procedure on each of the four samples, assembling the glassware and checking the hood vents for new plugs. *None today.*

She prepared for a few hours of heating, measuring, and telephone calls to her other refinery managers. *This time you can't leave the room.*

The sample from S4 behaved peculiarly when she poured it out for distillation. It poured slowly, much more slowly than a thirty-gravity crude should.

13 Days: The Pythagoras Conspiracy

At 8:00 p.m. she turned off the mantles and finished the weighing for the second set of distillations.

She wasn't surprised when Preston appeared in the doorway. The engineering VP's tenacity meant he kept the same weekend hours she did. "I just opened my e-mail. I think you should see one of the messages." Preston hunched over, his urgent posture, and slid a printout across the lab counter-top. "Notice when she sent it."

"Oh no!" Jean-Marie's e-mail showed she'd sent it at 7:45 p.m. last night, after she left Lynn's office. Lynn smoothed the paper and read:

"Preston, see the report Catanalyst sent to Dwayne. I also located the security video of the pretreater accident but haven't viewed it yet. They're both locked in my desk in case you see this before I see you again. The password to open the lock is NOLAinEXILE.

"The rate of pretreater-catalyst poisoning is too high. Also, I have a note from one of the night-shift operators saying he saw Farrell Isos around the pretreater near where we found Armando, LaShawna, and the others, but much earlier, about 5:00 a.m. Let's talk in the morning. Jean-Marie."

They jumped up, locked the lab, and walked quickly to Jean-Marie's office. *Her office when she was alive,* Lynn thought grimly. Preston kept watch in the hallway while Lynn unlocked Jean-Marie's desk.

"The original of the security video! I've been asking Farrell for copies of that for days and he's been saying he didn't have it. Wonder where she found it? What's going on with that jerk Isos? I'll get Tyree down here to start him talking." She locked Jean-Marie's desk and walked with Preston back to the lab.

"Let's forward the e-mail to Alex Stinson and Mark."

"Look at the Catanalyst report," Preston handed Lynn the report and she read it as they walked. She turned to the written summary and table of results. The pretreater catalyst was indeed overactive—it

287

was encountering high embedded sulfur and was much further along in its useful life than it should have been. The report also showed higher metals deposition, particularly vanadium and nickel, than what Lynn expected.

"So shortly the cycle will reverse," Preston said.

"Right." Lynn continued to read. "Catalyst activity will drop. Then the sulfur and the metals will stay in the crude, leading to even more downstream fouling. With excess vanadium throughout the refining units, failure of critical units is imminent. We're looking at more deadly fires and explosions here soon."

"Shit." Preston's shoulders slumped low and his hands covered his eyes. When he looked up, her face was a mask of pain. "When we find the asshole who killed Jean-Marie I'll take him out myself. We owe her that much."

"Not your fault."

"I shouldn't have said anything to her. Then she wouldn't have stayed late. She couldn't let anything go."

"It's not your fault," Lynn repeated. "It's the fault of whoever killed her."

They sat still for several seconds.

You need to divert him. "Preston, if Jean-Marie were here she'd be working nonstop to find and solve this crude oil problem. All the sulfur, all the metals that we're not supposed to have. I'd say we owe her that, don't you?"

Preston looked up, eyes red. "Yeah."

"Look, I need a hand with these comparisons. I've entered the results on these forms. Do you remember where the assay file is?"

Preston tapped keyboard buttons for a while, then said, "What would be your guess?"

"The results for the tank S4 sample don't match the Oriente assay."

"You're right. Who should we call?" He hunched over again.

"No one yet. This refinery is being sabotaged, and it's not the only one. But someone here is nervous about what we're learning. We must find out who. The crude in S4 is heavier, more sulfurous, and a more metallic crude than Oriente. Someone's making a substitution. We're in exactly the same place as before, but this time it's without Jean-Marie."

"You're saying Jean-Marie is dead because I spilled the beans yesterday," Preston said bitterly.

"No. That's not what I'm saying. Whoever would blindfold, gag, and shoot a woman and lock her in a cooling tower where no one could hear her scream isn't human by any measure," Lynn heard her voice rising. *Isn't human at all.*

She closed the blinds one by one. "Will you finish washing glassware? I'll be upstairs watching the videotape in the conference room." She heard Preston lock the door after her. She fingered her cell phone, ready to call Preston or refinery security if necessary.

In the conference room, Lynn rolled the tape, upset again by watching LaShawna, Armando, and the others fall. She thought about what Jean-Marie's last e-mail said about Farrell being near the pretreater the morning of the leak. She rewound the security tape to a point further back in time, to 4:20 a.m. And gasped as the scene unfolded.

The tape showed Farrell Isos trying the bypass valve in different positions. His white hard hat bobbed when he moved the valve to direct the poisonous gas out of the open pipe into the air where it killed four of the five operators. He pulled a flag from his pocket. The tape was black and white, but it must have been the orange flag. Then the boyish security guard wrapped the stem of the flag near the open pipe. The flag lured the operators, who thought they had a legitimate repair, over to the gap spewing deadly hydrogen sulfide.

It was Farrell who had tried to sabotage the refinery. The resulting leak killed four people. Then, someone—Farrell again?—tried to murder Armando by calling him out into the hydrogen sulfide gas. If Armando Garza hadn't survived and closed the valve, dozens more would have died. When the hydrogen sulfide didn't kill Armando, Farrell must have finished the job in the hospital by substituting nitrogen for the oxygen Armando so desperately needed.

Shit, the head of Dallas security just told all the TriCoast and Centennial officers about the threats against you. Isos knows everything.

Intent on watching Farrell in the videotape, Lynn hadn't heard the door open. The scrape of a chair startled her.

"Preston, spare my heart and knock next time. Watch this. Now I understand why Farrell's never made copies of the tape. He was probably hiding this original!" Lynn rewound the tape and rolled it again. Preston clenched his hands as he saw Farrell test the bypass valve in different positions.

"Time to get that boy outta here, I'd say," Preston drawled in a pitch-perfect imitation of Cody. Then he was serious. "I can get the tape copied right now. Six copies. I'll bring the original back to you, send one to Mark, send one to Kyle and Gina at the CSB, and hold on to the rest until we see who else needs them."

"I'll call Tyree Bickham and ask him what the steps are."

When Lynn called Tyree in Dallas he was emphatic. "Notify HPD. They or plant security should arrest Farrell for a suspected felony. I'll tell Mark he's got a bad apple in his group. The security videotape is evidence, and I'm glad Preston thought to make copies. Keep the original with you but not any of the copies. I'll be down on a corporate plane tomorrow after church to handle the situation."

"Tell me the steps with Farrell in the meantime."

"If HPD doesn't get him, then next time he sets foot on the property, get the security guards to hold him like you're planning. You also need a guard with you to get all his keys, ammo, badges, passwords, and so forth."

She called the plant's security office. No one answered. She decided to try later. She called Alex Stinson at HPD and left a brief message on his voicemail about the need to question Farrell.

You're out of time. Jean-Marie's been murdered. Armando, murdered.

13 Days: The Pythagoras Conspiracy

Four operators dead at Centennial. Sabotage up and down the Channel. Farrell's the key, but likely he's not the only one.

Indeed, Armando said he'd seen a person with a yellow hard hat in the utilities area a few days before the leak. Unless he'd borrowed it, that wouldn't have been Farrell, whose hard hat was white.

Only five people—Reese, Jean-Marie, Dwayne, Jay, and Riley—owned yellow hats. And now Jean-Marie was dead.

35.

Sunday afternoon, Houston

The next day arrived with a storm watch, perhaps the reason she continued to be unable to reach Centennial's security office. The Weather Channel predicted the storm wouldn't strengthen and would sideswipe Houston, not hit directly, bringing heavy rains to the area. It appeared an evacuation wasn't needed. *The only good news this week.*

She stopped at the Post Oak Empire Bakery for a newspaper, orange juice, and a few slices of chocolate-cherry bread. Humidity painted the sky gray.

At her office at Centennial, she called her other TriCoast managers and arranged to borrow the gasoline, jet fuel, and truck diesel needed to meet the refinery's contracts. Lynn wasn't the only one scrambling. Because of the surprise refinery shutdowns, everyone was hitting the phones, calling in old favors. Prices were spiking further; as with last year's hurricanes, there weren't enough working refineries to spin crude into gasoline, jet fuel, and truck diesel. *But it's not hurricanes this time*, she thought sternly.

The President had again temporarily suspended sulfur regulations and granted new import licenses so that foreign companies could supply US airports, gasoline stations, and trucking terminals. If the shortage continued into the fall, heating oil would be needed, too.

Many Houston refineries had been damaged in the last week by electrical outages, the *Gulf Coast Herald* reported, and quoted Reliant, the main Houston utility, saying it was not the source. *But all it would take is one or two rogue utility engineers. Enron proved that in California.*

Lynn found a large chip of smooth chocolate in the bread and bit into it.

When she checked her online news summary, an article in the international section about European bombings stopped her. "Parisian development group claims responsibility."

Paris. Oh no.

As she scanned the list of demands, she reached for the telephone, trying to restrain her panic. *Had to be Robert's group. Does Ceil know the danger she's in?* Besides Tolf security, the CIA and every aggrieved country's police would want to talk to her sister. Or worse.

No one answered at Ceil's apartment. *It's Sunday evening. She's probably out eating or walking.* Lynn decided to keep trying every few hours. She pushed her wheat-blond hair out of her face repeatedly, and remembered she'd seen the gesture from Ceil.

She summarized what she knew.

Armando Garza, LaShawna Merrell, and the other three operators encountered a higher-than-expected hydrogen sulfide concentration in the gas outlet from the catalytic cracking pretreater. *So high it killed four of them almost instantly.* She stood and stretched against the wall, pressing her hands against the cool cement block and her heels into the floor.

Brian's analysis and your distillation results show the crude mix doesn't match what TriCoast is supposed to be running, and that the crude in tank S4 is heavier, more sulfurous, and more metallic than the costlier Oriente.

Dwayne had said the crude was gobbling too much hydrogen. Dwayne and Jean-Marie had identified the overproduction of coke, Number 6 fuel oil, and sulfur. Despair cut through her. She still thought of Jean-Marie in the present, expecting to see her duck through the door.

Lynn circled the floor in the outside hallway, thinking. The pretreater catalyst was changed on schedule, but now the catalyst showed overactivity, which would change to underactivity from metals poisoning. The corrosion analysis showed high corrosion levels, consistent with excess hydrogen sulfide encountering water to form sulfuric acid. Next were the out-of-kilter refinery weight-balance, the rough operations Adric reported, and the difficulty meeting product specifications.

Jean-Marie also identified the high metals level in Texas Cement's bricks before she died. *She didn't just die, remember? Before she was murdered. After Armando was murdered.*

A rogue crude could explain everything. *Except the murders. Or the murders, too? You have to compartmentalize. Focus on the technical issue. Forget someone's been trying to kill you, too.*

Lynn twisted in her chair but found no comfortable position. Heavy crude would account for the coker being overloaded and dumping vacuum resid into the cat cracking system, she deduced. Heavy crude with metals in it would poison the pretreater catalyst. Sulfur, metals, and coke would pass through to the cat cracker, poisoning its catalyst, too. If the cat cracker—the heart of the refinery—cratered, so would the refinery.

Jesus. No wonder Centennial is stumbling. She looked out the window to see that the cloud cover had become total. But when she checked Houston's weather forecast, the storm's predicted landfall was still hours and miles away, in Port Lavaca. Still, she felt the tense silence of waiting all around her. She confirmed that Bart and Reese had implemented initial tropical-storm protocol—no nonurgent work, no equipment testing.

Lynn clicked on the crude assay file and sorted it by atmospheric resid, the heavy, undesirable part of the crude. Then she looked at the unexplained distillation curve for the S4 crude. By volume, seventy percent of the crude in tank S4 was atmospheric resid. If it were Oriente, the atmospheric resid would only be fifty percent.

That's it! She sorted the assay file by resid content. The crude oil in S4 could be any of at least fourteen crudes, and it could be coming from Canada, Indonesia, Venezuela, China, Iran—or even California or Mississippi. But not Ecuador, where Oriente originated.

She eliminated six crudes with low sulfur and vanadium content, leaving eight: one Canadian, five Venezuelan, one Chinese, and one Iranian.

You need a more complete assay on the crude in tank S4. Jean-Marie had mentioned Jay's confirmation assays. *You still haven't heard from him on those.* She called his office and left a message he would likely pick up tomorrow.

Then she sat back. The image of Jean-Marie's gunshot, water-bloated body filled her mind. Of her last conversation with Armando Garza. Of the visits to each family of the operators killed in the accident. LaShawna's husband and children. Her conversation with Ceil.

She tried Ceil again. Still no answer.

The locked door rattled.

36.

Sunday night, Paris

Le Monde:

"Several bombs yesterday that damaged buildings but caused no injuries confounded authorities in Paris, Rotterdam, and London.

"In a statement received late last night from an unnamed group claiming responsibility, Western countries, particularly the United States, are called on to reduce energy consumption by increasing taxes on gasoline and diesel and applying the additional tax revenues to building refineries in less-developed countries that have none.

In particular, the statement suggests, "the energy-hogging juggernaut of the United States, symbolized by its massive electrical plants and enormous automobiles, should be put on an energy diet. Americans should learn to walk again and should share their *pétrole* with those who truly need it."

Robert was pleased to see *Le Monde* featuring the story precisely as he'd envisioned it. The bombs were small and set for off-hours, designed this time to destroy property, not maim or kill people. One of the explosives he directed be put in the center of TriCoast's Rotterdam lobby. Robert imagined its Cosmati mosaic broken into hundreds of pieces, returned to its original fragments of lapis lazuli and marble.

TriCoast . . . the thought of Lynn Dayton briefly crossed his mind. *She will be here soon enough.* He would focus on her further after meeting Sansei's deadline in two days. They didn't know of his plans for Lynn, nor did they need to.

The Rabbit and the others were progressing with their "capacity reductions." He was pleased that gasoline, diesel, and jet-fuel shortages had resulted from damage to so many Houston refineries—damage he, Robert, commanded. The States had temporarily lifted its strictest environmental requirements for gasoline and diesel so that food and vital materials could keep moving. Sansei had received a special import license to deliver its off-spec gasoline into the States. Xin Yu at Sansei indicated his satisfaction with Robert by immediately depositing hundreds of thousands more euros into his accounts.

Pirates in the south China Sea disrupted some of the first relief gasoline shipments. Coincidentally, the captured shipments had consisted of better-quality gasoline made by companies other than Sansei.

❖

Ceil seemed surprised to see him, he thought, as well she might at her scabrous hovel of a Goutte d'Or apartment.

"I saw the news of the bombings. They seem to have the effect you desired," she said, recovering from her surprise. She invited Robert in for tea.

He was here to enjoy himself, and that's what he would do. "Let's talk of the next steps we should take."

"Would you like to include Guy and some of the others? Shall I call them?"

"No. Let us, how do you call it? Brainstorm." He leaned closer to her, smelled her just-washed hair.

When the ringing of the telephone interrupted them again a few hours later, he heard it from the shelter of Ceil's warm, narrow bed.

He had kept all his anxiety at bay, and their lovemaking had been slow, serious, and fulfilling.

The last sound he heard before falling asleep was of Ceil unplugging her telephone.

37.

Sunday afternoon, Houston

t's me," Preston called to her from outside the locked door of their office.

Good. After she let him in, he found a perch at the edge of the desk and pointed at the numbers on Lynn's screen. "The margins are still negative, aren't they? This refinery's cratering, not to put too fine a point on it."

"I wish you were wrong." Lynn told him what she surmised about the crude oil feedstock, relying on evidence Jean-Marie had contributed.

"So you've got it down to eight crudes, none of them Oriente. And the financials confirm what we see operationally," Preston said.

"The rogue crude explains the operations problem. The rogue crude ties to everything else. Farrell is following orders. He didn't mastermind the leak, switch Armando's oxygen, or murder Jean-Marie by himself. So who tells him what to do?"

"Why didn't Dwayne and Adric figure out the crude?"

"Yes, they're on-site all the time. They see the bumpy operations. Do they have something to hide?"

"Dwayne is preoccupied with his wife's cancer. And running the refinery well is important to him. He and Jean-Marie seemed to have had a good working relationship, despite their mutual complaints. But I can't rule him out." Preston frowned. "What about everyone else?"

"There's Adric. Like Dwayne, I don't understand what his incentive would be, but I can't eliminate him either." Lynn counted.

"Reese is an old buddy of yours, but could he be directing Farrell?"

Lynn was surprised. "I don't see why."

"Your relationship could be blinding you." Preston hunched over further.

"A man I've known for twenty years? I've gone to his grandchildren's christenings!"

"Exactly," Preston said, with a sharp glance at her. "But I have to say he isn't acting differently than usual."

"Leaving Jay and Riley."

"Riley's a jerk, but I don't see his motivation, nor Jay's," Preston said.

You can't announce it yet but Riley won't have his job long. He must sense that. He's the one with the least to lose.

Dwayne appeared in the doorway, rumpled as always. "I heard your voices," he said.

Lynn hoped he hadn't heard their discussion of him. *Wish his smoky breath had told you he was nearby like it usually does.*

"We're talking about the refinery. Who killed Jean-Marie?" In case Dwayne was their man, she wouldn't tell him about the tape that showed Farrell's complicity.

"What if it's Greenpeace?" Dwayne said. "Or punks vandalizing things. Maybe Jean-Marie caught them at it."

"Occam's razor," Lynn said.

"What?" He appeared annoyed.

"A fancy term for keeping it simple," said Preston.

"You could at least tell me when you're insulting me," Dwayne whined.

"It means the simplest explanation that fits the facts is better than a more complicated one," Lynn said. Dwayne's sudden appearance jolted her as much as Preston's had. She remembered the telephone death threat. *"Bitches who screw around in refineries don't last long. Especially when they trust the wrong people to help them. And they die such interesting deaths."*

"How can you talk like a pointy-head when we got six dead bodies and we're not sure who's next? Hey, you're looking a little white. You feel okay?"

"I'm fine." She pressed her foot down to forestall the cramp she felt starting. "And rushing to a conclusion doesn't make it the right one."

Dwayne glanced at the note he was holding. "Whoa, doggies! The control center says Jean-Marie came through at five after eight."

"A security guard put out the alarm at eleven thirty when she didn't check back through," Lynn said. *Easy. Not too much info to Dwayne yet.* "But not Farrell. He said he was off-shift. We have other reasons to suspect him."

"So who's holding Jean-Marie's marker?" Preston broke in, evidently not yet trusting Dwayne.

Dwayne balled one hand into a big fist. "She took care of her brother. Bailed him out a few times. She hasn't—hadn't—seen either of her exes for years. Can't think of anyone."

"This is frustrating," Preston said. "Like one of those dreams where the harder you squint, the harder it is to see."

Finally Dwayne offered, "Weather's ugly as a buck-toothed buzzard. I'm not staying. Lynn, what are plans at the Four Seasons?"

"For the tropical storm?" she asked. "Ride it out, I think."

"Maybe you could stay in Jay's new house," Preston said. "It's big. Southampton neighborhood."

"Where does he get the money?" Lynn asked.

"Good question," Dwayne said. "I don't think the rumor's true that he inherited nothin' when the old man died."

"Bobby Gans?" Preston stood.

"Yeah. Even though Bobby never forgave Jay for flunking out of Texas A&M."

"Tell me about this." Lynn drew big squares on a piece of graph paper. "I thought he had an engineering degree." *How will you explain to the board that one of your supply vice presidents, responsible for purchasing hundreds of millions of dollars of crude oil, is untrained for the job?*

"Nah. He never got a degree there or anywhere. He started premed, flunked organic chemistry, then just lived at the frat house and drank beer."

"Sounds good to me," she quipped to hide her dismay over Jay's fabrications.

"A&M finally threw him out. All the old man's millions didn't make any difference."

After Dwayne left, Preston said, "I need to go, too. Will you be okay alone?"

"I'll be here only a few minutes longer. Security's around."

"Security, yeah. Have they picked up Isos yet, one of their own?" Preston asked sarcastically.

She called the security office and got a gruff, but familiar voice, one of the guards she'd seen the morning Jean-Marie's body was discovered. "No, ma'm. We haven't seen Isos but we'll arrest him if he shows up. You call us if you need us."

She nodded at Preston.

He said, "Telephone me when you get back to your hotel so I know you're safe." He left and she locked the door.

Lynn stared at the screen in front of her. She left another message for HPD Officer Stinson about Farrell Isos. She called Ceil. Again no answer.

As she prepared to leave, the telephone rang.

"Lynn, Brian Tulley. I didn't expect to reach you, but I'm glad I did."

"Why?"

"We couriered the report to the Four Seasons. I got concerned when I didn't hear from you. It has some diagrams that are hard to scan and e-mail, so I'll fax another copy to you now. What's the number of the nearest machine?"

"There's one at Shelby's desk, near the conference room."

After she gave him the number, Lynn moved down the hall with her laptop and the precious videotape into the conference room, so she could hear the fax machine when it cranked up. She dialed the control center while she waited. Adric answered. *Your luck is holding.* "Do you have anyone on shift tonight who was there the night before last?

"The night Jean-Marie was killed. Skyler Knowles."

Is Skyler part of this? Adric? "Let me talk to him."

After a moment the receiver switched hands.

"Skyler, did you see Jean-Marie when she came out to your area Friday night? She checked in through your control center."

"No. I must have been out on the unit. But I called her before she came out."

"You did?"

"Yes. She told me she'd see me shortly. She was meeting with someone in her office. Then she said she'd come to the control center so we could look further at the hydrogen sulfide alarm."

"But you never saw her."

"Right."

After she hung up, Lynn's foot cramped and she jumped up to stretch it. *Wish he'd told you sooner. Why didn't he?* The sky outside the conference room window was darkening from both the oncoming sunset and the growing storm. The whole afternoon, time she didn't have, had disappeared. *Forget your deadline with Mike, your career. This place will never make it.*

Jay. Jay got no family inheritance yet he drove an expensive car and parked where a boil over could ruin it. He claimed a Texas A&M engineering degree Dwayne said he didn't have. *Connect the damn dots!* Now that she thought about it, he hadn't used any of Jean-Marie's magic engineering passwords—efficiency, consistency, or feasibility. *A crazy basis for suspicion.*

She wished Preston had stayed; he was always a good sounding board. *But it's better if he takes a break from this. He'll be fresher tomorrow.*

She heard the fax machine grinding at Shelby's desk and walked out to see what Brian had sent.

In addition to his fax, she found one from an oil brokerage company named Latin American Crude Traders, the company that supplied Oriente. Except it wasn't Oriente. The fax was short: "Expect 400K barrels of Heavy Lag in 150K shipments at agreed-upon Oriente market less $3.00/bbl."

Whose message? Heavy Lag?

She remembered her list of crudes matching the distillation of whatever TriCoast had in tank S4 and bounded the ten steps through the door to the conference room where her laptop sat on the table.

One of the eight crudes on her short list was Venezuelan Lagunillas Heavy. *Heavy Lag.*

Venezuela produces considerable Lagunillas oil, up to a couple of hundred thousand barrels a day. Lynn reread the assay. *Lagunillas contains fifty percent more resid, twice the sulfur, and five times the vanadium of Oriente. That's it!* Similar to the Mexican Maya crude, everything about it required more treating and refining. If Centennial was running Lagunillas Heavy instead of Oriente, all the settings, the catalysts, the temperatures, pressures—everything was wrong.

She raced through more calculations. *Even if you are the EVP you have to be sure what you're dealing with before you single-handedly order full-scale modifications in the operation of a 150,000 barrel-a-day refinery.*

Each degree difference in gravity—there were about twelve between Oriente and Lagunillas Heavy—was worth, jeez, how much? Fifty cents? Eighty?

Josh Rosen might know, she thought. She looked up his cell number.

He picked up on the fourth ring. "Lynn, what's going on?"

"Sorry to call on the weekend. One fast question. What's the gravity differential now?"

"Crude prices have been high since we found out the IEA inventory numbers were wrong. Refining capacity is tight—I don't have to tell you that—so gravity's worth about a dollar a degree. With Nigeria and some of the Saudi crude off-line, my stats show much more heavy crude coming into Houston from Venezuela."

The heavy crude exports Ceil talked about.

"Why do you want to know?"

"Fitting a puzzle together and a few of the pieces don't snap right in. More later. Thanks."

At a dollar a degree per barrel that multiplied to twelve dollars a barrel. So even if Jay acquired Lagunillas at three dollars a barrel less than the price of Oriente, the refinery was still paying nine dollars a barrel too much for the crude it received. Assuming Latin American Crude Traders was buying Lagunillas Heavy at the market price—a price twelve dollars a barrel lower than Oriente—and assuming Centennial was paying three dollars a barrel less than Oriente, that left a considerable sum of money on the table.

Jay's most recent deal was four hundred thousand barrels. $3.6 million. And he'd completed five or six other deals recently.

TriCoast had overpaid millions of dollars for the Lagunillas-instead-of-Oriente crude just in the last few months. Jay and Latin American Crude Traders likely split the proceeds. *A partial replacement for the lack of inheritance from Bobby. Indeed, the operational problems started showing up after Bobby Gans' death.*

That explained the refinery's financial squeeze. TriCoast's bad yields resulted from the poorer-quality crude. Farrell must be on Jay's payroll.

So why the sabotage with the deliberate H_2S leak? Why shut down the sure income stream from his crude oil switch?

Lynn recalled what LaShawna told her husband about seeing someone who looked Hispanic in the utilities area. Her husband thought it was Armando. Jay wasn't Hispanic, but his golf-tanned skin and black hair might make him appear so from a distance. What was he doing in utilities?

Jean-Marie must have asked Jay about the confirmation assays. *But then what happened? Jay killed Jean-Marie? Armando, too? With Farrell's help?*

Damn, you're alone. She relocked the conference door and closed the blinds over the glass curtain wall.

Slouching uneasily in her chair, she realized there was little time to decide what to do next. Home phone numbers for Preston and Reese, and her cell phone, were down the hall in her temporary office. *An ocean when you don't know where Jay is.* Her temporary office door wasn't secure, anyway. Then she heard an unmistakable clanking of someone outside the conference room trying keys in the locked door.

38.

Sunday night, Houston

Goddamn Dayton bitch." It was Jay Gans' voice outside the conference room, no longer warm or reassuring.

Lynn grabbed the phone and punched the refinery's emergency number.

"Security," said a thin, reedy voice. "Isos."

What the hell's he doing here? How'd he get to his post without being arrested? What happened to the other guard? This is worse and worse. She hung up the phone without speaking.

Another key rattled in the lock. Her calf seized with a lightning-fast cramp and she sprang to her feet to walk it out.

The more people you alert, the better chance you have to get help. Your computer.

She e-mailed an SOS to the plant-wide distribution, hoping someone might be near a screen, even at this late hour on a Sunday.

The lock clicked open, and Jay entered, the dark-haired, sun-lined, no-sweat man. A gopher-faced grin never left his mouth, but never reached his eyes. He looked crazy, as if no amount of reasoning, or pleading, would deter him from his purpose.

"Lynn, what are you doing here so late? Now that you've bought the refinery, I'll give you the real tour of it." He laughed at his own joke.

"Jay, just the person I was thinking about." *Weak.*

"That sweet bullshit might work on flyboy Reese or your boss Emerson, but I'm not a fool like they are," he sneered.

He grabbed her right arm.

She yanked it away and backed up.

He lunged, grabbed her arm again and twisted it behind her back, then moved around behind her.

"Did you really expect I would give up my game? You and Jean-Marie are alike. You think you're tough. You're overeducated saps."

"What happened to Jean-Marie? Did you kill her?"

Lynn couldn't see him behind her back, but she heard the satisfaction, and insanity, in his voice. "Farrell said she was leaving the refinery without checking out."

"After you lured her to the pretreater? It took two people, Jay, to blindfold her, gag her, shoot her, and get her inside that cooling tower."

"Think so? Maybe." He saw the original of the security videotape Preston had returned and scooped it up. "Farrell won't be glad I got this back but it keeps him in line."

"You had the videotape all the time?"

He nodded. "Never hurts to have a little something to keep the boy loyal. That New Orleans bitch stole it from my office."

As appalling as the news about Jay's blackmail of Farrell was the change in the way he talked about Jean-Marie. No more joviality. *You'd never know they worked together for years. Is he on meth?*

"Jay, we've made copies."

"That's a lie. You're desperate to finger a suspect, save your job, save yourself. And if you're not lying, we'll get the copies back. Simple." Then he slammed her shoulder. "Let's go."

"I'm not going."

His gun came out of nowhere. She felt the cold metal behind her right ear, snagging her hair. *Good God!*

"I thought you and Farrell liked hydrogen sulfide and hydrogen fluoride. You've changed methods." She struggled to overcome her shock.

"It works better, doesn't it? Acids and gases aren't as specific as bullets. Now move. Down the stairs to the truck." His tone was nastier. With a chill, she heard an exact match to the low snarl of the threats left on her voice mail.

"You are the one who called and threatened me."

"You should have listened then." He pushed her in front of him. "The hall, to the side exit. It's too bad refineries are such dangerous places for women."

The truck. What if? Did he mean a run-down red one? The one time you need one of those suckers to fail while you're driving, will it?

He opened the passenger side of a red truck, shoved her in and said, "Slide over and drive. The keys are in the ignition." He shifted the gun down to her ribs.

Her heart lifted at seeing the red truck, then fell when she saw its number. He'd chosen a reliable one. She started it. "What about the hydrogen sulfide alarm? What about the four operators?"

His gopher grin returned. "Isos deprogrammed the alarm. Easy for him to do from a security console. The operators? Well, my timing was off. I didn't think the H_2S would build up that fast."

You sure as shit didn't, you soulless bastard.

"Armando Garza?"

"He saw something he shouldn't have."

Her brain buzzed. "*You* killed Armando!"

"If too many people know a secret, it's not a secret."

"What was the secret?"

"You figured it out. Part of it."

"How long have you been buying Lagunillas instead of Oriente?"

"So you haven't gone soft in that big Dallas office. We're heading to your favorite place, the oil storage tanks. Shut up and drive."

A refinery is never completely deserted. But there are places that seem to absorb all sounds. *Jay's picked the most soundproof place. Like he did with Jean-Marie.* Although Centennial's gasoline and diesel tank farm was near LaPorte Freeway, its crude oil storage tanks were near the Ship Channel, and far away from everything else. Worse, the space around the tanks was wide open. *But it's near sundown and the storm clouds reduce the light even more.*

When they got to the guardhouse, it was Farrell Isos who opened the window. Lynn couldn't see what, or more likely who else, might be concealed behind the guardhouse partition.

"You're not supposed to be here," Lynn said, choking. "Alex Stinson knows about you. You're supposed to be held for questioning."

"Alex did call me. I convinced him the stress of the job had gotten to you, as it certainly seems to have done."

Her blood raced. Her watch blinked eight fifteen. Nowhere near a shift change, so they were unlikely to see anyone.

The gun bit her ribs as Jay leaned over to talk to Farrell. His juniper-soap scent intensified. "Don't worry about her. We're going to the crude storage tanks. It'll be easier to dispose of the body," Jay told Farrell.

"You're kidding, right?" Lynn tried to keep her voice from sounding as scared as she felt.

"I'm sure Preston would be willing to lay good odds," Farrell said.

"So that's why you held Preston up the day we ran our first distillations in the lab. You made those bets with him to give Jay time to plug the fan intakes."

"The cornerstone of our safety process is the buddy system," Farrell sneered.

"You stay here and start the second part in about fifteen minutes," Jay said.

"So, did you ever hear from your friends in HPD about fingerprints on the valve?" Lynn asked Farrell.

"No fingerprints," he said. One freckled arm tapped impatiently on the side of the booth.

"Or no friends." She saw his hand tighten, drop toward his belt.

Your joke won't be so funny when he shoots you, or does whatever he's planning with that hand.

"Payday's next Friday," Jay said.

Regular plant payroll was scheduled in another two weeks. *So Jay is paying off Farrell. So what, Sherlock?*

Farrell leaned against the booth. "Glad you found someone to take care of you after your call from the conference room a few minutes ago, Ms. Dayton. And I saw your e-mail. I sent a follow-up message telling everyone you were fine," he said languidly.

Shit.

Despite the gathering gloom, she could see Jay's scowl.

"Farrell, what happened to Jean-Marie?" she asked, afraid to hear his answer.

"I shoot at trespassers who don't identify themselves," he answered benignly.

Jay snorted.

"See you later, Jay," Farrell said with finality and closed his guardhouse window.

The two of them killed Jean-Marie. Two to one. This time Farrell is staying behind for some "second part" you may not live to see. So you and Jay are one to one. That doesn't take care of his gun, though.

Lynn fought her panic and drove as slowly as she dared. *If Jay kills you, who'll take care of Dad? And Ceil? How can you escape? Surely Jay has an ego.* "What's the second part?"

"Don't worry about it. Your lungs will be full of that crude oil you love so much by then."

She couldn't keep from swallowing. *Think!* "Were you the source for the *Gulf Coast Herald?*"

"A few telephone calls."

"And you were the one in the lab the other afternoon while Farrell delayed us?"

"Indeed."

He didn't want Centennial, only money. He knew nothing about what he was doing. The substitution of Lagunillas for Oriente was wrecking the refinery. It would crash any moment. His gun nicked her ribs. Despite the humidity, she felt cold. *You were right. Jean-Marie's killer isn't human any more.*

A thought slid away. *Grab it!* "What did Armando see, Jay?"

"He had no business in the utilities area."

The yellow hard hat in the utilities area. *That's what Armando remembered in the hospital as unusual. Why was Armando's seeing Jay there so important that Jay murdered him? And LaShawna saw him there, too.* "What were you doing in the utilities area, Jay?"

"My French partner and I found another way to make money from this pissant refinery . . . keep driving."

When they passed through the gate into the crude storage area, he directed her toward the back, close by the Ship Channel.

"Who's your French partner?"

He looked at her, appraising. *Figures it won't hurt to tell someone he expects to kill.*

"He calls me the Rabbit. I think of him as the Robber. You wouldn't know him. Robert Guillard."

"Robert?" She choked and her shock turned to horror. *Robert Guillard? So that's why he's interested in Ceil, and you. But if Jay works for him, and Jay's about to kill you, that means Ceil's in danger too.* Another chill went through her. *He's telling you all this because he really will kill you.* Her foot came off the accelerator.

The car's slowing prompted him. "Turn off the ignition. Give me the keys. Get out."

When he pushed her out of the truck, she saw a ten-inch pipe wrench glinting in the gravel under mercury vapor lights that had started to come on. A small refinery was sometimes called "pots and pans." A phrase from a game echoed in her mind. "With the wrench, in the kitchen."

In one motion, she dropped down, grabbed the wrench, used it to hit Jay's gun hand, and started running, hanging onto the wrench.

She heard his cursing. Then nothing.

The time she'd spent memorizing the refinery's layout paid off. So did the running and the upper body workouts. She moved quickly through a pipe alley toward the steam line for tanks S4 and S2. Then she moved down the line until she found a valve. It was locked. She moved farther down and found another valve. *No lock yet, despite our instructions. Thank God.*

She adjusted the wrench and tried to open the valve in the dark. Stuck. She wrestled with it until it turned.

Suddenly Jay materialized across the steam line from her, his gun aimed at her chest.

"You had your chance to escape. You blew it." He grinned a buck-toothed grin she could barely see in the growing gloom. *Not gopher. Rabbit.*

She ducked, gave the valve a final twist and slid to the ground as far from the valve as she could. Superheated, high-pressure steam exploded through the open valve. Jay screamed when the steam found its mark.

She jumped up and ran toward the tank-farm exit.

Then her arm was yanked back, almost out of its socket, and the gun nestled under her left ear.

"Up the stairs. Drop the wrench this time."

Jay waited until he heard the clunk of the wrench. He forced her around and around, up dizzying, saw-tooth metal stairs on the side of the big tank. They climbed twenty feet up, then thirty feet. From behind, his arm jerked hers like a spastic cockroach. A sulfurous smell lingered everywhere.

He's going to shoot you at the top and dump you into the tank, just like he told Farrell. She felt too numb to do anything but follow his directions. Giant rotors swirled slowly at the bottom of the tank, fifty feet below.

The platform at the top was about six feet above the top of the tank. The floating "roof," which floated on the oil in the tank, could be from ten to thirty feet below the top of the tank.

His breathing.

Ten steps from the top Jay panted like a dog after a run. He sounded surprisingly winded. *Dayton, do something or you're dead meat.* She focused on the rhythm of the climb.

One, two. Three steps from the top she screamed, half turned, and rammed her elbow into his chest. She slammed her other arm down on his gun hand.

He stumbled only for an instant, but dropped the gun. She kicked it off the stairs and pulled away. The gun clattered when it hit the ground fifty feet below.

"Stupid move, baby."

Damn! You can't get past him. Jay blocked the stairs below her. If she jumped over the side, she'd hang up on the saw-tooth stairs on the way down or die after she hit the ground.

But you could push him over.

She backed up the stairs to the top landing, facing him. A cramp seized her leg and she cried out.

In that instant, he was much stronger and faster than she expected. He lunged, trying to grabbing her. The Rabbity teeth bared. "Know-it-all bitch. You're dead."

His soft street shoes caught on the metal grill of the narrow catwalk, giving her barely enough time to step aside as he fell toward her.

He caught himself.

She looked inside the tank. The floating roof bobbed and scraped against the walls about twenty-five feet below.

Jay pushed her down the slippery stairs inside the tank, and she felt rust crumbling under her fingers.

Then he lunged again.

She shrank flat against the tank wall and slammed her elbow up into his chin.

He groaned, lost his balance, and fell back off the catwalk and into the tank. He thumped onto its metal floating roof, fifteen feet below where she stood.

The roof dipped. Metal roof screeched on metal wall.

He cursed, picked himself up. The floating roof swayed some more.

If Jay studied engineering, as he claimed, he understands applied force, acid chemistry, and metal fatigue. The acid from the heavy crude had likely eaten the metal of the floating roof into the thinnest of surfaces. *If he does know, he'll move only inches at a time. But Dwayne says he doesn't.*

"Don't move too fast!" she shouted.

"You're still scared of me? Good girl!" Jay scrambled heavily toward the ladder on the inside of the tank wall.

He screamed when the metal floating roof, corroded indeed by the months of too-sour crude and resulting sulfuric acid—for which he was responsible—began cracking.

He tried to grab a side, but like thin ice, the force of his struggle widened the cracks. She watched in horror as he fell through.

She heard the rotors continuing to turn. He was being swept down and away from the hole in the roof.

Jay Gans would never find the airhole, the place he'd fallen through, again. Not even his juniper-soap smell remained.

She leaned against the rusting handrail to catch her breath. Tears wet her cheeks. Shock, anger, and sorrow mixed crazily together as she climbed the inside stairs to the top of the tank.

A flicker of light in the distance pricked her numbed senses. She saw its source. It was in the same location where LaShawna had seen the stranger and Armando had seen the person with the yellow hard hat. Suddenly she knew the second part of Jay's plan for Centennial, and for every other Ship Channel refinery.

39.

Sunday night, Houston

Lynn heard cursing and the clank of a metal bicycle frame shaking as it hit the speed bumps. From the top of the stairs, she looked down fifty feet over the side of the giant 150,000-barrel S4 crude oil tank. *Adric, thank God!* Preston, Reese, Tyree, and Dwayne followed behind in Reese's truck. *Someone saw your message. And Farrell's not with them.*

She raced down the sawtooth metal stairs. When she was close enough for them to hear, she shouted, "There's a fire at utilities! Near the turbogenerators! Reese, get some men and equipment before it spreads. Preston, call the fire department, Tyree, call the refinery volunteer unit. Dwayne, come with me and make sure everyone's safe! Adric, turn off the heat and the rotors for S4 here. Cut any flows into or out of the tank! Jay's in there."

"Oh Christ!" Dwayne said. "You okay?"

"Yeah."

After quick calls on cell phones, responses came back.

"Paramedics and fire crews on the way," Preston reported.

"I radioed the control center to shut down and isolate the tank," Adric shouted. "I need to get back there to supervise the process, make sure we do it right."

"Preston and I will stay here to meet the crews, tell them about Jay," Tyree said.

"Backup operators are on the way," Reese told Lynn. They'll meet us at utilities. I'll go with you and Dwayne."

A fire in the utilities area would interrupt the power supply. That would kill all the pumps, leading to loss of cooling water and electrical energy, catapulting into loss of steam and air pressure to the refinery. Without cooling water, pressures in the reactors would build immediately. If even one or two valves failed, fires and explosions could spread throughout the refinery. *Jay and Farrell tried a couple of tricks that didn't work, so they go for the juice. Same as the other sabotage on the Channel. Robert Guillard is Jay's partner. As you suspected, their plan is bigger than bringing down just Centennial.*

Lynn jumped into Reese's truck with Dwayne, and they plowed along the half mile of asphalt roads to the boxy, white utilities center. A slight figure raced out the door. Lynn didn't need to look twice. "It's Farrell! Get him!"

Dwayne jumped out and moved faster than she could have hoped, low and fast like a T-Rex charging prey. He leapt onto Farrell and knocked him down. They struggled on the road, a mass of arms and legs. Although Dwayne was twice Farrell's weight Farrell kept squirming away. Finally the big man landed squarely on Farrell's back. He pinned the guard's arms and snatched his gun.

"Reese, call HPD!" Lynn yelled. "Then help Dwayne hold Farrell."

Preston and Adric hurried over, panting from their run from the storage tanks. Just inside the utilities building, Lynn could see a larger orange glow, the same one she'd seen from the top of the storage tank. She despaired. *The refinery is just big kegs of raw fuel, we're smack in the middle of it, and Farrell tossed in the match.* "We can't wait! Adric, where are the fire extinguishers?"

Adric, Lynn, and Preston burst through the doors of the utility building and Adric pointed out the red extinguishers. One was mounted on a board and two were in corners of the room. "They're heavy. The corner ones weigh about seventy pounds, the one on the wall is forty."

Lynn knelt and pulled a red cylinder from a corner. *Seventy pounds, at least.*

"They're all carbon dioxide, so we have to be within eight feet of the fire," Adric told them.

She spotted the blaze fifteen feet away at turbogenerator 2, zipping toward all three control boxes on threads of gasoline.

"There!"

"P-A-S-S," Preston yelled. "Pull, aim, squeeze, and sweep!"

They ripped the pins from the tops of their extinguishers. As if united by one thought, they moved forward and aimed at the three different lines of fire, spraying the popping waves of orange with compressed carbon dioxide.

Lynn's hands felt cold. She glanced down at them. Ice had formed around the nozzle of her extinguisher.

They swept back and forth, reaching the fire feed, a slower-burning pool of lubricant. Adric backed up, coughing, and Lynn felt a huge presence at her elbow.

"Go. We'll finish."

Lynn looked around to see firefighters bigger than football linebackers and similarly bulked up, with solid helmets, massive coats, enormous boots. Next to their gear she had the sensation of wearing little more than a cocktail dress.

Adric was stumbling. Lynn and Preston put their shoulders under his arms and helped him outside the cement-block utilities building. The red and blue fire engine lights swirled. Tyree had joined the group and relieved Dwayne, keeping a wrestler's hold on Farrell while Alex Stinson of HPD handcuffed him.

"Wait!" she said.

Tyree turned and waved his massive hand, the Howard University ring flashing gold and orange under the moving lights.

"Procedure is we take him in, read him his rights before questioning him." Tyree spoke before she could. "I'll call you as soon as I can."

"The original videotape. It's in the truck by S4. Jay took it from me, and he left it there. Preston made copies, but you'll still need it." She moved closer to him and dropped her voice. "And you need to get the word out to everyone on the Channel to guard their electrical equipment. Jay's pattern of sabotage." *But you can't tell Tyree about Robert since your sister's been dragged in. You have to get to her first.*

"We'll do that now," Tyree said. He climbed into the back seat of the police cruiser Alex Stinson was driving, his eyes on Farrell Isos. They sped off toward the tank farm.

Lynn gathered her coworkers. "Let's go to S4, too."

They tumbled into trucks and arrived at a scene very different from the one they'd left. The paramedics had set up searchlights and were slowly sweeping the tank. As Lynn and the others arrived, they saw Tyree ahead of them, returning to the police cruiser holding the videotape aloft and pumping his other hand. He bent and leaned into the window nearest Farrell. They could all hear his single word.

"Gotcha!"

Tyree climbed into the cruiser next to the slight security guard, slammed the door, and Alex drove off again.

The huge, dark storage tanks loomed between them and the Ship Channel. Except one. Searchlights trained on S4 from several directions. *If Jay'd had his way, it would be you in there instead of him.*

"Dwayne and I got calls from Adric at the crude unit, then from Preston at home," Reese said. "Both saw your emergency SOS."

"You never called from the Four Seasons, so I worried. I was home, online, when I saw your message," Preston said, breathing shallowly.

"High-stakes poker," Dwayne muttered.

Preston moved closer to Lynn, not responding.

Must be true. But he saved you because of it.

"After your e-mail SOS came through, Farrell sent one saying you were fine," Preston said. Lights from the fire department rescue-squad truck swirled behind him, backlighting him red, then white, then red again.

"You didn't believe Farrell," Lynn said. She peeled her smoky, sweat-soaked shirt a few inches off her shoulder and flapped it. *Pointless. Air's so humid your shirt will never dry.*

"No," Preston said. "I sent an e-mail to everyone in the plant except Farrell telling them this was an emergency and to find you. I called Dwayne and Reese, then drove here, running every red light. They met me at the guard's shack. The real guard on duty had been knocked out. We called an ambulance for him."

"Farrell wasn't there? He was when I drove through. Jay had a gun on me. They had a friendly little chat about how convenient it would be to dump my body in the tank."

Preston shook his head. "That's why we still have our cell phones. No one to take them. We started driving around searching for you. Thank God we found you, although you took care of yourself."

"I couldn't have kept Farrell from blowing down the refinery by myself," Lynn said.

Adric joined them and passed out bottles of water. "We all need these." Then he added his version. "When I saw the leak on our monitors in the two-hundred-pound steam line to the tanks, I headed outside. Then I heard a scream. That must have been Jay."

"Jay, or his body, is in S4." Lynn squeezed her eyes shut for a moment and took a long drink of the cold water. "So is the crude he was lying to us about. We don't have Oriente. We've got Lagunillas Heavy with five times the vanadium and twice the sulfur."

"Holy shit!" Dwayne yelped, an operations man to the core.

Adric said, "I've cut the flow out from S4, so there's no more Lagunillas entering the system, but . . ."

"Right, in about ninety seconds we go back to the office and reprogram for what's really all through this place," Lynn said. "It's been ruining our equipment and catalyst. It's also been ruining our margins, because Jay got kickbacks from the broker who supplied the Lagunillas. He used Centennial money to overpay for the crude. Then he and the broker must have split the extra. He told us he was buying Oriente, but instead it was lower-quality Lagunillas."

Reese said, "He's been trying to hangar this jet for months! Why?"

"Trying to build his bank account. Jay's not even the engineer he claimed to be. A&M forced him out for cheating." Lynn glanced at Dwayne.

"Jay came apart when his daddy didn't leave him anything," Dwayne concluded.

"Now I have a question for all of you," Lynn continued. "I found a ten-inch pipe wrench out by tank S2 that came in handy. Any idea what it was doing there?"

"That belongs to Skyler," Adric said. "He's been missing it since you two took samples there, said the truck's back gate was open when he returned it. The wrench must have fallen out of the truck bed. Either that or Jean-Marie was watching out for you."

"I like the second explanation."

After two hours in Centennial's conference room grinding through calculations for the heavy crude and calling operators to reset controls on each unit, they were finished.

"Man, I need that smoke right now," Dwayne said.

"I'm calling it a night," Lynn agreed. "You both should, too."

"Adrenaline overload?" Preston asked, a smile softening his eyes.

"Probably just like you feel after a big day at the track," Dwayne barked at him.

"Yes, but usually nobody's dead at the end of it," Preston said. Then he gasped and cut his eyes to Lynn. "Sorry."

Lynn nodded and her heart sank. The firefighters' rescue squad still hadn't found Jay Gans' body.

The humidity broke about eleven thirty. Rain from the outermost edge of tropical storm Adrian smacked her car's windshield. *What a night.*

Cy. She had to tell him. *More ammunition against your job. And how will you answer the question he's really asking?*

You were almost killed tonight. She pushed away the thought that if she could take a chance like that, she could easily take a chance again on marriage. *And what about his kids?*

She kept driving, nearing the warehouse district at the downtown end of the Houston Ship Channel. Her thoughts returned to all those who had died, even Jay. Then she thought about Cy again. *Stop being so responsible. You hide your feelings at work so well you don't know what you really feel anymore. Be honest. You love him.*

The rain splashed harder now, wind gusts eddying around the car as she pulled through the gate into the hotel garage. She switched off the windshield wipers and relished the quiet, then found a parking place and turned off the car. Shock hit her. Jay and Farrell had wanted her dead. *Tried to kill you. Killed Jean-Marie, Armando, and so many others.* She wrapped her arms around the steering wheel, holding it tight while she shook with sobs.

❖

Back in her room at midnight, she saw the message light blinking.

Cy's recorded voice was tinny. He had called at seven, about the time Jay walked into the conference room.

"Call me as soon as you get this message. Um. Whenever that is. I'm sorry about our last conversation. We'll sit and talk when you come back to Dallas. But call me now. Please."

She took several deep breaths, wiped her eyes, and dialed the familiar number. Cy reacted instantly when she told him about Jay and the fire. "Good Lord, Lynn, that's horrible! Are you okay? Of course you're not! I'm flying to Houston right now!"

If she started really crying she wouldn't stop. "No, don't." She laughed through tears. "Even I appreciate how difficult it is to find a babysitter at midnight. I want to see you, but don't fly down. I'll finish here tomorrow morning and fly to Dallas in the afternoon. And Cy . . ." She took a deep breath. *Okay. Here goes. Tear open the scar.* "Let's give our relationship more of a try. Can we? Should we get serious? Set a date?"

"Engaged? Yes, of course! Are you sure?" He sounded awake and happy. "Good. I mean, yes."

"I love you so much, Cy."

"And I love you, Lynn."

40.

Late Sunday night–Monday, Houston and Paris

Sleep would feel good. Unbelievably good.

The air conditioning roared. The hotel room was freezing. Lynn longed to flop on the bed, climbing under sheets and blankets. Instead, she paced the small room. Although it was only 6:00 a.m. in Paris, she called Ceil. No answer.

Small bombs had been set in Europe by a French pro-development group. *The one Ceil mentioned. Robert's.* Jay Gans said Robert Guillard was his partner in taking down Centennial. *Probably all the Ship Channel sabotage was linked through Jay to Robert. Robert, to whom Ceil is so attracted. Robert, who brought her to Paris and asked Vandervoost about you. Whose name, in its French pronunciation, sounds like Jay's name for him, "robber."*

Jay made several million dollars from his crude oil substitution scheme. Robert must have offered so much more that he persuaded Jay to give up the steady income to instead shut down Centennial and the other refineries. *What's Ceil's part? Does she understand what Robert's doing? Damn it, is she involved in sabotaging your refineries and killing your people?*

Her telephone rang, but it wasn't Ceil.

"Lynn, Tyree. I'm still at HPD with Alex Stinson. They found Jay's body."

She shivered, surprised she felt bad about the death of someone who had tried to kill her.

Tyree interrupted her thoughts. "Jay didn't have fingerprints on file, but since they had the body, they got 'em. He matched to a couple of partials on the knife you turned in, the one used to cut the block of wax."

"So that was him. Did you also tell Alex about having all the Ship Channel plants keep extra watch on their electrical equipment?"

"Yeah. In the meantime, Alex has been talking to Farrell Isos. Or listening to him. He won't tell me what Farrell is saying, but says the man's attitude has done a one-eighty. Alex has been pissed at you, at everyone at TriCoast, because Farrell was feeding him lies and antagonizing him to slow down his investigation. Now Farrell's a changed man. And he's saying there's still danger. Alex wants to talk to you. Listen, Lynn, if you talk to him, I may have trouble using you and him as witnesses against Farrell. I'd like to nail the numbnuts. Testimony from both of you could be crucial, but Alex insists on talking to you. I have to ask if you want to talk to him, but I want you to say no."

"Tyree, the lives of my people and others on the Channel are at risk. If Farrell can help us keep them alive, that's my first priority."

"I still think it's a bad idea."

Lynn heard a door slam.

A new voice on the phone. "Lynn, Stinson. I'll wait until Tyree is out of earshot. . . . First, congratulations on your quick thinking. Those goons have been a two-man crime wave. They obviously didn't expect you to fight. And now I understand why Isos was such an SOB every time he talked to me. Okay. I'll set up the background quick. Farrell knew about Jay's kickback from a Latin American Crude Trading broker. It's been going on since Jay's dad cut him out of his will, Farrell said."

"Can you find the broker?"

"Already checked. He hasn't been seen since receiving the most recent payment from Jay." Stinson groaned, sounding as exhausted as she felt. "There's more. According to Farrell, Jay was hooked up with a guy named Robert Guillard in—get this—Paris. Guillard has some crazy idea about directing development money to third world countries to build oil refineries."

"Ah . . . is that so?" She stopped herself from telling Stinson she knew about Robert. *You don't want Ceil investigated.* She almost missed what Alex said next.

"But that's not the worst. Farrell said Guillard was paying Jay to sabotage several refineries here."

Yup. But she said, "All those deaths and injuries linked to one man?"

"Sounds extreme, but we confirmed it. Farrell said Guillard was pushing Jay to knock out not only Centennial but other Channel refineries. He, and maybe others, got big bucks if they did it fast."

"Jay was already making money with his crude switches. What did Guillard offer?"

"According to Farrell, Guillard paid Jay $10 million whenever they shut down a refinery."

"Since he had to split with the broker, Jay was probably walking away with only around a few million dollars for each shipment of Lagunillas he substituted for Oriente. Guillard's money was better." Despite her logical response, Lynn felt her dread escalating. *Jesus, who is this man your sister's locked onto?* "From Guillard's standpoint, the H_2S leak at Centennial and the first Meletio tank fire were failures. Then Jay and Farrell, maybe others, decided to slice electricity, which can blow a whole place apart. Guillard must be a wealthy man."

"Yeah. Another wealthy terrorist. I used to think that was a contradiction in terms." Stinson laughed. "I'll start the paperwork to get Jay's bank records subpoenaed tomorrow. But, in the meantime, this is too big for TriCoast security and me. I'll tell the rest of HPD and the other refineries what's up. The feds, too."

You have to tell him. No way around it. "Officer Stinson, could you hold up those calls? For a few days anyway?"

"Why?"

"I have a younger sister, Ceil. She's involved with Robert Guillard."

"You're shittin' me!"

"He lured her to Paris with a job when she really needed it. Let me try to get her away from him."

"I can't wait a couple of days. Hundreds, even thousands, of lives could be at stake right now."

Same as you said to Tyree a few minutes ago before you knew how deeply Ceil was involved. She felt nauseated. *There's nothing remotely moral about trying to save Ceil if you're risking the lives of so many others.* "Please, Officer Stinson."

"At eleven tomorrow morning I'm making the calls."

Twelve hours. Her relief combined with fear at his deadline. "Ironically, I talked to the FBI a few days ago. Special Agent James Cutler. He thought my conspiracy theory was bullshit. Maybe he won't now." She gave Stinson Cutler's number. "Did Farrell say Jay was directing the sabotage? Maybe he's the only contact here. Maybe with him dead nothing more will happen . . ."

"Farrell thought Robert had other American contacts," Stinson said. "I have sisters and brothers too, Lynn. Two of 'em work at Meletio. Fortunately, neither was hurt when it crashed. I'm just starting to feel warm and fuzzy toward you and your TriCoast buddies. Don't blow it. I'm not waiting past eleven in the morning."

As soon as Alex hung up, Lynn tried calling Ceil. Still no answer. She opened her purse, grateful to find her passport still inside from her last trip.

She packed and checked out of the Four Seasons. As the cab drove her to Houston's George Bush Intercontinental Airport, she began calling. None of the long-range TriCoast airplanes were anywhere near Houston. The next commercial flight to Paris was hours away. The stormy weather might delay it even further.

She called the TriCoast hangar again.

One of the pilots found a charter company that could fly her to

Paris now, before the winds and rain got worse. The TriCoast pilot would vouch for her credentials and ability to pay. It would cost Lynn everything she'd saved in the last year, but the charter could leave within an hour. She booked it.

Once aboard the plane, she e-mailed Mike Emerson that she'd resolved Centennial issues, would be gone a few days on family business, and that she'd give him a full update soon.

She left a message on Cy's office voice mail so as not to wake him at home. *Or have him try to dissuade you.* "Cy, Ceil's life is in danger. I'm chartering a plane and flying to Paris to find her. I'll be back as soon as I can. I love you."

Sleep suddenly was far away. She paged through the several dozen e-mails she'd accumulated in the last few days. One from Bart, the early-rising manager of TriCoast's second Ship Channel refinery, jumped out: "We planned for more production from Centennial. Since TriCoast can't meet gasoline and diesel contracts from our own production, I've taken bids from importers. The Sansei consortium just got import approval and its bid is the lowest, tho its gasoline and diesel quality is worst."

Lynn groaned. Bart should have given her a heads-up before taking bids. *Sansei? Same people Vandervoost said had tied up shipping capacity? Is Sansei backing Robert? If their quality is bad, you'll be screwed the first time someone's car gums up.*

Lynn replied: "No on Sansei. Too much customer risk. We need gasoline that meets normal specs, even if price is higher in the short run. Alt 1) time trade; Alt 2) take physical delivery of NYMEX gasoline from Josh Rosen or others."

Lynn confirmed with the copilot that their arrival was several hours away. Her neck muscles cried with exhaustion. She turned off her BlackBerry and computer and moved her luggage aside. The last thing she felt was the rumble of the charter's jet engines.

41.

Monday, Paris

Sun warmth skimmed his eyelids. Robert was startled at the unfamiliar walls. He heard Ceil in the kitchen.

"How did I come here?" he asked when she appeared in the doorway.

"Quite well," she answered, a Madonna-like smile curving her lips.

Robert didn't understand what she meant, and he felt the frown on his forehead.

"American slang," she said. "I'll get croissants at the bakery two doors down."

No. She couldn't. "Don't leave me."

Last night's light had been too dim for what he now saw. Six long slashes scarred her right forearm. "Your arm. What happened?"

Ceil touched the gashes and hesitated. She finally said, "*Pas grand chose.* Nothing much."

He realized his Gabonese operatives must have slashed her. Maybe she struggled more than he'd expected. There was no point in feeling squeamish now, but he didn't want her leaving him. She might be his insurance.

She shrugged and her beautiful, worn face turned serious. "I'll go to work soon. Remember? The job you obtained for me." She took his hand in hers and pulled him from the bed.

His back hurt from sleeping crammed next to her in the narrow bed. He'd forgotten the holiday until now. "Not today. It's Whit Monday. Neither the ministry nor the IEA will be open."

"Whit Monday?" She stepped toward the sink and he followed.

"Yesterday was Whit Sunday, Pentecost. For many it marks the beginning of the Christian Church. Today is a public holiday."

They could stay here a few hours more. Then he would contact Xin Yu and the Rabbit.

❖

The copilot awakened Lynn before landing at Orly, the closer-in airport she'd requested.

"Today is some Northern European holiday. I've never heard of it before," he told her, "but it'll slow you down. They always do."

When she checked voice mail, Reese's message was the first she selected. "The fire department dragged the tank and found Jay's body about 3:00 a.m. Martinez, the medical examiner, has it. The tropical storm really did veer off, so we'll get some flooding, but nothing major. Now that we have the right instructions, the refinery's operating better than it has in months. Severe clear all the way."

For a change, everything at Centennial is fine. Maybe Jay and Farrell didn't do permanent damage. She remembered how Jay's last angry scramble tilted the floating roof. How he'd crashed through the brittle metal he himself had thinned as truly as if he'd poured acid directly on it.

Jay and Farrell were nodes on a network. Is Robert or Sansei its center? Or both?

She left her luggage with the pilots and agreed she would call them to have it delivered once she knew where she was staying. By the terms of the charter, the pilots would wait for her up to three days. She told them her sister would be returning with her.

While in the customs queue she tried to call Ceil at the only two numbers in Paris she had for her sister. No answer at Ceil's apartment. She called the IEA and realized it was closed because of the holiday. *God, you have to find Ceil. What if she's with Robert when the CIA finds him?* They might assume Ceil was an accomplice. Or, Robert might take Ceil hostage.

Can't you get to Ceil's any faster? Where is Harry Potter's floo powder Marika told you about? She took a train from Orly to the Gare du Nord station. In her rush to get on a plane she'd left her maps behind and her laptop was with the pilots. But she'd written down Ceil's address and thought she remembered how to find it.

Lynn walked quickly. She came to a street she recognized but was unsure which way to turn. "*Excusez-moi de vous* . . . ah, disturbing you, ah . . . *déranger, Monsieur, j'ai un problème.*"

The man she stopped looked so serious she thought he hadn't understood. Then he responded in French so rapidly she felt more lost. *Don't cry just because you're running out of time to find your sister and you can't understand this obnoxious jerk.*

"*Par où?* Which way?" She pointed to the handwritten address.

His lips lifted in an exaggerated smirk, but he pointed left.

"*Merci, Monsieur.*"

The man strode away without replying.

In minutes she was knocking on Ceil's door, thinking of all Ceil told her when she'd been here before. *When was that, only four days ago?*

She was unprepared for the handsome man who answered. His jet-black hair contrasted vividly with his light-blue eyes. His first glance at her was one of surprise. His gaze shaded into familiarity, as if he knew her. Then he stepped back and assayed her so completely she felt heat climb her neck into her face. His eyes stripped her.

So this is how "the look" feels when practiced by an expert. "Uh. Um. *Où est* Ceil Dayton?"

❖

No one should be disturbing them, he thought, angry at the woman standing there. Then his anger turned to recognition, and calculation.

The woman he wanted had come to him. She was just as he remembered from New York, just as depicted in the TriCoast annual report. Lynn Dayton. Short, blond hair, but not nearly as well-dressed as he'd expected. What was she doing here? He wasn't ready for her now.

While these thoughts fought for dominance, he directed all his energy into looking her over to properly evaluate her.

"*Non. Attendez.*" He slipped behind the door and began to close it.

He couldn't have predicted what the woman did next. She threw herself against the door as he tried to close it and screamed.

"Ceil! CEIL!"

The pale-eyed bastard has to be Robert.

He began closing the door. Desperate with fatigue, Lynn screamed.

Ceil appeared by the man's side. "Lynn? What are you doing here?"

Thank God. Lynn forced her voice quieter. Otherwise Ceil might withdraw, might even close the door herself. *And why is Robert here so early in the morning?* That must mean Ceil's interest in him had advanced. *If your sister slept with him she won't believe anything you say.* "I've tried to call you several times. Why didn't you answer?"

"I was out. What can be so urgent you would just show up here?"

"That I would charter a plane to get here as quickly as I could?"

Ceil didn't react.

Hold on. No ranting. Jay probably didn't understand French, so Robert must understand English to have communicated with him. "Is this your friend Robert Guillard?"

"Yes."

Robert nodded nearly imperceptibly, his eyes not leaving Lynn's.

Okay. Go for it. With effort, she kept her voice deliberate. "He's responsible for killing several people, maybe dozens. You're not safe with him."

"What could you possibly mean?" Ceil rocked back on her heels, and moved closer to Robert.

"When I asked for you just now, he would have shut the door."

Ceil squared her shoulders. "Killing people? Absurd."

Ceil doesn't know. You have to tell her. Lynn spoke fast. "Robert and the people working for him are sabotaging oil refineries, killing and injuring dozens of people, maybe hundreds if their plans play out. Your friend here," she said, trying but failing to keep the sarcasm out of her voice, "has been ordering people murdered."

Robert took Ceil's elbow and looked calmly at Lynn. And spoke in English. "I am not a killer. You are confused after your long trip. Perhaps you are thinking of someone else. Ceil, if she is your sister, we should invite her to come inside."

"No!" Lynn said. *Inside, away from other people, is dangerous.* "We must walk. Um. Ceil, where can we walk?"

"We haven't eaten yet," Robert said as if he hadn't heard her, except that he spoke English again.

Ceil looked at Lynn like her big sister was crazy but said only, "Let's find a fruit market."

How had this Lynn Dayton learned so much so quickly? He did not expect that from her. His mind raced.

Ceil trusted him. She would flee with him, he was certain. If he attempted to lose Lynn, perhaps in the crowds around Sacré Coeur at Montmartre, Lynn would become more determined to stay with them to protect her sister. Exactly what he wanted. It would later be easy enough to keep both under control by threatening to kill one or the other. All he needed was to get across the border. He would reestablish his communication with Sansei, although he would now have to explain to them Lynn's role in his plans. If the Sansei operatives recognized her, they'd know she was too important to harm. Better. Additional insurance for him.

"Sacré Coeur is nearby," Robert said. "Shall we walk to it?"

"How could you listen to him? He's a charlatan. A murderer!"

Lynn whispered in her sister's right ear. The three of them walked abreast with Ceil in the middle.

Ceil smiled beatifically.

The more insistent you are the less Ceil will listen. Paris was warmer than she'd expected. Her fatigue and her frustration with Ceil increased her temperature. She envied Ceil her sleeveless blouse, although not the six broad gashes it exposed. *The gashes from the rape attack. She should be home with us.* "Your gashes haven't healed. Won't you at least return with me to see Dad? He's not well."

Ceil put her hand in Robert's, the color in her eyes flattening. "It won't change his health whether or not I'm there. I didn't help Mom."

"Yes, you did!"

Despite the crowds, when they turned the corner onto Boulevard Barbès, Robert recognized three of Xin Yu's agents. The two men and the woman walked a few meters behind them, not bothering to conceal themselves. He wondered if they had already been to his Palais Royal apartment. What could he do?

He nudged Ceil and Lynn toward the next open door he saw, a neighborhood bakery. His fear mixed with giddiness. Lynn, his target for so long, had come to him exactly as he had planned!

As they lined up to order, he saw the doll-faced man, the dumpy man, and the woman who'd attacked him with a bat pause and sit at a table outside.

How would he escape with Ceil and Lynn from the trio that waited for him?

Sacré Coeur dominated the view. Lynn could see the gleaming, white, fat-turreted basilica long before they arrived at its great lawn and long hillside of steps. "It looks like it's from another continent. And it's so white!"

"Roman-Byzantine style. Its stone bleaches white as it ages," Ceil answered.

Lynn thought they would never reach the top of the steep hill with its many steps. *Ceil is acting like she's on vacation, instead of walking with a murderer, a terrorist!* "This is worth the climb?"

"Yes. Highest point in Paris," Ceil said. "Sacré Coeur was built where Saint Denis was beheaded for his religious beliefs in the third century."

She saw Robert clutch Ceil's hand so hard her sister's fingers whitened. "Charming." *What will happen if you just pull Ceil away from him?*

Families picnicked, children skated. Noisy radios and clacking roller blades filled the air around them.

"*Ici, mademoiselle,*" a voice said.

Lynn turned to have Ceil translate, but Ceil and Robert weren't there. Terrified, she looked around. There!

Robert was dragging Ceil toward an alley. They were about to disappear into the mass of artists, tourists, chairs, and awnings. She pushed away from the crowd and screamed. "Ceil! CEIL! Don't go with him! Please, for God's sake! Someone stop them!"

People stared at her, recognizing her desperation but not her words.

Robert hustled Ceil along, scraping her right arm against the white wall of the basilica. Even from a distance Lynn could see the gashes on her sister's arm open as she struggled to pull away from him. Blood surged from her old wounds.

He held her more tightly.

Lynn burst into the crowd, seeing only the two of them. When she was ten feet away she screamed the only thing that might surprise Robert. "JAY'S DEAD! FARRELL TOLD US EVERYTHING! YOU DON'T HAVE A CHANCE!"

"Yes I do. I've got both of you," he said in English, putting his arm around Ceil's neck. He started squeezing and backing away.

Lynn raced closer, now five feet away from her sister and Robert.

"Come with me or I'll kill her," he hissed.

Lynn followed them down the alley. Ceil was gasping.

"Fight him! You can get away! You're strong enough!"

Robert tightened his grip on her neck. "Stop talking or you'll have a dead sister."

He's going to kill her, no matter what you say.

Ceil forced her right hand between Robert's elbow and her neck. Lynn saw her take a deeper breath. *Good, Ceil!* Several red lines streaked Ceil's arm. Blood from her opened gashes dripped onto Robert's white shirt.

He grimaced at the stain, then retaliated with a boast. "My friends set up her rape in Gabon for me, then sent her here to me. Now you're both here, as I planned."

"You chickenshit!" Lynn shouted.

Ceil's look showed she felt the blood streaming down to her fingers and remembered the rape from which she'd tried to defend herself. Her face hardened in fury and she jabbed her free elbow back behind her into Robert's ribs.

He stumbled but kept his grip.

Lynn screamed, "Ceil, break away! I LOVE YOU!"

Ceil twisted side to side.

Lynn closed the distance between them. All she could think of was their old signal. "Stop your bike!"

Ceil didn't hesitate. She stomped her foot down on his. His hold loosened and Lynn yanked Robert's arm away from Ceil's neck. He cried out in pain and reached for Ceil, but she ducked. Firecrackers sounded and dozens of Asian bus passengers streamed down the alley toward them.

Lynn enfolded Ceil, covering her head, and pulled her toward the subterranean entrance to the dome as the crowd ran past. She sobbed, "I'll take care of you. Nothing will happen."

Robert shouted angry words in French.

At the second volley, Lynn realized she was hearing gunshots.

Suddenly, Ceil seemed to understand the source of the shots in a way Lynn didn't. "We have to get out of here."

Three people, two men and a woman, emerged from behind the group of bus passengers, caught Robert by the shoulder and began pushing him out of the alley and toward the hill.

The sharp pain in his foot felt like glass piercing his skin in a dozen places.

Ceil and Lynn had betrayed him.

The Rabbit dead? That couldn't be.

Tourists jostled in front of him. He took advantage and swerved, limping, to the right of the Sansei agents. Steep, narrow stairs stretched below.

He called upon the most powerful moment he knew, and he leapt far out over the stairs, away from the basilica.

He willed himself to think of nothing but flying, of the tremendous soaring in a wing suit, with a long, slow, luxurious glide back toward the earth.

Maybe he would be suspended forever.

He heard more shots.

One slammed his back and knocked him out of his perfect arc. The foolish, graceless earth rushed up to meet him.

Thérèse bent over him. How could that be?

"*Thérèse, je t'aime,*" he said, and slid into blackness.

Epilogue.
Tuesday

Ceil took Lynn to Versailles, but that was the only request to which Ceil acquiesced. When they rowed the Grand Canal, Ceil explained her refusal to return stateside. "I love France. It feels like home to me. And I need to be away from the memories of Mom dying. Dad's smoking killed her. You realize that, don't you?"

"She had bone cancer, not lung cancer."

Ceil lifted a hand from an oar and waved it, as if she were brushing away crumbs. "The doctors said inhaling smoke increases the risk for all cancers."

"Dad tried to stop many times. He finally did." Lynn paused, then asked, "Will the IEA keep you on?"

"They'll understand. Robert hid everything from everyone, though he did tell me more about his plans last night. Sansei funded him, but threatened him, too."

"Why was Sansei funding Robert?" The Sansei gunmen hadn't hesitated to shoot Robert in a crowded public space. Lynn didn't want to think about what they might try next.

"He told me they want to shut down US refineries so they can sell their gasoline and diesel in the States. He arranged the . . . shutdowns."

What a goddamned euphemism. The words tumbled from her. "I saw Robert and Sansei's work. A father with two little kids who wanted to know when their mother was coming home, and she wasn't—because they killed her. A man poisoned before he could say good-bye to his son. A woman trapped and dying in a water tower where her cries couldn't be heard. Robert was nothing but a cheap murderer." She heard her voice rising in anger and did nothing to stop it. "Why the hell would you want to be involved with that?"

Ceil's voice held sorrow. "I didn't understand until last night. Nobody but Robert knew about Sansei and the sabotage and the killing."

Lynn felt cold. "If Sansei was watching Robert, they saw you. They could assassinate you."

"Their only connection to me was Robert, and he's dead."

When the sisters rode to the airport, Ceil silently pointed out a news article about Robert's death. One theory was that this important treasury official had become disoriented, perhaps ill, and had been randomly murdered when he ventured too close to a *banlieu* notorious for its high crime.

"Omigod," Ceil gasped. "This says his distraught wife—wife! He never told me he was married!—consented to a search of their apartment. His e-mails suggest he ordered the deaths of US citizens. He called them Pythagoras projects."

Same as on the scrap of paper found in Armando's room.

Ceil looked stunned, and Lynn wrapped her arm around her. "I . . . what . . . how does Pythagoras equal murder?"

Lynn explained the story of Pythagoras and his cult. Then she strained to keep her voice down so the taxi driver couldn't hear her. "Ceil, the police will want to talk to you. You were the last one to see Robert alive. How will you persuade them you weren't an accomplice? Ceil, please come back with me!"

"Running away won't solve anything. It will only make me appear guilty."

"You're smart but you're not acquainted with the French legal system. You could be in jail forever." Lynn felt sweat sliding under her arms. *And to be selfish, it will hurt you if your sister is accused as an accessory to murder.*

Ceil tapped ashes into the ashtray and went on as if she hadn't heard. "There's one other item about him in the article, which is no surprise given his reference to Pythagoras." She indicated the bottom of the page.

"Robert was a mathematician."

"Yes. This article even quotes a mathematician, John Paulos: 'Abstract thinking is another characteristic of mathematics . . . it has been associated with various dissociative pathologies, and it is easy to see how one trained in such reasoning and in thrall to an ideal could come to justify vicious and murderous acts as a nebulous 'good'."

"Sounds like the author of the article sympathized with Robert."

"Robert was a graduate of the École Polytechnique. He was excused many things."

"Murder?" Lynn shook her head. "No. I saw too many dead bodies."

Ceil turned her face toward the door. When she turned back, her eyes were red. "You weren't there every day watching our own mother die. Don't lecture me on grief."

Shit. We're almost at Orly. You can't end the visit on this thought. "You did everything you could. No one could have done more."

Ceil directed the driver to the private plane terminal. She stepped out of the cab with Lynn and threw down her cigarette before they hugged.

When they embraced, Lynn felt Ceil's heart beating against her own. "I'll miss you. I love you. Take care of yourself. Call any time." Lynn squeezed her sister's good arm.

"I love you too, Lynn. Come see me any time." Ceil climbed back into the cab.

Lynn watched until her sister was out of sight.

"I'll help you with those bags." It was the copilot of the charter. "Just you? No little sis?"

"Can't drag her away from Paris."

"You're not the first."

Airborne, she called her father and reassured him of Ceil's safety, but reported on Ceil's decision to stay in Paris. "Now, tell me about the lung reduction surgery."

"Renfro says I'm . . . too old," he said, sounding much too cheery for the news he was delivering.

"Oh no!"

"But . . . drug study . . . may help."

"I want to hear more about it. I'll be back later today, in about six hours."

"Good. See ye . . . love ye."

"Mike's not in now. He and Sara are in a board committee meeting."

Worry chilled her stomach. She hoped they weren't talking about Centennial or any of her other refineries. Probably Reese had kept Mike up to speed. *You were so focused on Jay, Ceil, and Robert, you forgot to talk to your boss the last two days. Good move.* "Don't break into the meeting, but when will he be free to talk?"

"Probably thirty minutes or so."

"Perfect." Maybe the Mike-Reese bond had strengthened, Lynn thought after she hung up. Maybe Mike would stop thinking of Reese as the outsider, the old-timer. Maybe he and Claude had wrapped up the testimony questions. *Maybe he'll give you a month extension on fixing Centennial now that you know it was being sabotaged three ways from Monday. Yeah, and maybe there's gold in them thar hills.*

She outlined the full sequence of events that she would need to tell Mike and Sara about Sansei, Robert, and her sister. She made a note to end by focusing on the good news about Centennial's improving operations and the budget she needed to finance the link with TriCoast's other Houston refinery. Perhaps after she explained Jay and Robert's sabotage, they would give her the time she needed to finish fixing Centennial—and allow her to keep her job at TriCoast.

❖

They met near the angular, green I. M. Pei building. In a silky green forest of bald cypress trees and a humid, wet concourse of fountains, water rushed everywhere.

Warm, familiar arms circled her from behind. Cy's starched. white shirtsleeves were rolled up to his elbows.

Lynn gripped his hands hard and touched each of his knuckles. He came around and sat next to her, never dropping her hand, and gave her a long kiss. Then he arranged Marika and Matt on his other side. They peeked around at her.

"I'm so glad to see you alive!" Relief tightened his voice.

"That's two of us," she said, closing her eyes to blink away tears.

"He's in his Daddy clothes," Marika interrupted in a serious tone. Cy had changed from his suit pants and dress shoes into jeans and running shoes—everything washable except the shirt.

"And here, these are for you," Marika said, as she and Matt reluctantly handed Lynn a bouquet of red roses.

"Roses? Did you pick them out?" Lynn asked her as Matt squirmed.

"No, Daddy did. Can Matt and I each have one? Please?" Marika asked in a tone that strained hard but didn't quite succeed in covering pure desire with politeness.

"Marika!" Cy appeared exasperated.

"Of course you can."

Matt and Marika carefully chose one rose apiece. They each stroked their red flowers, smiling at the scent and the velvety feel. Then they began pinching off the petals.

"Matthew, Marika! Hold them," Cy pleaded. "Just look at them."

"Lasers!" Matt exclaimed. Instantly the children began fencing with their long-stemmed roses.

"It's okay." Lynn laughed. "They like the roses, too."

Cy tried again. "Marika, Matt. Sit here with us . . ."

The array of three hundred-plus water jets resumed their choreo-graphed dance in front of their bench.

"Daddy, wook!" Matt shouted.

Roses forgotten, the children edged closer to the square bank of holes in the pavement, then raced into the middle of them. They laughed as columns of water randomly popped up and soaked them.

Lynn finished her story, glad Cy's kids couldn't hear her.

"Tell me more about the prosecution of Ceil's rape."

Lynn gave Ceil's explanation, that Gabon's legal customs were generally modeled on the French, but rape couldn't be tried.

"How good can Gabonese law be?" He tightened his arm around her shoulder and choked a little. "I asked to hear everything, but this is terrifying. The Sansei gunmen could still come after you."

"Ceil thinks their interest stopped with Robert. So do I." Lynn traced Cy's face with her fingers.

"I didn't realize the danger of your situation. I almost lost you." He pulled off his glasses and wiped his eyes.

Her tears matched his when she leaned over to hug him. She locked her arms around his back. "You couldn't have stopped me. Jay was trying to prove himself to his father. Once his father died, it became impossible, and he cracked."

"So anyone in Jay's path was a target." He wrapped her hands in his.

"Ceil was in danger, more than we realized. Robert's idealism was untempered by conscience. He'd made Pythagoras his god, and he was willing to sacrifice any number of real, living people to pursue his vision."

"Until he himself was killed by Sansei. He was trying to pull you in to him, too."

She took one of his hands and put it on her thigh. "What time did you say your sister is babysitting the kids tonight?"

He caressed her leg. "In a half hour or so, but only for an hour, she said."

"We'll make the best of it."

Cy swatted at a mosquito on his neck.

Grabbing his hand, she pulled him into the middle of the fountains. The water sprang up in jets around them, and they kissed until they were drenched.

"Yuck, Dad!" Marika shouted.

Lynn's watch dripped water. Two in the morning in Paris. She'd give Ceil a few more hours to sleep before calling. But only a few.

"Time to go see your aunt," Cy said. "She's got a DVD and ice cream for you." The children squealed at this perfect scenario.

Lynn followed Cy's Volvo in her Maserati. She waved at his bouncy children each time they turned to look at her. At Cy's sister's house, she put the car keys in her purse next to a folded piece of paper. Preston's printout about Pythagoras and Hippasus.

Robert, too, was killed by the Pythagoras Conspiracy.

END